Myths and Lies of Ithyion

Lost Kingdom Saga Short Stories

Laura Carter

Additional Information

<u>Trigger Warnings:</u>

Your mental health and experience whilst reading this book matters to me. This book contains death, violence, explicit sexual content, references to child abuse, self harm, non graphic but on page sexual assault and rape. If these are topics you find difficult to read, please approach with caution and at your own discretion. If you read this book and feel there are other trigger warnings missing, please notify me via my social channels so I can amend this page. Due to the themes and presence of sexually explicit scenes, this book is classified as 18+

<u>Glossary and Pronunciation Guide:</u>

If you wish to check the pronunciation of character and place names as you read them, you can find a pronunciation glossary at the end of the book.

<u>Playlist:</u>

I do some of my best writing after listening to music and as a result have created a very large overall series playlist. I have taken the songs relevant to certain chapters and placed them in a Myths and Lies Playlist. You can find the playlist linked in my socials. At the rear of the book, you will also find a guide for which songs relate to which portions of the book. I recommend only listening after you have finished the book or finished the relevant stories, otherwise the lyrics of some songs may act as a spoiler.

For anyone that needs reminding there is someone out there that will sacrifice everything for you and your love

THE KINGDOM OF
ITHYION
STATE CAPITAL
ASYNTHOS
VASTURIA
XYLIA
THE ISLE
EXORIA

O'OHAR
SAHRIH
ANDOR
GODS
ERESYDON
CARVYRE
LEHORYA

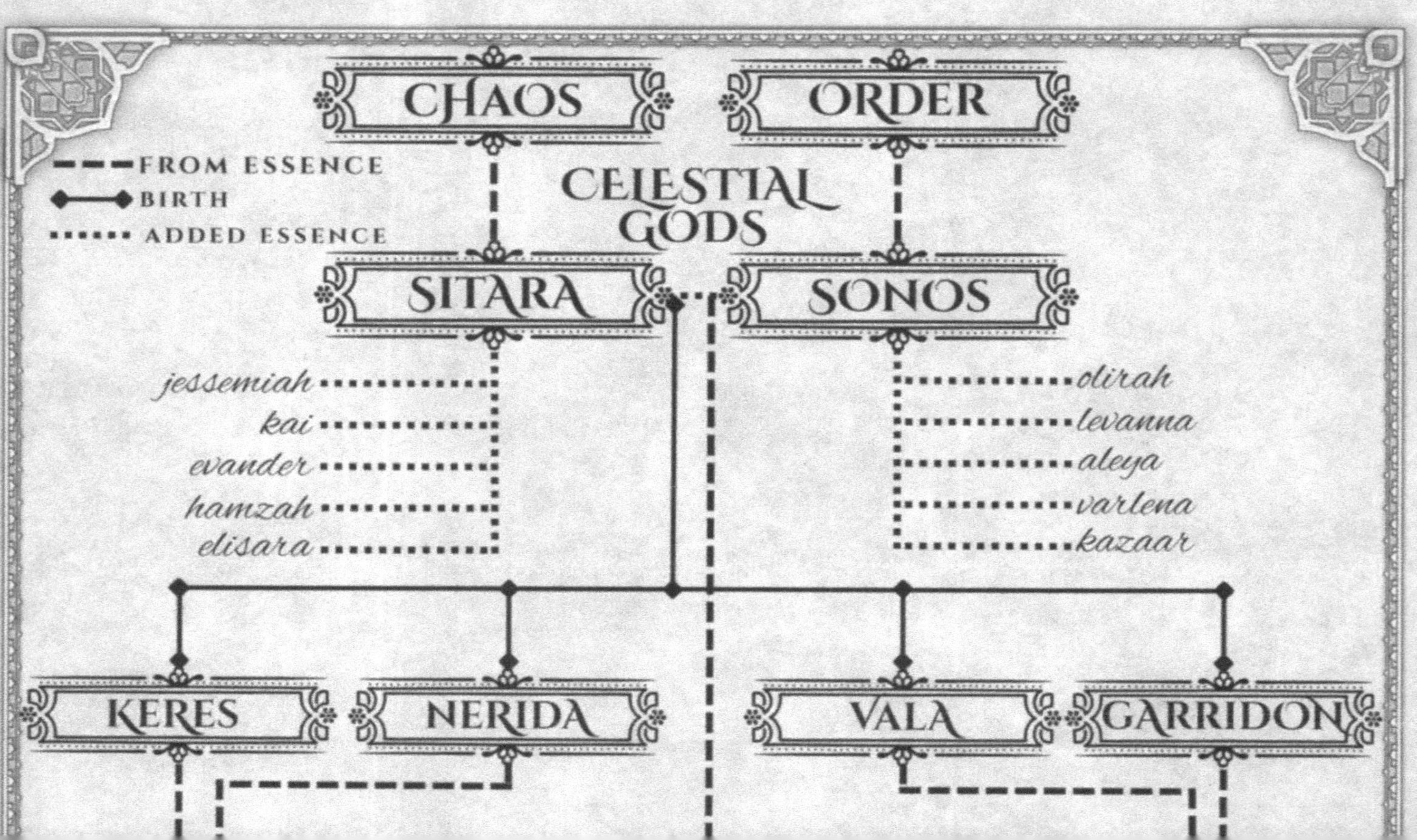
CHAOS
ORDER
CELESTIAL GODS
FROM ESSENCE
BIRTH
ADDED ESSENCE
SITARA
SONOS
jessemiah
kai
evander
hamzah
elisara
olirah
levanna
aleya
varlena
kazaar
KERES
NERIDA
VALA
GARRIDON

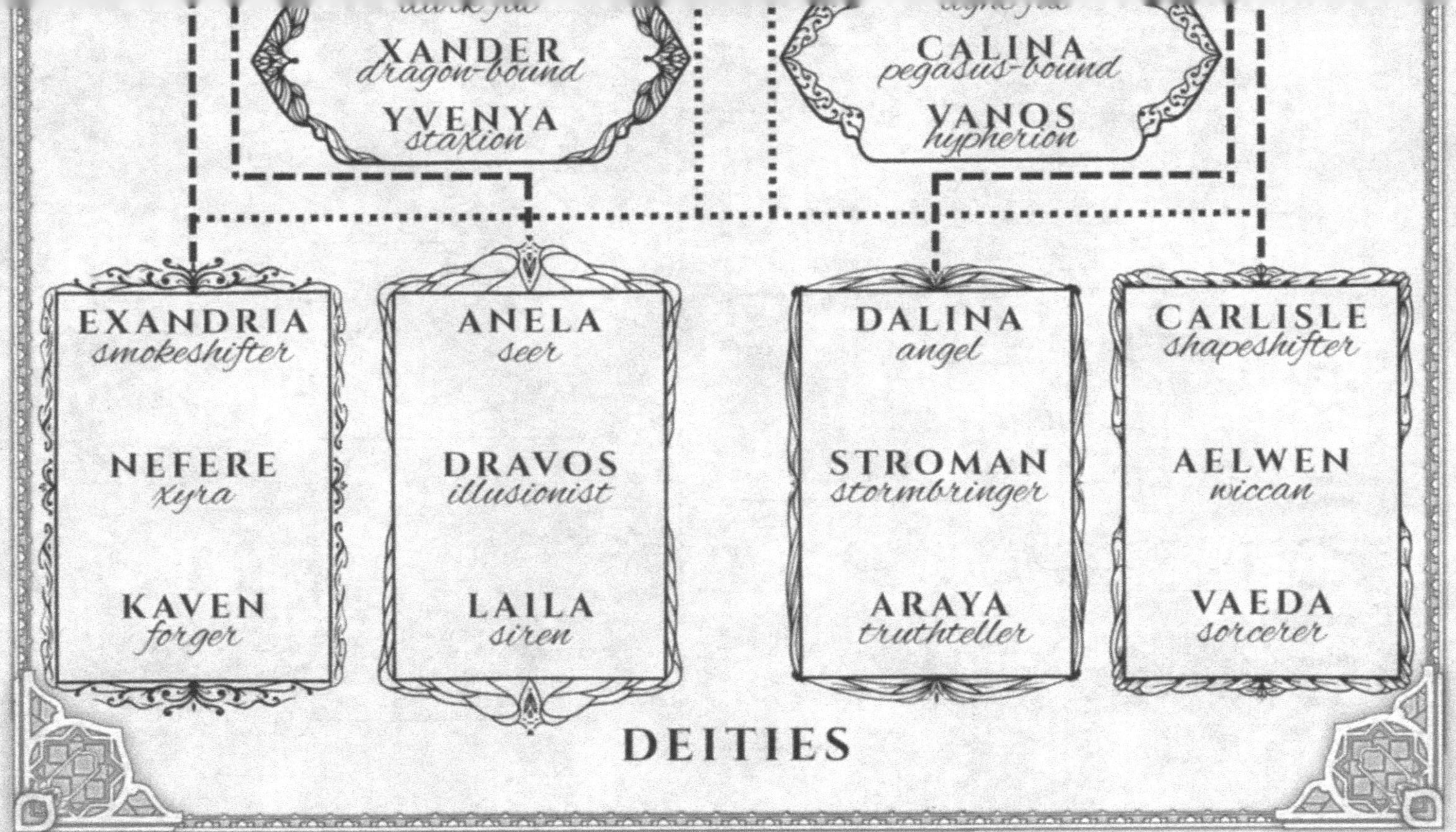

XANDER
dragon-bound
YVENYA
staxion

CALINA
pegasus-bound
YANOS
hypherion

EXANDRIA
smokeshifter
NEFERE
xyra
KAVEN
forger

ANELA
seer
DRAVOS
illusionist
LAILA
siren

DALINA
angel
STROMAN
stormbringer
ARAYA
truthteller

CARLISLE
shapeshifter
AELWEN
wiccan
VAEDA
sorcerer

DEITIES

HISTORY OF ITHYION

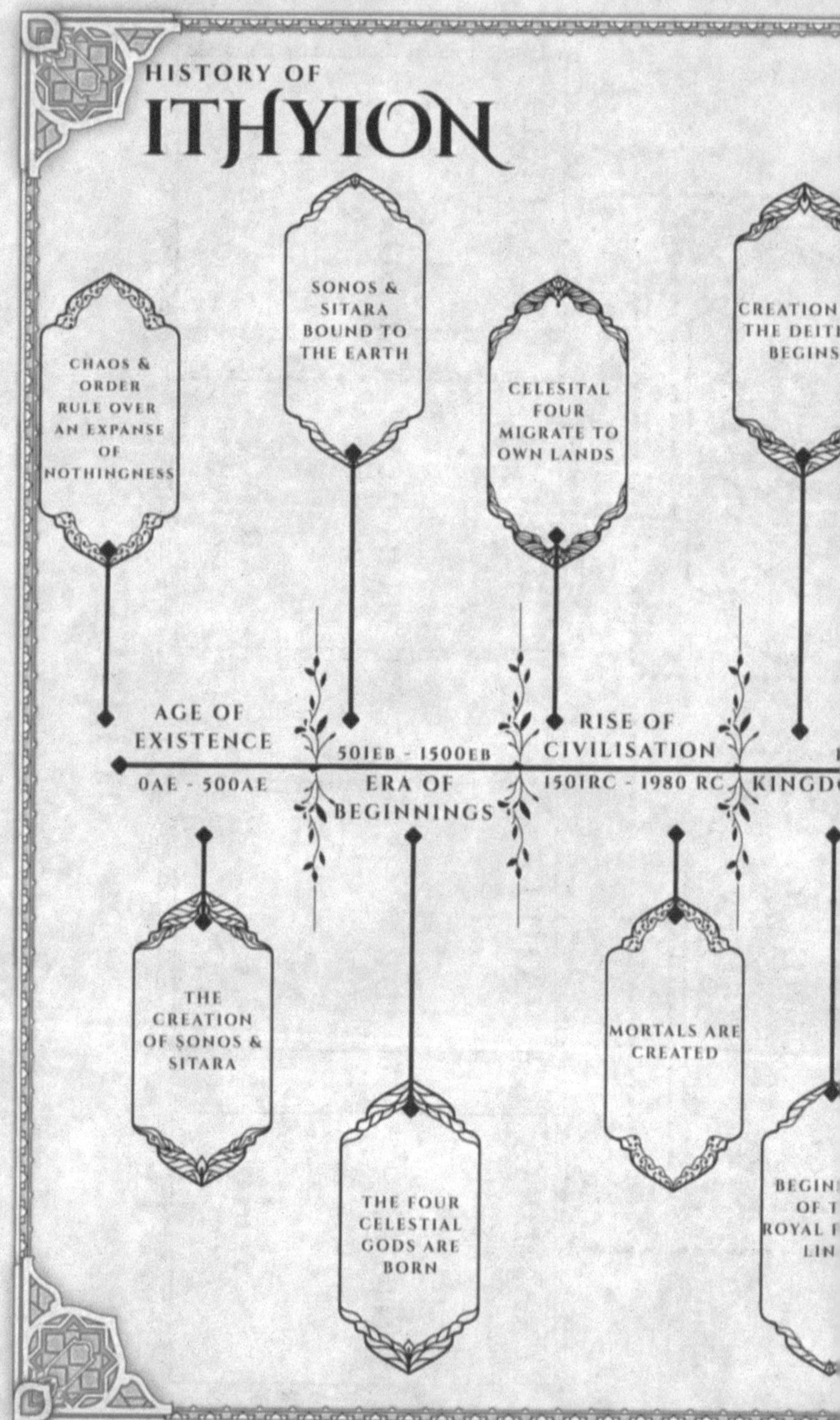

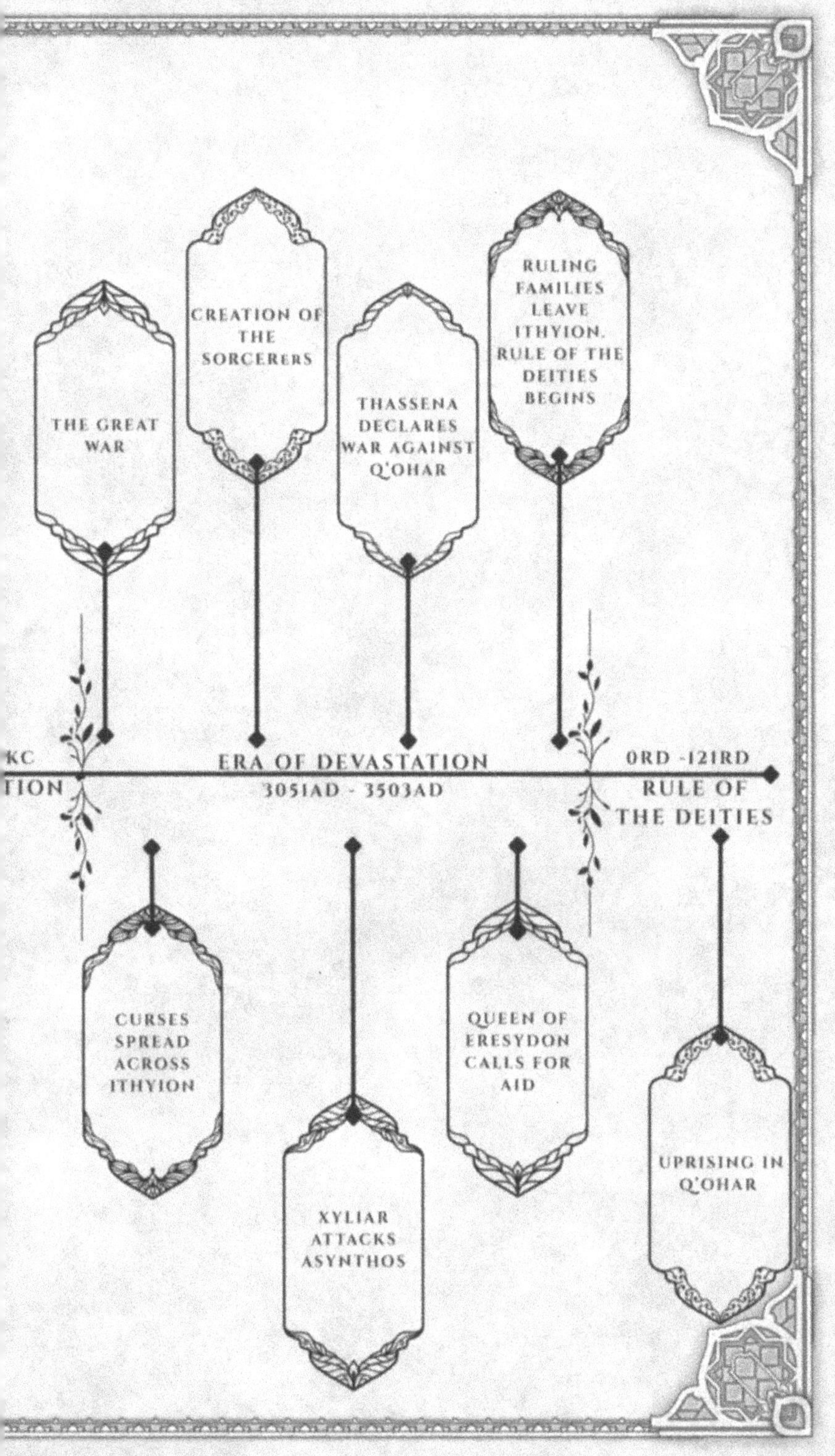

THE GREAT WAR
CREATION OF THE SORCERERS
THASSENA DECLARES WAR AGAINST Q'OHAR
RULING FAMILIES LEAVE ITHYION. RULE OF THE DEITIES BEGINS
KC
TION
ERA OF DEVASTATION
3051AD - 3503AD
0RD -121RD
RULE OF THE DEITIES
CURSES SPREAD ACROSS ITHYION
XYLIAR ATTACKS ASYNTHOS
QUEEN OF ERESYDON CALLS FOR AID
UPRISING IN Q'OHAR

XYLIAR

KINGDOM OF CREATION
[1981KC – 3050KC]

THE SIXTH STATE
XYLIAR
OF ITHYION
NOTABLE SETTLEMENT
SETTLEMENT
CAPITAL
KARDYN
LAXIA
TALLOS

ASYNTHOS
ZANDYN
LOW HEALERS
FIELD OF EMBERS
RYOX
HATCHING GROUNDS
EXORIA
TO THE FRACTURED ISLES & CARVYR

Chapter One

When a person spends their entire life in darkness, it's hard to imagine anything different. It's near impossible, one might say, to differentiate the guiding shadows from those there to punish you, or from the persistent shadows mirroring the taunts of others until you believe them to be true. Darkness like that sets deep in your bones, your entire being, to the point you begin to wonder: is there a reason for life at all?

Weak. Useless. Powerless. A disappointment to the lineage of the first deity. That was Valon Abexu's entire life, all ten years of it. At first, he had recounted the failures of his life to distract his mind from the pain. Now, the memories acted as a reminder of why he deserved his siblings' treatment. He started with his earliest memory. He was only five. Tears streamed down his face as his short legs carried him down the blackened hallways, his bare feet catching on the jagged stone floor, prompting more tears.

"Run, Valon. Run before they eat you!" Laughter erupted from the end of the corridor but was quickly drowned out by the snarls approaching the backs of his heels. The shadowed wolves his brother had created nipped at the trail of his fluttering cloak as he ran as fast as he could. If he had been older, he would have known the shadows couldn't really bite him and would dissipate at the wave of a hand. He would know they had used their Staxion-born power to invade his mind and enhance his fear. But to a five-year-old, who knew only to fear the darkness, Valon was running for his life.

"Gods, he's actually going to make it," said his eldest sister,

Cecilia, as he pushed his legs further to where all twelve of them stood watching. Eight brothers and four sisters—twelve children his mother was proud of. Yet she wanted him to be better. Valon screamed as his hands collided with the stone dragon statue towering above his siblings. Between them, they exchanged dull zonri, the coins clinking against one another. They groaned when Valon threw up blood on the stone floor.

At age seven, he wished he were five again, a time when he could flee the torture instead of facing it. It was the reason he still didn't go outside, even now. He learnt to fear the bitter winds of Xyliar and the threats of upsetting a dragon. "Perhaps we need to try something more physical." One of his brothers, Viserius, had suggested, as though he actually cared for their desired outcome and not just the joy it brought him to torment his youngest brother. That one suggestion landed Valon a week balancing atop a landing platform. Larger, singular dark rocks jutted out from the ground that surrounded the castle of the capital, Exoria. His brother had left Valon atop the tallest, narrowest peak, where he sat in the middle, his knees clutched tight to his chest and his head buried between them, bracing against the wind he was adamant swayed the rock. He was so high up, the clouds began to comfort him, when another gust of wind and flapping wings caused him to shake. At age seven, he stopped screaming. He stopped speaking completely until the age of twenty. If he screamed, a dragon might hear and devour him, so he became silent.

Noiselessly, he wept atop the platform for seven days until it became too much. His body had weakened. Flat on his back, he stared up at the morning sky, the rocks cutting into his skin. A grey, dull day. Rain dropped onto his face, plastering his hair—several shades lighter than his family's—to his forehead, when a dragon soared across his vision. He didn't have the energy to move, so he simply stared. He usually found dragons terrifying, but for a moment as he watched it, truly watched it, he admired the creature. Its scales were so dark it matched the rocks comprising the mountain and castle, but the glint of deep purple shone on its wings as it approached. Perhaps it was exhaustion, finding beauty in the darkness, or the fear of the repercussions if the family's experiment failed, but Valon gave up. As the dragon flapped its wings and lowered onto Valon's platform, he rolled until he tipped over the edge. Valon Abexu, at the ripe old age of seven, was ready to die, and he smiled as the wind whipped past him and the rock blurred, waiting for the inevitable collision with the walls of the castle estate below. But the sudden darkness wasn't the end. Shadows cradled him seconds before impact, and then there was nothing. He lulled his head to the side to find his siblings waiting.

"You didn't think it would be over that quickly, did you?"

Other memories were scattered in amongst those two—starvation, sleep deprivation, the murder of his beloved animals and a servant he'd befriended—all of which led him to the dark cell he was in at age ten.

"Dragon still got your tongue, Valon?" his brother sniggered as a shadow lashed his back again. Still, Valon did not scream, did not even grunt.

"This is getting boring," Cecilia whined from where she leant against the cell walls, examining her fingernails. "Nothing has ever worked. I don't know why she forces us to keep trying."

"Because he's a disappointment to the royal family otherwise. She can't have the other states discovering that one of her sons is not only a mute but has not an ounce of power in his veins."

"She should just kill him then and be done with it." Valon didn't react. He was used to being talked about as though he were not there. "We'll continue to outlive the other ruling families anyway," his sister added. She was right. Their near-immortal state was a constant reminder to Valon of the further suffering he might have to endure unless someone ended his torment. He was only ten, but his brothers and sisters varied from twenty-five to six-hundred-and-ten.

"You're right; perhaps we should suggest leaving him down here and, when the next generations arise across the kingdom, we wipe him from the history books," his brother chuckled. Valon knew they relished their cunning, a trait the other states failed to see. When the whip came down again, he barely trembled.

"It's certainly an idea," a dark voice echoed. Feet padded down the spiralling staircase to their left before someone entered the arched walls of the cell, a cave closing in on him. Valon's brown eyes fluttered open as his mother came into view, lit beneath the moonlight. His siblings bowed their heads. At least the pain would dull for a moment with her arrival. "We have at least another thirty years before we need to consider changing our faces again, though," said Kylara Abexu, though she was currently known as Vyla Abexu to the states. Even at age ten, Valon could acknowledge it was a smart plan for one craving power. As generations changed, so did the Abexus': changing their faces and names, falsifying their deaths, all to keep their seat of power. The other states would not stand for one person maintaining control for an entire existence, especially when they believed they had murdered Kylara centuries ago after fearing the extent of her power. So, the family fooled an entire kingdom. They adapted, changed faces, and fooled an entire kingdom into believing they aged slowly, but the reality was even slower.

"Perhaps you need to try, mother," his brother said, gathering his shadows and stepping aside. Kylara stepped forward, her silver gown pooling at her feet, matching the moonlight shining over her long, sleek black hair. As Valon dangled in chains, she trailed her sharp nail down his cheek before tilting his chin to meet her gaze. "I don't like having them do this to you, Val," she murmured, her black eyes glistening. "You know it is only because I care and want to ensure you have the means to protect yourself, to change with us and lead a long, happy life." Valon leant into her touch. "But we cannot do that if you do not show us your power." Her shadows leaked from her skin, crawling along his pale and bony arms toward his neck, holding his head up as she withdrew her hand. He mourned the fleeting moment of comfort her contact brought him.

Valon clenched his eyes shut and searched within himself, as he had countless times before. Everyone had a soul, the essence of their being, but for many it was also the essence of their power, a bright and blinding light within that centred a person's abilities. It was not unheard of to come across mortals, those with no power. Sonos and Sitara, the first celestial beings, bestowed elemental essence upon their children, and their own powers of light and dark when they created Makaria and Oxyron. But when they deemed the new creations, those first deities, too powerful, they gifted their children with mortals to fill their lands first. While the celestial gods eventually succeeded in creating their own deities within the kingdom's elemental states, it was not uncommon for lineages to mix with mortals until some were born with no power, others with weakened abilities or only the elemental gifts of their celestial god, and many with both that power and that of a deity. But Makaria and Oxyron had been left to fend for themselves with no mortals to call their own when the land they were abandoned on, Styros, was still whole. So, they set about to create their own. The process resulted in the first Staxion Fae, Yvenya with the same shadows as Makaria and the ability to control mind. As well as the first Hypherion Fae, Vanos that wielded Oxyron's light and the ability to walk through dreams. Whilst Makaria and Oxyron believed them to be deities in their own right, for their level of power and creation from their own essence, those of the other five states didn't always recognise them as such. Makaria continued to create more Staxion Fae, this time pulling from Yvenya's essence rather than her own to ensure they were not as powerful as she. It ensured everyone in Xyliar in the present day should possess power, all having descended from the first deity Makaria created and those afterwards. There were occasions where mixed bloodlines, born from those that visited from other states, woke with no power but there was no other reason for a citizen to be born without any. Particularly one whose lineage was from the first and only royal family, there was no reason that when Valon searched within himself, he found no power in the essence of his soul. His lip quivered, and his mother tutted.

"Leave us and wash up for dinner," his mother said. His siblings smirked before obeying.

"I don't know what else to try, Val," she sighed, creating a chair out of her shadows to sit upon. She crossed one leg over the other. Her onyx crown glittered in the moonlight. Valon opened his mouth, but nothing came out. "And now you do not even talk, so we cannot work together to find a solution." The shadows crawled up his neck, caressing his cheek. He wanted to believe the gentle lilt of her voice, that she only acted in his best interest. But he had never witnessed one of his other siblings being tortured. He had seen no one else endure pain like he did.

"I-I-m—" Valon's mouth tried to form the words, raising his mother's eyebrows a fraction. "S-s-s-orr-y-y."

Kylara hung her head and sighed. "You can stutter or be silent all you like if you just did as you were told, Val." She tapped her fingers, willing the shadows to creep toward his mouth and ears. "Perhaps darkness will awaken darkness."

Valon flinched against the chains and tried to shake his head as the tendrils of her power pushed into his mouth, ears, nose, forcing themselves into his body as though they could find something he knew was not there. Valon's eyes watered as he tried to scream, tried to form the words to beg his mother to stop. Reminders that he deserved this came flooding back. His mother had lived over a thousand years as the first daughter of the first deity, and yet he was the most disappointing thing she had ever witnessed. Weak. Useless. Powerless. Valon Abexu, son of Kylara, grandson of Makaria, the first deity, was a disappointment to his lineage.

Chapter Two

One hundred and twenty-six years later

Anela's skin was as radiant as the sun. When his fingers met her cheek, warmth surged through him as though he was born anew. What a grand feeling it was, to be in love, to look into one's eyes and fall into their soul, over and over again.

"Marry me," he whispered. Tears pooled in her eyes as a grin stretched across her face. She giggled. "Promise to spend every day until your last by my side." Anela nodded and pressed her hands to his cheeks, pulling his face down into a kiss he wished would never end.

"I will love you from this day until—"

"What are you reading?" Cecilia asked from across the table, staring down her angular nose, so different from the rounded structure of his. Valon finished chewing the piece of meat and breathed deeply.

"M-medical j-journ-n-al," he lied, nudging his glasses up his nose. Cecilia wrinkled her nose and turned to their sister, Firella, instead. Despite experimenting and torturing Valon as a child, Cecilia seemed more disgusted by his work now. Firella remained indifferent and smiled politely. As the only daughter in the family without the Staxion abilities of control, and only dark magic, she kept as quiet as possible. Valon did not blame her; she had seen the treatment he had received for his absence of power. He turned the page of the novel, the sigil of Thassena etched in the top right-hand corner: a ship with three sails. The novel was from the queen's private collection, a gift to his mother the last time she had visited under the face of Vyla Abexu. He had read this one before, for it was one of the many in the grand library's collection with a happy ending. He didn't like the ones without. The absence of a happy ending drew Valon back into his own melancholy. Reading was his only distraction; words were a medicine far more effective than any provided by healers for the lashes he received. Though he hadn't completely lied about the medical journals, for that was what he largely read during the day.

Medical journals, travel logs, historical accounts—always non-fiction texts to aid in the experiments he'd spent the last sixteen years working on at his mother's request. The only thing he was good for. The only way to prove himself. Valon wondered how different his days might look if she had never found him experimenting with the fast-healing blood of dragons, combined with stalactite water from Asynthos. He had overheard his sisters talking of the healing properties in the water after a visit to the Sturmov royal family of the fourth state, a visit he, of course, had not attended. Valon did not exist. It had piqued his interest, hoping it would permanently clear his scars. It had not. Though it had lessened them, for the experimentation led to his current work and far less time in the cells.

"How is your research coming along, Val?" His mother asked from the head of the long dining table. She sipped on a glass of wine. His heart warmed at the affectionate nickname, but it was quickly squashed by his fear of taking too long to reply. He cleared his throat.

"I-I believe th-the study into d-d-dragon anatomy." His siblings sniggered. "C-com-m-bined with h-historica-a-l accounts of sh-shape-sh-shifters will prove h-helpful," he finished, quickly bringing the wineglass to his mouth to avoid further conversation.

"Perhaps an assistant would be useful," Kylara said. Valon glanced around the dining table. He didn't know which sibling would be the most tolerable to work with. Valon did not envy the work of his siblings. He did not think he had the stomach to ride a dragon and command the scouting ranks guarding the coast like his Dragon-Bound brothers. Nor did he think himself capable of engaging in conversation to garner information from influential lords and ladies across the kingdom like his flirtatious sisters. He most definitely was not strong enough to train armies and did not have the stomach to lead in torture. However, Viserius's recent tasks did make him envious. He had been journeying to the isles that separated Xyliar and Carvyre, believing he had discovered a substance that could inhibit a person's power – Tungstyn. He would happily take a look at that if ever asked. "The others are far too busy with other matters. No, I was thinking of bringing someone in just for you." Kylara smiled. Valon watched, trying to determine the angle and figure out what she gained from offering him help and company. "If you had someone else read through your research, you may move onto experimentation far quicker."

There it was. He was moving too slowly. Valon shifted in his seat. "I-I'm s-s—"

"Do not grovel, Valon," she snapped. "It is unbecoming of an heir to this family."

"Like he would ever be on the throne." His brother barked a laugh, and Valon prayed someone would take the attention off him.

"An a-a-s-sistant would be h-helpful. Th—thank you." Valon opened his book again and hoped it was enough to end the topic. Outside the towering arched glass windows, a dragon roared, marking its arrival on one of the platforms. Valon flinched as the windowpanes rattled under the force of the sudden rush of air but quickly masked it by piercing another chunk of meat with his fork while staring at the words on the page before him.

"The Dragon-Bound have returned." Cecilia clapped her hands eagerly and pushed away from the table, her sisters quickly following suit, all lifting frivolous, lace-laden skirts in various shades of grey before running.

"They have an unhealthy obsession with those men," Viserius snorted.

"Can you blame them?" their mother asked. "They will need false husbands soon, given the ages they present to the other states. Who better than the men who protect this land?"

"We protect this land. They simply ride around preparing for another war, just in case," Viserius scoffed.

"Without those men, there would be nobody to tame the dragons from simply burning you all alive." Kylara pointed her fork at Valon's brothers. Valon had read countless historical works from the scholars of Exoria over the years from long before he, the youngest of his family, was born. Many of the texts could, of course, be verified by his family given their age, not that the citizens knew of that secret. The dragons were born when the land, originally named Styros, was split during the war between Makaria and Oxyron. The war that created Xyliar and Carvyre as they knew it today.

Dragons spawned, emerging from the fissures created by the breakage across Styros. History, and his mother, claimed the dragons were the universe's answer to protecting the land and its people from the ruling Fae of Carvyre. The same reason for the sudden birth of the first pegasus in Carvyre. Balance between light and dark, always. What the accounts did not say, though, and what his mother did not know, was why exactly the land was split in the first place and the cause of the rift between Makaria and Oxyron, who should have been as drawn to one another as Sitara and Sonos. What had forced them to draw on their essence to create beings bound to their respective creatures? The first Dragon-Bound Fae, Xander, and the first Pegasus-Bound Fae, Calina. Something had forced the two to build powerful defences around them, whilst creating families to rule over each land instead of themselves, a legacy of power. The Abexu's of Xyliar and the Nylaria's of Carvyre were the very beginning of the ruling families in Ithyion.

Yet, the triggering events for what was the entire royal structure of the kingdom of Ithyion, was lost to history.

"Valon," his mother called, rising from her place to beckon over a serving boy for another glass of wine, his hand trembling as he lowered the tray. "I will have your new assistant brought to your workspace in a week." She smiled. Valon nodded. As he savoured this rare moment of kindness, he almost forgot she had whipped him only two days before for his failure to provide an adequate update.

***

The desk squeaked as Valon pushed it against the western wall, the fourth wall he had attempted. Resting his hands on his hips, he analysed its position before the window that sat just two inches higher than the splintered wood. He would never complain about the state of the furniture and equipment that had been pulled from abandoned stores rather than made brand new. He was just grateful to possess something that belonged only to him. Sighing, he approached it again, shifting it an inch to the left until it was central. This was the right spot. It wasn't a window he often gazed out of, overlooking the landing platforms and Exoria down below with its dark spires and grey stones that created a web of streets. He preferred the eastern window of the tower, with its expansive ocean view and fantasies of freedom and a life elsewhere. Given that he usually worked late into the evening, the western window provided a view of the sunset, offering more natural light while he worked at his desk.

Valon's hands trembled as he continued setting up the desk: a large quill with a feather from a pegasus—his mother's reminder of the royal family she claimed would threaten them one day—and a copper pot of dark ink. Its pure white, tipped with the occasional pale lavender, contrasted the usual black of the birds used in Xyliar;

the fine bones scattered through the silken feathers were iridescent in the sunlight. Valon winced as he thought of what his brothers must have done to capture and pluck such a creature.

He collected the next books he needed to take notes from: *A Study in the Anatomy of Angel Wings* and *The Myths of Shapeshifters* and *Anatomy: the Development of Children* and stacked them to the left of the tabletop. Valon tidied the other tomes scattered across the room into neat piles on the shelves and straightened the glass vials and liquids on the centre table. Despite the room being reasonable in size, the sheer volume of deep mahogany wood furniture and work materials made the room seem smaller. He might have found the room claustrophobic were it not the only place he was free from his mental cage. Staring at the mounted, preserved adolescent dragon wings, only a tenth the size of an adult's, he scratched the nape of his neck. Should he have removed them? He knew nothing about his new assistant; they might find it rather gruesome. What if they were friends with or related to a Dragon-Bound and took offence? A knock sounded at the door to his tower, so far from any public space in the castle, and ended his contemplation.

"O-one m-moment," he called, unrolling the sleeves of his shirt and placing the family sigil pins back on the cuffs: an amber flower on copper, a symbol of the flowers blooming along the state's coast, where it had once connected with Carvyre. He tutted as he attempted to flatten the crinkles where his shirt met his trousers. He should have arranged the room last night instead but had stayed up far too late, using reading as a means to calm the anxiety he felt for this very moment. Valon wrung his hands together, trying to stop them from shaking. He had never met someone from outside the castle. He rarely even spoke with the guards or the servants, not after one was killed for befriending him. How was he to know the best way to instruct an assistant? As sweat beaded on the back of his neck, Valon twisted the engraved copper handle of the door and attempted a smile.

The smile dropped when he saw Viserius on the other side.

"Valon!" his brother exclaimed, barging past him with a petite woman in tow. "I love what you've done with the place," he said, prodding vials of Angel blood and the saliva of the strongest dragon in the royal fleet.

"D-don't t-touch th-that," Valon said. "It b-burns b-b-one." His brother picked up the vial.

"Huh, this would have been useful years ago when we had our fun together in the cells." Viserius grinned, and the quiet woman, still being dragged by her wrist, glanced between the two brothers. "This is Luxiana." He pushed the woman in front of him with a vice-like grip on her shoulders. She flinched, bringing her hands together and twisting them in a way that mirrored Valon. Her hair was lighter than most women he had met, a warmer chestnut compared to inky black. Her eyebrows were full and framed her eyes perfectly. He tilted his head. He had never seen such unique eyes. One green, and one such a dark shade of brown it was nearly black.

"Hello," Luxiana whispered, smoothing down her simple grey dress. The collar was high around her neck, seeming to elongate it, and the fitted sleeves covered her entire arms until looping around her middle finger to keep them pulled over the backs of her hands. Hands he noticed trembled the closer his brother neared her side. The dress was woollen and fitted to her torso, where it gently cascaded outward and down to the floor. He felt like he recognised it as a memory tried to resurface in the back of his mind.

"Well," Viserius said as silence stretched between them. Valon realised he had not returned his greeting. "I'll leave you two to become acquainted." He released Luxiana's shoulders and trailed a hand down her back before squeezing her waist. Leaning down, Viserius brushed her hair back to reveal a rounded ear. She was not Fae. Valon wondered if her family had moved to Xyliar or if she was an orphan taken from one of the other states by a wealthy lord of the sixth. "I'll miss you," he whispered, albeit not so quietly. Valon tensed as Viserius clapped his shoulder before exiting the room, leaving Valon alone with another person, other than a member of his family, for the first time in over a hundred years. Luxiana rubbed her arm as she stood in the centre of the room, looking around her. She cocked her head at the dragon wings on the wall.

"Uh, th-this is y-your d-desk," Valon said, his stutter worsening as he rushed to get the words out. Stepping around the room, he gestured at the western window. "D-do you h-have any b-belongings w-w-ith y-y-y—"

"No," she said politely, approaching Valon with slow steps. "Viserius said my possessions would be brought to a bedroom on the floor below." She placed a hand on the desk and leant forward, staring out the window. Her eyes glistened as a dragon flew past. He hoped he had chosen the right window.

"Y-yess. The r-room n-next to m-mine." Valon nodded, and Luxiana tensed. Panicking, he added, "It l-l-locks from th-the in-inside." He pushed his glasses further up his nose as Luxiana nodded slowly, still staring at the view. A small smile curved her lips, making Valon's stomach flip.

"What is your name?" she asked, finally turning to face him. He stepped back, not wishing to invade her space. He took a deep breath and tried to keep his mind empty, preparing to annunciate.

"Valon," he said, smiling as he accomplished it without stuttering. She reached her hand out to him, and Valon stared at it.

"Luxiana, but you may call me Lu."

Valon clenched and unclenched his fist. When had he last touched another person? What if he squeezed her hand too hard, or she flinched at the coldness of his skin? Before his anxiety spiked further, he reached out to take her small hand in his. He hoped she couldn't feel how sweaty it was.

"Val," he said. "C-call m-me Val."

Chapter Three

S*ix months later*

"Two drops of dragon's blood," Luxiana murmured, ticking the ingredient in the journal. He knelt before the beaker, carefully holding it at eye level, before taking the pipette and adding two drops inside. He winced as he hunched his back, his glasses slipping down the bridge of his nose. The rest of the liquid remained stable. "It didn't bubble this time. That's a good sign," she murmured, jotting down notes in a different, smaller journal. Valon nodded, looking to her for the next instruction. He caught her slight frown as she glanced at his back. Her hair was pulled up in a mess on her head, held together by copper pins and clips he had swiped from his sisters' afternoon tea tables when they weren't looking.

"Four ounces of Shapeshifter marrow," Luxiana instructed next. Valon unscrewed the metal tin and placed the beaker on the scales before dropping in the mixture, slowly adding additional drops until the beaker rose in perfect line with the iron weights on the other side. "Careful," she murmured. Valon's lips quirked. This was usually the part that led them to start from scratch again. "Perfect," she said, reaching for the beaker as he stood and stretched his back. He swallowed his grunt of pain as the wounds from his most recent lashing tore open.

"H-how l-long th-this time?" he stammered, dipping his hands into the washbasin, his fresh scars still red and bright on the backs of his wrists and arms.

"Three hours," she said, turning the glass on his desk where the morning sun shone directly onto the mixture and the dark wood of his desk. "Three and a half boiled it, two and a half solidified the mixture, but it was the golden amber hue we needed by that point." She returned to her desk, scribbling away in her journal as she always did after they attempted to create another dose of the growth stimulant. Her regular glances in his direction did not go unnoticed.

"Food?" he asked, clearing his throat. Luxiana tucked a stray hair behind her ear and smiled as he uttered the word, stutter-free. She was a healer; it explained why he recognised the grey, modest woollen gown when he first saw it. It was the same one worn by the women who tended to his scars when he was a child, before his mother determined he was old enough to manage the pain himself. Though he had never seen her in the hallways; he was yet to ask why not. Shorter words, brief sentences. That was what she said on day three of knowing him. That was her advice for improving his speech—start small. At Luxiana's nod, Valon reached into the cupboard on the wall, pulling out a jar of the floral apricot jam he quickly learnt was her favourite, and a loaf of wrapped bread.

"What was the reason this time?" Luxiana asked. Valon's hand stilled, tightening his grip on the knife as he sliced.

"What d-do you mean?" he asked, trying to force a positive lilt into his tone.

"Val," Luxiana's voice softened, and he sighed, turning his head to look at her over his shoulder. "The wounds are bleeding through your shirt."

Valon's hand trembled on the knife as he continued slicing. She would be able to see the shape of the blood, the harsh streaks. There was no denying the cut of a lashing.

"Too slow," he murmured, beginning to spread jam. He said nothing else, and Luxiana didn't push him. She never did.

"I have a good feeling about this dose," she said, changing the subject. Valon licked the sticky residue from his thumb as he placed the plate of bread, laden with golden jam, on her desk. Removing her chin from her clasped hands, she stared out at the cityscape below, like she always did. "Though if it does fail, we will need a Dragon-Bound to extract more blood for us. We are running low on a new batch." She bit into the bread, and Valon cleared his throat as she licked the jam off her full lips.

"I w-will ask," he said, biting into his own slice.

"I can go. Where are they housed?" she asked. Valon frowned.

"Next to th-the h-healers' quarters," he said. Luxiana paused her chewing for a second before continuing, but he noticed.

"Y-you did n-not sleep th-there?" he asked, brushing crumbs off his shirt. Luxiana picked at the crust that she never ended up eating.

"I was a private healer," she said. "For Viserius." Valon's hand paused with his bread mid-air.

"Did h-he have m-many in-injuries?" He suspected he knew the answer.

"No," Luxiana breathed, looking down at her plate and nudging it away. Valon nodded slowly, knowing the kind of attention Viserius usually preferred from women.

"I-I'm s-s-sorry."

"Don't be. It's not your fault the healer I was a servant to, and later trained under, was placed in the castle. He took an interest in me immediately. Nor is it your fault I've spent the last ten years in a windowless room." Luxiana rubbed her eyes and rested her head on her palms, continuing to stare at the view Valon had chosen for her.

"Why windowless?"

"He liked my skin pale. Said the sun would ruin its porcelain perfection."

Valon realised then why her eyes had glistened when he showed her the window above her desk, and why she sat at the desk every moment she could to gaze longingly out at the view.

"Never been to c-city?" he asked. Luxiana shook her head.

"I came from the Hallow Healers in Zandyn." While Valon had never left the castle, he knew from the maps it was the most northeastern town of the sixth state, located in the centre of the dark woodlands. He also knew from reading a journal on the medicinal properties of Xyliar's native plants that the Hallow Healers condemned the use of pain relief in healing. Valon wanted to ask Luxiana all she knew of their rather secretive practices but recognised now was not the time.

"I've never been either," he said, and her head turned from the view to face him. "Or to Z-Zandyn." Her thick brows pinched together.

"Why not?" she asked. Valon cleared his throat, rubbing his arms; his rolled-up sleeves exposed his scars. Luxiana's eyes trailed over the scars, and she nodded slowly, understanding the reason without him verbalising it. She turned back to the window.

"Maybe you could take me one day, Val," she sighed. "Two broken birds finally set free."

"One day, Lu," he whispered.

***

"It's ready," Valon said from his desk, turning the glass beaker one last time as the sun finally shifted from his window and moved above the tower. Luxiana leant over his shoulder, and his skin prickled where her hand gently rested on him. The scent of apricot jam and soap drifted from her. "Seems stable," he said. Luxiana hummed, turning the beaker in different directions. The mixture had paled to a golden shade of amber and had maintained its velocity, sticking to the edges of the beaker only slightly before dripping back down.

"Then it's time for the next step," she said. Valon took a deep breath as she walked to the door and murmured to the guard outside. Six months, and they had finally made it to the next and final step of the experiment. Valon's hands grew clammy as he wondered what would happen to Luxiana after this. Would she be returned to Viserius or the healers' quarters? What would be expected of him next if he finally accomplished what his mother had asked of him for the last sixteen years, just after his one-hundred-and-twentieth birthday? Would she be reminded that he still had no power and remained a disappointment? The door creaked open, and a second pair of light footsteps joined Luxiana. "I didn't realise she would be so young," Luxiana's voice wavered. Valon turned.

A young girl with dirt coating her pale skin and bright green eyes stared back at him. Her blonde hair was matted, and her simple brown dress was torn along the hem. Valon frowned.

"W-was told a woman in r-return for twenty zonri—"

"Yes, zonri," the girl said eagerly, her eyes widening. "I need the money for my brothers." Valon frowned again. If she had siblings, and they too, were Shapeshifters brought over by his own brothers after their last trip to Eresydon, why had they not come instead? He would feel more comfortable injecting the growth stimulant into an older male. Medical journals proved they had higher pain receptors during shifts.

"P-perhaps we a-s-sk for a brother," Valon said.

"No, no, no," the girl rushed. "It must be me. I was told I would only be paid if it were me."

"It's okay." Luxiana hushed the girl and sat her down on a stool. "What's your name?"

The girl looked between Valon and Luxiana. "Sophia," she said.

"And how old are you, Sophia?"

"Sixteen."

"She is technically an adult. We cannot tell her no if this is what she wishes," Luxiana sighed. Valon shifted in his seat, still uncomfortable. He did not want to inject such a young girl, but what troubled him more was knowing there were people in Exoria so desperate for coin they would come to the castle in this state willing to do anything that was asked of them.

"Are y-you sure?" Valon asked Sophia. She nodded eagerly as Luxiana handed her a glass of water. Sophia's eyes widened, and she gulped it down in seconds. Luxiana and Valon shared a look. She turned to slice some bread and spread it with jam.

"Eat it slowly, or it will bloat your stomach and cause pains," Luxiana said, rubbing the girl's back, who practically salivated at the sight. Valon tilted his head, directing Luxiana to come to him. He turned on the stool to face the window as she brought her face close to his.

"Sh-she may not be s-strong enough," he whispered.

"If we say no, she returns to her family with no money," Luxiana replied, though her eyes glistened, clearly torn by the decision too. "Who knows what might happen to her if we call for one of your brothers and ask for someone else." Valon shivered and nodded. They were Sophia's best hope of getting her out of the castle with money in her pocket.

"Ready?" Valon asked as Sophia wiped the back of her mouth with her sleeve. She smiled; her stomach full. Such an innocent smile.

"I need to unbutton the back of your dress, is that okay?" Luxiana asked. Sophia nodded, and Valon dipped a syringe needle in dragon saliva to burn away any other residues before filling it with amber liquid. He approached slowly, but she did not flinch or eye him warily. Luxiana wiped a cloth dipped in the saliva of an adolescent dragon and dragged the cloth along her back to clean away the streaks of dirt. The liquid was weaker than an adult's, that would burn her skin completely.

"Two s-small pinches," Valon said. Sophia nodded as Luxiana knelt before her to hold her hand, smiling gently. Her eyes flickered to Valon. He nodded and slowly inserted the needle at the edge of her left shoulder blade. Sophia whimpered for a second but then exhaled deeply. Valon counted as the liquid slowly bled into her skin. One, two, three, four, five. "One more," he whispered, moving the syringe to the edge of her right shoulder blade. One, two, three, four, five. He wiped her back again with the cloth. "Done."

"Is that it?" Sophia asked, rolling her shoulders back.

"You did so well." Luxiana smiled, patting the girl's cheek. "Now, the serum Val used concentrates your Shapeshifter powers. So, where do you normally feel the essence of your power manifest?"

"Here," Sophia said, pointing to her stomach, where most people felt it.

"Okay. When you feel it, the sensation should transition from your stomach to your upper back instead."

"Where the pinch was?" she asked. Valon moved back to the edge of his desk, picking up his journal to take notes. Luxiana nodded.

"And when you feel that, I want you to stare at the wings on that wall behind me and focus on only growing the wings. Can you do that?" Luxiana asked. The girl nodded while Valon made notes about her stable temperament. No changes to skin colour or temperature yet.

"Can they be any colour?" Sophia asked, staring at the deep purple wings on the wall.

"What's your favourite colour?" Luxiana asked.

"Green," the girl said with a smile. Dark green like the Hybrooke Forest of Eresydon." Luxiana's back stiffened.

"A beautiful choice."

The three of them waited. A minute passed, then five, then ten. Valon was losing hope when the girl let out a small gasp and straightened her back. Luxiana squeezed her hand and backed away as the girl's eyes narrowed with concentration, staring at the two adolescent dragon wings on the wall in front of her. Valon scribbled, his handwriting nearly illegible as he took notes. The girl hunched, though did not appear to be in pain as two deep green stumps slowly formed from her back.

"It burns a bit," the girl said, gripping her knees. The wings slowly grew from the stumps, spanning throughout the room. "It doesn't normally take this long," she said, panting a little.

"You're doing so well," Luxiana murmured, reaching for the girl's hands as she straightened. "Can you move them?" The girl pinched her brow together and, slowly, the deep forest green wings flexed and then retracted, hanging behind her back, matching the size of those on the wall. "Magnificent," Luxiana breathed.

"We did it, Lu," Valon murmured.

"We did, Val."

Chapter Four

S everal emotions hung in the air of the throne room—intrigue at the young girl, with dark green wings, standing in the centre. Hatred from Valon's siblings for doing something worthy for once, and relief from Valon and Luxiana as the queen, his mother, paced around the girl, grinning.

"Extend them again," the queen requested. The girl's hands clenched as she spanned her wings. The queen ran a finger along the leather like material. "Do you think it would be possible for scales to form with a more experienced shifter?"

"Perhaps, though the adolescent dragon wings used as a model for the shift do not yet have scales; they only form in adulthood as they lose the protection of their mother," Luxiana said, her voice shaking slightly. Viserius stared at her from beneath one of many large stone dragon heads protruding along the stone wall of the long throne room, lit by the light falling in from the wall of window panes opposite. Valon did not visit the throne room often, given he was never invited to meetings on matters of the kingdom. He was thankful for that as he glanced sideways at the stone eyes seeming to scrutinise him and the true-to-scale stone teeth poised as a reminder of the dangers outside the castle.

"But would it be possible to request they try? Nothing would need to change about the serum?" the queen asked.

"No, your Majesty, the serum is stable," Luxiana said. Valon brushed his finger against her palm, a silent thanks for leading most of the conversation. Sophia's shoulders were beginning to shake. For several hours, she had displayed the wings for Valon and

Luxiana, and now for the queen and her family. It was longer than he would have liked for her first partial shift. The queen clapped her hands.

"Well, you both have worked wonders. I am proud," Kylara said, smiling at Valon. He straightened his back and inclined his head, hiding his shock at the praise passing her lips. Warmth spread in his chest. "I should like the girl to stay in the castle for a while, to test her ability to retract the wings before calling them forth again."

"I—" Valon began to speak as Sophia turned to look at Luxiana, her eyes wide. This had not been agreed.

"I will have Cecilia and Firella provide her with a room. Now, you two"—The queen pointed a finger at her son and Luxiana as Valon's siblings took the girl's arms and guided her toward the arched exit. He turned his head to watch her, but a shadow licked his cheek, and he flinched, turning back to face his mother—"deserve a reward. Name it." She looked at Valon expectantly. Luxiana's pinkie brushed his hand in silent reassurance. He would never have reached this milestone without her; it was Luxiana who deserved something, a gift to make her smile.

"I would like..." Valon swallowed, evening his breathing. "To take Luxiana into the city," he said. Kylara grinned unnaturally at the perfect pronunciation of his words; he bit his lip to keep it from wobbling.

"A wonderful idea. It is a beautiful afternoon. You may go now but be back at dusk. I will send guards with you should you need directions." The queen turned back to her other children. Viserius and Valon's other brothers had their heads together, whispering. "Well done, Val," she said, waving a hand in dismissal. Valon turned with Luxiana, but her gaze was fixed down the hallway to where Cecilia led the girl away.

***

Leather and parchment. That's what the sixteenth store they visited smelt like, and it was the first scent Valon had enjoyed, its familiarity easing his anxiety. Though he would be remiss not to credit Luxiana's patience and reassurance for offering him a moment of reprieve; his breathing had become shallow, his skin pale and clammy upon stepping out of the castle. When the wind whipped against his skin, he was immediately transported to being seven years old atop the landing platform. Luxiana had gently looped her arm in his, waiting for his breathing to slow.

Despite the fast pace of his heartbeat and the regular glances skyward for dragons, Valon, along with Luxiana, was in his element. They trailed their hands over the leather-bound journals and admired the glass vials of ink in a myriad of colours. Bakeries, apothecaries, stores dedicated to glassware, one that specialised in taxidermy, another that traded in dragon-scaled protected chests, one that sold illustrated maps of the continent, and numerous book stores had all contributed to the purchases filling up their leather satchels.

"Which one?" Valon asked, pointing at the array of smaller journals, the exact same size as her favourite, which he knew was nearly filled. Luxiana smiled, bumping her shoulder against his; she pointed to a small forest green. Valon signalled to the shopkeeper, a Fae who appeared in his mid-forties. He reached for the top shelf.

"Engraving? The man asked, taking the journal over to a small stand holding a variety of brass letters and a hammer.

"Lu," Valon said with confidence. Luxiana smiled beside him as the man hammered the letters into the bottom corner of the journal.

"Each journal comes with a free inkpot," the man said, setting the journal down on the raised counter at the back of the narrow store. Valon reached for the highest shelf, pulling down a sparkling amber, the same shade as Xyliar's sigil.

"Something special," he said to Luxiana.

"You need one too, so we can match," she said, reaching for a deep chestnut journal on the bottom shelf and taking it to the engraving stand. "Val," she said joyfully to the shopkeeper, who smiled.

"You're a charming couple," he said. Luxiana giggled, and Valon blushed. The shopkeeper smiled at Valon. "If you want to take her someplace nice, the Garden of Statues at the west of the city open to the public every first rest day of the month."

"Thank you," he said, accepting the paper bag containing their journals and pots of sparkling ink.

"And the market four streets west of here is closest to the gardens, the food will stay warm if you fancied eating amongst the statues." The man waved his hand, and a shadow reached out, pulling the shop door open for them with a tinkle from the brass bell. A dark Fae. Valon wondered if his identity extended beyond that, if he had also been gifted the powers of Xander the first Dragon-Bound or Yvenya the first Staxion. Though he couldn't imagine a Dragon-Bound would have been permitted to do anything other than enrol into the armies. The pair inclined their heads in thanks and ducked out of the store. After Luxiana relayed the information to the two guards in copper armour, they began a march through the streets, heading west. Luxiana looped her arm through Valon's, the harsh wool of her gown brushing against his velvet jacket. He blushed when she smiled up at him.

The cobbled streets were slick with the late-morning shower. That's why she held his arm, or at least that's what Valon told himself as his clammy palms struggled to keep hold of the paper bag. Or perhaps she noted his calmness at her contact, though surely she did not care for his wellbeing that much?

Still, the sun hid behind dark clouds, a similar shade to the brickwork that made up most of the city. The buildings were all even in width and height, four stories tall. The further out of the city they ventured, the grander the buildings would become, with wrought-iron gates protecting property lines, intricate spires reaching toward the clouds and stone creatures lining ledges. The inner streets of the city were far simpler. Mahogany wooden signs hung from each store, with some painted in black and amber ink to give them the appearance of superiority. Couples filled the streets, walking arm in arm; men donned the same velvet-tailored jackets as Valon's, while women in gowns wore lace far more expensive than the woollen dress on Luxiana. Despite the evident wealth of the couples, the clothing in Xyliar appeared far more modest in style than the colourful illustrations Valon had seen of Q'Ohar, or the silks that his sisters travelled with when visiting Thassena. Even in a dull grey, Luxiana shone the brightest, and the several men who stole a second glance did not go unnoticed as they walked through the streets.

"Do you smell that?" Luxiana asked, squeezing his arm. The air was thick with the delicious scents of food.

"Do you k-know what you w-want?" he asked as the street opened into a square filled with stalls. Valon hoped so, for he was overwhelmed by the options. He had eaten better at the castle since becoming an adult. Even so, his mind could not comprehend the endless options and foods that appeared to originate outside of Xyliar. Long string-like dishes coated in sauces, rice laden with some form of meat, handmade pastries, filled with a variety of mixtures. All seemed far more intriguing than the usual meats and vegetables he was used to. Luxiana interlocked her hand with his and pulled him toward a stall in the corner.

"Two Andor game stews, please," she said, holding up her fingers to the Fae woman behind the stall. Valon waited patiently. He pushed his glasses up his nose, shifting closer to Luxiana as the noise in the square became more overwhelming with each passing second. Nearby, a stall owner yelled as a group of men chased two children darting away with a loaf of bread. Their plain clothes and dirt-streaked faces reminded him of Sophia. He hoped Cecilia was taking care of her. "Valon." Luxiana tugged on his sleeve while balancing two bowls tied with cloths to trap the heat. "I said, shall we find a spot in the Garden of Statues?"

Valon nodded, his eyes following the children as the men, breathless, dodged down an alleyway.

The stationery store owner was right; the walk from the market to the gardens was short, and it was only a few minutes before the guards escorting them stopped before a set of large wrought-iron gates, held open with chains. A small group of citizens trailed out of the stone chapel at its entrance, with moon engravings etched at the peak. It was where one would go to pray to Sitara, the Goddess of Dusk. Unlike most citizens, who believed their powers originated from the celestial goddess, Valon had never been one to partake in such traditions. The Abexu family was taught to worship their grandmother, Makaria. His family held a grudge against Sitara, led by their mother, for discarding Makaria to this land without a second thought.

Couples promenaded down the wide gravelled path along its centre, many stopping at the fountains dotted every few minutes, spurting water that was definitely dyed blue to appear more beautiful under the lack of afternoon sun. Valon and Luxiana veered off the main path and into a hedged maze, where each turn presented a new statue.

"Who carved these?" Luxiana asked. Valon shrugged. He had spent little of his life researching the city he could see from his windows and far more time dreaming of places further away.

"Most of th-the sculptors in the c-c-ity descend f-from the wealthiest families. Tirus, the s-son of the Lord of Kardyn, is k-k-known to be the m-m-most dedicated. I w-w-would not be surprised if he c-contributed a number of p-p-pieces." Valon only knew such information from listening to his brothers' jesting about the heinous things that occurred at the lord's annual ball, and how dull Tirus was for refusing to partake in their fun.

"If you could be anything else, what would you be? Would you sculpt?" Luxiana asked, unwrapping the bowls as they sat down on a stone bench opposite a large fountain in the maze's centre.

Two bodies reaching for one another, separated by spurting water in the centre, never quite touching.

"I am nothing n-now," Valon said, accepting the spoon from her and stirring the stew. A rich and herby scent drifted to his nose.

"You are an innovator, are you not?" Luxiana asked, spooning the stew into her mouth and closing her eyes with a sigh of contentment. Valon's smile was lopsided while watching her. "You research like a scholar, and you create like an artist. Your mind is developing theories like a philosopher. That makes you an innovator. So, what would you be instead?" she asked, taking another spoonful. Valon copied her, letting the thick stew warm his throat as he contemplated her question. The flavour harboured far more herbs than he was used to.

"A w-writer," he said, licking his lips.

"Like stories? Or articles?" she asked. Valon blushed.

"Stories."

"What kind of stories?" She smiled, scraping the sides of her bowl with her spoon. Valon cleared his throat before taking another bite. "Do you read a lot of stories?" she probed, clearly noting the way he avoided the question. Valon shrugged.

"I read to h-help myself s-s-sleep," he said, placing the emptied bowl on the floor by his feet.

"My mother used to read to help me sleep," Luxiana said, placing her chin on her hand. She rested her elbow on her leg and stared at the fountain.

"Where is she?"

"Probably dead," Luxiana said, though her face was not sad. "She's the one who handed me over to the Hallow Healers in the first place, in exchange for enough zonri to last her six months with only one mouth to feed instead of two."

"Why?" Valon asked, hoping it was not an invasive question.

"She said I was a reminder of the man she loved and lost," Luxiana sighed and leant back, planting her hands on either side of her. Valon stared at the small gap between their fingers.

"Who was he?"

"Some man from Eresydon, where I'm from," she said, moving her hand slightly until their pinkies touched. They had held hands and linked arms in the market, but not like this, not without reason.

"When d-did you a-rrive?" Valon asked, glancing at their fingers.

"When I was four. Apparently, my mother was convinced Xyliar would offer us a fresh start."

"A Wiccan?" Valon assumed. Other than the Shapeshifter they had injected, and the Stormbringer Cecilia had been married to when she was five-hundred years old and bore a different face, Valon had never encountered someone of a different Ithyion race. Slowly, Luxiana nodded.

"What about your father? Do you know who he is?"

Valon shook his head.

"My mother never s-speaks of our sires."

"So, we are both fatherless with mothers who show us no love," Luxiana murmured, hooking her pinkie with Valon's. She leant down with her other hand, picked up a rock, and began carving onto the bench. *Lu and Val.* "Two birds freed from our cages." With one green eye, the other near black, she looked up and stared intently at him, their faces so close they felt each other's breath. He memorised the light crinkle of her eyes when she smiled and the quirk of her lips. The light behind her green eye sparkled, while her dark eye promised entry to her soul. "Perhaps we will experience love one day, too."

Chapter Five

N*ine months later*

"Am I the strongest shifter you've tried this on?" The man's voice was already grating on Valon, and Luxiana rolled her eyes from behind his muscled shoulders. Valon stifled a laugh.

"Shifter, yes. Man, no," Valon replied.

"You've tried this on men who aren't shifters?" the man asked.

"Don't flex," Luxiana said from behind him before Valon could answer. He couldn't hide his smirk this time. The man relaxed his stocky frame as Luxiana wiped the sterile cloth between his shoulder blades.

"We've started trials on those native to Xyliar using a modified elixir," Valon confirmed as he feigned writing in his journal, hoping the man would stop asking questions.

"What's modified about it?" he asked. "Ah!"

Luxiana injected the needle between his shoulder-blades. It wasn't a question Valon could answer. His mother would punish him if she learnt he'd disclosed their testing methods on Xyliar Fae and Staxions. It had been over a year since he last felt a whip of shadow against his skin; he refused to tempt her. They had modified the elixir at his mother's request. The queen didn't particularly want to start a war with Eresydon when it became noticeable shapeshifters were going missing, and so they needed an elixir that could be tested on their own people. The ingredients were largely the same: dragon blood, marrow of a Shapeshifter, thornberry for acidity, moonlight fungus for stability—to be left in direct sunlight for two and a half hours. The only adjustments made in the recent batch for the volunteer soldiers were a larger marrow supply, the blood of a Shapeshifter, and remnants of failed attempts at extracting a Shapeshifter's essence. That was where both he and Luxiana drew the line, though they did not know how much longer they could get away with stalling. They both knew why it wasn't working on the Fae of Xyliar. Their essences were tainted with the power of Valon's mother after she took it from them. They needed a small amount of essence to be given freely by the Shapeshifter. Valon did not think anyone would volunteer.

"Okay, Wrenford," Luxiana said, placing the syringe down on the desk. "We need you to focus on those wings on the wall there, but we want you to imagine scales on them, like this," Luxiana said, placing a tray to his right with a display of various stacked dragon scales that had been provided to them by a bonded.

"Scaled wings, got it," Wrenford said. "Do I receive payment after? Or are there more tests?" he asked. Luxiana and Valon shared a look.

"More tests," Valon said, his lips pursed as he avoided the man's eye and focused on scribbling in his journal. "Different part of th-the castle." Valon cleared his throat as Luxiana placed a delicate hand on his shoulder. Nine months had passed since the start of these experiments; injecting men and women of different ages, Shapeshifters from different parts of Eresydon, Xyliar Fae of different locations, dark Fae, Staxion Fae, Dragon-Bound too. All in the name of tracking varied trends and changes to find a permanent solution for Xyliarans to grow and maintain wings. An army for the queen, for his mother. The man's muscles tensed.

"Oof, it burns," he grunted. Valon sighed and slammed his journal shut. He removed his glasses and rubbed his eyes. The burning always meant the same thing; he wouldn't be able to permanently maintain the wings. Based on the subject's muscle mass and young age, he would likely manage to retract and protract for about three months. Luxiana opened the door and waved to the guard as deep grey wings protruded from the man's back. No scales, just leathery skin. The usual.

"Thank you for your time, Wrenford," Luxiana said. "Sascha here will show you to the next test." The guard who was always at their tower gripped the man's arm. Luxiana closed the door and leant against it. This was always the part they found hardest, not knowing where the test subjects went next. A few months ago, Valon had broached the subject at dinner after Luxiana sobbed when sending a thirteen-year-old girl away. The look he received warned him that one more stuttered word would land him chained and back in a cell.

"He was the last for today," Valon said, his voice clear. His stutter had lessened in the last nine months. He still preferred shorter sentences, for it reared back up when he was nervous, but he felt far less inferior now around the dinner table. "It is the first rest day of the month. We could go into the city?" he asked. Luxiana offered a gentle smile, one that told him she appreciated the suggestion, but would still think about the man even as they breathed in the smell of leather and parchment or when they sat on their bench in the Garden of Statues.

"That would be nice." She smiled before washing her hands and removing her apron. Valon grinned at the colour of her gown, green for Eresydon. She had bought it on their last monthly visit to the city. His freedom from torture came with a weekly pocket of coin, which Valon took any opportunity to spend on Luxiana. Just as he intended to today, to free her mind of worry.

***

The wind whistling around the landing platforms outside the castle windows was louder at this time of year, so loud it could be heard through the glass windows. Below, the usually dark grey stone of Exoria—and the mountain the castle was built into—was blanketed in snow. Luxiana pulled her cloak tighter around herself as Valon fished gloves out of his cloak pocket, ready to wind through the final hallways before braving the cold ride down the mountainside. Luxiana stopped abruptly in front of him, and he collided with her back, holding her shoulders to prevent either of them from falling.

"Is that..." Luxiana's voice broke off with a croak. Valon looked ahead to find the reason for her abrupt stop and failed words.

"No," Valon breathed. His hands slid down Luxiana's arms, reaching for her wrists as she tried to run from him down the corridor. His Fae blood made it easy to maintain his grip on her, as much as it pained him to have to. But he could not allow Luxiana to be collateral damage to his mother's fury.

"You monsters!" Luxiana yelled. "She's a child!" Her voice broke. Valon knew tears would fall down her cheeks, mirroring those blurring his vision now. He pulled Luxiana back, wrapping his arm around her chest to keep her from acting rashly. Slowly, his mother approached from the other end of the hallway. With the shadows pooling at her feet, this would not end well. Two healers walked with the patient, their hands resting on the lower back of the young girl with forest-green wings. Sophia. Her hands cradled her stomach, swollen after nine months.

"This is why you wanted a constant supply of elixir sent to the healers!" Luxiana spat. "So you could inject her through her pregnancy in the hope she will birth a new race?" Luxiana stopped fighting and cried in Valon's arms as the girl's lips quivered. Her face was hollow, nothing like the typical glow during pregnancy. Her hair was limp around her shoulders, and dark circles lined her red-rimmed eyes. She had just wanted money for her brothers.

"Who is the father?" Valon asked, holding his chin up over Luxiana's head. His mother whispered quietly to the healers, who then steered Sophia back in the direction they had appeared. The girl glanced over her shoulder repeatedly, her eyes pleading.

"You should not distress a pregnant woman," the queen said, briskly approaching the pair. The hallway darkened. Shadows crept up the walls and windows, hiding the snowfall outside.

"Woman?" Luxiana screamed. "She is not even seventeen!" Shadows whipped out toward Luxiana then, and Valon shoved her to the floor, taking the blow of the whip that coiled around his neck. Kylara tugged, pulling her son forward.

"If you had found a way for the elixir to permanently change our Fae races, I would not have resorted to such measures." The queen's eyes darkened, the black of her irises nearly swallowing the whites as she shifted her gaze from Luxiana on the floor to Valon balancing on his tiptoes. The darkness teetered at the edges of her irises, toeing the line between Kylara relinquishing the control of her power, releasing it in full force. A dark cell flashed in his mind. "Have you found a way, Val?" she asked, emotionless. "Perhaps we should end your experiments completely and proceed with my plan." The queen tightened her shadows' grip, and Valon choked for air.

"No, please! I—" Luxiana stopped speaking from where she still knelt on the floor, her glistening eyes shifting between Valon and the hallway where Sophia had been taken.

"You know something," Kylara said, loosening her grip on her son. "I can sense it at the edges of your mind, girl. I can easily rip it from your thoughts or force you to write it out in your own blood." Luxiana's face, if possible, paled even further at the mention of using her Staxion abilities. Valon tried to mouth the word 'no' as his mother flung him to the ground and lashed a whip of shadow across his back. Valon did not cry out; he had learnt to stifle his pain over a century ago. Nor did he want Luxiana to hear his anguish as a result of defending her. The whip came down again, ripping his jacket and shirt. He knew Luxiana could see the blood trickling down his skin.

"I know how to fix the elixir!" Luxiana screamed. Valon breathed in a gulp of air as the shadows retracted. Resting on his hands and knees, his fingers became wet with his own splattered blood as he turned to face her and shook his head again. "I can get the consensual essence of a Shapeshifter," she said, pursing her lips. The queen watched, remaining silent, waiting for the pair to explain their secret. "It must be consensual. No matter what means you use currently, whether that be torture, or false promises, it will be tainted. I can get it wilfully."

Valon frowned, waiting for her to meet his eye so he could try to decipher her plan. She finally stared at him. One black eye, one... green, complementing her gown and the journal she loved so much—the Eresydon goods she always sought in the market. He had assumed it was merely a nostalgic memory of her childhood home, a place she had last been happy. *I reminded her of the man she loved and lost.* Luxiana said her mother was a Wiccan, but never said her father was too. She never confirmed if he was a Wiccan or a—

"I can get it, just please don't hurt him," she cried. A Shapeshifter. Luxiana's strong emotions were not simply empathy; she was a Shapeshifter. Fear rippled through Valon. If his mother deduced the same thing, there was no telling what she might do, or what experiments she would force Luxiana into, or *who* she might involve. He had to protect her and keep her from both his brothers and the darkness. Something even they could not deny.

"Wait," Valon choked, forcing himself to stand. His mother's shadows crawled across the floor, poised and ready to inflict another punishment with a single thought. "If she is to trade this information, I want something in return," Valon said. "Something that offers her protection against any secrets she has kept from you or I during this experiment." He added himself to the equation to steer his mother into believing he knew nothing of the secrets kept from her, making it more believable they kept nothing else from her. This was the one thing he could think of—a link to know when she was in danger.

"Your speech has improved," his mother said. "As has your confidence. You almost look like your brothers." Valon tried not to wince. To him, it was not a compliment. "Very well, Valon. What do you want?" Valon looked at Luxiana with tears still streaming down her face.

"I request a celestial-bound marriage."

Chapter Six

This marriage was nothing like the ones Valon had read about or imagined. Luxiana wasn't in a white gown and veil, carrying a bouquet of her favourite flowers as they did in Asynthos. Nor was Valon standing before an altar with a tear in his eye as string music signalled her entrance, ready to wrap their hands in the fabrics of their families as they did in Eresydon. There was no ocean lapping at their waists like the ceremonies of Thassena or a pyre honouring the deities of Q'Ohar. They weren't surrounded by friends, nor were they in love with one another—at least, he didn't think she loved him. A part of him was pained; his guilt-shrouded logic deduced this as the best way to protect Luxiana. The only way to keep her safe was to be bound to him. There was little documented about celestial bindings, only handwritten journals that once belonged to Makaria, and the myths passed through Ithyion's other states. Each believed them to represent different things. All he knew from his grandmother's journal was the binding of this marriage would allow him to *feel* Luxiana, to know she was safe. He just hoped she wouldn't resent him for the binding of their souls, their essence, their lives—their incredibly long lives now she was tied to his Fae lifespan.

"Kneel," his mother commanded, sounding just as he imagined the daughter of Makaria should, the granddaughter, by essence, of Sitara. Darkness, temptation, the sound of the night dripping from her words. Valon's hands trembled, but he did as he was told. The polished rock beneath his knees was cold from the recent snow, which had fallen only hours before his mother granted his request. His unbuttoned black shirt billowed in the wind where they knelt on the highest rooftop point of the castle, as close to the sun, the moons, and the stars as possible. As close to Sonos and Sitara, the God of Dawn and Goddess of Dusk. The first celestial gods.

Though she was still a head shorter, as Luxiana knelt, her eyes met his. He pursed his lips to hide his emotions from his mother, keeping his resentment private. But no resentment showed in Luxiana's eyes, only a steely determination as she gave him the smallest nod and extended her hands. Valon had thought she was beautiful from the moment she walked into his tower, but she appeared as a goddess now, perhaps one who might strip him of his self-hatred and fears.

The moment his mother granted the request, she took Luxiana away for preparations, despite Valon's protests. His brothers arrived at their tower shortly after to provide him with the loose black trousers and the shirt he wore now. But Luxiana—Lu—was being presented as a gift to the gods, and Valon was prepared to sacrifice everything to keep her by his side. Her hair was still damp; soft ringlets curled around her face, the rest cascading down her bare back. The gown was not a gown at all, but a simple, golden, silk slip with a low-cut back and lace detailing under her breasts and along the curves before forming thin straps. She was like the sun itself, sparkling under the light of the full moon watching over them now. The sky was cloudless and the stars blinking as they took in the performance soon to begin.

Below the stone dais, waiting against a wall, were his siblings. Viserius's scowl confirmed one thing to Valon: their mother would not allow him to pursue Luxiana in any way. Regardless of what they all thought of Valon, a celestial bound marriage was sacred.

"Who presents the gifts to the gods?" his mother called. Cecilia and Viserius stepped forward, the eldest daughter and eldest son. They both bowed their heads and raised polished platters up to Luxiana and Valon. Two still-beating hearts sat bloodied on a gold and silver platter. Valon tried not to think about who had been murdered for this ceremony. Luxiana's lip wobbled; she looked like she was about to empty the contents of her stomach. Valon squeezed her hands before releasing them. He reached for the darkened heart on the silver platter and the thin dagger engraved with the moon on its hilt. Luxiana followed his actions, her hands trembling as she held the much smaller heart and the golden dagger. The face of the sun glinted as she gripped it fearfully in her hand, as though she might accidentally wound herself.

"To the celestial beings who grant us all, we present the heart of the corrupt and the heart of the innocent. Two hearts awaken; two souls found. In return for two lives taken, we ask for two lives bound." His mother's palms were turned outward; shadows danced across them as she nodded at Valon. With trembling hands, he took a deep breath and plunged the dagger into the heart, waiting as Luxiana did the same. Her tears watered as the beating slowly faded until the organs were cold and still in their palms. They returned the hearts to the platter.

"You will now paint the symbols of the celestial two on one another's chests," Kylara commanded. Valon blushed as he glanced at Luxiana's pale skin. She leant forward, saving him from the hesitation, and slowly, using her bloodied hand, painted an interlocking sun and moon on his chest where his shirt billowed open. He mirrored the action, her skin soft and pebbled in the cold air. His hand shook at touching a different part of her. "Interlock your hands and repeat after me." The pair did as they were told.

"I give myself endlessly to you."

"I relent the hold on my soul."

"I ask my body to be made anew."

"I give you ultimate control."

"I call upon the celestial two."

"I ask that they see my word is true."

Valon's hands warmed where they met Luxiana's, a faint light beginning from their fingertips and seeping between their clasped hands.

"Sonos and Sitara have heard your plea. We must wait and see if they deem your essences a match," Kylara said, her eyes intently watching the glow between their hands. Valon knew this was why she had agreed so readily to the request. Witnessing the celestial binding would confirm whether he possessed some power deep within, even if it was not enough to manifest, because why would the gods bestow a tie to someone with no power, someone unworthy? It had been a risk to ask for such a marriage. Every being had a soul, an essence, but only those with power had a white glow. Those with no power, descendants of the first mortals created by the gods to fill the other states, would show a simple translucent thread, barely visible to the naked eye. If his mother could, she would rip it from him to inspect, but as she was not a god or a deity, she risked killing him. The very fate that had befallen the Shapeshifters she had stolen from. This would confirm to his mother if there was hope for him yet, if more must be done to awaken his power. Slowly, the white light trickled from beneath their palms, painting the floor with streaks like lightning. Valon loosed a shaky breath as the light began to twist and spiral, wrapping around them both, bathing them in white. He glanced sideways at his mother and wished he hadn't. The smile on her face was one only of calculation, not happiness or joy, as the celestial binding was granted.

"With this blessing from the gods, your marriage is recognised as sacred. Your souls are one. May you feel what one another feels, may your thoughts intertwine, may you know of one another's presence at all times from this day until one of you passes." Valon gave Luxiana a small smile, one she returned as the white glow around them faded and the weight of someone else's mind became present. Snow fell around them as they turned their palms, the interlocking sun and moon visible on their palms.

"Hi Val."

"Hi Lu."

***

As a child, Valon longed to read his family's minds, to fully comprehend why his lack of power was such a problem for them. Now that he saw into another's mind, he wished to rid himself of the gift immediately. It felt like an invasion. A single thought could manifest a memory or image that was not his own. He apologised countless times, despite Luxiana's reassurances that he did not need to. The wall between their rooms was knocked down. Each side had been near identical, the only furniture a single wooden bed, a chest of drawers, and a writing desk, all the same deep mahogany as the furniture in the top room of their tower. Valon had spent many sleepless nights staring up at the brick ceiling, wondering if she too was wide awake. Open books still sat on his desk, from where he had used his sleeplessness to read. The only difference in the room now was the removal of the two single beds, replaced by a larger one smothered in black sheets. Small pieces of rubble remained on the floor as the two of them leant on the opposite sides of what had once kept them apart at night.

"I'm sorry I forced this on you," he whispered in his mind. Luxiana shivered, still in the thin golden slip that emphasised the lighter highlights in her hair under the glow of the room's lanterns.

"If I had wanted to say no, I would have."

"But I have signed you to a life as long as mine, with nearly no way out. Only a god or deity can sever a tie without killing the bonded partner." Luxiana smiled at his words, and he frowned. He didn't ask why, but she would have sensed the question. *"Your voice is confident. Sturdy."*

"I don't believe I ever stuttered in my thoughts." He smiled, prompting a giggle from Luxiana that lit up her face. She was magnificent. Luxiana blushed; she sensed that thought too. He rubbed the back of his neck.

"You are magnificent too," she said aloud this time. "You did not have to protect me from whatever may have come when I gave up the information about the essence."

"I did," Valon said. "It is my fault you are in this position." He looked down at his feet and kicked a piece of rock. "If I were not a disappointment to my family, I would not have been r-relegated to that tower to ex-ex-periment. If I had not been slow, my m-mother would not have f-f-found me an assistant; you wouldn't h-have been sent to me; we wouldn't have c-compl-leted the experiments and found out what was m-missing; you would never have known to offer u-up—" Valon choked on his words and pressed his hands to his eyes in frustration, stinging with unshed tears. He could sense her move like a light in the back of his mind. Luxiana's hands were gentle as she cupped his wrists to pull his hands from his face. She planted a kiss on the celestial binding on his palm.

"We can never know which direction the threads of fate will tug us in," she whispered, holding his hands above her heart. "But I think we would have found one another, either way." Her movements were slow as she stepped closer. His hands fell to her waist, hesitant, before planting them softly on her hips as she cupped his cheek. "In the old language, still used by the deities and the gods, there is a saying." Luxiana reached up on her tiptoes and planted a kiss on his cheek. Valon sucked in a ragged breath as she moved and kissed the other one. As he leant down to rest his forehead against hers, she said, "*Adeti caligh et alu servusian.*" Her voice caressed each word as her eyes pierced his before she planted a gentle kiss on his lips. "After creation and before severing," she said. Valon frowned, slowly trailing his hands up her ribcage.

"What does it mean?" he asked, his lips hovering before hers. Luxiana smiled. "It has lost the rest of the passage over time. But it is a reminder that you can only control that in between your birth and your death. Fate may put us on our paths, but only you and I, Val, control what we allow to taint our marriage, and what we allow to ignite our love."

"*Love?*" he asked silently, waiting for her to bring her lips closer. "*From the moment you told me to call you Val. From the moment I knew with you was exactly where I should be.*"

Chapter Seven

*S**ix months later*

"You can't give anymore, Lu," Valon said, rubbing his wife's back as she hunched over at her desk. Luxiana sniffed and added a tally to her green journal.

"We have no choice, Val. There is a war; they need more soldiers."

"Then they can take more foot soldiers or work better rotations with the Dragon-Bound. The Fae's powers work just fine without the advantage of wings."

"Do you want to be the one to tell your mother that?" Luxiana asked, spinning on her stool to face him. Valon grasped her hands and knelt before her. She was paler than normal. Beads of sweat marked her forehead from the energy of drawing from her essence daily and willingly extracting pieces of it. As Luxiana was not a Shapeshifter with the elemental powers of Garridon, they had no way to measure if the constant withdrawal of essence would affect her abilities. Having shifted so infrequently in her life, her strength was hard to measure.

"She cares more about seeing the outcome of this than putting your life in danger," Valon murmured, resting his palm on her growing womb. "As much as it pains me to say, we know there's a high likelihood our children will be born with wings."

"It was a necessary risk to inject myself before..."

"I know, I know," he reassured her. "We do not need to rehash that discussion. I understand why. You wanted to give them the best opportunity in the future, to not be seen as a disappointment like..." Valon stopped as pain pierced his chest, stemming from Luxiana's anguish at the reminder of what he'd endured as a child and what they were attempting to prevent for their own children. Luxiana was to be the first experimental subject to conceive and give birth to a child while using the elixir enhanced with her own essence. Knowing their children would be unique, that his mother would want to keep them alive as a result, was what he held onto as he debated telling Kylara they needed to stop withdrawing her essence. He would not punish Luxiana for his request, not when she carried a potential new race.

"If you keep going, we might not have any children," he whispered, stroking her cheek. Outside, a flurry of roars announced the return of the Dragon-Bound. They had been gone for three weeks, their numbers split from defending the oceans surrounding Xyliar. They were inconveniently placed next to a state that had sided with the deities. Carvyre was united with Thassena and Eresydon, while Xyliar, Asynthos, and Q'Ohar had sided with the celestial gods. It had been a surprise when his grandmother, Makaria, had sided with her mother. Given she had wanted nothing to do with her, Valon wondered if it was an attempt to impress her. As a result, the Abexu family and all Xyliar backed the gods and goddesses. Xyliar was aligned with not only Sitara and Sonos, but their children, Nerida, Keres, Vala, and Garridon. At least their state was unified on the decision; many of the others faced uprisings as the people, those who wished to defy the deities and support their original celestial god, rebelled.

"Can you make it to the throne room?" Valon asked. Luxiana reached for the wet cloth in the bowl on her desk and wiped her forehead. She nodded.

"We need to know if things have escalated—*and whether we wish to proceed with the alternative plan.*" She added the latter suggestion in their minds.

"It could still be too risky to do it now. Perhaps we should wait until the babies are born."

"It will be more difficult with two screaming newborns." It would be difficult either way. By her estimation, Luxiana was only three months pregnant. Upon discovering her pregnancy, had they known war would begin across the kingdom, they would have fled immediately. Fleeing now, when they were both such a large part of the efforts, was near impossible. The doors to their tower were constantly watched, with Valon's mother expecting them to work day and night to build the ranks of the winged army. The very winged creatures that unwittingly started the Great War.

It all began with a message from the Queen of Asynthos. An Angel had spotted a dark Fae permanently changed by the elixir. She had called on her deities—Dalina, Stroman, and Araya—and alerted them to the emergence of a new race. In the past, only the celestial gods and two others had created such a feat. Sonos and Sitara with the first light Fae, Oxyron, who in turn created the Hypherion Fae and Pegasus-Bound, and the first dark Fae, Makaria, who then created the Staxion Fae and Dragon-Bound, all direct parallels to one another, mirroring the two first gods. Vala and her Angels, Stormbringers, and Truthtellers. Nerida and her Sirens, Seers, and Illusionists. Keres and his Xyra, Smokeshifters, and Forgers. Finally, Garridon and his Shapeshifters and Wiccan, the only god to have created only two deities. It was not an absurd deduction for the deities the Asynthos queen called on to assume one of the celestial gods had created a new race.

The blame was first pointed at Vala and Keres, for both had created deities with wings. Next, they accused Garridon, for Shapeshifters could, of course, shift into birds. After that, Sitara was blamed for the darkness in their wings. Sonos and Nerida were the only ones left unscathed by the deities' fury, which resulted in Carvyre and Thassena's royal families siding with their cause. Their fury was fuelled by envy at their inability to create new races themselves. Fury fuelled by the possibility that if another race now existed, were they now deities too? A new deity for citizens to worship, drawing attention from the others? The more a deity was worshipped, the more enhanced their powers became; they did not want to share any more than they had to. But at least they were united in their fury against the celestial gods, who seemed happy to keep their hands clean while their people died for their cause. Now, Valon and Luxiana would attend the hearing to understand just how many more had been lost at their hands.

***

Every new name spoken added another splinter to Luxiana and Valon's soul. Glancing around the throne room, and at each of his siblings who stood below one of the carved dragon heads lining the room, he knew none of them cared. If it was up to them, this would not be included in the spoils of war. They would simply plan the retaliation. But Kylara had lived long enough to see rulers fall because of the neglect toward their people. It was laughable, really, how she cared not for the poverty of those in her capital, or the bodies she so easily threw at experimentation, but keeping people happy during war; that she apparently cared about. So, when soldiers returned from their new missions overseas, a handful of citizens were selected at random to visit the castle, where they would hear the names of the fallen and dine with the royal family in their honour.

When the sobs died down and the citizens were escorted from the throne room to one of the sitting rooms for refreshments, the queen conjured a table of shadows and the Abexu royal family all took a seat.

"It is less than the last mission," Viserius said. His face was stern, and his age—despite being well over six-hundred years old—was only now beginning to show.

"It is still more than was lost on Carvyre's shores," Kylara snapped, resting her chin on her interlocked fingers. The plan had been to capture a fleet of pegasi that were regularly journeying to the Fractured Isles that lay between Xyliar and Carvyre. Instead, they had fallen into a trap and lost three dragons. Kylara's eyes found Valon's. "Where are we up to in creating more elixirs?"

"Don't," Luxiana begged silently. Valon squeezed her knee under the wisps of shadows.

"We have reached the capacity Luxiana can provide, given her condition. Until the pregnancy is complete, she cannot draw any more essence," he said, holding his chin high. Future fatherhood emboldened him. Protecting Luxiana gave him confidence. His mother narrowed her eyes. "Any more risks losing the babies and all chance of understanding what the future of the Abexu family may hold," he added the latter part with an internal grimace, words spoken for his mother's benefit alone. Her frown smoothed; she understood the risk.

"It's your wife's fault we're in this mess to begin with," Cecilia snapped. Luxiana flinched. She already blamed herself. Even if she was not the one to personally command the Fae who was caught, it was her wilfully given essence that had successfully created him. It was Luxiana who had suggested he needed to test long distances to ensure his wings were strong. Yet she had not been the one to tell him to fly to Asynthos; that had all been Viserius.

"Don't listen to her, Val. She's just bitter because her betrothed was one of the Dragon-Bound who died this time." Viserius rolled his eyes, and Valon gave him a tight smile. His brother had become friendlier since their success with the elixir, ever since a war erupted because of it. Valon placated him with polite smiles and nods, hoping to keep him as far from himself and his wife as possible.

"Excuse me for being upset! I lost the love of my—" Shadows whipped across the table, rapping the back of Cecilia's knuckles. It was far less punishment than he would have received.

"You think every man you sleep with is the love of your life," snapped their mother. "Your complaints don't help us plan our next steps."

"We could return to making elixir with essence taken... unwill-ingly, again." Viserius grinned, and Luxiana flinched beside Valon.

"The last time, it worked, but most were unable to sustain the wings for longer than a few weeks," Valon interjected.

"Long enough for missions to Carvyre," Kylara mused. Nausea rose in Luxiana's throat—Valon felt it. The idea of harming more Shapeshifters for their essence was unbearable; she was already burdened with so much death already. "Is there a way to adapt the elixir, a way to prolong the effects?"

"Not that we—"

"I'll try," Viserius said. Valon furrowed his brow.

"You don't know the first thing about the measurements or the technique or—"

"Then you can give me your notes." Viserius smiled, watching Valon. His eyes turned to Luxiana, trailing down her body. "You wouldn't want to slow down our opportunity to win the war, would you, brother?" Valon gritted his teeth. When he did not reply, his mother clapped her hands.

"Very well. Valon and Luxiana can take a break from their work to ensure Luxiana's pregnancy is healthy. Viserius will take over the experimentation and testing." His mother waited for them all to depart. Viserius's smile was menacing as he passed Valon and Luxiana and headed toward the corridor they knew hid the young female Shapeshifters.

"We need to leave, and we need to set them free," Luxiana said silently, reaching for Valon's hand.

"We can try, but there is no way we'll be able to now, not before the babies are born. Viserius will come to us with questions about the elixir and my notes. Before, when he left us alone, it would have been easier to find a pocket of time, but now, he'll be too unpredictable," Valon replied. The pair slowed as they passed the turning for the corridor Viserius had taken. There were fewer lanterns, the hallway filled with crawling shadows, all stemming from below a doorway

at the end, which Valon knew led down to the cells he was well acquainted with. A muffled scream sounded, and Luxiana squeezed Valon's hand harder.

"Perhaps we could say we want to monitor the new subjects. We can still work; I just can't draw on my essence," she said.

"Would you be able to cope with that? Seeing whatever suffering they have endured because of our guidance? Valon pulled her away from the corridor and toward their tower. *Because I don't know if I could bear feeling that from you, Lu. It is already hard absorbing your pain as well as my own."* Guilt washed over him, leaking from her like tears. He rubbed her back. Once again, Valon wished he had never been born without power. Although his celestial-bound marriage showed something lay dormant within him, it had yet to come to the surface, and his mother had given up on bringing it forth. Instead, she waited to see if something would trigger it. If he could unlock it by himself, perhaps then he could get them out.

Chapter Eight

It had to work. It had to. Valon repeated those words over and over in his mind, but the doubt was firmly cemented in every part of his body, even with the newfound confidence Luxiana gave him. Why should he be able to awaken the power that was somewhere within him when his own mother and siblings could not? Despite the question of doubt worming its way around his mind, it was also the reason he was telling himself perhaps he *could* do this. Their methods had always been incited by fear, in forcing his power to come forth as though it would be triggered to protect him. Instead, it had hidden further away, having known nothing other than fear.

Valon was trying a different route, a direct route—straight to the source.

The moon was merely a sliver, it felt sensible to call upon power in complete darkness. Under a full moon, he would have feared someone might watch him, his siblings, his mother, grandmother, or perhaps even Sitara herself. Valon wanted to keep their involvement as far from his power as possible. They were all the same. Power hungry, self-obsessed, egotistical. Valon simply wanted power to protect his family and save those who had befallen their fate because of his and Luxiana's work.

Valon had only been a part of a celestial ceremony once, in his binding marriage to Luxiana, but he had seen two others in his lifetime. The first occasion was when Kylara tried to conceive a child after Valon proved unworthy. The physicians had warned that perhaps Valon had no power due to the many children she had birthed before. Her solution was to call on as much blessing and power as possible. Naked and painted in the blood of a sacrifice, Kylara knelt on the stone rooftop of Exoria's castle and directed as much of her dark power as possible skyward to the moon. Kylara begged Sitara to listen to her pleas, to bless her with a healthy pregnancy. Sitara did not listen.

The second celestial ceremony he witnessed was his mother trying to revive the stillborn baby. There was a moment, when Kylara raged at him the night his dead sibling was born, that he thought he would be the one sacrificed. But alas, she took the life of a baby born the same day. Valon watched as she sacrificed the babe and painted the moon with its blood, crying to Sitara to bring her child back to life. Valon had never truly seen his mother cry until then, and to this day he still did not know what emotions were behind the tears. Anger for failing? Resentment and blame toward Valon? Grief at another loss of potential power for her family? Or some sudden maternal instinct she had never shown Valon?

Both ceremonies had taught him what not to try. So, there was no sacrifice, no power used to call on another, and no shouting or crying. Atop the roof of his turret, Valon sat cross-legged in as close to complete darkness as possible. He faced the east with his back to the distant city glow, the darkness of the ocean ahead. It was a cloudy night, with barely a star visible above. Dark. Quiet. Untainted.

Valon pulled the object from his shirt pocket and passed it back and forth between his hands. He closed his eyes and breathed deeply. At the core of his theory was the land—the world's natural beginning. Power was passed down in lineages, but to summon the highest being possible, he needed to show he understood who truly started it all. Valon picked up the dagger from the rooftop and carefully sliced his palm, the one without his celestial bond. What was another striped scar on his skin? Slowly, he allowed his blood to drip, only his blood, to show he was sacrificing his inner fears and chaotic emotions. When he opened his eyes, blood coated the lump of rock. To any regular citizen, one might think it was simply that—a rock. But to Valon, it was one of the rare artifacts his family had collected over the years. A fallen star. He needed something that had existed for as long as Sitara and Sonos themselves, to prove he sought the thoughts and help of the oldest beings that he could think to attach an object to. The night before he had used the same dagger to carve the old language into its face. A single word, one of two that were rarely used now, not when so many knew the rule of these lands to belong to the celestial gods and deities.

Valon smeared the blood until it filled the cracks of the word. Chaos.

***

"Did whatever you plan, work?" Luxiana asked, gripping Valon's hand tighter. She glanced over her shoulder as they hurried down the hallways of the castle.

"No," he sighed. It was the truth; his calls to Chaos had not worked. They could not have, for his only memory of the night prior was falling asleep on the rooftop while waiting before awaking the next morning to the rising sun's warmth on his face.

"What did you try—" Luxiana stopped talking as Valon pulled them into the door of a nearby room; the sounds of guards' footsteps followed briskly after. His wife's eyes widened as they waited. "I thought we counted out the patrols accurately; there shouldn't have been another one down here for at least thirty minutes," Luxiana said. She rubbed her hands together and began pacing as Valon cracked open the door and peered into the hallway.

"They must have started a new rotation," he murmured. "But that means it should be quiet for at least fifteen minutes. We can't risk any longer in case they have changed the time between patrols." Valon grabbed Luxiana's hand and pulled them back out into the hallway, hurrying along the stone floor and rounding corners until they paused at the final one. There would be two guards in front of the door, and they needed to distract them.

"*Ready?*" Valon asked silently. Luxiana nodded and pulled a glass orb from her pocket. The pair brought cloths to their faces before she threw it around the corner. A light smash followed, and then coughing and two distinct thuds. It had worked. The pair rounded the corner and made a dash for the single door at the end of the hallway. Valon glanced at Luxiana to ensure she was okay. He had not wanted her to take part in this plan, but she had insisted. They stepped over the two men knocked out from the gas they had concocted from sleeping herbs, heightened by the addition of dragon smoke.

Valon's hand trembled as he pushed the heavy door open, knowing the spiral stairs down the cave like cells all too well. Instead of venturing all the way to the bottom, they paused on the first floor below. It was silent behind the door that had become Viserius's workspace. Luxiana turned the doorknob.

"*We don't have time,*" Valon said silently.

"*You go down and release the prisoners; I'll see what I can find out about his experiments.*" Luxiana did not wait to listen to Valon's objection. She gently pushed his back toward the next step before creeping into the workspace. As the spiral steps narrowed and a chill settled, Valon focused on the feeling of Luxiana's soul intertwined with his, sensing for any fear or pain. All he gathered was curiosity as she looked around the room above.

A low growl sounded from the bottom of the staircase, behind the pillar, only a few steps away. Valon froze. A shiver ran up his spine as his hands reached out either side of him, using the rock to steady himself. The growl stopped, replaced by the sound of claws scraping across stone, echoing further with each step.

"*What is it?*" Luxiana's voice echoed through his mind; she felt his apprehension.

"*Some kind of creature.*"

"*Are the prisoners okay?*"

"I don't know; I can't hear them." Valon took another slow step down, and then another, and then another, pausing with each step to listen and ensure the creature hadn't turned back. The only sounds were crunching followed by a snuffling sound. His hand trembled as he peered around the wall on the penultimate step.

Every single cell door was open. Not a single prisoner. Upstairs, he felt Luxiana's heartbeat quicken. Something was wrong. In his rush back to her, Valon's foot slipped; his knee resounded with a crack as he fell with a thud, his palms grazing the walls as he tried to steady himself. In the darkness, the crunching stopped. As Valon scrambled to his feet, the scraping of claws began, quickening toward him until a face that would haunt him for the rest of his life lunged from the darkness. It had the usual bone structure of a human child, the cheekbones, the nose, albeit flattened, the forehead with skin like black leather pulled taut over its face, accentuating the gaping sockets where eyes should have been. Whatever the thing was roared, spraying saliva over rotten canine teeth.

"Valon!" Luxiana screamed in his mind, though he could not tell if she was in danger or if her fear was for him. Despite the roaring pain in his knee, he flung himself up two steps, still facing the fast-approaching creature. It grunted, its leathery wings slamming into the walls as it realised it could not fit onto the narrow staircase. Valon did not take another moment to examine the creature or understand what he saw and turned, half limping, half crawling up the staircase until he reached the floor above.

The door to the workspace was open, but Luxiana did not stand at the threshold. Instead, he came face to face with dark polished shoes as he hauled himself up the final step.

"If you had wanted to visit, you only needed to ask politely." Viserius smirked down at his brother. Valon waited, his heart beating loud in his chest as he sought Luxiana's emotions.

"I'm hiding in a cupboard."

Valon held his hand out in front of him and tried to feign confidence.

"Well, that w-was the intention," he said. Viserius did not immediately reach for his brother's hand. "But when I a-arrived, your g-guards were unconscious." Valon swallowed hard, trying to level his breathing from the fear still shaking his bones. Viserius narrowed his eyes, and Valon wondered if this was how he would die, kicked back down the stairs to be eaten alive by that *thing*.

A hand reached out to him, a copper signet ring on the index finger.

"They were awful guards anyway, whoever attempted to break in has given me a reason to kill them," Viserius chuckled, tugging on Valon's hand to help him to his feet. He brushed dust off the shoulders of his jacket. "Now you're here, perhaps you can help me with understanding my little problem downstairs." Viserius steered Valon into the workspace. Valon's eyes immediately scanned the room for a cupboard and found it next to the window and a wall coated in different tools he could only assume were for torture.

"The c-creature?" Valon asked. Viserius hummed and pulled a large open book toward them on the centre table.

"I've been experimenting with the unwilling essence of a Shapeshifter." He pointed toward a sketch of a Xyliarian Fae with leather wings. "I've succeeded in getting it to work with no burning sensation upon injection, so now we must wait to see if they lose their wings or not. But each time I inject, there is a fifty-fifty chance."

"Fifty-fifty chance of w-wh-what?" Valon asked. He did not know if he was more uncomfortable that his brother had found a way to work with the stolen essence, or that he was speaking to him so... normally.

"Of success," he said, rubbing his chin. "None of them experience burning, but half of them turn into those things within a few hours; the others seem fine and able to focus only on their wings."

"A side effect?" Valon asked. "Of an unstable elixir?"

"I've been experimenting with raw Tungstyn metal found on

the isles. But too much or too little either stops the transformation from happening at all or creates that thing."

"I could look at the compound…" Valon was cut off by the sound of shouts and a roar above, followed by screams coming from their sisters' afternoon tearoom. The exact same roar he had been faced with moments ago.

"For fuck's sake," Viserius cursed, slamming his fist on the table so hard that Valon jumped. "I told the fools at the rear entrance of the cells to double up defences so they couldn't break out into the tunnels up to the main castle floors." Viserius slammed the book closed and stormed from the room. Before Valon could overthink whether his brother would turn back, he hobbled to the cupboard and lurched it open. Luxiana stumbled out, wrapping her hands around his neck as she cried silently.

Chapter Nine

*T*hirty Years later

"Ossie!" Luxiana called down the tower's winding staircase. Valon chuckled to himself. He had told her he wouldn't listen. "Osiris Abexu, get up here immediately or I'll be telling your mother all about the trick you played on your grandfather, and then she'll stop you from going into the city at the weekends to see that girl in the markets!" Luxiana blew a tuft of hair from her face and smirked at Valon at the sound of frantic footsteps.

"Okay, I was wrong," Valon said silently.

"He doesn't just like her, he loooooooves— Ow!" Sallos cried out as a ball-shaped blur of sparkling darkness flew through the doorway and hit the boy in the arm, sending him sprawling over his chair. Brushing his floppy, dark hair from his face, Sallos readied a returning ball of shadow, though this one lacked the unique coppery threads that Osiris's power held, which they attributed to his mixed lineage.

"Not near the vials!" Valon scolded. He should really tidy them away when the boys visited. The current vials all contained his own attempts at adjusting the elixir that he and his wife had created over thirty years ago. To this day, he had not been able to manipulate it in the ways Viserius had, nor had he ever been invited back down to his brother's workspace and cells. Whatever normality that had briefly existed between them had never returned, though it was safer, mentally, for Valon and Luxiana to try to pretend they did not hear the screams from the cells late at night or the occasional roar with a higher pitch than dragons. They had a family now; that was their priority.

"Sorry, grandfather," Osiris said, though his lopsided grin had already earned his forgiveness.

"Help your brother tidy away the study books you should have been reading," Valon said with a raised eyebrow. Osiris did as he was told; he always did. Eventually.

"We need you to stay in your rooms this evening, boys," Luxiana said, wiping the sticky jam marks off her desk. It seemed an eight-and ten-year-old had no concept of cleanliness.

"Will my father be back by then?" Sallos asked. Osiris's smile dropped.

"He won't. He'll be attending the meeting with your mother and us," Valon said. Only in the past year did Osiris notice the extended Abexu family treated him differently from Sallos because of their different fathers. Their treatment was also Valon's fault. He should have known letting his first daughter, Salvia, fall in love with a man from Carvyre would enrage his mother, especially upon discovering her pregnancy and the sullying of the Abexu line with Osiris's birth. It wasn't the fact that he had mixed lineage; were that the case, she would have been angered first by Salvia and Viola, Valon and Luxiana's daughters. Salvia's punishment was a forced marriage to the new Lord of Kardyn, the sculptor, Tirus. Valon wasn't against the man; he was polite and cared well for his son, Sallos and treated Osiris as his own in private. He tried his best to put a smile on Salvia's face, despite her perpetual state of grief after her love, Osiris's father, was presumed murdered. Much of Tirus' time was spent in the city though, working on sculptures for royals across Ithyion—not a profession Valon's mother approved of, despite his title of lord for one of Xyliar's most affluent areas. Salvia was expected to host many affluent families in the castle as a result, leaving Valon and Luxiana to care for her sons.

"Your Aunt Viola will be back from Eresydon in a week, though, and you know she is far more fun," Luxiana said. Their two daughters couldn't be more different. While Salvia favoured education and scholarship, which was her reason for travelling to Carvyre in the first place to see the libraries, Viola favoured adventure and field research; she had been eager to see the homeland of her mother's people from the moment she could talk. She had been there a year now, but the regular letters made up for her absence. He still worried, though, as any father should when his youngest child wished to travel alone in the midst of war. It ended three months ago when Sonos was injured. The great God of Dawn was struck by the combined power of eight deities, three from Thassena and Carvyre, two from Eresydon. It wasn't enough to kill him—Valon wasn't sure what would—but it was enough to pierce straight through his chest, with the after-effects felt across the kingdom. The earth shook; the sky bled; oceans wiped out coastal settlements. The world suffered from the imbalance caused by injuring one half of a whole. It was then the deities realised the kingdom could not exist without him; injuring Sonos or Sitara would have catastrophic effects, and given they had sided with the other celestial four, the deities stood no hope of doing any real damage.

Today marked the surrender, three months after wounding the God of Dawn and realising the consequences. It was why this evening was so important. Xyliar was hosting all the deities and all the celestial gods for peace talks at Sitara's family seat of power. Valon was going to meet his great grandmother.

***

The air in the throne room was thick with the weight of power. The sound of the soldiers' armour clanked when they shifted, accompanied by the occasional roar of a dragon landing outside the castle. A tapping began on the long mahogany table spanning most of the throne room. At one end sat the Abexu family: Valon, Luxiana, Salvia, her husband Tirus, Valon's twelve siblings, their various husbands and wives, and his mother, Kylara. She sat poised at the head. At the opposite end were two rows of deities. Their larger bodies consumed their chairs. On the side backlit by the windows were the deities of Carvyre, Thassena, and Eresydon. Oxyron with his flowing white hair and crown of gold whispered to the first Pegasus-Bound Fae, Calina, with lilac feathers in her blonde hair, interspersed with thin braids and sun-kissed skin extenuating her muscles. On Oxyron's left, the first Hypherion, Vanos, was trying to tempt Thassena's deities into conversation. His hair was cut far shorter than Oxyron and Calina's, and his grin was blindingly white, revealing dimples that finally caught the eye of Lailor, the first Siren.

The Thassena deity did not blush at his grin. Instead, she smirked and batted her eyelids in a way that suggested she could very easily be his demise if she opened her mouth to sing. Anela, the first deity of the first state, slapped Lailor's arm, drawing her back to a more rigid position. The Seer sighed and tucked a strand of hair back into the pearl clip holding back her white curls, starkly contrasting with her umber skin. On her left, Dravos glared at a jug of water, furious he could not use his powers to create an illusion, one to invite some entertainment to the atmosphere as stiff as the backs of the two Eresydon deities. Carlisle, the Shapeshifter, and Aelwen, the first Wiccan, clasped hands beneath the table, warily eyeing the other deities. Valon wondered if they always feared something happening to them when they gathered, if they saw themselves as weaker for being only two representatives for their state rather than three like all the others. Valon's question was answered by the way Nefere was looking them up and down on the opposite side of the table.

Valon's gaze drifted to the woman two seats down from Nefere with night-black curls pinned extravagantly atop her head. Her eyes sparkled, but they shot daggers at Oxyron opposite. His face was stony as he watched her, but there was something sad in his eyes, something missing. Makaria had not acknowledged the Abexu's—not even her daughter—leaving Valon to wonder if his mother's cold and heartless treatment towards him as a child was a learnt behaviour.

"They're late." Luxiana jumped next to Valon at how deep the deity's voice was. Nefere looked around the table. His pale blue eyes were piercing under a dark, strong brow and stood out against the warm undertones of his brown skin encompassed with golden cuffs around his biceps.

"You always say that," a female voice said further along the table. Dalina, the first Angel of Asynthos. Her pale white wings were magnificent with her arches towering high behind her silver hair and the feather-like gown she wore. "Not all of us have a strained relationship with our gods." Heat surged through the room as Nefere released his wings. Valon's eyes widened in admiration. They had a dragon-like quality—sleek, aerodynamic, perfect for agility. Angel wings were strong, designed for long distances. But as the first Xyra, Nefere's wings were a display of power. They spanned behind the other two Q'Ohar deities' backs, though they did not flinch. In fact, Exandria, the Smokeshifter, smiled, leaning back into the warmth as sparks jumped from the flaming feathers. The orange glow brightened her ash-toned skin and gave some life to her grey eyes and hollowed cheekbones. Kaven, the first Forger, smirked while examining his fingernails.

"Live through a hundred years of torture as an experiment at your god's hand, and then talk to me about strained relationships, Dalina. At least I was able to put my history aside and correctly join you and their side during the war." Valon flinched at Nefere's words, which hit too close to home.

"Will you both—" Makaria's shout was cut short as five orbs of light grew at the head of the table where six thrones had been placed. While the Abexu family bowed their heads, Valon secretly glanced through his lashes to see which deities showed reverence.

Only those of Xyliar, Asynthos and Q'Ohar bowed, shadowed by the dragon heads on the wall.

"Your respect is noted." An ethereal voice floated through the air, power radiating from each syllable as Sitara permitted them to raise their heads. On one side of the table sat Nerida and Vala, with Keres and Garridon on the other. All four wore elaborately draped fabrics in the colours of their states: Nerida in a deep blue of the oceans she created, Vala in the pale greys of her skies and clouds her winds blew through, Garridon in the greens of his forests, and Keres in the oranges of flames.

On the onyx throne sat Sitara, her dark skin glowing beautifully against the golden creams draped over her skin and the crown of stars atop her head. Though too far to see her eyes clearly, Valon had heard them described as crushed stars. The throne on her right remained empty. "Please excuse Sonos's absence," she said, sending a look at the deities in front of the window. "He is still healing." Her smile was tight.

"We can still ask for justice without him present," Nefere said. A handful of the other deities sucked in sharp breaths at his boldness. Sitara's smile made Valon decide he never wanted to be on its receiving end.

"And what would constitute justice, Nefere?" she asked, glancing at her son Keres, as though blaming him as well.

"The abolition of any more elixirs, a register of those born as a result of the experimentation, and the death of those responsible so that such creations may not continue," he said. The Abexu family all straightened. Even his mother's face paled.

"That is extreme when the tensions have been squashed," Kylara said.

"Were you spoken to?" Makaria asked, staring at her daughter. Kylara pursed her lips and glanced at Valon and Luxiana. His wife's hand went cold beneath the table.

We approve the abolition of the elixir," Luxiana said.

"Lu," Valon hissed.

"I apologise; she misspoke," Kylara said, glaring at her son to get his wife under control.

"It makes up for the damage we—"

"What Luxiana means"—Kylara interrupted—"is we are open to discussions on how the elixir is used moving forward." The room fell silent, and Valon felt the pressure of all seventeen deities, including his grandmother, bearing down on him. "You cannot mean to—"

"Enough!" Makaria snapped. Shadows whipped out across the table, splintering it in two, and forcing the Abexu family to fling themselves back before it fell on top of them. The deities did not move, though some smirked at the entertainment.

"Luxiana, is it?" Sitara asked, rising from her throne. The white and gold fabrics draped along the floor as she walked barefoot down the centre of aisle created by the splintered table until she towered over Valon and Luxiana. Opposite them, their daughter trembled, leaning forward in her chair as though she could do anything. Tirus gripped her shoulder, pulling her back gently. Sitara's head turned toward Garridon and his deities. "A child of Carlisle's lineage, a Shapeshifter, and..." Sitara met Valon's eyes. He felt the pulsing of her power, searching, identifying him. "Valon Abexu, a child of my line, but.." Sitara trailed off and tilted her head, seeming to recognise there was something off, given the lack of power for someone so close to her lineage. Sitara turned away, surveying the rest of the Abexu family. Her eyes lingered on his mother, her granddaughter through essence. "It pains me to inflict such a tragedy on one of my own," she murmured, weaving down the aisle created by the cracked table. "But justice," she said, turning back to face the Abexu family, "is justice."

A crack sounded through the room.

A single lash of shadow.

A flash of darkness that nobody would have been able to stop even if they wanted to.

There was no markings across any of the hands placed in their laps. Nobody had been tugged forward at the command of the whip. The crack was not from the sound of the shadow or a flash of lightning striking outside alongside Sitara's quiet anger.

The crack was Luxiana's neck snapping.

A single crack before she thudded to the floor.

Murmuring began in the room as the conversation changed. Though it all drowned out as Valon fell to his knees; pain jolted through his body as he reached with a trembling, scarred hand, to brush the chestnut hair from his wife's face. A glow emanated from his palm as he turned her head from where it lulled against the stone floor and, slowly, the celestial binding of their marriage began to fade.

"Lu." Even in his mind, his voice trembled.

"Lu," he said aloud this time. Opposite him, screams began, and he vaguely saw Lord Tirus covering Salvia's mouth and holding her back as she tried to crawl to them. "Lu," Valon's voice cracked. He looked up as he pulled his wife toward him, cradling her dead body in his arms. Tears fell as he rocked her, calling out to her in his mind.

She wasn't there. Never again would he feel all the emotions she crammed into her body, all the empathy and love she had for others despite what she'd endured. Never again would he hear her laugh at him as he dropped apricot jam on his shirt or see her smile when he bought her yet another journal in the city. There would be no more rest days on their bench in the Garden of Statues or—

The pain began as the last of the light faded from his palms, as his body felt her soul being ripped from within him. Images flashed through his mind of a night so long ago he could not focus. Darkness. Blood. A lump of rock.

Valon looked up. Someone needed to help him, to bring her back. His siblings all faced the other end of the table, listening to whatever conversation was happening between the gods and the deities. He didn't know why he expected more from them. This was yet another form of torture they subjected him to; another pain to hinder his joy. His eyes found his mother's. Although she faced the gods and deities, her eyes flickered to him; there was a sadness there, as if she did possess some affection for him after all. Where was that affection as a child? When he was beaten and tortured for his lack of power? Where was the affection that might have nurtured something within him instead, preventing his constant need to prove himself in other ways, to experiment, to have an assistant, to bring Luxiana into all of this? This was her fault, his family's fault, Sitara's fault.

As Luxiana's soul tried to return to the skies, Valon shuddered a breath at the fire raging within him. An image of Valon from above appeared in his mind. He was kneeling on the rooftop of his turret, his eyes rolled back in his head, his hair was darker, his features more angular.

"No," he murmured, cradling her body tighter. "No," he whispered again as the pain made its way through his chest and along his arms. Justice is justice. The pain twisted within him, stoking the fire of rage he felt deep in his stomach. Rage at his part to play, rage at his family, rage at the deities, the gods, everyone who had caused this. His hands cramped around Luxiana's body, and a wisp of darkness skated over his knuckles as the rage and pain grew. Valon tried to latch onto her soul to keep it from fleeing. "*Adeti caligh et alu servusian*," he whispered, kissing his wife's forehead as the shadows crawled inside him, reaching for the light she had brought him. "After creation and before severing," he murmured against her skin. "I will find a way to defy it all." He lowered Luxiana's body to the floor and rose. His body was on fire as he stumbled over the broken table and stood in the aisle, waiting for Sitara to turn. On his left, his grandmother leant forward, her head tilted as though she could sense it, sense the destruction that was about to unleash. Another image flashed in his mind, his skin crawling with black veins. She took from him, and so he would take from her. Finally, Sitara turned, narrowing her eyes at Valon.

"Justice is justice," he said before exploding with one hundred and sixty eight years of suppressed darkness.

SONOS

Chapter One
AGE OF EXISTENCE [0AE – 500AE]

Existence always seemed a futile thing. An expanse of nothingness, left only on a faded plain to watch the shifting colours of the sky. The only entertainment was speculating how the colours might appear. Naming them provided some enjoyment at the beginning. He called the first one blue, the one that faded from the dark and slowly erased the stars when he rose. The colour that signalled the beginning of the shift, the shift through time and space, through the expanse of nothingness, in a shade he called beige. His favourites were pink, orange, yellow, gold, but he preferred when they all merged into one colourful blend upon awaking, as though they were fighting for the title of who was most mesmerising without realising their battle created a masterpiece. Those were his favourite times of the day—at least they were until Sonos saw *her* for the first time.

Sonos would float around the beige world, watching his creator down below. Order. He always hovered directly above, lighting her way as she walked. He felt nothing but warmth until the colours shifted and darkened. That's when dusk, the blues of mystery that turned to the black of desire, became his favourite time. He remembered the moment he saw her, her translucent form bathed in a light so different from his own, serene rather than illuminating. She was the embodiment of the night and the secrets it held, but just like the night, he was destined never to reach her.

Every day, he willed Order to walk faster and faster, begging her to sprint so he might reach the serene light in the sky before he shifted, and dusk appeared. Every evening, she brightened the night just as he faded, and every morning he awoke, grasping as she blended into the darkness. Why must he be alone in this existence when he knew there was another who ached for company? So, Sonos screamed at the sky until it reached his creator's ears.

"You are unhappy, my son," the voice called from below, a musical echo that could draw life from the very sound if she so willed it.

"I am lonely," he called back, his brightness glaring down at her. "And I know she is lonely, too."

Order tilted her head. "Sitara?" she asked. *Sitara.* He tested the name in his mouth, dragging it out like a sigh of contentment.

"Is that her name, the name of the beautiful light I can never reach?"

"It is," Order said. "You wish to meet her?"

"There is this feeling I cannot describe—this pounding in my being that strengthens when I reach for her. I believe she will only make me stronger, brighter," he said.

Order hummed. "I am not her creator, Sonos, but I will speak with him."

And so, Sonos waited, hoping that his evening glimpse of her floating form would be the last time from such a distance.

Three days passed; three more days of watching Sitara fade while Order ignored his cries for answers until eventually a different figure appeared. A man stood opposite Order as the sky changed to dusk. His image shifted regularly, as did Order's, never staying still long enough to glimpse their true forms and faces.

"Order," he said. Voices were the one consistent sound from these first beings, and whilst Order's musicality could breathe life, Chaos' deep husk threatened to crush anything in his path.

"Chaos," she replied, her tone not as bright as when she spoke to Sonos. "She convinced you then." Order looked up above, to where Sitara hovered in the darkening sky above Chaos.

"Apparently, the love of a daughter is enough to convince you of anything, no matter how much you may not wish it," he said, his voice haunting.

"We sacrifice our forms so they may live a life together. For us all to exist topples the balance; for none of us to exist would destroy all. We watch from a distance so our influence is felt but never seen," Order said. The two beings in existence clasped one another's wrists and muttered in the first language.

"I make no promises," Chaos echoed his final words. Sonos felt a pull, a heavy weight tugging him downward as the pair lifted off the ground. Golden threads twisted around them, sparkling and tugging to determine exactly what should happen to them next. The threads spilled outward, shooting off in different directions across the sky and drifting into the universe until Sonos felt sturdy ground beneath his feet. He watched the sky as Order and Chaos faded like sparkling dust when a delicate voice spoke.

"Hello."

Sonos averted his gaze from the sky, where dusk darkened further, and the bright light that had so often been the essence of Sitara floating across the sky became the moon. He looked down. She was real. She was there. She was magnificent. Sitara's corporeal form was shorter than his, her head resting just below his chin. Thick black curls fell down her back, and her eyes glistened like crushed stars as she looked up at him. Her full lips parted with a smile. Under the light of the moon, her skin was luminous, contrasting the golden creams of cloth draped over her like a star. He reached out to stroke the fabric between his fingers.

"Golden, like you," she said, reaching to the dark cloth draped over him.

"Dark, like the night you watch over," he murmured, drifting his hand to her shoulder. Beside his, her skin was soft and her features delicate. Looking down, he noticed his pale muscles showing beneath the black cloth and the white hair hanging over his chest. "You look..." Sonos's voice trailed as the moon brightened until he no longer felt Sitara's skin. He frowned.

With a whispered "no," her grip on him loosened, and he faded.

***

Trapped in bodies on the same land, but still separated, was worse. Knowing he could feel her skin, hear her voice, but only in the fleeting moments when the day turned to dusk, and the night turned to dawn, was torture. Every day, he ran, hoping to reach her quicker so they would have longer together. Every day, he failed. Every day, he reached her and grasped her cheeks while her hands gripped the fabric on his chest. They rested their foreheads against one another, only for him to fade with the morning and wake to her, running to him again. An endless cycle of desperation. He needed to tie them together, as Order and Chaos had done when they wrapped the golden threads around themselves. So, the next day, he tried it.

Sitara faded in his grip, but instead of running, he imagined those threads of light and searched within himself for something similar, something that would cement the beating in his chest that increased every day for her. He sensed it in the pit of his stomach, the ball of light that Order had used to create him, the essence of his being that had once been up high, watching the beige, plain world below.

Sonos tugged and tugged, trying to break it free until a soft glow formed in his palms. With soft movements, he imagined reaching for Sitara and pulled the light free, manoeuvring it in an arc of power. As he walked, he practiced, twisting the light in different shapes, learning the way it felt and moved, the way it connected to his body. When he reached Sitara that evening, the threads of his power met her cheeks instead of his hands, and she smiled under its light. She nodded slowly; she understood.

When Sonos awoke the next morning, Sitara greeted him, bathed in shadows that dripped off her like the moonlight. It moved differently to his power. Where Sonos's light was harsh and sharp, her shadows were soft and caressing. Their powers reached for one another, their eyes widening with smiles as the threads of their darkness and light twisted in a tower between them. Her power felt natural against him, like it was destined to always be a part of his world. Sonos pulled the power closer, and she did the same until a white light emanated from their chests, crawling back along their powers, their souls interlacing as they became aware of one another's presence in their minds and hearts. As the sky brightened from deep blues to the cascading display of yellows, oranges, and pinks, Sitara did not fade.

A single tear fell down her cheek as she closed her eyes and felt the sun on her face. Sonos leant down and kissed it away.

"Hello," Sonos breathed. Sitara giggled at his breath tickling her cheek.

"Hello," she murmured back, leaning into him. The sharing of their essence had cemented their souls together, linking and maintaining their power and control over the rise and fall of the sun and moon, a balance that provided them with one another. Their powers fell away as they interlocked their hands together and strode toward the sunrise.

"It's so warm," Sitara said as Sonos pulled them to a stop. They sat beside one another, watching the sky's colours change.

"Is it cold at night?" he asked.

"It is, but not in an uncomfortable way. It is peaceful," she replied. "And the stars make it worthwhile."

"What do you think stars are?" he asked, curious about the bright lights reminiscent of his power but nestled in a darkness similar to Sitara's. She hummed, considering.

"I think they are simply possibilities we may never know," she said. Sonos stared, interpreting her words in their many ways, literally and figuratively. He wondered if they would ever have a firm answer. "I have counted and mapped them all."

"You'll have to show me," Sonos said. Sitara lay back down on the faded ground, and Sonos lay with her.

"It took me years," she said, turning her head to face him.

"We have years," Sonos said until their noses touched. Sitara's eyes lit up as she reached to stroke his cheek. "Eternity."

"What will we do with years?" she asked.

"Anything you wish."

Chapter Two

ERA OF BEGINNINGS [501EB- 1500EB]

"Take a deep breath," Sonos said, resting his hand on Nerida's abdomen, above where her hand rested. "Search for the light within you, the core that is the essence of your power, the essence we blessed you with during your creation."

"I'm trying," Nerida said, stamping her foot. Sonos smiled at her impatience, her desire to do everything immediately and perfectly. Gently, he smoothed his hand over the curls that resembled her mother's. Of their four children, Nerida resembled her parents the most. For the most part, it appeared each of their appearances were distinct, due to the way Sonos and Sitara's merged essence had manifested in them during the births. But the signs of the pair were still in each of them. Vala's long, straight white hair mirrored Sonos'. Garridon's physique was slowing growing into that of his father's and Keres' strong bone structure was as angular as his mother's.

"Breathe in," Sonos said, their chests rising, "and out."

His daughter mirrored his instructions while sniggering sounded nearby.

"Keres," Sitara snapped. "I'll remember this when you attempt to access your power and have the same troubles. How would you feel if we mocked you for it?" Their youngest son shut his mouth, earning a smirk from Garridon and an eyeroll from Vala. They had been practicing for years now, focusing on their breathing while searching for the location of their powers to see how it might manifest. Nerida, the calmest and most logical of their four children, was to try first. Sonos dreaded Keres' turn.

"I've got it," Nerida said, quiet and gentle. Sonos released his hand from hers and stepped back to join his family, watching patiently. Her fingers were methodical as she lifted them in different ways and twisted her wrists, calling on her power in her veins. Sonos and Sitara did not know if it would work. Although Sitara gave birth to each of their children naturally, they had drawn on their essences during their creation. They expected the children to eventually wield. Whether it manifested the same as Sonos and Sitara's light and shadows remained to be seen.

A frown appeared on his daughter's face as she concentrated until something clear pooled at her feet. She opened her eyes and guided her hands until it moved with her, forming a ball. It was not the same as the light of Sonos or Sitara's dark shadows. There was no harsh lines from the light or a shadows' blurred edges. It was clear and moved with a smooth fluidity. Keres approached, poked a finger at it, and then withdrew it immediately.

"It feels... odd," he said, not like either of the gifts he was accustomed to seeing.

"Leave her be, Keres," Sonos said, pulling back his son's shoulder-length brown hair. He held him in place as Nerida twisted her power into a towering plume. She split it into strands and sent it outward. Somewhere in the distance, it landed. As Nerida spread her palms out, Sonos's brows lifted at the demonstration of her power.

"Wow," Vala whispered beside him in genuine amazement. She was the most emotional of their children, and Sonos could always hear her true thoughts in her tone's minute changes, and the lies in the twitches of her face.

"Wow indeed," Sitara said. The family watched as the pools of her power expanded in different directions, reaching as far as the eye could see until the patch of tinged beige they stood upon was all that remained, surrounded by a deep blue that reminded Sonos of dusk.

"Water," Nerida said. "I'm going to call it water," and she ran toward its edge.

"Wait for us!" Garridon called, running after her, his golden hair flopping from side to side as it always did when he was running high on energy, whether from fleeing his sisters—after relentlessly teasing them—or bouncing up and down while telling his parents an imaginary story. Sonos reached for Sitara's hand. They smiled and followed their children.

"It's my turn next!" Garridon said, bobbing in the water. Droplets flew into the air for Nerida to catch and send toward Keres' cheek.

"You need to be as quiet and calm as Nerida was," Sitara said, though Sonos wasn't sure he agreed. With all four of their children being so different from one another, he wasn't certain Garridon's playfulness would align with Nerida's serenity. He was right. Garridon curled his toes at the edge of the water and jumped, slamming his fists down simultaneously. Their world shook. Sonos held his love tighter as Nerida and Vala reached for one another's hands to keep from falling in the water.

"He always has to be more dramatic," Nerida mumbled, as the shape they were standing on rose, breaking through the water. Garridon slipped on the water residue left by Nerida, and as he stumbled to maintain his balance, his hand sliced downward, and a piece of the land they stood on fell away, breaking off into a narrow strip alongside it.

"Steady yourself," Sonos warned. Garridon blushed but held his hands outward. In the surrounding distance, masses emerged from the waters, sending it rolling toward the edges of their land. They grew and grew until some were level with where they stood and others flatter.

"Look there's one for each of us!" Garridon exclaimed, counting the five pieces of land he had conjured. "Well, one for each of us and one for mother and father, unless they want this one," he said, jumping up and down on the land.

"What if one of the other lands is far nicer?" Sitara asked, ruffling her son's hair and placing a kiss on his freckled cheek. "Wouldn't you want your parents to have the best pick of them all?" Garridon waved his hand, and the land nearest spawned towering shapes in a colour Sonos had not yet seen, as though the blue dusks had melted with the yellow of the sun. Green. Sonos turned his head, examining the five pieces of land around them. In a blink, Garridon slapped his hands together and the lands moved further across the oceans until only the edges could be seen, the trees a blurred line on the lands. A loud crash sounded through the sky, and the water shook.

"Uh, I think those two collided," Garridon rubbed the back of his neck as the family looked to their right, where two of the pieces of land had indeed crashed together. "That can be ours, Keres! You can have one half; I can have the other!"

"Okay, my turn!" Keres exclaimed, punching his fists through the air toward the greenery in the far distance. The next minute, it burned a bright orange as dark puffs like Sitara's shadows spiralled skyward.

"This is exactly the kind of thing we said for years would happen!" Garridon exclaimed. Vala tilted back her head and gave a frustrated sigh at her brothers. The breath rippled against their draped clothing, turning into a gust that surged toward the orange, slowly disappearing until blackened shapes remained. The gust continued though, blowing and blowing, so strong the lands shifted again until they were no longer visible on the horizon. An entire ocean away.

"There you go," Vala muttered. Spirals of air floated above her palms, gently blowing back her long hair. On her left, Nerida sulked, and Sitara placed an arm around her.

"Why did it take me so long?" she said, kicking her feet in the water.

"Because you are the most logical, you wanted to understand where it came from. The others are driven by their emotions," Sitara said, tapping the side of her head. "You are driven by your mind." Warmth shot over them as Keres punched the air again. "What next?"

***

Spending millennia with only family for company proved difficult. As Sonos and Sitara's children aged, so did their individual needs for space and solitude. Eventually, as Garridon had joked as a child, they each took a land and gave it a name. Nerida claimed Thassena and filled it with lakes, rivers, and streams; Vala claimed Asynthos for its high mountain peaks, providing cooler air; Garridon and Keres remained close, dividing the land in half: Q'Ohar and Eresydon. Sonos and Sitara were offered the remaining land, which the children named Styros. They were content to remain on the smaller island in the centre of the vast ocean, a reminder of where they had started and how far they had come.

"They'll be here as the sun rises," Sonos murmured into Sitara's ear before playfully nipping at her skin.

"Then we should make the most of our peace and quiet," she replied, leaning back into his chest where he cradled her amongst the blankets. She stared into the fireplace of the carved home their children had created on the strip of land Garridon had accidentally sliced from the island. Initially they had wanted to stay on the main island, but before their children had moved, they had used this long strip to practice their powers. Now, Sitara and Sonos felt their children in every piece of their home. The carved mountain that housed cascading stone stairways and hollowed out rooms in a towering mountain was evidence of Vala's strong touch. The waterfall within the throne room and the lake outside was a serene addition from Nerida. The land was lush with grass and scented flowers that attracted what Garridon had named butterflies. The trees were a burnt red leaf, the result of Keres accidentally setting fire to them and Garridon quickly trying to bring them back to life.

Sonos and Sitara had added their own touch when they decided to make this small isle their home, weaving their magic into the sands of the beach, creating a sparkling black dust that resembled starlight. Home, even if it felt empty at times without their children.

"Don't lie. You have been desperate to see them again," Sonos said, stroking back her curls as she turned to face him.

"And when will the next time be if our attempts today are successful?" she asked, her voice quiet and low—sombre. It pained her not to see them, but they now understood their childrens' desire for company, who longed for people of their own to guide and nurture, for bodies and laughter to fill the lands they had turned into homes. Today, Sonos and Sitara would attempt to fulfil that wish by creating a new race, a less powerful one, but new all the same. If they succeeded, then their children would do the same.

"They're probably still in bed; you know what they're like." Garridon's voice carried through the open expanse on the other end of the hallway. The rush of the waterfall hid the throne room from view, a beautifully carved room with onyx and marble flooring to match the thrones Vala had carved. Black flowers now climbed the walls, hiding what had once been entry points to their children's rooms. They had not slept in them for years.

"They know we're here. Give them time," Nerida said. Sonos suspected she was pulling out a chair at the round stone table to patiently wait.

"That's our cue, my love," Sonos whispered, kissing Sitara's cheek as they donned their robes, wearing the colours of the other, and walked through the waterfall hand in hand. Sitara had woven her magic into it long ago, lacing the water in shadow so that it would not drench them, marking it an inky black. Their children greeted them with warm hugs, and Sitara clung to each and every embrace for far too long before they took their seats. They waited expectantly for Sonos and Sitara to begin. When they created their children with their essence before, it was during a moment of love, passion, desire—not like this, and not with an intent to control the level of power they passed to their creations.

Together, they bowed their heads and drew on their merged essence from deep within their chests, pulling out two threads of light that pulsed with life. It twisted above the table as Sitara and Sonos focused, sharing an image in their mind of the two beings they tried to create until the light twisted into the form of two bodies—a female body, similar in age to Nerida and Vala, and a male similar in build and age to their sons. The light faded. A woman with skin the same shade as Nerida's floated above the table, her eyes closed. Shadows drifted off her skin, and Sonos frowned. Next to her, a male with blonde hair and pale skin was encased in threads of light.

"That's too much power," he murmured. They had not intended to relay the same gifts as either of them.

"There's something wrong with them," Keres said, squinting his eyes at their heads. Sonos followed his eyeline. They were right. Their ears were not shaped as they should be; instead of rounded ears, pointed tops peeked through their hair.

"If you wish for them to be weaker or without visible power, perhaps draw from their essences instead. We could use that," Nerida suggested.

"It could work," Sitara whispered into his mind. Sonos nodded. With their eyes closed, the two creations floated. Sonos and Sitara radiated their power outward, searching for the essence that now belonged to the beings and tugged until two much smaller and dimmer tendrils broke free from their chests. But they still pulsed and glowed brightly. Power emanated from the tendrils as they were placed in a glass bottle.

"It's still too much," Sonos said, his eyes narrowed as he turned the bottle, analysing the glow. "We cannot give you this. What if you split it and it creates beings powerful enough to harm you?"

"That wouldn't happen, Father." Nerida tried to rationalise. "We were born from you with your essence; we are as close in power as is possible. You have already split this essence; they would not be more powerful than us." Her siblings nodded their agreement.

"And if you added your own essence to it?" Sitara asked. "Whilst you might mould them to your will, you would be adding additional power." Sonos sensed his wife agreed with him. This felt far too dangerous.

"If the essence was split again into four, how many might we create from one of those piece? Each creation would surely dilute the power further." Garridon leant back in his chair.

"One or two perhaps. We won't know for certain until you try," Sitara said. "As your powers and essence vary, you may find your creations would too, that you only manage one while a sibling manages three. There are far too many factors. I think we should try again." The children's expressions saddened at their mother's words, evidently impatient to take what had already been drawn from their power and use it for their own creation.

"I think we should create beings without power to keep our children from risk—mortals," Sitara said silently to Sonos. He did not look at her.

"I agree. Perhaps if we use our essence to create sands like we did on the isle, each grain would have a fraction of an essence to give it life, but nothing else. It would take time for it to form into any mortal being under our children's guidance, but the length of time would surely guarantee they had no power." Sitara hummed silently in agreement, and the pair twisted their power in the centre of the table until it disintegrated into falling, sparkling dust.

"What is that for?" Keres asked, wrinkling his nose.

"Vala," Sonos said, turning to his daughter, "If you could cast it outward, splitting it evenly to land on your homes." Their second daughter nodded, though her brow was furrowed. She blinked, and the dust spiralled upward through the circular opening in the carved mountain, disappearing through the air.

"That was your future mortals," Sitara said. "It will take time, perhaps hundreds of years, but each grain is blessed with our essence. Slowly they will take life and become the mortals you desire."

"Mortals?" Garridon asked.

"No power," Sonos said. "No threat." The children were quiet, and Sonos sensed their disappointment; they had taken their chance to create beings themselves. Sitara's sadness rippled through him as Garridon and Keres rose to leave.

"What will you do with these two?" Vala asked, prolonging the speed at which she rose, likely to avoid upsetting her mother. Sitara shrugged.

"We will send them to the abandoned land. They can do as they wish there," she said, folding her hands in her lap. Sitara wrapped an arm around her and kissed the side of her head. Keres quickly embraced his father next to the table, before Garridon did the same, both rushing away quicker than usual, even for them.

"But they are technically your children now too," Nerida said. Sitara looked from the two floating beings to her daughters standing at their chairs and her sons already heading for the door.

"They are not my children. You four are the only ones I need."

Sonos pulled Sitara into an embrace to hide her tears as her children left.

"You'll see them again, especially when they realise how difficult it will be to manage so many mortals on their lands; it was hard enough managing four children with power," Sonos chuckled and kissed his love's head. He pulled back and cupped her cheeks. "Do you want me to take these two to Styros?" he asked. Sitara nodded and pulled back. She stilled, her eyes scanning the table where the two beings floated above.

"Where is the glass bottle with the split essence?" she asked. Sonos mirrored her action, scanning the stone. It was nowhere to be seen. He recalled the brief embrace from his sons.

"The boys took it."

Chapter Three

RISE OF CIVILISATION [1501RC – 1980RC]

Lightning struck the darkening skies above, scattering the clouds with streaks of light as water fell in a torrential pour. Sonos wiped the water from his eyes as Nerida shoved her hands skyward, forcing the rain back up before redirecting it in a cascade toward the army of shapeshifters approaching from their left. It knocked them from the raised hills of the valley, forcing them to twist and turn as they attempted to regain their balance amongst the gusts of wind being wielded by a group of air benders atop the hill.

"This is foolish!" Sonos roared over the winds. Nerida nodded her agreement. "More of their people will pointlessly die over something none of us began." They had been at this for thirty years now. Sonos, Sitara, and their children fought against the deities of Thassena, Carvyre, and Eresydon, for they believed it was the celestial gods who created another race, taking power and offerings from them. Sonos and Sitara knew nothing of it, too blissfully wrapped up in one another to keep tabs on the deities they had never claimed as their own. Yet their children had essentially stolen from them, taking their withdrawn essence without permission to create these beings they now warred with. Had they been content in this world with just their family and mortals, a war would not rage now.

Despite wishing the deities had never been created, they managed one success. The first being they had created, Makaria, rightfully sided with her mother, though Sitara refused to be called 'mother' so openly. She distanced herself as much as possible from the lineage that shared her dark power. She laid no claim to Makaria, nor the beings she created and called Fae, the name she had given them to differentiate from those created by the celestial gods. She had no desire to involve herself with any of them, which Sonos respected. It was why this war was even more absurd, knowing Sitara and Sonos had kept as far from them as possible. It was their children's meddling and their creations, who possessed gifts none could have predicted, that started all this. They became involved only when their children were at risk. This was exactly why they had refused to give them the essence they had split from Makaria and Oxyron. It had taken them centuries to forgive them.

"What do you want us to do?" Vala asked, creating a spiral of air that knocked through a portion of Carvyre's army. Sonos's eyes searched for Sitara's on the other side of the valley. The valley on Eresydon had never originally existed. The war had been drawn here as it had the smallest population, a result of Garridon only ever creating two deities, rather than three. The valley was a recent consequence of vast power colliding, carving itself into the land.

"We could just kill them all," Sitara suggested silently, cloaking the Xyra in a blanket of darkness as they flew for the Pegasus-Bound Fae, their flaming wings sparking with each flap.

"That could turn the other deities on us. They view one another as siblings," Sonos replied. He sensed her frustration down their bond.

"If each of us takes one of the compass points, we can funnel them all into the valley. If we can trap enough of them, they may back down and surrender," Keres called as his eyes followed a cloud of smoke before Exandria. The Smokeshifter appeared in front of Garridon's Shapeshifter. If it wasn't for Carlisle's quick transition into a hawk, his throat would have been sliced—even so, it would not have killed him. Nobody had successfully killed a deity yet, but Sonos theorised that getting close enough to rip the essence from them should do it. Sonos, nodding his agreement, directed his children, with Nerida and Vala flanking the east as Keres and

Garridon took the west. Sitara remained in the north where the valley had funnelled into a cave, and Sonos in the south where it flattened into an expanse of fields.

"If you blind them, I'll blanket them in shadows as they try to focus. It should disorient them enough for the children to force them closer."

"See you in a moment." Sonos smiled down their bond and funnelled all his power into his arm before he brought it down in one swift arc, sending a ripple of light over the battlefield. What he hadn't prepared for was Oxyron, the first deity of Carvyre, anticipating the attack. He shielded himself, Calina, and Vanos, and the deities of Thassena and Eresydon against the blinding white, his power the closest thing to Sonos's and the easiest to protect against it. In a circle, the group clutched one another's hands, their heads bowed as the light faded, and a ripple of darkness formed at the other end. Sitara was building her power, sending it toward them. But before the shadows reached the group, they lifted their arms into a point in the centre, and a glowing light emerged from each of them as they released a fraction of their essence. It merged into a blinding beam. As Sonos raised his arm to draw his power, they angled the beam downward, straight through his forearm and chest.

***

When you have lived for as long as the world, and longer than its people, it's easy to forget the value of time. Sonos had seen it all from the very beginning, and he assumed he would one day see the end, if it ever came. What he hadn't anticipated was feeling fear for the first time. Fear of never seeing his children again, of never holding Sitara. Fear of nonexistence, as immediate as a mortal's death when struck with an illness or the blade of a dagger. Sonos had watched death and the pain it caused, yet he had never considered how it would feel or what happened next. This world, his kingdom, Ithyion, was all he had ever known, and flashes of it rushed through his mind when he was struck.

Sonos remembered nothing about what came next. One moment they were trying to end a war, and the next a searing pain felt like it tore him in two. Sitara's pain surged alongside it as she watched. Then there was nothing but complete and utter emptiness until he opened his eyes, blinking against the sun shining through the window of the bedroom he shared with Sitara. She wasn't there when he first awoke, something he knew she still hated herself for even now, three months later, whilst at peace talks with their children and deities. When Sonos finally felt the sun on his face, Sitara had been called to Thassena to help Nerida with managing the unexplainable tidal waves striking the coastal towns. He would later learn that was not the only naturally occurring disaster to arise while he was unconscious.

Earthquakes had struck parts of Q'Ohar, where lava burst free from the fissures with no mercy, forcing people from their homes. Asynthos' temperatures had risen drastically, melting the stalactites at a pace that hindered harvests and wasted precious healing water. In Eresydon, drought had struck the farmlands with such ferocity that even the power gifted by Garridon failed to invite new growth. All these consequences directly resulted from the imbalance caused by his unconsciousness. At least it had been enough to stop the war.

The world's order had returned when Sonos awoke. It was how Sitara had known to return to the Isle of Gods so quickly. First, the waves had suddenly dropped mid-air; next, she had sensed the beating of his heart within her own. It took her only thirty seconds to make the connection before appearing at his bedside. Three months later, he still felt the effects of his injury. When the deities' combined essence struck him, it extracted a piece of his own essence when it pierced through his back. A missing piece. He felt its absence in the way his power felt lighter, the way it took additional time to position himself before calling upon it, otherwise his aim was off; he also felt it when he did too much in a day, exceeding his limits. Sonos, the great God of Dawn, felt somewhat mortal. The threat of death hung over him, compelling him to bring about change.

Pushing himself up from the bed, Sonos changed into the deep night fabric that served as a constant reminder of his love. His chest was stiff as he stretched and peered out of the window. They had built a second residence on the mainland of the Isle of Gods, reserving the split land and carved home just for the two of them. This newer, pale-stone temple structure sat in the centre of the main isle. They had built it as a location to host visitors, particularly during the war when they needed to meet with representatives of Xyliar, Q'Ohar, and Asynthos. It was where they would have hosted today's peace talks if Sonos had not been injured. He had agreed to stay here, in this newer building, for it was smaller and easier to navigate in his recovering state. If he was being honest, he hated it and would beg Sitara to return to their usual home as soon as possible.

Sonos stared out the window and tilted his head. Someone was here. Nobody ever visited the Isle of Gods without invitation, only his children. But whoever approached had some connection to Sitara, evidenced by the way his steps tinged the land from brown to black. Veins of smoke and shadow crept out around him. Sonos flexed his hands until protective rings of light hovered around his forearms. He jumped from the window and landed with a shudder, waiting for the man to approach. Sonos, having encountered many faces, could not be expected to recognise them all, but something told him he should know someone who possessed as much power as this man did. It radiated from him.

"Usually an invitation is required to visit the isle," Sonos said, crossing his arms. The man's face was red, and his eyes swollen, as though he had been crying. "Do you need assistance?" Sonos asked. The man nodded.

"I do not know if you can assist with what I truly need," the man said.

Sonos slowly approached. "Perhaps if you tell me what you require, we can see."

"Theoretically." The man clasped his hands behind his back. "If Sitara were to leave, would you do anything to bring her back?" he asked. Sonos checked his bond. He sensed her there, though she was quiet. She was likely talking, negotiating peace with the others.

"Of course. I would have to; the balance of the kingdom depends on it," Sonos said. "Though whether it would be possible, I do not know."

"What would you try?" the man asked.

"Have you lost someone?" said Sonos. The man clenched his jaw, waiting. "Sitara and I are in a unique position. Our essence is a direct creation of the beings who created the universe. I would use my essence and any that remained of hers to tie us back together."

The man rubbed his face, contemplating Sonos's words. "Could your essence be bound to others to give another essence life again?"

Sonos frowned, recalling the imbalance his unconsciousness had on the world. Would such an act, defying death itself, do something similar?

"You would need both mine and Sitara's for balance," Sonos said. "One without the other could have consequences. But I have seen what has happened to this kingdom as a result of meddling with life and creations; the same can be said for reviving someone whose time has come."

The darkness drenching the floor flew up into a wall around the pair.

"It was not her time," the man snapped, his voice a deep husk that scratched a memory in Sonos's mind. His cloak blew back with the strength of his power, revealing scars littered across his arms. "It was your precious Sitara that took her from me."

"Sitara does nothing without cause," Sonos said, though he felt pain for the man before him, imagining the agony of losing the other half of his soul. "Come," Sonos said. "Drink with me and tell me of the love you have lost." He had no intention of placating the man's desires. Once he stepped inside his home, he would bind him with light until Sitara and his children returned. "Do you have a name?"

The man's eyes shifted to black, but not the same onyx Sonos witnessed in Sitara's or those who descended from her line. There was something void-like about them, dark and old.

"Caligh Servusian."

ASYNTHOS
AGE OF DEVASTATION 3051AD - 3503AD
[PRESENT YEAR: 3360]

BOZNAYA RANGE
BORNOVO
LAKE Z
FOREVER FIELDS
K

THE FOURTH STATE
ASYNTHOS
OF ITHYION
CAPITAL
SETTLEMENT
NOTABLE LOCATION
TO THASSENA
PORT MARZOV
STURIA
VERA
TO XYLIAR

Chapter One

OLIRAH

Olirah had two tasks at the top of her list that day, her mental list that was. Once, she had used a feather plucked from her own back as a writing tool and her blood as the ink, but parchment would be a luxury she would lose the second her temporary home of the day was raided following her departure. Not that she had any thynai to purchase any as it was, and wasting a single coin on parchment would not be wise. But letting her mind run away with possibilities and outcomes was one of the few techniques she had available to distract from the pain in her stomach. Hence item one on her list: find food. Item two: find shelter. Those two tasks were her first thought upon waking and the last before sleep, yearning for the night to ease her body's aches and pains.

The morning wisps of mist and cloud twisted around Olirah's body, caressing her arms as they trailed up to form a halo around her brow. When her stomach rumbled again, she instead imagined the damp halo was a diadem, picturing herself as a princess of the state rather than a starving thirteen-year-old girl in the capital's slums. Princess of Asynthos. Olirah scoffed as she pushed back the tangled grey strands of hair, with shaking, bony hands, from her face and shoulders. *Princess.* That was a far-fetched daydream, even for her. The only way Olirah would ever step foot in the palace towering over the mountaintop capital, Vasturia, would be if she broke a serious law. It was likely she would die of starvation or during a brawl for the most sheltered spot in the Eamon District—named after a boy who had risen from orphan to lord—long before she committed a crime worthy enough of being presented to the queen.

The wind picked up as she crept around a corner toward the morning market. A chill ran up her spine, reminding her to focus on her task for the morning rather than allowing her mind to run away with her. The wind rushed forward again. An urgency graced it today and ruffled the feathers of the lilac wings protruding from her back. Far too weak to retract them, Olirah was past caring about the dirt marring the once-bright gold tips of her wings, dulled from constantly dragging them across the cobbled streets. She could not remember the last time she hadn't felt burdened by them—perhaps when she had last seen her parents. Though that too was so long ago, she could not recall how old she was then or even picture their faces. Did Olirah's mother have the same grey locks that drew disgusted looks from those who saw her dirtied blood, far different from the pristine white locks revered in Asynthos for its similarities to the celestial goddess, Vala? Did her father have the same pale, sickly complexion, scattered with light freckles that would become so prominent beneath the sun in Thassena or Q'Ohar, making her appear more tanned and alive? Did both possess the same silver eyes that frightened the children on the streets, particularly when streaks of white tendrils flashed within during her moments of anger? Eyes that made the drunken men leer at night and tell her she was either a curse or a blessing and that a night together would decide the answer. "Never been with an Angel with such interesting eyes and wings," they'd say.

"Never been with an Angel only thirteen either, I'd hope," Olirah usually snapped back.

The wind whistled in her ears again, whipping up around the mountain the city sat upon, beginning its song for the day as it weaved higher through the streets, its tune smoother and wealthier the more it climbed, until reaching the sparkling opal-encrusted palace at the summit. *Focus, Olirah.*

"Runts will be sniffing around any minute now," a gruff voice complained as Olirah peered around the pale stone of the dingy alleyway. The rancid smell drifting from the puddles she had walked through was slowly replaced by the scent of fresh pastries, though she imagined they smelt nowhere near as heavenly as those in the bakeries further up the city. Her silver eyes scanned the market, the already narrow street narrowing further with the rows of stalls lining the right-hand side. The left was free for the busy morning workers, who tossed thynai in exchange for their rushed breakfast on the way down the mountain toward the first checkpoint for the stalactite harvest. The wind carried the sound of clinking, but it was not the clinking of thynai in one's pockets; it was the sound of a coin landing against stone. Someone had dropped money. Crouching down in the corner of the alleyway, she scanned the boots stomping past. A single thynai would be enough to buy her a loaf of bread from the furthest stall—the stalest on offer, but an entire loaf all the same. Enough bread to last a week if she rationed it well, provided no other child saw her with it and stole it while she slept. A glint of silver finally caught her eye as a boot stepped off the coin. Four stalls down.

First, she would have to make her way past the fruit and vegetable man, who prepared the winter's harvest of frostberries for the mothers making pies at the weekend; then, she would slip by the healer, who claimed her stalactite healing water was just as good as any harvest from the royal mountain—though Olirah knew it was water from the communal spring, which she'd boiled down and filtered. Another dark alleyway briefly broke up the stalls before she could pass the butcher with the dried deer meat that he had slapped her last week when she tried to take a scrap that had fallen into a puddle. Only then, after all that, would she reach the coin on the floor before the pastry stall.

"Here's one of them now," the same gruff voice said, smoking a pipe as he spoke with the man displaying the frostberries. Olirah followed his gaze to the opposite alleyway. Olirah never dared venture to the western side of the city because of the number of guards patrolling, protecting the royal family's private path to the castle. It was far more likely she would be ratted out for theft and hauled off to either prison or the stone mines deep in the Boznaya Range at the state's centre, home to the production of marble across Ithyion. Olirah shivered. No child taken to the stone mines had ever returned. The older children of the streets told horror stories of what happened in the dark depths of Asynthos. Raids on transport, stolen children taken by other states, while others were killed trying to escape the mines, fleeing the dangers of their duties. Some said they weren't mines at all but homes for the three deities, Dalina, Stroman, and Araya. Tales told of children sent there as payment, the three deities' price after the ruling family of Asynthos sided with Vala and the celestial gods in the Great War. Yet the war had ended over three hundred years ago, and peace talks and agreements had left Asynthos free to worship whomever they chose, or so was the messaging still conveyed by the royal family, who hosted festivities in the name of both Vala and the deities.

Olirah eyed up the 'runt' the two men jested over. She was definitely lanky enough to attempt outrunning any guards. Perhaps that was why she lived on the riskier side of the city. The girl's skin and hair were far darker than Olirah's. She was likely labelled an outsider too. Based on her colouring, Olirah would bet that either or both of her parents hailed from Q'Ohar. Or the girl herself might have fled Q'Ohar, though that would have required travelling a great distance and an ocean to flee the third state of Ithyion and arrive at the fourth.

The girl narrowed her eyes as she tucked a strand of dark hair behind her ear, revealing the jagged top. It had been chopped off. Olirah tensed. Only fighters gained injuries like that on the streets. Olirah, weak and frail, couldn't fight the girl for the coin her eyes were also clearly fixed on. Her skin prickled as something crawled within her, a tingling sensation that always seemed to skate in her veins whenever she thought of her weakness or having to fight for herself. Perhaps that was how it felt for Stormbringers before the curse on Asynthos. If Olirah was an Angel blessed with the power of the second deity, Stroman, lightning would crackle across her fists and brow, giving her the strength she lacked. But the state was cursed never to bear another child with such power, a curse that had been in place for three hundred years ago. Nobody knew why.

Olirah's wings ached as she straightened, placing her palms on the wet stone and preparing to run as the girl opposite glanced between Olirah and the thynai still on the floor. The pair locked eyes—Olirah's silver on the girl's warm honey. The girl relaxed her shoulders and tilted her head, scanning Olirah's high cheekbones and bony shoulders before moving to the unusual lilac shade of her wings. Suddenly self-conscious, Olirah anxiously tugged at the golden tips. She wished she had the strength to hide them, to hide how different she was from the other white-winged Angels of Asynthos. The girl's eyes softened across the alleyway. She cracked her neck before wings slowly emerged from her back, so much slower than normal Angels, seeming to deplete her remaining strength. Olirah's eyes widened at the magnificent feathers coating the wings, a stark contrast to the wings gifted by the first Angel, Dalina.

The black feathers were not quite as dark as the night sky; streaks of varying shades of grey interspersed throughout, creating wings that were a much different shape than Olirah's, and different from the Angels of the state. Pushing her shoulders back, the girl hid her wings in the shadows, far enough that the jesting men would not see them from behind the wall. Her fingers tugged at a feather before brushing over the silver tips. Like Olirah, she was solitary. Abnormal, as she was often called by the other orphans in the Eamon District. Olirah swallowed back tears as the girl retracted her wings until nothing remained of them but shadows. Olirah wished she had memorised their beauty. With the girl not venturing into the market, the men grew bored and distracted by the many voices filling the street. She curled a finger, beckoning Olirah over. Olirah shook her head, and the feeling under her skin returned. The girl rolled her eyes and quickly peered down the street before darting to Olirah's spot.

Neither of them said anything for a moment as they surveyed one another. The girl reached for Olirah's hand, who moved to pick at her feathers again and recoiled into the wall at her touch. She winced as her wings crushed the stone. The girl raised her hands in surrender.

"I was just going to tell you to stop. You shouldn't pick at something so magnificent," said the girl, her voice rich and silky like honey. A deep lilt confirmed Olirah's earlier suspicion; the girl was not Asynthos-born but had been raised in Q'Ohar. Her imagination threatened to run away with her again with all the theories and stories of how this girl, no older than thirteen, had travelled such a distance and why.

"You think they're magnificent?" Olirah whispered, slowly pulling her hand away from ruffling the feathers. The girl smiled.

"Who would want wings of white when uniqueness is far more appealing?" the girl asked. Olirah shrugged.

"I would rather not stand out so much."

"Why do you not hide them away then?"

"I am not strong enough to."

Slowly, the girl nodded. "Or perhaps fate wants your wings to be noticeable; perhaps they will lead you to your destiny."

"Is that what you tell yourself?" Olirah asked. "That your abnormality destines you to become great? Free you from the torment of poverty?" An angry tone laced Olirah's voice now, enraged by this girl's hope that she might somehow escape the life Olirah knew she herself would die in.

"Who said destiny is always something great?" The girl's eyes darkened as she looked away from Olirah and around the corner again for the thynai on the floor.

"What is your name?" Olirah asked. The girl did not answer as her honeyed eyes flitted in different directions through the street.

"If you follow my plan, we can share the thynai," the girl said, turning her head back to face Olirah.

"How are we to share one coin?"

"We can buy one loaf and split it. I have some old frostberry jam we can add to disguise the staleness," the girl said. Olirah narrowed her eyes. Where on earth could she possibly hide food? Nothing ever stayed hidden on the streets. The girl tapped her fingers on her knee. A faded patch on the loose black fabric suggested she did it often.

"What is the plan?" Olirah asked first, and the corner of the girl's mouth twitched upward. Olirah's heart rate spiked, and she refrained from jumping at the tingling feeling building beneath her skin.

"It's risky, but believable. I'll walk along the edge of the pastry stall and pretend to browse. They'll know I'll be waiting for someone to drop something, so the owner will be focused on me. You walk past me and graze your finger on my back so I know it's you. I'll step back to pretend to bump into you, which gives you a reason to fall to the ground and grab the thynai. We pretend to get into a fight to make it clear we have no stolen food in our hands, and then you sprint back to this spot. We'll have to wait and then spend the thynai tomorrow or walk to one of the other markets on the western side, where no one will have seen what happened."

Olirah nodded slowly, her hair falling in her face as she took in the plan. The wind brushed the two girls, pushing their hair away so they could see one another properly. The girl held out her hand to Olirah.

"Deal?" she asked. The whistling of the wind picked up again, and the uneasy tingling under Olirah's skin intensified as she stared at the girl's hand. She tilted her head at Olirah, her eyebrows raised, as though she sensed something in the air as well. With a gulp, Olirah reached for the girl's hand. Something sparked between their palms, and Olirah flinched, but the girl held on, a warmth spreading from their palms and up Olirah's arms. There was something comforting about the feeling as it wrapped around her until a tingling spread over her abdomen. Olirah reached for her ripped shift and lifted the hem, her right hand still gripping the girl's. Gasping, she stared at the raised scar on her abdomen, the clear sign of the Goddess Vala, red and raised on her skin. Olirah shoved the girl back, but she was far stronger and stayed rooted to the spot as she lifted her own shirt, revealing a matching, paler scar etched on her abdomen.

"I told you. Perhaps fate wanted you to have your wings out for a reason," the girl murmured.

"There is no such thing as fate; there is no reason behind what happens to a person other than misfortune or determination." Olirah snapped. The girl was infuriating.

"Why do you care so much? It's just a sign that Vala sees we're tied to a similar destiny. For all we know, the scar will be gone by the end of the day. Whatever events our deal triggers might seal the destiny of others." The girl peered around the corner. "Either that or we go our separate ways after sharing some bread, and it remains on us for years, disappearing once our destiny is completed. A destiny that would not have occurred had we not met and planned to steal a thynai." The girl shrugged.

"Celestial ties are considered a blessing according to the queen, they deserve more respect than ignoring it for years." Olirah snapped, and the girl scoffed. Olirah rolled her eyes at the insolence. Everyone in Asynthos had heard the way the queen spoke of her ancestors and the celestial tie that helped save the Angel captured by Keres to create his first Xyra. The woman, whose name was not spoken out of respect, had received a celestial tie with the Angel as children. It was later, when they were adults, that the tie enabled the woman to locate where the Angel was being held prisoner.

"Oh, they are a blessing now?" the girl mocked. Olirah gritted her teeth and steadied her breathing. Perhaps they had different views on ties in Q'Ohar. But in Asynthos, ties were not granted lightly. Every story she had ever heard ended with death; even the woman tied to the Angel Keres had taken died during the rescue.

"Ready?" the girl asked, rising from her crouch. Olirah kept her mouth shut, letting her frustration whirl within. But she nodded as the girl stepped onto the market street. She turned her head back briefly, locking eyes with Olirah.

"Jessemiah," she said with a small smile. "That's my name." She left to stride down the street. *Jessemiah*. Something stirred inside Olirah as she whispered her name on the wind and watched her back, imagining the beautiful black and silver wings hidden within her. Olirah grazed her hands over the scar on her abdomen and counted to five before following her into the street.

Olirah kept her head down as she weaved through the crowd, her wings catching the attention of men, who looked her up and down. Someone's hand grazed her feathers, and she flinched, pushing forward quicker, away from their leers. Jessemiah stood only three steps away, tapping her chin as she surveyed the pastries while the woman behind the stall assessed her closely. Olirah's breathing quickened as the wind rushed past, carrying the scent of pastries and something citrusy. When Jessemiah stepped back, her hair brushed against Olirah's cheek in the breeze. The citrus wafted off her dark locks as Olirah raised a finger ad brushed it against Jessemiah's spine.

A gentle warmth radiated between the two. Olirah paused, her eyes on the silver coin to the left of her foot, bracing herself to fall. A loud laugh jolted Olirah's attention at the same moment Jessemiah stepped backward as planned. As Olirah fell, her eyes locked on a tall man turning into the street. Ice blue stared back at her, highlighting his cropped white-blonde hair, which was almost as bright as the wings towering behind him in his pale blue uniform. Guards. Guards had seen the abnormality of her wings. This was why she stayed on the eastern side of the city, in the poorer districts.

Olirah let out a genuine yelp as her side collided with the stone.

"You got in my way!" Jessemiah shouted, feigning frustration. The bodies in the street moved quickly, and Olirah heard the shouts of guards. Jessemiah's eyes widened as she looked down at Olirah and reached for her arm. "Run!" she hissed.

Silver glinted in Olirah's eyeline as she snatched the thynai, wrapping her hands tight around the small hexagonal coin before Jessemiah hauled her up and pushed her ahead. "Run!" Jessemiah urged.

Olirah's knees scraped, tearing open, as she scrambled up with Jessemiah's help.

"Halt!" shouted the guard behind them, his voice dripping with authority. If he was an Angel in the guard, then he had to be high-ranking. Only air wielders and mortals were in the basic ranks that patrolled the city. An Angel in uniform was so rarely seen in the city's lower levels.

"This way!" Jessemiah called. Two strides ahead, she ran toward the western alleyway she had first appeared from. Olirah glanced to the east, to her own, but gulped as the owner of the frostberries stand stepped aside to obstruct her escape into the safety of the Eamon district that so few guards wished to wander.

"Olirah!" Jessemiah yelled, gripping the edge of the wall. She turned back without any of her former confidence. Olirah had no time to contemplate a different route as Jessemiah's hand gripped tightly to hers, pulling her into the western alleyway. The guard's shouts echoed loudly behind them amidst the splash of puddles and the girls' rapid breathing. Clinging to Jessemiah's hand, Olirah focused on the warmth of her skin rather than the anxious tensions in her body and the fear in her chest. Perhaps misplacing her trust, Olirah followed the girl as she weaved them through dark alleyways, the sound of thudding boots behind them growing. There was more than one pursuer.

Olirah's back twinged at the pain of her dragging wings, and her lungs roared as she continued running with Jessemiah, whose even breathing suggested she slowed only for Olirah's sake. The dark alleyways began to widen and brighten as the usual smell of poverty eased, only panicking Olirah further. If the staple signs of the slums were fading, that meant they were reaching a wealthier side of the city, where more guards were stationed.

"Jess–" Olirah tried to halt her, but still, they ran. They ran until the path inclined and the stone brightened, until the odd twinkle in the walls signalled they were not only farther west in the city, farther than Olirah had ever been, but also higher, richer.

Bile rose in Olirah's throat, her stomach churning as she choked. Jessemiah pulled them forward, the light blinding, and the smell of fresh air overwhelming as it slammed into Olirah's face, pushing her back. Tugging her forward again, Jessemiah shoved her against a stone wall just in time for Olirah to empty what little was left in her stomach over the side of the mountain. Tears filled her eyes, and her head continued spinning when she looked down at the rocky paths below, winding to the multiple checkpoints that led into the stalactite caves and the snowy forest floor miles below. Wisps of clouds caressed her cheek, seemingly wiping away the saliva and tears from her skin. A soothing hand rubbed her back between her wings, but it did little to ebb the feeling of fire in her veins or the pain that resembled thundering rain in her mind.

"We need to move again," Jessemiah said urgently. Olirah shook her head.

"I can't," she stuttered, knees wobbling. Her hands became icy as the wind picked up, whipping the girls' hair. Olirah winced, and Jessemiah gasped before stepping back from her. Olirah collapsed down onto her knees and rested her head against the stone.

"Olirah," Jessemiah stammered. Olirah sighed, her hands falling to the floor to grip the grass; the silver thynai fell from her palm into its blades. She hadn't ever seen grass in the city. "Olirah," Jessemiah croaked again. Head still lowered, she turned to Jessemiah, who anxiously glanced between her and wherever, they had run from. Olirah frowned.

"I never told you my name," Olirah murmured, the pain in her head subsiding as raindrops fell onto her wings, dampening them before hardening into flakes of snow. A writhing sensation continued through her veins again as the grass at her feet appeared to lengthen, and the wind whipped a mix of rain and snow into her face with the lift of her head. There was a warmth at her back suddenly, and Jessemiah's eyes widened as the sound of boots echoed closer. Olirah could make out the stone semicircle they had reached, with a row of eight different openings around its curve—eight different places for guards to arrive.

"I didn't know, I didn't," Jessemiah stuttered, gripping her hair as she grunted and looked between Olirah and the openings. Methodical stomping sounded nearby, signalling the arrival of more than just a few guards.

"You led me here?" Olirah's voice cracked, the tingling of the scar on her abdomen increasing. Heavy guilt fluttered through her chest, though Olirah had nothing to be guilty about. Jessemiah, on the other hand, radiated pain and remorse. She swallowed back tears and cast Olirah a pitiful look.

"I'm going to fix this," she whispered, and her black and silver wings burst free. She turned to face the openings, the sheer size and magnificence of her wings shielding Olirah from view. Olirah paused, overcome by calm as the silver tips of Jessemiah's feathers glinted in the sunlight breaking through the clouds. With the rain finally easing, the wind returned to a graceful blow that was cold at her back, all warmth suddenly gone. Olirah's hands were icy again as she peered down at the stone. A silver thynai stared up at her; the grass she must have imagined had vanished.

The sound of boots halted, replaced by the hum of swords. Thunder rippled across the sky, and tension thickened the air. Murmuring began from the guards Olirah knew stood in the opening, staring at the anomaly of Jessemiah's wings. A crackling sound filled the space, and the thunder ripped across the sky again before light blinded Olirah's vision. Lightning crackled across Jessemiah's wings as she clenched her fists. The turn of Jessemiah's head caused a crown of bright blue light to ripple across her brow, woven with a white glow that was stark against the black of her wings.

"This is the best I can offer you," Jessemiah murmured, turning her back to face the guards. She released her palms, and lightning exploded, skittering across the stones. Olirah cried out as the lightning reached her, and her wings retracted for the first time in years. However, she was not thrown back against the wall in pain, rather in surprise, as the power caressed her skin before pain exploded behind her head and darkened her vision. The last thing she saw was her hand wrapping around the silver thynai. A blackened hole pierced clean through it.

Chapter Two

JESSEMIAH

Jessemiah was only eight years old when she determined that her destiny in life was to become a saviour. She had rescued a little boy from a cage, who was set to be transported across the Burnt Sands, named not for the scorching temperatures of the sand underfoot, but for the fact many who ventured through were found burned to death. He would surely die there. She had been ten years old when she first failed, her hands stained with the blood of her parents after failing to save them. Now, at thirteen years old, the reminders of her past failures led her to sacrifice her secrets to save the girl, Olirah, who was passed out behind her, cradled by Jessemiah's power.

Jessemiah had never seen nor heard of the girl before, and while she was good at conveying that she cared for no one but herself, the reality was far from it. It was why she was so ruthless with gathering and hiding food for the ten orphans she had taken under her wing on the western streets of Vasturia. There was less competition on the western side of the city. Most of the poverty-stricken children and the few adults, fearful of the richer, heavily guarded side of the city, favoured the Eamon District. While Jessemiah had often ventured to the market street dividing the east and west, and sometimes further into the other streets to steal, she had never seen Olirah before. Jessemiah would have remembered. She would have remembered the only other Angel with wings so different from the norm. She would have remembered the way the lilac softened the harsh bones of the girl's face, the way the gold-tipped feathers would surely cast her in a heavenly glow had they not been coated in dirt or picked in places, an anxious habit. If Jessemiah had seen Olirah before, she never would have agreed to the proposal. Jessemiah would have denied the Goddess of Dusk had she seen Olirah even once before Sitara visited her in a dream.

Lead the girl to the Crescent; let the guards take her. That was Sitara's only instruction during their short interaction. Who was Jessemiah to deny the first celestial goddess? If it had been a deity, she would have been more inclined to say no. Citizens were free to choose who they worshipped in Asynthos, and Jessemiah, under no circumstances, would choose the deity from whom her power originated. Asynthos, cursed never to birth a new Stormbringer again, yet here Jessemiah was. And had the deity, Stroman, the first Stormbringer, thought to seek her out or guide her? No, he had not.

She did not know why or how she was an exception to the curse. Perhaps it was because she had not been born in Asynthos, but in Q'Ohar, to a father who hailed from a mixed lineage of Xyliar and the third state, and a mother who hailed from Asynthos. It was the only way to rationalise the Angel wings that bore the colours of the sixth state. But she assumed the queen of Asynthos could have—and would have—tested such theories by having Angels of Asynthos marry those of other states, hoping for the birth of a Stormbringer. And yet, no success had been reported. So it remained to be seen whether Jessemiah's theories were, in fact, correct. Olirah could have helped her work it out, with her wings the shade of Carvyre's emblem, but the power the girl had released only furthered her uncertainty.

For the entire morning, Jessemiah told herself it would be easy to fulfil Sitara's request. In return for one girl, a stranger, she would be granted the ability to provide for all ten orphans. She wavered when the celestial tie had appeared, for she could have sworn she sensed the girl's emotions, the pain residing in her heart. Even so, she had persevered, knowing the guard would arrive, and she was to convince Olirah to run. But when what little strength

Olirah's body had been using to shield her power, crumbled away, Jessemiah knew she could not sacrifice the girl. The girl with wings of beauty, the heart of the wounded, and the power of all four celestial gods needed to be saved.

The wind felt different the moment Jessemiah tugged them into the Crescent, the semicircular balcony built into the mountain face that was often used for ceremonies. There had been a wedding on this very spot only a week ago. It rippled with energy, a reminder of when she first discovered her ability. A moment later, as the rain poured and grass sprung through tight cracks in the stone, a blazing fire blossomed across the wall's edge, coating Olirah's hair. She knew immediately that Olirah was wanted for her power; why else would anyone want an orphan? But how would anyone know she wielded the elements of all four gods? Did they simply suspect it because of her magnificent wings?

But what was Sitara's involvement? Why did she wish for Olirah to be taken by the guards? Did the queen want her? Regardless of all the questions, Jessemiah took a risk. They were to take someone with power from the Crescent that day, but the guards did not know who, and Jessemiah was just as much of a prize. Before her resolve shattered at the thought of the ten orphans she would not return to that day, Jessemiah did what her soul instructed and sacrificed herself for the sake of the girl blessed—or cursed—by the celestial gods.

Energy rippled through her, the crackle of pale blue lightning flowing across her skin, her wings, and crawling across the stone floor toward the guards. She forced it forward, and the guards raised their shields, her power licking at their protective armour. Behind her, Olirah did not move, but Jessemiah somehow sensed she was alive, despite the pungent smell of blood. She glanced back at the crimson trickling into the grey hair of the girl bound to her, a girl she shielded with her wings. Was this their destiny? Was Jessemiah fated to protect the girl from the life she now sacrificed herself to? Would she awaken, the scar long gone, with only the memory of lilac and gold wings?

"Wall!" the captain of the rank shouted to his comrades—at least that's the position she assumed of the sneering, blonde-haired man. The clank of silver echoed as thunder rumbled above. Moving in sync, the guards created a wall with their shields in each of the eight openings to the Crescent. Behind them, four more guards raised their shields through the gap, expanding the wall until it was four shields wide and two high. Finally, the row behind shuffled closer and lifted their shields to form a protective cocoon. Dents appeared in the armour as Jessemiah's lightning pommelled it. But with her only sustenance being the small meal from the night prior, her strength was quickly fading. Even if she had eaten and trained regularly, nothing would have prepared her for the sudden appearance of tungstyn chains that propelled toward her arms and cuffed her wrists, cutting off her power. It was the only material strong enough to inhibit powers, found deep underground in the central point of each state, like the universe's balance to all existing power. Her lightning scurried across the floor, retreating to its source until only a crown of the power remained around her brow. It slowly fizzled out as the silvery-white metal tightened around her wrists. In Asynthos, Tungstyn could only be used by the royal guards, confirming Jessemiah's suspicions. She would be taken to the Queen of Asynthos.

From within the shield wall, the captain shouted, "Kneel!" Slowly, the seven other groups edged forward, forming a circle of entrapment. Jessemiah snarled but did as she was told, lowering to her knees as the chains were pulled taut, twisting her arms at awkward angles. They pulled again, and the captain sneered. Jessemiah would not give him the satisfaction of crying out in pain, even as another set of chains was wrapped around her wings, keeping her from flying toward freedom.

"Aleksandr," an informal voice called from behind. "The one who was to be paid is unconscious." Jessemiah clenched her fists and remained silent. It had worked. They assumed Olirah was the girl who led them here, and she was the one to be captured. The captain scoffed.

"Keep the coin and share it amongst yourselves. We'll pass on that this one killed her in the commotion with her lightning," he said. The guards closest to Olirah grinned, elbowing one another. Jessemiah quickly deduced they were friends. The others still in formation looked uneasy, outsiders of Aleksandr's inner circle. Jessemiah noted the grey strips of fabric around the arms of those exchanging coin; it differed from the seven formations without it. The captain stalked toward Jessemiah and cupped her chin, scanning her face. He appeared to be in his mid-thirties, though as an Angel he could be far older for all Jessemiah knew. His striking blonde hair was slicked back, and his beard was cut short to his fading jawline.

"Don't you have better things to do than capturing children, *Captain?*" Jessemiah sneered. Yanking on Jessemiah's hair, Aleksandr spat in her face. She kept her expression neutral.

"Oh, you're mistaken, sweetheart. I'm not captain of the city guard; I'm captain of the Queen's guard," he chuckled humourlessly. "You are to become favoured by the queen for what you can do but just remember where you came from and how easily my men had you in chains. Do not cross me in the palace," he sneered before dropping her hair. Jessemiah blinked. She was to be favoured? By the queen?

"You can't be very good at your job, given the queen is nowhere nearby," Jessemiah said through gritted teeth.

"Seems the queen is gaining an idiot for her collection," Aleksandr gave a cold laugh. "You are the firstborn Stormbringer in three centuries. You are worth leaving her side for." Jessemiah did not react, waiting for more information. "She'll either treat you like a daughter and parade you around in riches for all to see, or you'll be forced into training, the best weapon we have for defending our borders should the tensions continue between the other states, and an opportunity arises to...intervene." Jessemiah wondered what exactly the queen had planned. Was he referring to the tensions in Eresydon? Only a year ago, the Wiccan had become divided after a woman close to the other deities of the second state, claimed she could enhance their abilities. She demanded she be recognised as a deity, the first of a new race but it created instability in the second state. Or were there tensions in other states she did not know about? Had something happened in Q'Ohar since she'd fled?

"The second I saw you I knew you came from the third state; the difference in your wings says it all. It's not the first time Q'Ohar's celestial god has stolen from Asynthos for ungodly experiments," Aleksandr said. The queen must have known something about Jessemiah's home state; otherwise, why would he mention it immediately after discussing the rising tensions?

It was not uncommon for Asynthos and Q'Ohar to be at odds. Animosity had existed ever since Keres stole one of Vala's most prized Angels and experimented on her to create his own winged beings. But most assumed those tensions had eased after the two states sided with Xyliar during the Great War. Things had been relatively stable ever since. Jessemiah ignored the insinuation that she was an experiment. She knew her parents and her wings, her power, had always been a part of her. Sitara had confirmed she was a blessing, even if she would not reveal how.

"Drop the other one at the holding pen on the way; she can be taken on this month's drop to the Boznaya Range." Aleksandr grinned before walking toward the opening of the Crescent on the far left, the one which would take him toward the path up to the palace. He tugged on a chain, and reluctantly, Jessemiah followed, staring at Olirah's limp form with wide eyes. A guard nudged Olirah with his foot. Jessemiah had just won herself favour with the queen, while Olirah was to be sent into the unknown. For the second time in her life, Jessemiah had failed to be a saviour.

Chapter Three

JESSEMIAH

"Who are you?" Jessemiah asked. Her voice was far younger in her dream. She realised then what she was replaying in her mind. The same dream that had been repeated on countless occasions in the last ten years. Haunted by the actions she had taken and the agreement she had made.

"I know I have not been heard from or seen in over three centuries, but am I really that easy to erase and my appearance so unrecognisable?" The woman smiled, a smile that did not reach the dullness in her black eyes. Jessemiah recognised the grief behind them. Her body was tense, her hands clasped in front of her long black gown. Jessemiah tilted her head.

"Sitara," she recalled. "I have only ever seen you depicted in gold and white." The goddess' smile slackened, and she rubbed her chest as if in pain. Nobody spoke of her these days, for their focus was on Vala or the deities in Asynthos. In Q'Ohar, the state was split. Some still worshipped Keres when she was growing up; others only cared about Nefere, the first Xyra. Jessemiah wondered where Sitara had been all this time.

"Wearing those colours was to honour someone... someone that..."

"Is gone?" Jessemiah finished; her youthfulness made her brash. "I understand. I lost my parents." She looked around but found only the dark streets of the city instead of golden sands and an oasis of nightmares.

"I know," Sitara hummed. "We have met before, but you were young. I have waited thirteen years for this, to ensure you were in the right place," Jessemiah frowned as the goddess stepped closer to take *her tiny hands in her own. She was cold, so very cold. Jessemiah tried not to flinch to avoid offending her.*

"We have?"

"What is important right now, Jessemiah, is that you do something for me." Sitara knelt until they were face to face. Her cold hands moved to tuck Jessemiah's loose hair behind her ears, the black lace of her draped sleeves slipping down her arms.

"Okay," Jessemiah said, somewhat apprehensively.

"If you do this, I can ensure you and the friends you care for never go hungry. This task comes with great reward. You are a blessing to me, Jessemiah." Jessemiah's eyes brightened at that. She thought of all the bread and jam she could buy for her family of fellow orphans. So, she nodded eagerly.

"You're going to meet someone like you tomorrow, in the market that divides the east and west of Vasturia. All you must do is lead the girl to the Crescent and let the guards take her."

***

Even a decade later, the rainbow whirling across the marble floor, reflecting off the opal-encrusted wall of the throne room, hurt Jessemiah's head and made her stomach churn. The lack of sleep from a dream that haunted her most nights only made it worse. The brightness was blinding, a stark contrast to the alleyways she had slept in as a child and those she visited on her days off. Sitara had not been mistaken. Jessemiah had been rewarded with the means to feed her orphan friends. The cost, however, was her loyalty, her power, and the daily guilt of knowing her actions condemned an innocent girl to the brutality of the marble stone mines. A brutal way of life, which Jessemiah had since learnt the full details of as one of the closest confidants of Avannah Sturmov, Queen of Asynthos.

"Name," Aleksandr called to the well-dressed man standing

in the centre of the marble floor, his head bowed to the queen. Jessemiah did not move an inch while analysing the man, whose boots shone with polish. He donned a deep navy cloak that covered a turquoise waistcoat and a white shirt. A silver sword was strapped at his waist that Jessemiah wagered had never seen blood. Not a thread out of place. His dark hair was braided close to his scalp. Jessemiah was certain that if he removed his cloak, the royal pin of Thassena would show on his left breast pocket. A ship with three sails, one sail for each of the three deities of Ithyion's first state. He was a messenger for the royal family, for the Sevia's. The man remained with his head bowed for a further three seconds before Aleksandr cleared his throat, breaking the silence. Jessemiah glanced out of the corner of her eye to where the Captain of the Queen's Guard stood on the right-hand side of the throne. He did not acknowledge Jessemiah—he rarely did in the queen's presence, unless to try to best her.

"Lorenzo Zerpane, your Majesty." The man bowed his head for the third time since entering the throne room and passing the giggling courtiers dressed in a rainbow of thick woven pastels beneath the windows and the guards lining the walls. Jessemiah's attention picked up at the mention of the family so close to the Sevia's, even if he was a lowly member of the family, tasked with simply passing on a message Jessemiah had already relayed to the queen two weeks ago.

"You have travelled far, Lorenzo," the queen said in the high-pitched, tinkling tone she always used when addressing the public.

"It took just one week, your Majesty. A testament to our honoured connection with the water, propelling us across the oceans to reach our wonderful neighbours." The man bowed his head. *Again*. This time, Jessemiah rolled her eyes. The queen's fingers tapped the arms of her throne. It had taken them a week to travel here, despite the royal family being privy to the information a week earlier before they bothered to send word to their fellow rulers.

The finger tapping continued, the queen clearly containing her anger at the insult while trying to appear patient, waiting for the man to reveal what they already knew.

"You needn't have concerned yourself with such travel, Lorenzo. I would have been arriving on Thassena's shores in ten days myself. We intended to set sail tomorrow morning for the prince's wedding to your..." The queen trailed off, waiting for Lorenzo's confirmation as to his relation to the bride, the future princess, and one day queen, of Thassena.

"Cousin, your Majesty. Sienna Zerpane was a cousin on my father's side." The man's voice quietened; he averted his midnight blue eyes.

"You come from a wonderful family, Lorenzo, though it's rare to meet a male. So often your forebears birth women into the family, blessing the kingdom with Seer after Seer."

"Indeed, it is a great honour to be a part of the family destined to reunite all of Thassena and break the bad omen left upon our lands after the Great War," Lorenzo agreed. The queen leant forward, clasping her hands together.

"Then why, good sir, are you on my doorstep instead of preparing for the celebrations with your family? Sienna is about to marry a prince of the Sevia line. She is due to fulfil the visions of your familes and break the omen you speak of. What could tear you away from such a momentous occasion?" The queen asked, her face an expertly crafted picture of confusion and concern.

"It is with great heartbreak that I come to announce the death, your Majesty, of Prince Darius Sevia of Thassena—"

"No!" The queen exclaimed, her hand flying to her head as she rose from her throne, trembling. "But he was so young, barely eighteen. The same as my son." A tear slid down her cheek as she reached for Aleksandr's hand, who assisted her down the steps. The rainbow of colours cast along the walls glistened against the queen's moon-white curls, the same shade as her feathered gown. "My dear boy, I am deeply sorry for the loss of your household,"

Avannah murmured, reaching with her lace-gloved hand toward the man's cheek. His eyes widened, and his body stiffened at the queen's closeness. "Tell me, how did it happen?"

Lorenzo swallowed with the queen's face so close to his before stuttering his reply. "M-murdered in his sleep, your M-Majesty."

"Such a dishonour! How cowardly of the knife wielder!" The queen moved her hand to rest on the man's shoulder.

"No knife, your Majesty." The man glared. "Fire," he whispered low, certain only the queen could hear him at such close range.

"Did it take any of the palace with it?" she asked, her voice trembling. The man shook his head.

"There were no flames when his servants arrived the next morning. Only a blackened singe mark through his chest, as though someone had set fire to him from the inside out." The man swallowed again and moved his hand to his stomach as the queen stepped away.

"You are not implying..."

"I am, your Majesty. The king and queen believe it is a direct attack from Q'Ohar. It is the reason for our delay in conveying the message to other lands. We wish to be certain of the culprit in Q'Ohar before any attack is launched in retaliation."

"Of course, of course. Completely understandable," the queen murmured, turning back to face the dais on which her throne sat. Jessemiah stood loyally at its side as the queen wiped a tear from her cheek and smirked at her confidante. Jessemiah did not react. The news was as they had expected. "Please, Lorenzo. You are welcome to stay in the rooms at the palace while you grieve before continuing your journey," Avannah said, lowering back into her throne.

The messenger shook his head. "I appreciate the offer, your Majesty, but I am to meet the fleet to convey the message to Eresydon's rulers before we journey south together to Carvyre and then Xyliar. We believe gathering as many men as possible is the most sensible choice before attempting to step foot on the sixth state."

The queen hummed in response. "A wise response. I have heard nothing from Xyliar's royals since beginning my reign, and my family before me had heard nothing since the borders closed after the Great War. You may very well be prohibited access."

"I agree, but we must try for traditions' sake." Lorenzo bowed his head as Aleksandr appeared at his side, turning to escort him from the throne room. The queen and Jessemiah remained silent until Lorenzo exited the doors. Aleksandr nodded once as he exited the room to determine if the next visitor was worth their time. The queen huffed with amusement.

"They insult me. They insult all the rulers with their delay." Avannah turned her head on her palm to face Jessemiah.

"His logic was sound, your Majesty. They will require proof before launching an attack on Q'Ohar," Jessemiah said. She offered a small smile, resting her hand on the pommel of her sword.

"And will they find any proof?" the queen asked with a raised eyebrow. Jessemiah glanced to her left at the guards ushering the courtiers from the room, leaving the throne room empty until only Jessemiah and the queen remained.

"If they are diligent in the inspection of his rooms, they should do, yes," Jessemiah confirmed. A loud grunt from outside the throne room sounded before a woman screamed. Unsheathing her sword, Jessemiah stepped closer to the queen as the sound of chains slammed against the walls, echoing in the corridor.

"Well." The queen clapped her hands together. "This is certainly piquing my interest." Jessemiah had to admit, it was piquing her own. Even when depressing or gruesome news was delivered to the queen during her weekly audience, there was always such decorum. Chaos never occurred.

"I'll wrap this chain around your neck and choke you before I let you touch me again," growled a female voice. Jessemiah raised an eyebrow at the queen before they both turned their focus to Aleksandr, who walked through the door with a dishevelled uniform and a split lip. Behind him, chains rattled as he dragged a woman along the floor.

"Aleksandr, really!" the queen scolded. "You're getting blood and dirt all over the marble!"

Aleksandr grunted. "Apologies, your Majesty, but she refused to walk or be carried. This was the best I could do after she stabbed two guards with their daggers."

"How... volatile," the queen commented, leaning forward again to peer around the head of her guard to see the woman. Aleksandr dragged her to a stop and stepped behind the captive, who lay face down on the marble. The ripped black fabric, that was likely once a dress, barely covered her pale skin. Aleksandr reached for the woman's shoulder to pull her upright, but she growled low again. The queen nodded once at Aleksandr, who grimaced before tugging the chain around her neck until she rose to a kneeling position, gasping for air. Her dark and matted hair hung before her face as she kept her head lowered, refusing to look up at the queen. Jessemiah could make out the prominent bones in her chest and shoulders. It appeared she had not eaten in weeks. Jessemiah's power wriggled under her skin. Something about the woman made it itch to be released. She clenched her fists.

"Tell the queen what you told the guards who found you in Port Marzov," Aleksandr commanded. The woman grunted but spoke.

"I am a citizen of Asynthos. I seek refuge and protection," she mumbled. Aleksandr tugged the chain at her throat again, and she spun her head to look at him.

"*All of it*," he commanded. Turning to face the queen, the captive slowly raised her hands to her hair to push it from her face. Jessemiah made to step forward but stilled at her silver gaze.

"I am a citizen of Asynthos; I seek refuge and protection," she said again. The queen waved her hand.

"Yes, yes. I can see that in your eyes—a rare and beautiful shade said to have existed among the first Angels. But what could you possibly be seeking protection from in Asynthos?" Avannah asked.

"I am a citizen of Asynthos—"

"Deities save me," Aleksandr mumbled. The woman bared her teeth at him, and he stumbled back a step. Jessemiah stifled a smile at watching another woman, other than herself, challenge him.

"I am a born citizen of Asynthos... and an escaped prisoner of Xyliar," the girl finished, her eyes pinned on the pale blue of the queen's. There was silence for a moment between the only four people in the room. Nobody left Xyliar. The queen laughed.

"Please, child. You expect me to believe that you"—she waved her hand at the woman's frail body—"escaped the sixth state that nobody has heard from in three centuries."

Aleksandr cleared his throat, seeking permission to speak. The queen nodded.

"There is a bounty on her head, your Majesty. It does not explicitly state it is from Xyliar, but men are being approached at every port and asked if they have seen a woman by her description. They say she is a danger to the royal family."

"Did it specify which royal family?" the woman murmured.

"Why do you say that?" asked the queen, replacing her former niceties with a stony expression.

"I may have... *offended* the Abexu family by leaving." The girl's arrogance wavered, her eyes becoming distant. She knew things; she had secrets.

"How did you end up as a prisoner in the sixth state?" Jessemiah finally asked. The girl's head whipped to the speaker, as if only now noticing she had been there all along. Something silent drifted between them, something urging Jessemiah to approach her. She ignored it. The woman cocked her head before turning back to look at the queen.

"I was sent as a gift from your royal family, along with countless other mine slaves. It was to attempt a response from Xyliar," the woman spat. She spoke the truth, Jessemiah knew it. The king had attempted such things several times in the past without Avannah's consent. The queen clenched the arms of her throne.

"How am I to believe you? There is nothing significant about you to identify you. You could hide anywhere, and the likelihood of being found is slim." The queen sat back against her throne to feign disinterest.

"Show her," Aleksandr commanded.

"I can't," the woman grunted.

"Show her—"

"It is the very reason I would be found. If I do this, I will be too weak to hide them again," the woman spat. Aleksandr narrowed his eyes, and his knuckles whitened around the chains.

"You are seeking refuge, are you not?" asked the queen. "Then if you remain in the city under my protection, you have nothing to fear by revealing whatever you keep hidden."

"Forgive me, your Majesty, but it is the very men of your city I once feared before I met a true monster." Jessemiah's skin crawled again, her power crackling at her fists. At the sound, both the queen and Aleksandr glanced at her. Meanwhile, the woman watched, a hand gravitating toward her abdomen. Then Jessemiah knew.

"Show her," Jessemiah commanded, leaving no room for negotiation or denial as she stepped forward and freed her wings. She spanned them wide, casting a shadow over the throne room floor and over the woman who looked so different now, with dried blood darkening the grey strands of her hair. The woman clenched her jaw but did as she asked with a grunt of pain. Her transition was nowhere near as fluid or as quick as Jessemiah's. The girl's wings grew slowly, so slowly Jessemiah was certain she could hear where her skin and muscle parted as lilac stumps protruded from her back, the angles wonky before her wings splayed out, nearly knocking Aleksandr aside. Though she could not see the gold tips under all the dirt, she knew they were there.

"Olirah," Jessemiah breathed, almost silently. Nobody else heard as she looked upon the woman she had failed to save. The woman with wings of beauty, a heart of the wounded, and the power of all four celestial gods. The celestial tie tingled under

Jessemiah's pale blue uniform, a scar that had never faded, even in ten years.

"Do you wield lightning?" The queen demanded, looking between Jessemiah and Olirah. She must have suspected the unique wings symbolised such a thing.

"I wield no power," Olirah grunted, her eyes flickering to Jessemiah, who towered atop the dais beside the queen. Jessemiah said nothing and waited for the queen to place a verdict. Yet the monarch remained silent too; something unsettled her. Turning her back to Olirah and Aleksandr, Jessemiah shielded the queen with her wings as she murmured.

"Have her join my ranks. She may not know she has power, or perhaps she is hiding it, but if she is close to me, I can see what she knows of the sixth state," Jessemiah suggested. The queen's eyes scanned Jessemiah's wings before she nodded.

"You report *everything* to me," the queen emphasised.

"When have I ever not?" Jessemiah smiled before turning back to face Olirah, beautiful Olirah, whose pain oozed off her in waves. Olirah, whom Jessemiah failed to save. She had not saved anyone since, either. Jessemiah was no longer destined to be a saviour but the executioner for the Queen of Asynthos. She had not saved Olirah, nor the Prince of Thassena when she struck him with lightning, leaving him to burn to death from the inside out.

Chapter Four

OLIRAH

A waft of citrus brushed Olirah's cheek as Aleksandr—as she'd heard him called—jerked her arm and pushed her into the woman, whose wings were far more magnificent than her own. Something about the scent was familiar, a comforting warmth tinged with a sharp tang. A melody of fresh air played beneath the fragrance, reminding her of a freedom she must have possessed once in her life. Freedom. A word that had drifted further from Olirah's mind over the years, though the exact number of years, she could no longer recall. Yet with every turn of the moon, and the seasonal change in temperature from the darkness of her prison, that word—*freedom*—slowly faded. It burst forth again when she escaped, but Olirah was no fool. Even if her mind was a constant haze, the trade with the Queen of Asynthos was not freedom. But she doubted any cage could be as taunting or as dark as the one she had snapped in.

"Careful," the woman hissed, grappling with the chains around Olirah's wrists. Her knuckles paled as she kept her from falling under the weight of her wings.

"After the fight she gave me, I wouldn't trust her not to break out," Aleksandr chastised, as though his rough treatment was justifiable. Olirah clenched her jaw, an automatic reaction to keep from rolling her eyes. *You do this to yourself, child.* Olirah's neck twitched, a slight flinch at the memory. *Do not speak, do not move, and do not react*, she told herself.

The month-long journey from Xyliar to Asynthos, stopping at more than one port on the way, had made her lax to consequences of her actions. Perhaps that had sparked her newfound confidence in the throne room when she was so vocal. Yet the moment the black wings, as dark as night, burst free from the woman, all confidence in Olirah had waned. *Feathers*, not leather, she reminded herself. But the colour was undeniably like those haunting her memories. The woman's wings were gone now. Olirah's were the only ones on show. She wished she had the strength to hide her own, to mask the marks others would assume were dirt from her travels rather than years of caked blood.

"Come now, Alek. We both know defeating you does not mean defeating me," the woman scoffed. A nickname, familiar, though the man's reaction suggested it was not friendly but taunting.

"You're forgetting, Jessemiah, the level of trust the queen places in me, and the strength that comes with that," Aleksandr scoffed. A muscle ticked in Jessemiah's jaw.

"Fortunately for you, you do not know what my role as commander entails. If you did, perhaps you would be more fearful."

Aleksandr said nothing as he spun on his polished shoes that did not look like they often saw a fight, and stomped away from the two women. Jessemiah wasted no time in dragging Olirah away. Her footfall was heavy on the sparkling floor, a contrast to the padding of Olirah's bare feet. The sun glaring through the windows lengthened their shadows, and Olirah swallowed at the dark figure forming on the wall. Keeping her head down, she used her matted hair to shield her face and hide the occasional glance through her lashes as she peered between the path and Jessemiah.

Olirah knew instantly where the woman originally hailed from. While her stowaway voyage had only parted in Q'Ohar for a week, she had seen enough enticing women to recognise Jessemiah's heritage. How did a woman end up leaving the third state to work in servitude for the queen of the fourth? Though when she spoke, the deep lilt of the fire state was less noticeable; her weak accent suggested she had been in Asynthos for some time.

The brown of Jessemiah's skin glowed in the sun streaming

through the windows as they continued their never-ending walk through the palace. Her uniform was a stark contrast to the light; it only exemplified her features and made her dark, braided hair glisten, while her lashes framed eyes the colour of honey. She radiated a warmth that Olirah would once have craved, though her uniform reminded her of ice. It was less formal than the polished silver Olirah imagined she would likely wear if she were to patrol the capital's streets. She'd tucked her cream shirt with its billowing sleeves into her matching, fitted trousers, and a tailored, powder-blue waistcoat fit snug around her waist, its lack of creases or lines suggesting protective armour underneath. Sparkling silver threading hemmed the edges, and a sigil of the state was embroidered on her right breast: three stars above three mountains, representing the three races of the state—Angels, Stormbringers, and Truthtellers. On her left breast was a grey metal badge in the shape of an Angel wing. Jagged blue lines of paint crisscrossed it like lightning. Olirah narrowed her eyes. Was the woman a Stormbringer?

"You aren't particularly subtle when you stare," Jessemiah mused, a teasing lilt in her voice. Olirah briefly locked eyes with her honeyed gaze before hiding behind her hair again. "I recognise the look in your eye, though." Olirah glanced back up at her, intrigued. This woman knew nothing about her. "You're analysing me. I'm unsure if you're trying to establish a weakness to kill me or merely figure out where I'm taking you."

Olirah kept her face neutral and looked ahead; they had reached the end of a hallway. All that faced Olirah now was an open balcony overlooking the city below. She could not help the deep inhale that pained her chest. The cold air—*free* air—rushed through her body and made her skin tingle. Afraid Jessemiah might tug her back by the chains still gnawing at her skin, Olirah slowly stepped forward and placed her hands on the cold opal. Delicate snowflakes landed on her knuckles, refusing to melt given her skin's coldness. Nobody had provided her with a blanket or new clothes when they found her stumbling behind crates at the port and captured her. Olirah admired the sparkling building tops before peering at the duller side of the city, one that seemed familiar. Then a different mountaintop came to mind. Bloodied dark rock, littered with carcasses rather than glistening opal dusted with snow.

"You can see why many call it the most beautiful capital in the kingdom, can't you?" Jessemiah asked. Her question brushed Olirah's memories aside.

"Do you not believe Sahrih is?" Olirah asked, referencing Q'Ohar's capital, renowned for the oasis it encircled. Its shape forced the city into a circular maze of streets. Jessemiah did not immediately answer as she stared off into the distance. She had been right. Olirah *was* assessing the woman, for she knew that haunted, vacant look all too well. Recollecting the past. The need to assess whether the woman was a threat outweighed Olirah's need to remain silent as she asked, "Have you lived in Vasturia for long?" Her honey-coloured eyes shifted back to Olirah, accompanied by the slightest furrow of her brow, so slight someone else might have missed it. Olirah cocked her head a fraction, trying to determine what was odd about her question. Was it because Olirah knew of other states despite having been captive in Xyliar? Was it because she was cohesive despite the pain in her mind and body? Perhaps the woman was simply contemplating different ways to torture her. As it always had, Olirah's mind ran away with her.

Though Jessemiah watched, she did not seem to care about Olirah's matted hair, darkened by layers of dirt and blood that disguised its true shade; nor did she scan the scars littering her bare arms and torso through the rips in her dress that held too many memories in its seams. No, Jessemiah's piercing gaze went straight through Olirah, like she was determining all the inner workings and worries of her mind, trying to understand the pattern of her soul. The intensity of Jessemiah's analysis as she beheld her captive made Olirah squirm; though perhaps only Olirah saw herself as such. After all, she had sought asylum, had she not?

"This way," Jessemiah finally said, spinning on her heel to a pale, arched door on their left. Olirah had been too fixated on the outside world to notice it. As Jessemiah stepped over the threshold first, whispering sounded from behind. When Olirah cocked her head, a door from behind abruptly closed. It was identical to the one she was about to walk through, and to the other six she now noticed in the narrow corridor. They were as high and far from the inner workings of the palace as possible.

"You can meet the others tomorrow morning," Jessemiah said, waiting patiently inside the room. The light reflecting off her made Olirah frown. At least from its appearance, it wasn't a cell. Yet Olirah would wait to pass further judgement on whether her new life offered any freedom, or if she would have to spend years hatching an escape plan. Tentatively, avoiding Jessemiah's inquisitive stare, Olirah stepped over the threshold. Magic tingled on her skin, an unseen barrier raising the hairs on her arms. She tensed.

"The queen has a Sorcerer that remains in residence at the palace to create and maintain barriers such as this one," Jessemiah explained. Did that mean the queen of Asynthos had sided with the Sorcerers in the tensions Xyliar's men spoke of when the new race emerged?

"So, it is a cell," Olirah murmured, glancing around the room. Still, it didn't look like one. Four windows lined the eastern wall, with two on either side of the balcony, inviting in the light that bathed both women now. Although they were high above the city, it was still an escape route if she could somehow lower the barriers. A large bed was pushed against the opposite wall, offering a view out of the window; the bedding was so thick she doubted anyone could feel the capital's cold air, even with the windows open. In the corner was a white dresser and a small writing desk nestled beside the fireplace with curved, engraved legs.

"The barrier is not to keep you in," Jessemiah countered. Olirah couldn't help the way her head tilted, her usual mask so easily slipping before this woman. "It is to stop anyone you do not wish from entering." Olirah dug her fingernails into her palms. She'd had no privacy over the years. She never had a place to call her own.

"This is your bathing chamber," Jessemiah continued, crossing the cold tiles to a second door. Although it was smaller, the room was just as bright. A large window filled the entirety of the right wall, a frosted glaze blocking the view. It was glaringly bright compared to the bedroom, and the soft blue walls were replaced with the same sparkling tile on the floor, reflecting the light flooding in. Olirah blinked, blinded by the contrast to her old cell. She frowned. Straight ahead was a basin; towels hung on the left, and a large space loomed before the window.

"You bathe with only a basin?" Olirah asked. Jessemiah smiled and walked to the wall beside the window.

"If you were in the usual guards' barracks, there would be communal baths and a private bathing tub for generals. But the queen affords us additional luxuries for all we do on her command." Jessemiah reached for the silver knob in the wall and turned it. Olirah jumped at the sound of water falling from the ceiling, splattering the tiles like the hammering rain during stormy nights in Xyliar. Jessemiah left the water running and stepped back toward the door.

"The queen collects residents from Ithyion. You will find many qualities from other states scattered throughout the palace: barriers from the Sorcerers, water systems from Thassena. In her private rooms, there is even a mirror for communications, designed by the Queen of Carvyre herself."

"Is that what I am?" Olirah asked, walking tentatively toward the water, her back to Jessemiah. "A collectable?" She reached for the water yet snatched her hand back at the warmth, expecting it to be ice cold. When a hand grasped Olirah's arm, she screamed and lurched forward. Turning, her eyes were widened and her back burned as she pushed herself as far against the wall as possible. Her vision blurred as the water streamed down her face. Jessemiah's eyes widened, her hand still outstretched.

"Don't-don't touch me," Olirah stuttered. The water flowed

down her shoulders as she stood there, frozen. The sparkling white tiles darkened as Jessemiah took a slow, careful step forward, raising a key in her hand for Olirah to see. She stepped under the falling water and did not react when the stream soaked through her clothes.

"I won't touch your skin, Olirah, but I need to touch the cuffs to unlock them." Olirah looked between her honeyed eyes and the key. Blinking the water from her lashes, she trembled and nodded slowly, pulling her head back further as Jessemiah, true to her word, unlocked the cuffs. They clattered and fell to the ground before Jessemiah knelt to unlock those at her feet. The Angel said no more before placing the key on the edge of the basin and leaving the room. Olirah did not know how long she stood under the water, letting it wash away every nightmare-soaked speck of dirt. She let it attempt to wash away who she had been for the last ten years while questioning how Jessemiah knew her name.

Chapter Five

JESSEMIAH

Five hours, eighteen reports, and a dinner at her desk later, Jessemiah finally heard the water shut off in the adjacent room. She placed her quill down with a sigh and cracked her neck, leaning back in her chair to watch dusk settle outside the window. Working was the only thing that kept her from knocking on Olirah's bathing chamber every ten minutes to check she hadn't drowned herself or jumped from the window. The warbled cries and sobs, barely audible over the falling water, told Jessemiah she was still in there.

It wasn't surprising. The woman had been caked in so much dirt and blood that, had it not been for her eyes or wings, Jessemiah wouldn't have recognised her. Her once-silver hair was nearly as dark as Jessemiah's now, while her skin was as dirt-covered as those in the forges of Q'Ohar, where her father had once worked. After the second hour of tears, Jessemiah knew the prolonged showering was for a reason other than hygiene.

In her entire employment, Xyliar was the one state Jessemiah failed to collect reports on. Nobody knew what had happened. The occasional whisper suggested the queen of the sixth state had killed her entire family—father, mother, cousins, aunts— driven crazy by the war. Nobody knew the genuine reason why though or what had transpired in the sixth state since. It was why Olirah was indeed a *collectible* to the Queen of Asynthos, though Jessemiah hated that word. Despite the stark contrast in Jessemiah's quality of life after she and Olirah had been forced to part ways, Jessemiah was not naïve. She knew she was the shiniest prize in the queen's collection. The others were indeed rare, but none of them, like Jessemiah, defied the curse on the state.

Despite the death and destruction the states had been forced to recover from following the Great War, it seemed the inflated ego and superiority of the deities had been passed down to the rulers of the kingdom. They were all driven by the innate desire to be at the top of the food chain. The exact reason the queen did not view Jessemiah and her cadre as abominations, like many in Vasturia did, was because she viewed them as something the other states did not have. A unique powerhouse.

"I knocked last time. It's your turn," sounded a not-so-quiet whisper from the other side of Jessemiah's door. Tilting her head back, her unbound hair fell between her shoulder blades, above where her wings would protrude if she had them on show.

"You're a fucking liar, Alyssa," a male voice sneered, though Jayesh was fooling no one with the veiled annoyance. He was besotted with the woman.

"Move, I'll knock," a gruff and quieter male voice said. Elias, always the mediator.

"No, it's his turn to get his head bitten off for interrupting," Alyssa snapped. Jessemiah slammed the leather binding of her reports closed and tossed the quill back in its stand.

"You do realise if I can hear you, she likely can as well," Jessemiah called, knowing they had come to ask about Olirah. Having grown up outside of Asynthos, her cadre frequently forgot that nearly all those from races in Asynthos were blessed with enhanced hearing, inherited from Vala's ability to summon sounds on the wind. Their muttering and bickering stopped until finally, a knock sounded. Three clear, evenly spaced, distinct raps on the wood. Different from the light, quick taps of Alyssa or Jayesh's pounding knocks that shook the door on its hinges. Elias continued to play mediator then. "Come in," Jessemiah called. She did not turn in her chair or attempt to redo the buttons on her waistcoat where it fell open. Instead, she stared out at the bruised colouring tainting the sky. She hated the dark. Feet shuffled in, and the door clicked shut behind them.

"Jessemiah, how has your day—"

"Ask what you really want to know, Alyssa." Jessemiah turned only her head to survey the three bodies. All three hid their wings, and none wore their pale blue uniforms. It confirmed to Jessemiah that they'd spent their day off in the city.

"What's her lineage?" Jayesh asked, straight to the point.

"Why do you assume she is joining us?" Jessemiah asked, earning a scoff from him. Alyssa rolled her eyes, as though it was absurd to pretend she could ever keep secrets from them.

"She's in the quarters, isn't she?" Jayesh proceeded. "Come on, I want to know if I have someone else to train with fire."

"How selfish." Alyssa turned her nose up. "Perhaps she shares my affinity for nature or water like Elias."

"Who's selfish now?" Jayesh scoffed. "Maybe she's a Stormbringer like Jes." Jessemiah glanced back at her reports, the ones which stated no other Stormbringer had been discovered in the last three-hundred years. The same reports also suggested there were no new collectibles for the queen to add to the list of individuals standing before her now. Jessemiah felt the weight of Elias's stare, focusing on the space between her shoulder blades where her black and grey wings, when unleashed, protruded. Their darkened shades differed from Asynthos' white wings or the burning red Jayesh boasted as a child of Q'Ohar, despite Jessemiah's parents being from the same state. Instead, her wings of shadows were closely associated with the very state no one had gained entry to or had heard from until Olirah arrived bloodied and bruised this afternoon.

"Lilac," Elias finally said. "Her wings are lilac, aren't they? The final missing piece of the queen's trophy case."

Jessemiah said nothing but offered a minuscule nod.

"Fuck," Jayesh cursed.

"Jay!" Alyssa scolded. "Do not curse!"

"Carvyre, then?" Elias asked as Jessemiah finally stood to face them all, leaning back on her desk and crossing her ankles and arms.

"The colour would suggest so, yes. Though she lived in Asynthos as a child, so I don't know for certain."

"I heard the chains," Elias continued. "What did she do to end up back in Carvyre before being shipped back here as a prisoner?"

Jessemiah glanced down at her boots, fixating on a spot of blood that needed cleaning.

Jayesh whistled low. "That bad then?"

Jessemiah didn't answer immediately. How much should she tell them? Usually, she decided on whether she could risk sharing information based on how likely it would get them killed if the queen discovered they knew the truth. She would never reveal that to them, though; the four shared an unspoken agreement that their emotions and care for one another were to be kept to themselves. To anyone who overheard or saw them interacting, they were simply colleagues.

"She wasn't a prisoner in Carvyre," Jessemiah finally said, deciding to offer some information. She looked at her three comrades, their faces eager for information, to learn more of the person who would now be thrust into their close-knit group. "She escaped Xyliar, where she has spent, potentially, the last ten years." Alyssa's eyes widened, Jayesh's mouth fell open, and Elias's eyes narrowed further.

"What was Xyliar doing with an Angel potentially possessing the power of Carvyre?" Elias asked. Jessemiah shook her head. Olirah could not walk through dreams or bond with a pegasus, nor had she seen the Angel wield an arc of light or communicate through mirrors.

"As far as she says, she has no known power." Not a complete lie. Olirah had said as much. Yet Jessemiah had decided to keep the true nature of Olirah's strength to herself for now until she determined why Olirah was hiding it.

"The queen wants her with us to gather their state secrets," Elias concluded. Jessemiah nodded.

"Is she likely to do that?" Jayesh asked. "What if she is a spy for them?"

"Did you hear her cries? They are not the sounds of a willing spy; it's the sound of a broken girl." Alyssa elbowed him before lowering her eyes, softening Jayesh's sceptical expression.

"Regardless of her motives, the only way we're going to gather any intel from her is if you"—Jessemiah waved her finger at the three of them—"make her feel welcome."

***

Olirah shone like a beacon on the palace rooftops. Despite how much she appeared to withdraw, she still seemed to pull and attract everything toward her. The usually rough winds atop the palace, rushing around the cadre while they trained, appeared to soften when they reached her, only fluttering the two panels of powder-blue gauze over her shoulders and breasts, cinched at her waist atop the billowing cream sleeves. The sun, high in the afternoon sky, filtered through the clouds yet streamed only on Olirah, bathing her in light and brightening the golden tips of each individual feather on her wings. Jessemiah counted each one, the tug on her abdomen, the celestial tie between them, prompting her to commit every inch of her to memory. She analysed the tug of her wings to her body when a weapon clattered onto the floor, or the tick in her jaw when Jayesh swore or Elias used his water as whips. Jessemiah memorised the way Olirah tried to hide the fact that, in her bones, she was terrified. But terrified of what, Jessemiah did not know.

Alyssa noticed it too. Whilst both men attempted to greet her, Alyssa offered merely a polite smile and nod before striding toward the weapons station. She had always been good at that, knowing exactly what a person needed. Jayesh, who overcompensated with humour, did nothing; Elias's polite attempts at conversation did nothing. Jessemiah's questions about her uniform did nothing.

Nothing coaxed Olirah to speak.

She simply sat on the very edge of the palace rooftop, with her back to the city, as though she might give up and topple backward any second. Her silvery-grey hair was no longer dulled with blood or dirt; it appeared to sparkle beneath the sun that was intent on warming her. Her pale skin was almost iridescent, and her silver eyes never once left the Angels. She watched, her eyes shifting between wary and curious, tense and admiring, focused and exhausted. For nine hours, Olirah sat and watched.

"What's the tally now?" Jayesh shouted as the rays of sun on Olirah slowly morphed into a light pink.

"For the month? Or the year?" Elias asked, wiping the sweat from his forehead. He returned his favoured sword to its place in the large alcove on the exterior wall.

"Month."

"Seventy-two to sixty-eight," Alyssa chimed in. Jayesh groaned. "He's beaten you in hand-to-hand combat seventy-two times this month."

Jayesh threw his sweat-ridden towel at Alyssa. She expertly dodged it and it landed in a bucket of water instead, one of the many placed around the rooftop to keep the fighters cool and regularly refilled by Elias's power. Nobody else in the city, or even the palace, knew they used the rooftop to train. Jessemiah doubted anyone else in the city even knew there was an accessible space up here, given the only access was through a turreted staircase directly from their quarters—or by flight. But an unauthorised Angel flying toward the palace rooftops would be captured or struck down immediately.

The cadre fell into their usual post-training routine, and still, Olirah watched, while Jessemiah watched her. Jayesh slipped through the only entrance and exit while Alyssa and Elias gathered supplies from the cupboards next to the alcove of weapons: plates, cutlery, blankets, stacked benches. Olirah's face was inquisitive as the pair laughed between themselves, carrying their collection of items to the far side of the long, rectangular rooftop, boxed in by walls that reached their torsos. Along the stretch opposite Olirah, archways formed a covered outdoor space overlooking the mountain range. There, Elias placed benches around a stone table while Alyssa meticulously laid out the plates and cutlery, straightening them all into exact, precise positioning, not a millimetre out of place.

Jessemiah's lips quirked as Elias walked past, shifting forks at different angles with his pinkie, teasing her in the subtle way he did when he finally considered himself off-duty.

"Alyssa!" Jayesh called, reappearing from the entrance with a tray wider than the doorway. It forced him to turn sideways to step through. "It's your lucky day." His grin was free and childlike as he kicked the door shut behind him. Alyssa squealed.

"Is Iris back from Eresydon?" She clapped her hands together, holding them in front of her lips with wide eyes. Jayesh placed the tray down on the table and lifted its large silver lid.

"Andor herbed game stew with freshly made dumplings for m'lady." Alyssa squealed again, earning a groan from Elias.

"The dumplings are always so heavy," he said. Alyssa rolled her eyes and slapped his arm.

"Oh, but the bowls of pasta she makes at your request aren't?"

"It's not the same; it's balanced with salads and fresh ingredients."

"What do you call that?" Alyssa exclaimed, pointing at the large bowl of stew. "Carrots, onions, potatoes—all fresh ingredients. Just don't eat the dumplings."

Jessemiah rolled her eyes at the usual disagreement, one that began every time their cook made a dish native to one of their homelands. She jumped down from her perched seat on the wall and locked eyes with Olirah before inclining her head toward the table. Jessemiah didn't look to see if Olirah followed. It seemed, for today at least, Olirah would do whatever suited her. The scrape of the benches as the others sat hid the sound of Olirah's footfall, but the scent of crisp soap rushing toward Jessemiah on the cooler evening breeze confirmed her approach.

"You can only get this herb in the capital of Eresydon; it's what makes the entire dish!" Alyssa continued. Jessemiah sat opposite the pair, with Jayesh taking the seat on her right. It left the head of the table free for Olirah, who looked cautiously at the stool, seeming to notice the chair put her at the centre of attention. The other Angels didn't look her way, as though she was a scared animal they could spook with a single glance.

Jayesh spooned stew into bowls while Elias filled glasses with fresh water. Jessemiah reached for the bowl of butter and began slathering it onto a piece of bread. Slowly, she slid it on a plate toward Olirah. When was the last time she had properly eaten? The tray left outside of her rooms last night had remained untouched, other than the two slices of bread that had been intended for the cream of mushroom soup.

Jessemiah watched as Olirah tentatively prodded a dumpling with a spoon before dipping the bread into the stew. A silence fell over the group, the only sound was the clinking of spoons against bowls and Jayesh's gods awful slurping of the stew's gravy.

"So..." he began. Alyssa shot him a look, a warning he was not to ask questions.

"How do you like the stew, Olirah?" she interrupted, an innocent enough question. Olirah glanced up through her lashes, seeming to want to hide her pained expression behind her hair as she chewed. When she cleared her throat, Jessemiah clenched her spoon in anticipation.

"It has a lot more textures than I'm used to," she said, her voice as delicate as the chimes in the palace hallways.

"That's a common response to game stew. It has several meats, so it's rather varied." Alyssa's eyes followed Olirah's hands, watching her pick at the bread. "If you prefer the texture of bread, you might like these dumplings better," Alyssa said, passing a plate of the crunchier, dry dumplings that were cooked over the fire rather than in the stew itself. Olirah tentatively reached out for one and pulled it apart. Her small smile told them she agreed with Alyssa as she sat and chewed.

"Are you from Eresydon?" Olirah asked. The mention of her home earned a grin from Alyssa, who flicked her red hair over her shoulder.

"I lived in Andor all my life, all twenty six years of it. I never knew my father and lost my mother in the War of Hearts last year, and when Jes came knocking one day, asking if I was interested in employment that would cover the cost of my grandparents care when they fell sick, I immediately said yes. I've been in Asynthos ever since."

"You don't miss Andor? And your grandparents?" Olirah asked, seeming to wonder how her parents had died, and if they had sided with the Wiccan or the Sorcerers in the war. Perhaps thoughts of her own family prompted such questions, though Jessemiah did not know what had happened to them to force Olirah onto the streets at such a young age. Jayesh tensed, and Jessemiah knew he gripped Alyssa's hand under the table.

"They passed two months ago," she said before smiling at the rest of the cadre. "But this is my family now." Olirah tilted her head, surveying those seated around the table. Her eyes seemed to brighten for a moment, as if imagining what her own life might be like here.

"To our family of crossbred abominations!" Jayesh cheered, trying to make light of the topic as he raised his glass. The clinking of their glasses was drowned out by the smashing of Olirah's as she stared off into the distance over the mountains, fragments of glass embedded in her palm.

Chapter Six

OLIRAH

Pain is good, it means you're alive. Olirah used to tell herself that in the early days of her life in Xyliar, but as the days soon became weeks and the months became years, numbness took over and distorted her reality. So, as Olirah collapsed onto the bed, staring at the red slashes on her hand, the tinge of pain she knew should be mingled with the blood absent, she wondered if she truly was in Asynthos, or if she was trapped in an eternal nightmare where the hope of freedom would be ripped from her when she eventually opened her eyes to darkness.

At first, nobody had said anything when Olirah ruined the cadre's moment of jesting, but once Jessemiah noticed the blood dripping onto the stone, marring the beauty with her disgraced blood, the talking began. Voices competed for Olirah's focus; someone asked if she was okay, while another directed someone to fetch a bandage. Above all the chatter and scraping of cutlery and benches was one voice, a female voice, trying to cut through Olirah's silent stare. Jessemiah. A soft and gentle murmur, a slow-moving hand reaching for hers. The memory of her touch under the falling water of the bathing chamber had Olirah jerking back and standing.

"May I be excused?" She repeated the question again and again, her head bowed and shoulders slumped.

A simple nod.

And that was all it took for Olirah to run, stumbling toward the turret door, down the winding stairs, and into her chambers. Hers. Her chambers, her bed, her nightgown that hung over her desk chair facing the window. All hers. Well, the queen's, if she was being particular. But it was hers while she remained in the palace. Nothing had been hers for as long as she could remember. Not even her body.

Abomination.

Cross breed.

Still, Jayesh's deep laughter ran through her like the cries of her fellow prisoners. Olirah clenched her eyes shut at the blood dripping from her hand onto the pristine silk sheets. Her eyes flew open again. What if she got into trouble for staining the bedding? A memory of different blood on different sheets crept into the corners of her mind, the red still noticeable despite the shadows of black silk. Olirah winced and stumbled off the mattress, tearing off the white bedding and crumpling it up before striding for the bathing chamber. She tossed the fabric on the floor and turned the handle as Jessemiah had demonstrated. As the water began rinsing the red from the silk, she dabbed at her hand with a towel and sighed. She tossed the blood-soaked material into the pile under the falling water.

Her hand trembled on the edge of the basin, gripping it so tightly her knuckles became as pale as the porcelain. Her eyes met her reflection, and she flinched. Before arriving in Asynthos, she rarely looked at her reflection. Anyone else might think her pretty, not as pretty as Jessemiah, but pretty nonetheless. She had been told so plenty of times. But hearing such words on repeat, when you were made to feel anything but, distorted one's mind. She tugged the odd blue gauze free from her belt and used it to wrap her hand, tying a knot and leaving the pieces trailing behind her. She returned to her bed with the water still running.

With the bedding drenched in the bathing chamber, only pillows crowded the mattress now. Olirah tugged one toward her, cradling it. Curling into a tight ball, she shrank into herself, focusing on the sound of hammering water. Last night, she had eventually turned it off after determining sleep would not reach her. Instead, she had sat before the large window, waiting for the sun to swallow the darkness for another day. But now, she let the water fall, filling the fear-filled silence as she awaited the next sound that might come in the darkness.

***

Light blinded the darkness as someone heaved open the heavy tungstyn door, bathing the curved ceiling of the cell with the glow of orange lanterns, brightening the room that felt like a cave. Olirah blinked harshly against the light, catching glimpses of the other girls in their torn, ragged garments as her eyes tried to adjust. Shuffling filled her ears as the other girls in the room flattened themselves against the walls, hoping that the further they were from the inter-cepting glow, the less likely they were to be the girls picked for the evening.

Yet after three years in the castle cells, Olirah knew it made no difference. She had clocked the rotation of bodies soon enough. The same three girls, the oldest three, for three nights in a row, then the second oldest three for the next three nights, and so on, until all thirty girls had been seen over the course of a month. Olirah used to use the rotation to track the month and year. When she was the youngest, she was taken on the last three days of every month. Over the years, girls would disappear, only to be replaced by new ones, moving everyone up through the rotation. Three years later, Olirah was now number twenty seven. When she was moved to the location, she was forced to wait patiently for two days as girl twenty-five and girl twenty-six first obeyed their duty. That was all she knew the girls as: no names, just number twenty-five and number twenty-six.

Number two caught her eye on the other side of the chamber, and the heavy rise and fall of her chest showcased her deep sigh as she bowed her head. Number one had not returned this month, which meant they would all move up again after the full rotation. Olirah would become twenty-six. What happened to girl number one? There was no evident reason why she was taken, nor a consistency in how many turns of the moon, but a new girl arrived each time, moving them even closer to the unknown. The lack of logic meant Olirah had no idea how long until she became number one and left the cell.

No one spoke to the girls as the three guards marched into the dark space. Olirah was silent as the guards gripped her arms. The touch, firm enough to appear forceful, held no malice. That confirmed it. Sascha was the guard tasked with bringing Olirah to her feet. Olirah flicked her eyes up, meeting the dark stare between the onyx visor, different from the copper soldiers she had seen occasionally roaming the hallways on the brief walk from one cell to another. Her eyes softened slightly before she gestured with her head for Olirah to start walking. If Sascha was on duty for the next three days, they would get more food—a win for the three girls. Olirah still hated her, though. Despite her small acts of kindness towards the girls, Sascha was still a part of the regime. Treating them like this for whatever reason.

The stone beneath Olirah's feet was cold as she followed the usual motions out the door, down a corridor, two lefts, and then a right into a small room. Five minutes to change into the black gown hanging in front of the mirror. The same style as always: thin silk clinging to her slowly developing sixteen-year-old body, a high slit up the right, a ribboned back that number twenty-five tied for her, knotting it as tightly as possible to delay the inevitable. With one minute spare, Olirah braided her tangled hair, which was more difficult than she would like, especially with her weak fingers.

"Time," a commanding voice called from outside the door. It was one of the male guards who accompanied number twenty-five and number twenty-four. The three girls looked at one another and completed their usual ritual. Standing in a tight circle, they held one another's hands, inhaled, and straightened their backs as they exhaled, plastering demure smiles onto their faces.

Sascha winced, as she always did, upon seeing Olirah's gown. The revealing dress accentuated her curves but also emphasised the sharpness of her protruding bones. The guards unlocked the box on the vanity, withdrawing three syringes. Olirah tensed as Sascha approached and moved her braid over her shoulder, wiping the centre of her back. Olirah stiffened as the syringe met her skin. She had no idea what it did; none of them ever seemed any different after the golden substance entered their veins, but whatever it was had to be key to why they were here. The soft strings of music flowed down the hall as they approached the same chambers as usual before laughter reached the girls' ears. Olirah tensed, as did the two girls on either side of her. He had company. Viserius never had company. Their pinkies brushed one another in solidarity before the chamber doors opened.

***

"It's okay" were the first words Olirah heard before bolting upright, sweat glueing the blouse to her chest. A lie. She would never be okay again. It took Olirah a second to grasp her bearings, though she stopped herself from catapulting to the other side of the bed, as far from Jessemiah as possible. A soft lantern glow in the hallway crept through the crack in the door. Moonlight streamed through the windows, bathing Jessemiah in a way that made her look kissed by the night itself. Her unbound hair fell over her shoulders and a thin shirt that matched her loose, creased trousers, which only creased further as she lifted one leg onto the bed to better face Olirah.

"It's okay."

"None of this is okay," Olirah snapped. Her hand flew to her mouth, as if hoping the action would take back the bite in her voice. Such a retort usually warranted a lashing. The strips of gauze hanging from her wrapped hand tangled with her legs as she tucked them up under her chin, creating a barrier between her and Jessemiah. The women were silent for a moment. The only sounds filling the room was the fall of water in the bathroom and the breeze rattling the windowpanes. The moon's height told Olirah she had slept for at least a few hours, though the memory of her life had felt far longer. She shook off the sound of laughter in her mind and pushed down the memories before the faces of the girls appeared again.

"No," Jessemiah murmured. "I suppose you're right. None of this is okay."

Olirah wrapped her arms around her knees and rested her chin atop them, glancing over at the woman, who sighed, as though her life had not always been one of palace luxury. Jessemiah twisted her hands in her lap. Faint scars lined her fingers and calloused palms. Perhaps life in the palace was not as luxurious as it first appeared. Olirah wondered then about the missions the Queen of Asynthos bestowed upon the commander and her cadre. Were these the kinds of missions Viserius had assigned his most trusted soldiers? The missions they bragged about? Leaving the state in secret to capture children? Was the woman opposite no better than those men she had known? The thought made Olirah tense. Noticing it, Jessemiah leant further away from Olirah.

"I am often plagued by nightmares, too," Jessemiah said. Olirah glanced sideways at her, the Angel who appeared so strong. Jessemiah cleared her throat. "When I was ten, I intended to meet my parents at the oasis in Sahrih. They told me under no circumstances was I to detour; it was vital that I went straight from my sword lessons to the oasis. I should have realised from their tone that there was something wrong. My mother was always so relaxed. Looking back now, it was unusual for her to be so serious." Jessemiah stared out the window, and Olirah watched her. "I never knew why they wanted me to go to the oasis. Maybe we were going somewhere afterwards, or they wanted me to meet someone. But on my route, I saw a little boy being pushed around by the city patrol guards. He was clutching a piece of bread; I assumed he had stolen it. I stepped in, handed over some coin as payment for the bread and tugged him away. It made me late." Jessemiah cleared her throat as her lip wobbled. "I just wanted to help him, but in doing so, I lost my parents. When I reached the golden sands, bodies were crowded at the water's edge. I couldn't see my parents yet, so I went to see what everyone was looking at." Olirah's brow raised slightly as Jessemiah wiped her eyes. "There they were at the edge of the oasis. The blood from their necks turned the water red."

"Did you ever find out what happened to them?" Olirah whispered. Jessemiah shook her head.

"No, and that's what haunts me most nights, not knowing why they were there, or if I could have saved them had I not wanted to help that boy." Jessemiah turned to face Olirah.

"The dreams never go away"—Jessemiah locked eyes with Olirah, who stopped her fidgeting—"but you find people that make the days easier."

Olirah looked away, but it did not lift the weight of Jessemiah's golden eyes boring into her as she stared out the window, across the city rooftops, beyond the oceans, and past the distant mountains to where a piece of Olirah still resided. Where her innocence remained.

Chapter Seven

JESSEMIAH

The shadows darkening the sparkling opal walls of the briefing chambers made the stone match the shade of Olirah's hair. When the sun dared peek through the clouds, it sparkled like Jessemiah imagined Olirah's eyes would were she not so haunted by her time in Xyliar. The first time Jessemiah woke her from a nightmare, she looked lifeless and had appeared so every night since for the last two weeks. They never spoke about the dreams, and neither of them mentioned Jessemiah waking Olirah to sit with her for several hours as she stared, hollow-eyed, out the window. It quickly became apparent that Olirah only ever wished to sleep when the sky had lightened to the deep blue of dawn. Understanding Olirah's fear of the dark, Jessemiah wished she could brighten every moment of Olirah's day.

"Commander," snapped a regal voice, pulling Jessemiah from her thoughts which so regularly strayed to Olirah. Jessemiah turned her head to the right at the tone. Queen Avannah sat poised on her throne, dragged by servants up the main flights of stairs to the briefing chamber. It would have made more sense for a guard to do it; at least those kissed with Vala's power could manoeuvre it with ease. Yet the queen seemed intent on reminding her powerless servants of their place.

"Yes, your Majesty." Jessemiah bowed her head, vaguely recalling the conversation about Thassena since Prince Darius' murder at her hands. "I am due a fresh report from my informants in the capital by the day of rest."

"Very well. It appears the escalation has not gone as planned.

The king has not called for Q'Ohar to answer for any crimes, which suggests they do not believe it was instigated by the third state." The queen's jaw ticked as she tapped her fingers on the arm of her throne. "We need a new plan; perhaps we need Eresydon on side. Their border with Q'Ohar means they are best placed for missions."

"The second state is still recovering from the War of Hearts. There is still instability over the way the land has been divided, with so many Wiccans having converted to the way for the Sorcerers. It would make it difficult to turn their attention outward to other states," Jessemiah added, trying to be diplomatic.

"I want retribution against the Elharars now," the queen sneered. Jessemiah held her tongue. The long-standing rivalry between the families was pointless. They hadn't even started it; the gods had. The Sturmov family's hatred was founded on Keres taking an Angel from Vala during the era documented in history books as the Kingdom of Creation. It was thousands of years ago, so why did it still matter? Avannah's family had even documented their right to Q'Ohar, claiming that the land should also belong to them as retribution, for the only reason it prospered was from the leadership of the Xyra, a race created from the theft of an Angel from Asynthos. A weak, watered-down claim to mask their greed. But those in power took any excuse to gain further standing, and a war against Q'Ohar, regardless of its foe, would benefit Asynthos' longstanding need for so-called *retribution*.

"Then I shall await the update from my informant and hope we can push the tensions between Thassena and Q'Ohar." Jessemiah bowed her head politely, hoping to put an end to the conversation. The quicker they made their way through the agenda, the quicker she could return to the rooftop and cadre. To Olirah. Jessemiah imagined her sitting in the same spot on the wall, studying her surroundings. Jessemiah was sure she made mental notes about her cadre's fighting styles: their strengths and weaknesses.

"Perhaps you will be more successful in providing an update

on the girl and Xyliar," Queen Avannah said. Jessemiah tensed. She had no updates; she had not been willing to push Olirah for information, not when her mind was so fragile and reserved. "Particularly given the events this morning."

Jessemiah's brow furrowed, and the queen raised an eyebrow, seemingly amused to have learnt something before her commander informed her of it. With a snap of the queen's fingers, the doors opened. Jessemiah rolled her eyes as Aleksandr walked in; he smirked when his eyes locked with Jessemiah's. He had lorded over Jessemiah ever since he brought her here at thirteen years old. As she aged, becoming the superior fighter, he had learnt when not to push too far, yet he took any opportunity to prove he was the more important of the two. It was laughable. His responsibilities were in title only. He believed himself the one in charge of the safety of the entire state, but if he knew what Jessemiah did for the queen, he would realise otherwise. To him, Jessemiah was merely a glorified gossiper, whispering secrets in the queen's ear. She was not surprised he withheld information to gain leverage with the queen. Despite knowing his intentions, Jessemiah chastised herself. Had she not been so exhausted from staying up with Olirah each night, she would have been up early enough that morning to discover this information first.

The queen crinkled her nose as four guards followed Aleksandr, dragging a large cart with them. Jessemiah tensed, the cart reminding her of those the king's guards used to transport criminals and children into the mines, the same one that would have taken Olirah before she ended up in Xyliar. The room's smell shifted, imperceptible to most, but not to someone from Asynthos. The change was undeniable. The usually sweet, floral-scented air, layered with the notes of roses throughout the palace, was replaced by something sour. Even Jessemiah's nose wrinkled when the doors behind the party closed, entrapping them all with whatever stench now permeated the briefing chambers.

Aleksandr gestured to the guards, who unhooked the silver pegs holding down the tarp. They pulled it back. It took five seconds for the room to react. The guards, advisors, the queen, and Jessemiah all widened their eyes with horror before they narrowed, filling with confusion at what they looked at. It took one second for everyone's eyes to dart toward Jessemiah, trying to determine the similarities between the black feathered wings protruding from her uniform and the dark, leathery wings of the mangled creature on the cart.

"Where was it found?" Jessemiah asked, steering the conversation. Her steps were even as she neared the carriage, attempting to tone down her senses as the smell ripened.

"It was discovered by the twenty-sixth unit on the eastern coast. It washed up with the tide," Aleksandr said, though his eyes were on the queen as he spoke, not Jessemiah.

"Has the cause of death been confirmed as drowning?" Jessemiah asked. Aleksandr did not respond. "You haven't had the body assessed by a coroner?" Aleksandr's brow lifted slightly as Jessemiah awaited his response.

"As it is not human, it was brought straight to the queen for her analysis," he said, as though the answer was obvious. Jessemiah kept her smirk to herself as she patrolled the carriage, surveying the creature.

"Its skin resembles that of a reptile or a dragon, though it is not as tough as the latter, nor does it have a layer of protective scales." Jessemiah clasped her hands behind her back. "Its skull has two raised bumps above its sockets, yet they are not rounded enough to suggest they would fully form into horns over time. Its claws are curved." Jessemiah pulled a dagger from her side and lifted the creature's gums. "As are its teeth, suggesting it is carnivorous." Jessemiah wiped the blade against her leg before returning it to its sheath. She lifted and extended a wing, forcing her to take several steps back. "Its wings are elliptical, allowing for fast take-offs and tight manoeuvring, yet they do not do well at maintaining speed over long distances. It could very well have struggled to maintain a long journey and fallen into the ocean."

"All statements that solidify the nature of the creature and the time that would be wasted by calling for a coroner." Aleksandr's smile was tight as he nodded at the queen. She raised an eyebrow at Jessemiah, who released the wing and stood to attention.

"Despite its animalistic features, its leathery skin is sheer enough to analyse the shape of muscles and tendons, all of which align with the structure and joints of a human. Its curved claws are attached to what are evidently five narrow fingers connecting to a palm. Its incisor teeth are sharpened, but counting confirms there are thirty-two, the average number for that of a mortal or a Fae. And while it has wings that are leathered rather than feathered, their extension and average length suggests the body has not fully grown into its sizing, confirming that, should a coroner have investigated, they would confirm that this was once a child aged between eight to twelve years old. Now"—Jessemiah turned her head to face Aleksandr—"would that not suggest we should call a coroner and have the body examined for a cause of death?" Jessemiah smiled as Aleksandr's face reddened, and his jaw ticked. A slow clap sounded from the throne as Jessemiah bowed her head to the queen in thanks.

"Is there anything you are unable to explain regarding the body?" she asked. Jessemiah frowned.

"I cannot quite determine how a child transformed into such a creature," Jessemiah glanced back at its face. "It has no eyes." The queen squirmed on her throne, her face crumpling with disgust. "You suggested this related to Xyliar, your Majesty?" Jessemiah prompted, eager to be assigned whatever task was required and retire to the rooftop to her cadre. To Olirah.

The queen looked at Aleksandr expectantly. Jessemiah knew it would further irritate him to provide her with information after the dressing down she had so expertly delivered before his guards.

"Based on the trajectory of the tides over the last week, it would have to have been within the water of Xyliar's border before being pushed northward toward Asynthos. It also resembles the descriptions in the written accounts of the Great War." Aleksandr's voice was strained as he recounted the only useful piece of knowledge he possessed. Jessemiah nodded.

"You would like me to confirm if Olirah has seen such creatures during her time on Xyliar, and if so, what she knows about them." Jessemiah didn't phrase it as a question, already knowing the answer. The queen nodded. Jessemiah's step faltered for a moment as she turned to move.

"You're hesitant," the queen said.

"She is struggling to adjust. Whatever happened on Xyliar..." Jessemiah glanced at the creature, "has caused deep-set trauma in her mind and body. I will ask but doing so this soon may delay her progress." The queen stopped tapping the throne to clench her fingers, her rings glistening in the light streaming through the windows.

"She has been here for over two weeks now, Commander, and you are yet to present any information on her history, her time in the sixth state, or if she has the power her wings suggest. Do you really think I wish to hear of any more delay when you have not taken a single step forward?"

"Perhaps I should take custody of her, your Majesty. I could have a Truthteller—"

"No," Jessemiah snapped. The third race of Asynthos was not one Jessemiah often wished to engage with. Their powers were useful, warping a mind to speak truthfully, but rarely did it leave the victim in a coherent, liveable state afterward. She would not do that to Olirah. The queen raised her chin, looking down her nose at Jessemiah, who always kept her emotions in check. Usually. "I will provide an update alongside the update from Thassena the day after rest." Jessemiah held her ground, waiting as the queen's icy eyes roamed her face, searching for the reason behind the slip of the commander's mask.

With a nod, she released Jessemiah from the meeting. Sweat

beaded along her back at the thought of Aleksandr's tactics on Olirah. She would need something from her—not the entire story, but enough to tide the queen over until Olirah revealed more. A tingling spread across her abdomen, and Jessemiah's hand fluttered over the celestial tie. She sensed Olirah wanted someone to talk to, but it was evident that experiences had made her hesitant to confide in anyone.

Instead of taking the steps to the roof, Jessemiah turned at the bottom of the corridor from the briefing chamber to the nearest balcony. Her heartbeat steadied as she launched herself off the side of the stone. Wind rushed through the feathers of her wings, calming her breathing. The sun warmed the spot between her shoulder blades as she flew upward, facing the palace. Normally, Jessemiah was a fast and efficient flier, set on reaching her destination as quickly as possible. But a silent tug on her abdomen again had her slowing, so as not to scare the woman she sensed staring out her chamber windows. It only took another minute of soaring for Jessemiah to halt, her wings beating behind her and holding her mid-air. Her form cast a shadow over the windowpanes, where the pale girl stood on the other side.

Olirah's head was cocked, and Jessemiah could have sworn a small smile tugged on her perfectly shaped lips. Her eyes roamed over Jessemiah, who shivered beneath her gaze, causing the light bouncing off the silver tips of her feathers to sparkle against the window's reflection. Olirah lifted a hand, pausing it a second before turning the silver knob on the paned door and stepping onto the narrow balcony of her chambers. Her movements were less rigid than they had been two weeks ago as she pulled herself up onto the stone ledge. Jessemiah slowly lowered until their gazes were level, and the breeze from the beating of Jessemiah's wings ruffled the lilac feathers on Olirah's, brushing her grey hair from her face.

Biting her lip, she asked, "Can you teach me?" and fiddled with a feather on the wings cocooning her body. Jessemiah frowned.

"Teach you what?" she asked. When Olirah slowly stretched her wings, Jessemiah's skin tingled at the magnificent colour, the sun casting a glow over their gold tips.

"To fly," Olirah responded just as softly, seeming embarrassed by her admission. Jessemiah's lip quivered, only briefly, at the realisation of just how little freedom Olirah had truly known in life, never experiencing what she was blessed with. Jessemiah reached out her hand, holding her palm upward in silent invitation. She didn't know if it was desperation to flee from the palace or some reassurance that Olirah could trust Jessemiah's touch—truthfully, Jessemiah cared little for the motive as Olirah's rough fingers glided her own.

"Don't let me fall," Olirah whispered, glancing down at the city below. Jessemiah reached for her other hand, interlocking their fingers. "Never," she breathed.

Chapter Eight

OLIRAH

Olirah was broken. That was the only explanation. Nothing Jessemiah revealed about her wings resonated with Olirah: the sense of her muscles that joined the tendons connecting her wings to her shoulder blades, how it should feel when extending an arm above her head. Olirah could do every exercise Jessemiah asked of her, but the moment she attempted using her wings, the most she achieved was displaying them for merely a minute before they fell and cocooned her body. They slumped on the grass now as Jessemiah knelt, examining Olirah's back.

Olirah tried to relax, focusing on the sensations of the sun beating down on her face rather than the fear of what someone was doing behind her. Jessemiah had flown them away from the palace. An innate knowing existed between the two, one Olirah could not place. It was as though Jessemiah understood the inner workings of Olirah's mind; instead of cradling her body as they flew, Jessemiah held Olirah's hands, allowing her to hang freely through the air. She should have been worried, concerned, in case Jessemiah purposefully dropped her, for that's what someone in Xyliar would have done. Did a part of her trust Jessemiah, or did she care so little for her life that nothing fazed her now?

They flew for roughly thirty minutes before Jessemiah lowered, lightly dropping Olirah onto the padded grass at the mountain's edge. The ledge was as large as a farming field, and Olirah wondered if a Stormbringer had once carved away the stone with their power for a place to call their own. The grass was moss-like, soft and cushioned under Olirah's bare feet. Delicate crimson flowers scattered the field like drops of blood. A patchwork of tree branches intertwined, their thin narrow leaves creating a kaleidoscope of sunlit patterns along the grass.

"When was the last time you fully retracted them? Before the queen had you display them in the throne room?" Jessemiah asked behind her while Olirah stared at the city, a sparkling gem in the distance. Olirah gave a single-shoulder shrug.

"I can't remember," she lied. Jessemiah was quiet for a moment before continuing.

"Weeks? Months?"

She opened her mouth to answer but paused. Revealing that they had been on display for years before she retracted them made no difference.

"May I... touch them?" Jessemiah asked, and Olirah tensed. The breeze fluttered over her wings and brought with it the citrusy scent of Jessemiah that calmed her mind. She nodded. Jessemiah's hands were slow and gentle as she ran her fingers along the curved bone protruding from her back, her hands slow as she squeezed gently at points, as though assessing their strength.

"They were retracted when I was sent to Xyliar, and once again when I escaped," Olirah said, pursing her lips. Why did she feel compelled to reveal anything to her? Her skin tingled over the unknown scar on her stomach, and Olirah pulled her knees close, wrapping her arms around them.

"From the stone mines?" Jessemiah asked, continuing her assessment as she slowly lifted the edge of her left wing, extending the muscles. Olirah nodded.

"I kept them hidden until I was number fifteen."

"What do you mean 'number fifteen?'"

Olirah picked at the feathers on her right wing as Jessemiah lowered her left. With the sun disappearing, Jessemiah's shadow fell over her until she sat cross-legged. Olirah glanced up through her lashes and then away, unable to acknowledge the look of concern on Jessemiah's face. Nobody cared about her, not really.

"I know you feel it," Jessemiah said, unclipping the belt at her waist. Olirah looked back, intrigued. "Do you remember the day you were taken from Asynthos?" Olirah frowned and shook her head.

"My memories are often fractured," she said. Jessemiah nodded and hesitated before lifting her blouse. Their eyes locked, and Jessemiah's breathing slowed as she leant back on one palm to hold the blouse higher at her ribs, exposing her stomach. Raising her eyebrows, Olirah leant forward, reaching with a trembling hand to trace the mark on Jessemiah's stomach. The women shivered simultaneously.

"You know I have one?" Olirah asked. Jessemiah would not have shown her otherwise. Olirah never knew the reason for the mark on her skin. The other girls in the cells questioned if it was a birthmark, a sign her family was blessed by the gods. The more bitter girls suggested she'd carved it into her own skin to appear more special.

"It's a celestial tie," Jessemiah said, her abdomen tensing under Olirah's touch as she continued to trace the shape. "A sign we have a shared destiny."

Olirah finally pulled back before drifting her hand to her stomach.

"We have met before?" Olirah asked. Jessemiah nodded slowly, wincing. "It pains you to have kept this from me."

"When you did not recognise me upon your arrival, I did not know if you intentionally pretended or truly did not remember," Jessemiah said. "But I told the queen to add you to my ranks so I could protect you."

"Why would you want to protect me?" Olirah asked, withdrawing. There was something Jessemiah was not telling her, though that was nothing new. They had met before, yet Jessemiah had kept that information from Olirah. Did she really want to protect her? Or merely use her like others had?

"Because there are far more people that would want you for your power with much crueller intentions than the Queen of Asynthos."

"What power?" Olirah asked; an emotion she had kept dormant bubbled inside of her. Anger. Anger at the cards she had been dealt, at the people who always wanted something from her. Perhaps Jessemiah did too. Jessemiah pursed her lips. "Is that why Valon wanted me?" Olirah spat. "Do my wings suggest I have a power I know nothing about?" Olirah resumed plucking her feathers before Jessemiah's hands reached for them.

"Who is Valon?" Jessemiah asked. Olirah frowned, tilting her head.

"Valon Abexu, King of Xyliar." Jessemiah's hands tensed. Dismissing her previous moment of distrust, Olirah's skin tingled. Surely a celestial tie would not be granted between two people who would harm one another. She had to believe Jessemiah's intentions were good when keeping their previous meeting secret. Or perhaps Olirah was just desperate to have someone who seemed to care. Regardless, Olirah offered a reassuring squeeze, intertwining their fingers to ease whatever had shifted Jessemiah's feelings.

"Olirah, I do not wish for this to sound condescending," Jessemiah began, tracing a pattern on Olirah's hand with her thumb. "Are you certain it is a man, Valon, who sits on Xyliar's throne?"

"Do you wish for me to recite the entire royal line?" Olirah tensed, fearing her memory could be wrong about this too. "Valon Abexu. He has one daughter, Salvia Abexu, who has two children, Osiris and Sallos. The heirs to the throne. The only other living member of the family is..." Olirah tensed again before saying, "Viserius Abexu."

"How often were you permitted to see the Abexu family?"

"I saw Viserius once a month, but I don't know over how many years. After that, I saw the entire family every evening," Olirah said, her palms beginning to sweat. "Why do you care about how often I saw them?" She glanced over Jessemiah's shoulder, her eyes becoming hazy as her mind shifted to her memories of Viserius, to the day her wings had shown for the first time since arriving in the sixth state. Jessemiah untangled one hand and brought it to Olirah's face, cupping her chin gently before pulling back to meet her gaze.

"Olirah, it's really important you tell me about your time in Xyliar, as much as you can remember," Jessemiah whispered. Olirah shook her head. She did not wish to recall memories she tried her best to hide. They surfaced only at night. "Olirah, as far as the rest of Ithyion is aware, the Queen of Xyliar went by the name Vyla Abexu. She had eight sons, four daughters, and none of them were called Valon. No one has heard from her or any of her family since the Great War."

***

Still as a statue, quiet as a mouse, innocent as a child. Olirah lived by those three expectations, which had been ingrained in her over the years, since her time in the chambers of Viserius Abexu. Focus on the other girls: number thirteen and fourteen. Do not disobey, Olirah reminded herself. That was how she made it to day fifteen in just a year. Too many girls had disappeared, never to be seen again, before the others climbed the pecking order.

Olirah's eyes strayed for a moment as rough hands gripped her shoulders. It was almost over. The minuscule sound of a fork scraping against a plate tugged her eyes back to Thirteen and Fourteen. They sat on men's laps, yet their eyes were on Olirah's, keeping her present, reminding her of the plate of food Fourteen held ready and waiting for her. Blood still ran down Fourteen's shoulder from where the whip broke her skin, punished for the sob that slipped past her lips. It was her blood Olirah felt pressed against her cheek on the black silk sheets as pain radiated through her; her body was trying to reject the events of the fifteenth day. The grip on her shoulder tightened as nails broke her skin. Then Viserius loosened his grip and shifted off the bed.

Thirteen and Fourteen tapped their feet, impatiently waiting to go to her. Olirah remained as still as a statue, quiet as a mouse, innocent as a child until she felt the damp cloth on her back, signalling she could finally turn around to clean herself. Thirteen and Fourteen moved, much to the frustration of the disgruntled soldiers at the table. Olirah kept her head down, knowing Viserius still watched from where he laced his breeches at the corner of the four-poster bed. Thirteen sat her up and supported her back as she untangled her hair and re-braided it. Olirah refrained from flinching at the touch on her already sensitive scalp. Taking the damp cloth, Fourteen wiped her cheek before attending to her thighs. Once she was clean, Fourteen tried to straighten Olirah's gown, hiding as much of her body as possible, but he ripped too much of the fabric this time, leaving her scarred skin and her left breast exposed for all to see.

"What is that?" Viserius asked, the deep drawl of his voice sending a shiver up Olirah's spine. Thirteen and Fourteen paused what they were doing and withdrew from the bed as Viserius approached. His eyes were on her stomach. The rips in her dress had caused a loose piece of fabric to hang freely, revealing the scar that had been there since her arrival, though she did not know how she got it.

"I said"—Olirah flinched as Viserius approached the side of the bed, tugging her braid back so her eyes met his. His gaze was as dark as the leathered wings protruding from his shirtless back—"What is that?" he sneered, pulling a dagger from the bedside table and pointing it at the scar.

"I don't know, I've always had it," Olirah said clearly, politely, her face neutral.

"Do not lie to me!" he shouted. "I have known you for over a year, girl, and I have never seen that before."

"Respectfully, Sir, you never face her." Thirteen's voice was strong as she straightened to look at him. The room fell silent. The soldiers at the table watched their leader, fingers itching at the swords still

strapped at their sides, waiting for a command to punish Thirteen.

"Kill her," Viserius ordered. "Have your fun with her first, if you so wish."

"No!" Olirah cried as a soldier tugged Thirteen back into his chest. Greedy hands reached for the hem of her gown as the second soldier watched Fourteen, begging her to say something with his eyes so that she would end up in the same predicament.

"Kill the other one too. There can be no witnesses to this one's death," Viserius said, waving the dagger back at Olirah, whose eyes widened.

"Please, Sir. I have behaved well; I have done everything that is asked of me. I—"

"You are marked!" he sneered, pushing the tip of his dagger closer to the scar. Olirah felt the blood trickle down her stomach at the same moment the door behind Viserius clicked shut. A flash of onyx uniform left the room.

"I will do whatever you wish—please!" Olirah begged, capturing his attention before he turned and noticed which guard had left.

"If my brother knows you are marked, he will take you, and you will divulge everything that goes on in these rooms."

"I will not," Olirah begged, tears filling her eyes. "I will tell him nothing. I will be loyal to you, your spy. I could gather information for you if he takes me," Olirah pleaded. Viserius removed the tip of the dagger, his eyes roaming her face, contemplating the suggestion.

"Unfortunately, silver one," he said, undoing her braid and combing his fingers through her loose waves. "It's too much of a risk." He raised his hand, and the dagger flew. Olirah jerked her head out of his grip, instinctively protecting herself. Pain exploded through her, but she could not place where she had been stabbed. Darkness enveloped the room. Something tickled her face as she tried to distract herself from the pain.

"How long were you planning on keeping this a secret, brother?" A voice echoed through the darkness. Only then did Olirah realise that the darkness was not from impending death, but from the shadows

filling the room. Slowly, she straightened as the darkness rescinded, leaving only ropes of shadow in her vision, wrapped around Viserius's arms and neck. Over his shoulder, Olirah's eyes locked with Sascha, the one guard who had shown the girls kindness over the years. "When I said we needed to work on the elixir, cross-breeding with children of Asynthos is not what I had in mind."

Sascha stepped aside, her black armour clinking as she stood to attention. A man appeared at her side, shadows stemming from his palms. He dragged Viserius against the wall with his power before black flooded the whites of his eyes. Viserius's eyes rolled back in his head.

"Explain what you have been doing," the man's voice echoed. Viserius kicked his feet as the shadows held him up by his neck.

"Injecting the girls of different races with the successful elixir to crossbreed with Xyliarians. Creating—"

"Abominations," the man sneered. "You are creating abominations. There is no need to mix so many lineages when we have a stable elixir to give our people wings."

"We need more than just wings; we need a superior—"

"You should have stuck to experimenting with your creatures instead," the man's voice echoed as he finally turned to face Olirah. She trembled. She'd heard brief stories from the other girls of the powers of those in Xyliar, but Viserius had never shown his Staxion abilities to control minds.

The man's eyes widened as he assessed the space around Olirah. It was only then, as an ache weighed on her back, that she mirrored his surprised eyes and noticed the lilac wings surrounding her, stark against the torn silk of her gown. The man tugged on his shadows until Viserius turned blue and collapsed.

"Sascha, take the two girls to the guest wing. The soldiers can take Viserius to my study unless they wish to end up hanging from the cliffs of Kardyn for the dragons' entertainment."

Olirah gulped, still trembling as the man approached. The similarities between him and Viserius were obvious—the same high cheekbones, dark eyes, dark hair, pale skin. But where Viserius's hair was long, this man's was shorter, flopping to one side. Wrinkles creased his eyes, suggesting years of laughter once, but the scars on his arms, exposed by his rolled-up shirtsleeves, suggested he had experienced much pain too.

"Olirah, isn't it?" he asked, slowly lowering himself onto the bed. He flinched as he looked at the stains and blood blemishing the silk sheets.

"How do—" Olirah cut herself off. Silent as a statue, quiet as a mouse, innocent as a child.

"Viserius kept records of you all. Sascha found them and had them copied for me." Olirah frowned. He knew then. He knew what his brother had been doing to them. "My area of expertise is experimentation. It is why my family has the wings they do, but this is not an experiment I would ever approve of, nor one I thought was taking place." The man's face softened, his eyes appearing kind, but he had mentioned Sashca more than once, which meant Sashca had known what was going on for months.

"My name is Valon, King of Xyliar," he said, his hand drifting to the loose, torn fabric on her abdomen. She flinched as his icy finger traced her scar. "It's time you and I looked for your counterpart."

***

The corridors were brighter on the upper levels of the castle, yet they were still dark, as seemed to be the preference in Xyliar, but the windows offered a glimpse of freedom, enough to keep Olirah moving. Her steps were uneven over the stone as she walked barefoot in her black gown. Her grip on Sascha's arm was tight as the guard helped her navigate walking with the wings on her back. She had wings. She was an Angel. When she showed confusion at her inability to move the wings, Valon said some Angels grew their wings later in life rather than their formative years, though it was rare. For once,

Olirah wished for memories from her past to answer her questions; usually, she was thankful not to remember, for it meant there was nothing to yearn for. Her eyes were focused on the ground, trying to keep from falling with the weight on her back.

"Take your time, you're doing very well," the man, Valon, he had called himself, praised. Olirah flicked her eyes up briefly to where he walked a step ahead. His scarred hands were clasped behind his back, and the gentle smile on his face made her nervous.

"Are you taking me to where the other girls disappear to?" she croaked, her mouth dry from fear and exhaustion. Valon frowned. Perhaps he truly did not know about Viserius's schemes, but a feeling in her gut urged her not to trust him. A muffled roar echoed from down a corridor to their left before Sascha steered right. Olirah glanced over her shoulder to look, but her wings blocked her view.

"That is the experiment Viserius should have been working on," Valon said. Olirah looked at him warily, too scared to ask any more as they approached a single, open door, revealing a staircase. "The elixir he was injecting into you is one I created. I know it is stable and would do no harm, but there is a second Viserius created when trying to adapt mine. It allows the Fae of Xyliar to grow wings, but there is a lack of consistency. He was meant to test a new batch this year." Valon began climbing the steps, which curved upwards. Olirah understood little of his admissions, nor did she think she wanted to know more.

"Where are Thirteen and Fourteen?" Olirah asked, her breath short as Sascha helped her up the steps. Valon was silent for a moment as they passed an open door containing a crumbled wall and a four-poster bed.

"Ah, safe. Sascha took them to a spare guest room and had maids attend them before returning for you."

"Can I see them?" Olirah asked as they reached the end of the stairs. Valon opened the door at the top of what appeared to be a turret. The room was bright but cold with the windows open. She tensed when she saw a line of syringes on a table.

"Let's get you cleaned up first."

***

"And then, he fell right off the dragon!" Sallos exclaimed, enticing laughter from Viserius. Olirah pushed the food around her plate, glancing up at where the Prince of Xyliar spoke with his uncle. She did not know how he stomached it, forcing civility to keep the peace at the dining table. His hair was similar to his grandfather's, Valon's, but in the light it appeared a deep brown rather than black; his stubble had grown out in the month he had been gone, and his skin was more tanned. Osiris looked so pale sitting beside him, looking anywhere but at his family. He raised his eyebrows briefly as he caught Olirah looking and downed his goblet of wine before leaving the table.

"Osiris, you should ask to be excused," his father, Tirus, called out. Osiris ignored him; he always did. Having spent two years at the dining table, Olirah had witnessed the strained relationship Osiris had with his family as a direct result of his mixed lineage, yet still he called the man father.

"I'll speak with him," Sallos said. Rising from the table, he winked at Olirah before jogging out of the room in search of his brother. Olirah's hand tensed around her fork. Only Tirus and his wife Salvia remained to keep Viserius distracted from Olirah. This was her last meal. She was leaving today. Valon had promised that if she continued with her mental tests, she would be allowed to leave for a home he selected for her in the capital, Exoria. He had treated her like one of his own, offering a life that felt like a blur compared to her days in the cells. She had eaten well and was dressed in clothes that must have belonged to past princesses; she took strolls around the garden with Lilia and Taria, numbers thirteen and fourteen. But she longed for a space that was only hers, that had not been touched by the man sitting opposite her now.

"Are you ready, Olirah?" Valon asked, wiping a napkin over his mouth and rising. He offered a hand to guide her back to the turret. She nodded with a genuine smile before taking it.

The walk to the tower she had become so familiar with was quiet, and she wondered if Valon was sombre about their final test. She took a seat in the leather chair he had brought up for her; they were without arms, allowing her wings to lounge comfortably.

"Shall we test my wings first? Or my mind?" Olirah asked, folding her hands in the lap of her grey woollen gown. Usually, they performed a series of exercises, while he experimented with the marrow taken from the bones that held up her wings, testing their reactions with other things. Valon sat down at his desk and turned his chair to face her. There was no smile. Her own wavered.

"Has something happened?" she asked, frowning. He had last acted this way when a ship, following one of Xyliar's, had tried to break through the barriers surrounding the state.

"Olirah, child, I have unfortunate news," Valon sighed, as though it pained him. "I know you were expecting to leave today, but with how little progress Viserius has been making with his experiments, and how much we have struggled to hunt through your mind for your counterpart, I just do not think I can permit it." He rubbed his chin while watching her, waiting for a reaction.

"But we could always continue with our tests. I could visit the castle once a week—"

"It would slow us down, Olirah. You know it would."

"I don't even know what you're looking for. You won't tell me what you want, so how am I to trust you will ever let me leave? First it is another month here, then another year, then—"

"Let me get you some tea before you become hysterical," Valon sighed, exiting the room. Olirah's breathing became rapid, her chest rising and falling as she struggled to get air. Suddenly the rows of mahogany shelving around the room felt suffocating. Lunging out of her chair, she unlatched the window and gasped in the cold winter air as the ocean roared. What she would give to be in that ocean *now. Freedom, a life of her own. Anger bubbled up inside her, and she slammed her hand against the desk. A recent vial of her blood shattered against the wood, the sound of the crack offering an outlet for her anger.*

Olirah spun, glaring at the vials of golden elixir filling the shelves. Experiments, tests, secrets. She wanted no part in it. In a thoughtless rage, she tugged the vials from the shelf and tossed them onto the floor, smashing the glass into pieces and letting the golden elixir trickle through the cracks in the stone. Her hair fell loose from its updo as she panted, and Valon's steps returned.

Olirah watched him like a frantic animal as his eyes roamed over his wasted elixirs. His knuckles turned white around the tray of teacups and bread coated in golden jam. Slowly, he walked to the desk overlooking the city and placed down the tray. He hung his head, and Olirah eyed the door. She could try to run.

Darkness seeped from his skin, crawling along the floor as though trying to gather what remained of the elixir before it climbed the walls.

"You did this to yourself, child." Darkness consumed her, and Olirah screamed.

***

"Three hundred and six, three hundred and seven, three hundred and eight." When a lock clicked, Olirah lost count. She smacked her head against the bricks, identical to those she counted in the cell to pass the time, until she knew a tray of food would be delivered. Perhaps they were early, and that was who opened the door into the dark cell. An image of a snow-coated city flashed in her mind. Asynthos. Home, or so she believed. In her cell, she had lost track of the passing time, though it was her only reprieve from Viserius and his damned experiments. He had taken too much blood last time, leaving her lightheaded. Though at least her back did not ache. She

had managed to keep her wings at bay for some time now, which only infuriated him. Recently she had heard him arguing with Valon. "Whatever you did has damaged the part of her mind that can summon them," he snapped. Olirah could not recall what Valon had done to break her mind. One day she sat at the dining table with the Abexu royal family, then tea with Valon, and then she was in a cell with Viserius. The only thing swimming around her mind was Asynthos, the fourth state of Ithyion.

"Hurry," a voice whispered. A familiar female voice. Olirah straightened against the wall, scraping her bare back against the stone. Dim candlelight filled the room as a young girl entered. Thirteen—no, she had a name... Lilia. "Get up," she said. Olirah flinched as she grabbed her arms and yanked her upward. The door cell closed, and Olirah jumped at the onyx uniform that stood alongside another girl, Taria.

"Where are you taking me?" Olirah asked. "He'll know you're here, he—"

"Sascha is getting you out," Lilia said, combing Olirah's dirt-ridden hair. She wore a servant's uniform. Olirah recalled Viserius once telling her she was lucky her friends had been offered employment rather than punishment.

"How? Don't under—" footsteps sounded down the corridor outside, and Olirah started to cry. "I told you, I told you—" Sascha grabbed Olirah, tugging her back into the darkness of the cell and covering her mouth as shadows seeped out from underneath her uniform and wrapped around them. In the faintest gap of the darkness, Olirah saw Viserius enter, look around the cell, and then at Lilia and Taria. Then she watched as, with a roar, he slit their throats. Their blood spraying in the darkness was the last thing Olirah saw before she felt a tug on her navel and nausea overcame her.

When the shadows pulled away, she wobbled atop slippery wooden decking, listening to birds and the rush of lapping water. Sascha lifted her visor and grasped Olirah's cheeks. "You're on your own from here; this was the best I could do." Then, as quickly as she had arrived,

Sascha disappeared in a plume of shadow.

Chapter Nine

JESSEMIAH

The crimson flowers of the Forever Fields lost their glow. The flowers, rumoured to have grown from the blood of Angels and Vala's tears after Keres had stolen from her, darkened under the shadows now cast by the trees. The day aged with exhaustion as Olirah recounted all she could remember of her time in Xyliar.

Jessemiah had witnessed countless atrocities in her time as Commander for the Queen of Asynthos, having committed many of them herself, but never could she begin to imagine what Olirah and numerous other girls had endured. It explained her reaction to Jayesh's playful jest about them being cross-bred abominations, because that was exactly what Olirah had been used for.

Jessemiah's knowledge of the royal families of Ithyion was extensive, unsurprisingly so, seeing as her role was to know everyone and everything. It was why she had confidently said there was no Valon in the Abexu royal family. Viserius, though, was a name Jessemiah was familiar with as a general of Xyliar's armies in the past. But if the rest of his siblings, as well as his mother, were dead, there was no knowing what his role was anymore, particularly as Olirah's story placed him as both a disappointment and an asset to his brother. It seemed Valon now ruled the state that had closed its borders for so long. But who exactly was he, and what had happened to extinguish an entire royal line, leaving only him, his brother, and immediate heirs behind?

"He never lost his patience with me, not until whatever I did that day led him to break into my mind," Olirah said, lying on her back. She twirled a tiny flower in her hand. Jessemiah sighed and lay back beside her, so their hands were side by side, and their feet at opposite ends. Their wings crossed over and under one another. Jessemiah had never been so close to someone else. The touch of their wings felt far more intimate than she expected.

"He needed you alive," Jessemiah said, turning her face to Olirah to watch the trees' shadows dance along her face. "To find me. Your counterpart."

Olirah hummed, the crinkles on her forehead relaxing, as if the weight of the trauma she carried in her memories had somewhat lifted since entrusting them with Jessemiah. The logistical and informative side of Jessemiah knew she needed to ask for more details, things she had heard or seen, the number of soldiers, the castle's defences, if she ever saw who reinforced Xyliar's borders. But right now, Jessemiah just wanted to relish the peace that overcame Olirah. Was this caused by the celestial tie? This innate presence drawing them to one another, inciting a trustful bond that neither could voice but both acknowledged?

"That's you, my counterpart?" Olirah asked, finally meeting Jessemiah's eyes. The light in her gaze appeared brighter as she studied Jessemiah's face.

"A shared destiny of some sort," Jessemiah murmured, her fingers twitching, wishing to cup Olirah's chin in her hands again. Olirah blushed, seeming to sense Jessemiah's train of thought.

"You mentioned a power... my power. Is that what he wants from me? Because I don't have it," Olirah said, her arm shifting next to Jessemiah's, the fabric of their blouses brushing against one another.

"Not anymore," Jessemiah said, though she remembered the bright glow in her eyes when she watched Olirah wield all four elements. "But you were magnificent when I saw you wield it," Jessemiah said. Olirah frowned.

"When we met? As children?" Jessemiah bit her lip, afraid of betraying herself by revealing she was responsible for Olirah's abduction and the life she endured after. Instead, she nodded. "What did it look like?" Olirah asked, her hand shifting just enough to graze her pinkie against Jessemiah's. They had held hands during the journey to the field, entwining their fingers while Jessemiah helped her to focus on her memories. It felt different this time. There was no reason for the touch, no necessity Jessemiah could use to justify the jolt it sent through her.

"Like a goddess reborn," Jessemiah whispered, her pinkie stroking Olirah's. "The vines that grew at your feet twisted as if they were raising their arms in prayer. The wind picked up at such a pace it was like it had to touch every inch of your skin, and your wings caught alight, bathing you in a glow like those on the altar at a festival to the deities of Q'Ohar. The rain kissed your brow as tentatively and as gently as a lover," Jessemiah said before hooking their pinkies together. Olirah's chest rose and fell more rapidly as her silver eyes flickered between Jessemiah's honeyed gaze and her lips. She gulped.

"He never kissed me," Olirah whispered. Jessemiah frowned. "Viserius," she confirmed. "Though nobody ever has." She reached up to brush Jessemiah's unbound hair from her cheek. "It's the one thing I have left I can choose to give freely."

As the sun yielded to the moon, Jessemiah clasped Olirah's trembling hand on her cheek, her hands cool.

"You should only give it to someone you trust," Jessemiah whispered, resisting the urge to tilt her head slightly and place a kiss on Olirah's hand. "After all you have endured, I wouldn't blame you for never trusting another again." Olirah's eyes watered at Jessemiah's words, and the commander feared she took it as a rejection. It was anything but.

"Does a celestial tie force trust on two people?" Olirah asked. She turned her body now to face her fully.

"Nobody knows the true purpose or power of a celestial tie. There are far too many stories and myths about it, placed by the gods or controlled by destiny. Nobody knows for sure," Jessemiah admitted. There were some things in this world that had no definitive explanation, only past tales and assumptions.

"Did you mean it? When you said you would never let me fall?" Olirah asked. "Because every day I think I fall further and further into the darkness in my mind."

Jessemiah turned onto her side to face her, their wings cocooning them in their own private sanctuary as she said, "I meant it. Whether it is this celestial tie, or another unknown force, I will never, ever let you fall."

Olirah nodded, her palm slipping from Jessemiah's cheek to wrap behind her neck.

"Then I trust you," she whispered against her lips.

Chapter Ten

OLIRAH

*O*ne year later

Fire ignited in Olirah's veins, a fire she had come to know all too well in the last year. One of determination, an engulfing feeling extinguishing any fear she once possessed at the sight of a flying dagger. Tucking her wings in tight, she ducked at the flying blade, raising her shield in her left hand as a gush of fire rushed toward her. Two seconds later, a heavy blow hit the shield, pushing into her body and forcing her to lower it. She spun away before she was compelled to submit. With her long braid whipping behind her, she pulled two long-bladed daggers from her hips, her pre-ferred weapons of choice. The kiss of a blade met her neck before she could use them. Even three months ago, Olirah would have flinched, but she laughed this time.

"Third time this week. Your spin is becoming predictable," Jayesh whispered in her ear. Olirah shoved her elbow into his side, where she knew he still had an open wound from his loss against Alyssa two days ago. The Angel had a twisted rule about leaving a wound unhealed during training losses, for it was a reminder of how he had gained it and what he had learnt. Grunting, Jayesh doubled over as Olirah walked away, wiping the sweat from her forehead before Elias tossed a soaked cloth in her direction.

"Three times in one week doesn't sound all that impressive when she's beaten you thirteen times this month, Jayesh," Jessemi-ah called. She sat on the ledge of the rooftop, her legs dangling either side against the backdrop of the slowly setting sun. She shook her hair free from her shoulders that gathered at her nape and began braiding it. Olirah paused, the cool cloth against her chest as she watched, captivated by the sheen of Jessemiah's hair against the white blouse. The pale blue of the rest of her uniform had already been removed, ready for dinner. A gust picked up over the rooftop training grounds, ruffling Jessemiah's loose attire, exposing her midriff and the tie that bound them. Her counterpart. The other half of her soul. At least, that was what Olirah told herself. After a year in Jessemiah's presence, she refused to believe it was only the celestial tie that made things so natural and right between them. They were fated for one another long before a celestial tie decided it.

"I *said*!" Jayesh interrupted Olirah's moment of fixation. "I suppose I'll set the table myself." Olirah blushed under his teasing grin as he joined Elias, who had already retrieved the large tray of food from the kitchens.

"Ignore his jests," Alyssa said, slinging an arm around Olirah's waist, dodging her wings. "I catch him staring at me the same way." She smiled and squeezed her waist before helping the men set the table, prompted by the sound of footsteps Olirah knew all too well.

"I have a new jar of healing salve from Eresydon to try in my chambers," Jessemiah whispered before she examined the joints of Olirah's wings. Three months after Olirah divulged her history in Xyliar to Jessemiah, she had visited the royal physician, who determined that the reasons she could not retract her wings nor fly was because of the injury she sustained when her wings defended her against Viserius's stab, combined with potential side effects of the elixir. Unfortunately, it had struck a major muscle. With it being left untreated, and with no rehabilitation or regular movement, it lost its full functionality. That hadn't stopped Jessemiah, though. Every assignment to another state had her seeking new healing products and practices, including her week-long mission to Eresydon that she had returned from only that morning.

"How was the mission?" Olirah asked, turning as Jessemiah finished her assessment. Her wings were out now, too, so Olirah felt less alone. It had not gone unnoticed that ever since their visit to the physician, the entire cadre ate dinner with their wings out, relaxing over the backs of the chairs.

"The wedding was like any other royal wedding I have attended."

"Was it really necessary for you to go when the queen was already attending?" Olirah asked, interlocking her fingers with Jessemiah's and squeezing gently.

"Why, did you miss me?" Jessemiah murmured, reaching to cup Olirah's chin. She grazed her thumb over her bottom lip in the infatuated way Olirah found endearing.

"Maybe." Olirah smiled coyly.

"Will the two of you be dining with us tonight? Or will you be satisfied with one another instead?" Jayesh called before grunting again. Alyssa had definitely elbowed him in the same wound. Jessemiah raised her chin toward the table as Olirah walked over to them, their hands still intertwined. They lowered into their respective seats beside one another.

"Fish? Again?" Jessemiah moaned, glaring at Elias. "That's the third time this week!"

"What can I say? The cook likes me." Elias' smile was lopsided as he pushed his hair back and out of his eyes and retracted his blue wings.

"I wonder why," Alyssa mused, and they all laughed, knowing his frequent trips to the kitchens of late were not only for food. Olirah didn't complain as she broke the flakes of fish with her fork. Knowing how many girls in Xyliar went without, she never complained about food.

"We exchange more than just physical favours." Elias grinned. "She has connections in Eresydon; she managed to find me a lord that had apparent records of the end of the Great War. Last night I was reading about a claim that the deities merged their essence—"

"Gods Elias, not this again. You're fascinated with the ins and outs of that war. What more is there to know?" Jessemiah groaned.

"There has to be a reason the curses swept the land only months after that war ended!" The other Angels groaned too as he recited his theories, but Olirah's ears developed a soft ringing as she listened. Wiggling her jaw, she wondered if Jayesh's knock to her face at the beginning of their fight had more impact than she realised. Yet when pressure festered in her head, she knew something was wrong. Olirah sucked in a sharp breath, dropping her fork with a clatter as her hands rushed to her temples.

"Olirah!" Jessemiah exclaimed, reaching for her. Darkness crept into the corners of her eyes, and it felt like the shadows were on the rooftop, reaching to tug her back to Xyliar. Her chair scraped back as she forced herself to stand, trying to back away from the shadows, the twists of familiar darkness. The darkness engulfed her as she fell back, her head meeting the stone floor.

"Olirah!"

***

Birds chirped overhead as Olirah opened her eyes with a contented sigh. The twisting branches above scattered slivers of moonlight over the field of crimson flowers, a comforting sight she knew all too well. The field had become her and Jessemiah's secret place, somewhere they visited together on their days off each week. A pinkie grazed her own, and Olirah grinned, turning her head.

She screamed.

She tried to launch herself up from the spot, to run, but dark shadows lurched for her body, holding her against the grass as the tendrils forced her face to his.

"That's not a very polite way to greet an old friend, Olirah," Valon murmured, allowing a shadow to reach up and stroke her cheek. The touch felt foreign now. "A year apart, and this is how you greet me?

The man who helped reunite you with your destiny." His eyes held no kindness now. His cheeks had hollowed, sharpening his features, and eradicating the kindness she had once seen. His former patience was gone.

"How did you find me?" Olirah stuttered. Valon tutted, caressing her cheek now with his real fingers. She struggled against the shadow constraints.

"I knew where you were all along, child." He smirked. "Why do you think I so easily let you flee the castle after I allowed Viserius to kill Lilia and Taria?" Olirah stilled. He had always wanted to reunite her with her counterpart; he had succeeded in finding Jessemiah in the memories she thought were long forgotten during all those times in his study. Or perhaps he truly found the memory the day he broke her, the day she pictured Asynthos. He had allowed her escape, and she had led him directly to Jessemiah. Had Sascha known? Was she asked to take her to that boat?

"Why did you wait so long then if you knew I was here, if you knew I found Jessemiah?" She was no longer still as a statue, quiet as a mouse, innocent as a child.

"Because this time, Olirah, I have lost my patience with you." He tightened the hold of his shadows, pulling her to stand as he rose beside her, his long velvet cloak hanging eerily with the lack of wind. Were they in her mind? The field looked out-of-place now as the twisting branches became shadows, the crimson flowers darkening to black.

"You should have unlocked your power by now. The two of you should have merged the essences of your souls, ready for me to take," Valon sneered. "We both need you together and at your fullest power, I will not let her get you first."

"Who?" Olirah asked.

"So many repressed memories. Did you ever wonder what really happened to your parents?" Valon's shadows tightened, suspending her midair until her feet dangled, scraping against the grass. She opened her mouth to speak, but the shadows twisted around her

neck. "They didn't die, Olirah. They abandoned you." She wanted to scream and call him a liar. Though she could no longer picture their faces, she knew they had loved her once. "She told them you were destined for a much bigger fate, but to achieve it, you would need to be left to fend for yourself. So, that's exactly what they did."

"Who?" Olirah rasped again, who was this woman he spoke of?

"And then there's the memory of her appearing to you one night, slicing your skin and placing a sliver of sunlit essence in your veins, the counterpart to the shadow of herself she hid within the woman you now love." Olirah was becoming dizzy. Nothing Valon said made sense. She could not recall the memories he spoke of or the mysterious woman. "But while she needs you alive and searching, I simply need your intertwined souls." When Valon finally released his shadows, Olirah fell onto the grass. Her knees thudded, and her wings instinctively drew close around her.

"I'm coming for you, Olirah. I'll bring an entire army to ensure I have you both." Valon knelt and tugged her hair, forcing her head up to look at him. "And once I can force both of you to merge your powers, there will be no need for you anymore." His smile twisted. "Maybe I'll let Viserius have you both after I'm done."

***

"Olirah, please. Please wake up!" Panicked hands roamed Olirah's face, their familiarity pulling her back into focus. Pounding remained at the back of her skull. "Thank the deities," Jessemiah breathed as a stray tear fell from her eyes and landed on Olirah's cheek. "Are you okay? Can you move?" Jessemiah asked, gently tugging Olirah forward until she sat upright, looking up at the three worried faces peering over her, the people she had endangered by being here.

"He's coming," Olirah croaked. The cadre frowned. "Valon will bring war to Asynthos."

Chapter Eleven

OLIRAH

Darkness overtook the skies of the capital three days after Valon had broken into Olirah's mind. The queen said it was unheard of for a Staxion of Xyliar to be so present from so far, which meant he was either on his way or had clawed into her mind all those years ago and never left. Olirah shouldered the blame, forever feeling the need to apologise. But even the queen, once learning everything Olirah had endured, said it was not her fault. Though it was a mystery to Avannah, and all the advisors of Asynthos, what Valon truly wanted by gaining Olirah and Jessemiah, and why he would be willing to go to war for them. Despite explicitly stating he wanted Jessemiah and Olirah's intertwined souls once their powers merged, nobody understood what that meant. Scholars exhaustively searched for retellings of merged powers, intertwined souls—anything on celestial ties—but found only myths and children's stories.

Their attempt at understanding was futile. Valon was coming for Olirah and Jessemiah regardless, and he brought an army with him. The other rulers of Ithyion had not taken Avannah's claims seriously, refusing to believe Xyliar was suddenly active and sending a war to the fourth state. Instead, Asynthos' capital was left to defend itself against the dark-winged soldiers soaring into the city.

"On your left!" Jayesh called from above Olirah and Jessemiah. A flash of copper uniform appeared from the alley on her left. Olirah ducked and spun as his broadsword came toward her, just as black wings landed at her back, approaching Jes. Olirah's long daggers were second nature now, and she pierced them through

the gaps in the soldier's armour, splattering blood against the metal uniform before pulling it free. Barely a second passed before
two more soldiers turned the corner out of the alleyway. There
was something familiar about the street in the lower levels of
the city, which usually housed a market. Yet there was no time
for distractions. Grunting against the strength of the soldier, she
slammed them with her shoulder to create space. Emerald green
wings dropped behind the two soldiers as vines wrapped around
their necks, tugging so hard they cracked right off.

"The city is overrun," Alyssa panted. "The foot soldiers have
taken every mine entrance, every entry point to the city, and are
filtering through every single gods-damned path." A second set of
pale aqua wings landed beside her, grasping his side. Olirah's eyes
widened.

"I'm okay, flesh wound." When Elias removed his hand, only
a thin trail of blood peeked through the gap between his silver
breastplate and the counterpart on his back. "They're funnelling
us up to the palace. We're trapped."

"Do we need to abandon the city; must we take the queen
and flee?" Olirah asked. The sound of marching soldiers drew
nearer with every passing minute. The cadre shared a look before
a scream interrupted them. Olirah knew the voice immediately.
Time slowed as she spun in the market street. Jessemiah pierced
a dagger into the skull of the man in front of her. Blood trickled
down his grey leathers and blackened wings. His body collapsed
with Jessemiah. Her palms hit the floor, and her left wing drooped.
A sword had pierced through the entire muscle until it came out
on the other side amongst the feathers at the bottom. Behind
her, two more winged soldiers appeared, skulking out from the
alleyway with their swords raised, shadows seeping from their skin.

Olirah's eyes flickered from Jes' anguished face to the approaching men and the hunger in their eyes as they sought their wounded
prey. The cadre had no way of moving toward Jessemiah. Nobody
had time or space to move at all as something inside Olirah shat-

tered. The fear of losing the only person who would never let her fall, consumed every wall within herself. Rage broke free.

Blinding light pierced the street as power broke from Olirah's skin. Flaming vines whipped free from her body, encircling the men's necks and tugging them toward Olirah as they choked on water spewing from their mouths. The wind picked up through the alley, whistling a battle cry that Olirah felt in her bones as she stared at her reflection in the man's widened eyes. Tendrils of light overwhelmed her irises; it was the same light twisting free from her body, moving across the stone street, searching for someone—her counterpart. Olirah wiggled her fingers, and the water that spewed from the men's mouths froze. Ice climbed up their bodies until she squeezed her fists, and they shattered. The blinding light emanating from Olirah slowly faded, leaving only the thin threads that slowly cradled Jessemiah's limp wing. She looked up at her from her knees.

"Like a goddess reborn." Jessemiah smiled.

"Holy shit," Jayesh cursed.

"We don't have time to marvel at her!" Alyssa cried, lifting Jessemiah. "They're getting closer!"

"Get us to the palace," Olirah panted, trembling. Her eyes still watched Jes, her wing twitching as Elias pulled the blade free from the threads of light nestled into her feathers. After latching onto Jayesh's hands, he propelled them into the air, with Alyssa and Elias carrying Jes between them. Screams sounded from behind. Olirah turned her head, watching the massacre of white-winged Angels below as hundreds of black wings advanced. A mixture of men and women with wings and mangled creatures like the one Jessemiah had described that had washed up on Asynthos' shores. The wind intensified as they reached the castle, the queen's only power creating a torrent of protection around the walls. It recognised the cadre and let them through.

Aleksandr and a wall of white-winged Angels lined the balcony and palace rooftops, ready and waiting as a last line of defence.

"She should have fled," Jes grunted as they landed.

"She's stubborn. She'd rather die than willingly hand over her state," said Jayesh.

"The king and the children got out. They're in Boznaya Range safe house," Elias added. Jes nodded with relief. The cadre fell silent, save for their breathing, which began to regulate as they looked out at the carnage over the city. Angels fell swiftly at the hands of Xyliar's warriors. Now and then, Olirah could distinguish a winged warrior from a deformed creature, and her heart raced at the reminder of Viserius and his experiments.

"We need a plan." Elias recaptured their attention. "He can't take Jes and Olirah if he's after their souls for more power."

"Then he won't have us," Jes said, her face stony as she looked at Olirah. A wave of knowing washed over Olirah, who glanced at the oncoming army and then at Jes with her wounded wing.

"He won't have us," Olirah agreed, reaching for Jes' hand.

"You three protect the queen," Jes commanded.

"But—"

"Now!" Jes barked, her eyes still on Olirah. The tears filling her eyes were telling. She could not look at her friends. Goodbyes were too painful.

"That text I was reading, that claimed the deities had merged..." Elias' voice trailed off as the three headed toward the throne room.

"Ready?" Olirah asked. Jes nodded and accepted Olirah's arm around her waist. Their wings brushed together as they took the long route up the wider stairs until reaching Olirah's chambers. The sky had darkened outside the windowpanes as the army surrounded the tunnel of wind that wavered now, allowing pockets of warriors to breach their defences. Aleksandr's Angels launched from the rooftops, an organised attack that was quickly overwhelmed by Xyliar's numbers. Thunder rumbled above, and the palace shook as if awakened by some power. A white light trickled down the windows as shadows exploded in the sky, heading toward the palace.

"Is that you?" Jes asked, watching the droplets of light that fell like rain. Olirah shook her head, but the light was soon consumed by the shadows knocking to break in. He was here.

"It would probably have been more helpful if I'd rediscovered my powers sooner." Olirah tried to laugh as she knelt in front of Jes, who sat propped against the bed.

"If I'd known all it took was for me to be stabbed, I would have let Jayesh win a fight sooner," Jes said, sniffing. Olirah stroked her hair back, away from the sweat beading on her forehead. "I said I'd never let you fall," she whispered, her trembling hands reaching for Olirah's.

"And you didn't," Olirah said. "I am choosing to fall with you." The windows cracked under the pressure of the shadows outside. "Are you certain?" Olirah murmured, cupping Jessemiah's face. She caught a falling tear with her thumb. Jessemiah nodded, resting her forehead against Olirah's, her dark hair tumbling forward.

"It is the only way," she responded, pulling Olirah into an embrace. Olirah winced at the cries outside the tower. Over Jessemiah's shoulder, the feathered wings of her comrades flew past as they fell to their deaths. A screech sounded again, and the room darkened.

"He is coming for us," Olirah murmured, withdrawing.

"This is the only way to save the state." Jessemiah smiled and reached for a dagger she had rested on the bed beside them. Olirah mimicked her action, picking up a matching dagger with a jewel-encrusted hilt.

"I love you," Olirah's voice cracked.

"From my first breath to my last, I was always destined to be yours," Jessemiah replied, angling her dagger into Olirah's abdomen, where the matching mark to her own lay beneath her clothing. Olirah did the same and kissed Jessemiah. The women clung to each other in a tearful kiss as they pierced their daggers to the sounds of the dying outside.

THASSENA

AGE OF DEVASTATION 3051AD – 3503AD
[PRESENT YEAR: 3400]

SALFI
ROSSO
ALORO
TO ASYNTHOS
STORA
COV
THE FIRST STATE
THASSENA
OF ITHYION
CAPITAL
SETTLEMENT
NOTABLE LOCATION

ADRICUS
TELIA
SACRIFICIAL STONES
CRIMSON MOUNTAINS
DRAVOS LAKE
OLIVE GROVES
SEYNA
LERA
OTILIE
IN SEAS
TO Q'OHAR

Chapter One

Fate awaited this precise thread in every lifetime. It was an exhausting existence, keeping hold of countless paths, so many sparkling and connected threads of hundreds of thousands of souls, to then release each individual one when it pulled taut, signifying the path the innocent, and not so innocent, strayed toward. It was an enraging existence at times too, especially when referenced only in passing as a vague *concept*—an excuse people used to justify their actions or the depressing turn their life had taken. It was as if Fate was not as worthy as the celestial gods or many deities, even though it was her very being and nature that blessed their creation. There would be no deities without the Gods, nor would there be gods without Sonos and Sitara. There would be no ruling king and queen of the skies at all without Fate. Fate, the forgotten third. The all-knowing being that had slipped through the cracks of history during Chaos and Order's sacrifice. But Fate decides. Without Fate, the balance between Chaos and Order would fall. Fate was the true storyteller.

She supposed that was why, out of all the millions of threads to oversee, it was this one she eagerly awaited. The moment a daughter of Thassena, a great Seer, walked through the Caves of Anela to discover their destiny. It was why Fate also favoured the Wiccan of Eresydon, for both felt like family, her own lineage, the small piece of her that had woven through blood and souls to cement itself in permanence. Fate saw all. Seers saw what was gifted to them in visions. Wiccan saw fragments through prophecies. All three seeing, and both races capable of altering which thread Fate would feel tug at her hands. And this thread... this thread was her favourite. It was the one thread, the only thread, that allowed her to plant her feet on the soil of Ithyion.

Fate waited, watching the slack sparkling thread in the darkness pull tighter and tighter, the light shining from it brightening. She waited eagerly. There it was—the familiar pull on her pinkie finger, the moment where she usually released it, allowing the thread to fall into place. But she held onto this thread until it tugged her sternum, sending Fate tumbling headfirst into the Caves of Anela—the caves of the first Seer, the first deity of Thassena, and the first creation born of Nerida's essence merged with that which was stolen from Makaria and Oxyron.

This cave was familiar to her, having seen it on countless occasions. She'd been here every time the firstborn daughter of this particular family line took her ceremonial trip to the caves, in the hope she would be blessed with the vision that would help them find their lost deity, Anela, and her greatest love. She had also been here each time before the curses swept the states of Ithyion, when the ceremonial trip was a rite of passage to being titled a Seer, blessed by Anela's hand herself before she disappeared. The tug of this thread signified the last daughter had failed yet again, which meant it was the turn of the newest heir to the family line. Fate had lost track of the women across the generations of Anela's lineage. But every single one had failed, having twisted the visions bestowed upon them to fit the narrative they had grown up hearing: that they would be the one to find Anela and her lost love.

Fate admired the beauty of the ten-year-old girl still looking around the sparkling cave in awe. She had not yet noticed Fate's presence, or the oracle, as those in Thassena called her. Her curls were still lusciously dark, as beautiful as the deep shade of her skin under the cave's green hue. The light caught the single white curl tucked behind her left ear, and Fate smiled. Her hair would become even more unique over time, as her destiny unravelled, and she grew into her abilities as a Seer. Each strand would lighten until she bore a head of bright white curls. No other Seer, only ever the firstborn daughter of the line.

The young girl halted suddenly, her small hands finding purchase on a glistening gem embedded in the rock. Her hand trembled, though the girl was not frightened. Exhausted was more likely after wandering aimlessly through the tunnels while trusting that the oracle would guide her.

"Are you the oracle?" her delicate but mighty voice asked, echoing across the cave opening. Fate did not answer. She was physically incapable of lying, for it could alter paths. Though this one was technically neither a lie nor a truth. She was Fate. But, to the people of Thassena, she was indeed named the oracle.

They spoke of a hidden being dwelling in the Caves of Anela, entrusted to keep the lost deities' place of origin sacred until her return. Fate had lost track over the centuries of how that particular tale came to be. Young Seers would navigate the caves of their deity after being gifted their first vision. They would wander until either finding the oracle or circling back out to the settlement of Aloro, where the cave tunnels began. Nobody ever questioned why it was only ever the first daughter in this family's line that succeeded in seeing the oracle. Fate supposed it was the lies of the immoral, who claimed they had met the oracle, that prevented such doubt and questioning.

"You look like you mother," Fate said, turning to face the shimmering wall behind that reflected her appearance. She tilted her head; her hair was pin straight and black today, her cheekbones pale and prominent, and brows sharp and arched. Last time she had been short and blonde, with a warm and welcoming face. One thing remained: golden eyes, like always.

"Our hair is different," the girl said, and Fate smiled.

"That is correct, though eventually it will fade, and you will look even more similar." Fate turned back to face the girl who had braved more steps into the cave, her eyes taking in the glow of gems around them. "Tell me, child. Why are you here?" Fate asked. The girl tilted her head, like it was an odd question.

"To be blessed with the vision that may help me find Anela and her lost love, so I might return honour to Thassena and free our lands of the curse." The slight lift of the girl's chin conveyed her determination. Fate knew all too well that doing so would not break the curse. None of the curses would be broken until a prophecy in the future came to pass, one between generations who were not yet even born. The threads of the future.

"You appear confident," Fate said, clasping her hands together and grounding her feet in the sand below. The girl's face wavered, a small frown tugging on her brow.

"I have to be," she said.

"Why is that?"

"Because if I don't succeed, then I will have to marry *him*." The girl rolled her eyes at the thought of the boy, who Fate knew was sitting in a lesson in the palace, being taught the correct table manners for a banquet.

"You do not wish to marry Prince Theon of the royal House Sevia?"

"I'm *thirteen*," the girl stressed, and Fate chuckled.

"You would not marry him until twenty-five, as is tradition. So you may focus on your visions."

"Exactly. Twelve years to find Anela," the girl said.

"You do not believe in the sacred pact between your houses? That the marriage between the children of each house will bless your people and help to alleviate the curse?"

"Why would the marriage between two people lift a curse preventing the Sirens from returning to land?"

"Why would a vision of one child break a curse?"

"Because it is Anela who will break the curse. I just have to be the one child to find her." The girl crossed her arms, and Fate refrained from laughing at her frustration.

"Well, you needn't worry. I don't imagine you will marry him either way." Fate smirked.

"Why?"

"Because something always seems to stop the wedding from taking place." The girl looked at her feet and began rocking back and forth. The marriage never succeeded. The girl's mother, Sienna, had been the closest, until the previous Prince of Thassena, Darius, was killed in his bed two weeks before the wedding and the woman forced to find a new husband.

"I don't want him dead," the girl mumbled.

"I never said he would die, only that I don't expect you'll marry him." The girl looked back up at Fate, narrowing her eyes.

"What do you know?" the girl asked. Fate laughed this time—loudly.

"Well, *everything*. Is that not my purpose? Is that not why you are here?" She smiled and perched on the edge of the rock pool in the cave's centre, holding out her palm for the girl to take. "Are you ready to be gifted the vision of your fate?"

The girl hesitated, seeming to realise the life-altering implications of this moment, and the weight of the vision. Her hand was soft and delicate as it slipped into Fate's. A golden spark ignited between the two of them. Fate grasped her other hand and squeezed lightly. "Ready?" she whispered. The girl nodded and closed her eyes as Fate shared the image of one of her strongest threads, revealing her destiny.

The girl's brow furrowed as she took in the vision, her eyes fluttering beneath her lids as Fate watched, knowing the vision was short. Young Seer's minds often latched onto pieces of a vision rather than the whole picture, meaning they would take elements very literally rather than dissecting the other possible threads linked to it. Fate's small smile faded as the vision repeated itself, and she saw the parts the girl latched onto, the false hope it would instil. Her eyes flew open, and her irises glowed.

"I'll do it!" The girl beamed. "I'll succeed. I'll find the river drake!" The girl drew back, clapping her hands together. "I'll find Anela's lost love, which will surely help lead me to the deity." The girl spun around in circles, hugging herself while Fate wore a sad smile.

"You will find the river drake." She nodded.

"I must go! I must tell my family the good news and begin studying so I might try to locate him!" she squealed. Fate opened her mouth to say more, to keep the girl near, extending Fate's brief moment on Ithyion. But Fate knew she would return to the Caves of Anela again one day. This girl would not succeed, and another firstborn daughter would grace her presence in the future, until, eventually, the final daughter would arrive. So, Fate lifted a hand in farewell as she watched Levanna of House Zerpane run from the caves with her glowing eyes of midnight blue awash with hope.

Chapter Two

Riverbed species. Rivers of Ancient Thassena. River Sirens: Differentiating Cultures. River Flows: A Study into the Enhancement of Foresight. Levanna stomped her foot and hung her head back. Closing her eyes, she took a deep breath to calm her frustration. Having traced her finger over the spines of the alphabetised books, searching for the mention of rivers countless times, she still could not see the book she wanted, despite the librarian insisting nobody had checked it out. The city library was only permitted to those over the age of eighteen, which was ridiculous! She had been an avid researcher from thirteen, with a notified certification from the Scholars Guild since the age of sixteen. It then took her another two years for her access request to be approved, something about supply and demand and limiting the number of hands that touched ancient books in a year. Though Levanna was certain her access was instead delayed because of a certain king trying to slow her progress, believing the marriage to his son the key to a thriving state and the reunion of the deities. On her first day in the capital's library, she would not have put it past him to misplace the books he knew she'd seek first. *River Drakes: A Compendium of Ancient Breeds. River Drakes and Tales of the Sea. River Drakes: An Anatomical Study.*

Levanna had read nearly every book in Thassena. She explored the coasts of Rosso, the marshes of Adricus, and had scoured every library in nearly every major settlement. None had offered any answers or insight into the vision the oracle had bestowed upon her at thirteen years old. And now the last library to check was the capital's, Lera.

A mirage of iridescent scales glided along the oceans of Thassena, specifically the Siren Seas off the capital's coastline, eventually becoming the central waters of Ithyion, The Ouro Ocean. A thrum of power washed through her veins, as though the ocean called to her. In return, she called to the river drake, swimming to the side of the ship she stood upon. The scales on its head formed a crown, complementing the purple of his irises. She knew it was him. Anela's nameless love.

With a frustrated sigh, Levanna refrained from recalling more of the vision, knowing it would only aid her annoyance, and strode out from the aisle of shelves to the small hexagonal table by the mosaic windows. With the sun setting outside, the pink sky glowed through the blue glass pattern, creating a scattering of purple light across the columns that had stood for far longer than the wooden shelves. The guards stationed by the doors in their silver armour tutted at the same time as the librarian when Levanna hastily dragged her satchel across the table, knocking over a pot of quills.

"Sorry," Levanna muttered under her breath, though rather insincerely. A small scoff broke the silence across the hall. Levanna watched the man as she unbuckled the engraved gold buckles from the worn brown leather. She knew the inside pockets from memory, rifling through the same papers her mother and grandmother had before her. If only her other ancestors had thought to document their findings and the links to their visions. Levanna was gifted the satchels and notes when she returned from her visit to the oracle, but it seemed her relatives had been nowhere near as thorough in their note taking as Levanna was now. Perhaps because none of their visions had shown them the river drake.

The scoff came from the man sitting three tables down, but he did not look up at her now. Instead, he combed a brown hand through his dark hair, where it flopped over his circular glasses a minute later, the tips lighter than the rest. He appeared to spend a lot of time in the sun. They tickled his high cheekbones, and he huffed, blowing the strands of hair from his eyes, yet they returned just as quickly. This time it was Levanna's turn to scoff. *Get a haircut if it bothers you so.*

His long fingers paused mid-turn of a page, and Levanna suddenly found the pages of her satchel rather interesting as he looked up. She had no time for her betrothed, let alone any other men, but it was in her nature to analyse people, to analyse everything and anything. She flitted her eyes to the hand-drawn anatomy of a river drake. In her peripheral vision, she knew he had taken his glasses off. Levanna dared a glance. Behind his frames, his brow furrowed as he read. Before she could over-analyse the shape of his lips, he set the glasses down and reached for a quill, dipping it in ink. As his hands scrawled across the top sheet of parchment, the tendons in his arms flexed beneath his red, rolled-up sleeves. It was Levanna's turn to furrow her brow this time. An unusual colour choice for a scholar of Thassena, unless—Levanna's thoughts left her as he lifted the book up and she caught sight of the title in silver along the spine. *River Drakes: An Anatomical Study.*

"I need that," Levanna said boldly before clamping her mouth shut under the librarian's stare. Slowly, the man lowered the book and turned to face her fully. His bronze eyes glowed against the purple hues dancing through the room. Levanna straightened under his scrutiny. His eyes skimmed the white streaks in her hair, the family crest on her leather satchel, and the papers she was certain he couldn't read from such a distance. She hurriedly slid them back into the leather, just in case.

"Unfortunately, *I* am reading it," he said. The corner of his lip quirked before he balanced the tip of his glasses between them again and returned to the pages. His voice was surprisingly soft. "I—"

"Miss Zerpane, you will be asked to leave if you cannot keep your volume to a minimum," the librarian scolded from her high-topped stone dais, as old as the room's columns. Levanna pursed her lips and scraped her chair back, though too harshly to make a point. She sidestepped the tables and sat down opposite the man, who did not look up from his book. He merely placed his glasses back on the bridge of his nose and continued making notes with his quill. Her sisters would have judged him for not apologising and offering the book at the sound of her surname, belonging to the second greatest house in Thassena. But based on the shade of his shirt, and how appallingly it stood out among the blues and creams of Thassena, she suspected this man hailed from Q'Ohar, which only piqued her interest.

Why and how had a scholar of Q'Ohar been granted access to Thassena's capital library? It had taken Levanna—a first daughter Zerpane and the betrothed to the prince—*two* years. What information about Thassena interested him so much that he couldn't find it in his own libraries? Secrets? Other ways to ruin the royal family? Her family, perhaps. While it had never been fully confirmed, her mother's betrothed had been burned from the inside out. Her entire family suspected the involvement of either someone from Q'Ohar or even their royal family. But an attack against Asynthos, instigated by Xyliar, had stopped the Sevia's from waging war against a different state. All efforts instead went into defence in case Xyliar turned on them next. They never did. Yet again, the sixth state had closed itself off over forty years ago, so nobody knew what went on within. Visits between states were largely sanctioned as a result for fear of being intercepted across the ocean, meaning this man opposite her was either deemed important enough to visit or unimportant enough to risk.

"I'll pay you," she whispered, leaning toward him. Still, he held the book, but he glanced up through fluttering lashes.

"You'll pay me?" he asked. His voice remained soft, innocent, but something caused a shiver to crawl down her back, bare except for the twisted fabric forming a rope along her spine, tying with the gauze around her neck to hold up the deep blue gown. Her mother would scold such attire when she returned home; it was far too casual for a library, particularly for the future Queen of Thassena.

"Anything." Levanna nodded. "I'll pay you anything for that book." She lowered her voice into a whisper, too. He raised an eyebrow.

"I suppose you would also like the collection in my satchel that I was planning to take back to my accommodation?" the man asked, closing the book and retrieving his satchel from the back of his chair. He had to be important if the librarian was allowing him to take books back to his quarters. He unbuckled the highly polished clasps. "Given they are on the same topic?" Levanna let out a soft sigh of relief and nodded eagerly, waiting for him to withdraw the books and pass the stack to her. The man stood, brushing down the crinkles in his shirt at the front, indicating how long he had been sitting hunched over the table.

He was far taller than she expected. He rested a hand down on the table, his tendons flexing. The closeness of his arm to her body forced her to look up at him in the glow of the glass mosaic. His hair flopped forward, framing his glasses. He smiled, a full smile, showing perfectly straight, pearl-white teeth. Levanna was dazed for a moment before offering a polite smile in return. She opened her satchel, waiting for the books. He looked between her face and her hands. Her excitement piqued at the thought of new reading material when he reached for his satchel, yet it came crashing down as he slung the leather strap over his shoulder and tucked the anatomical study under his arm. He leant further toward her and whispered, "You can have them when I've finished."

"But I—" She was cut off as he flashed a dazzling smile at her again and turned on his heel, leaving her dumbfounded in the library.

"Insufferable son o—"

"Miss Zerpane!" The librarian scolded, her cheeks flushed from raising her voice. "I think you are done for the evening. You may return in the morning."

Taking a deep breath, Levanna counted to ten, cooling her temper that grew with each passing year. She repeated the motion a handful more times, partly to ensure the man would have made it down the staircase and out of the library before she did something that would most definitely have her hauled in front of her future in-laws. Reaching into her satchel, she pulled out the large topaz ring and spun it between her fingers. She watched it sparkle as she left the third floor and paused at the window, slipping it onto her ring finger. She found the mop of floppy brown hair almost immediately, bouncing down the steps outside and into the throngs of the city without a care in the world. Levanna inclined her head at one of the guards she was forced to keep with her at all times.

"Follow him," Levanna said.

Chapter Three

"A nd *then* he said there was no one else with eyes as beautiful as mine." A chorus of swoons and affirmations echoed from across the breakfast table, where Levanna's youngest sisters, Lyla and Lanaya, sat with porcelain cups from Asynthos, filled with tea from Q'Ohar. Levanna rolled her eyes and stabbed another piece of fruit with her fork.

"You do realise," Levanna said between chewing, "the three of us all share the exact same eyes, so one might deduce he is lying." Levanna quirked an eyebrow, watching her sisters and their friends stare at her. It wasn't only their eyes that were the same. Other than the fact Levanna was much taller than her sisters and their hair had never gained more than a single white streak, they could have been triplets. Their matching midnight-blue eyes and wild curls captivated most men and women. Levanna wasn't egotistical enough to assume it was because of beauty. Everyone in Thassena knew the Zerpane family, and so it was their expectations weighing on Levanna's shoulders as they stared. She shrugged. "Just an observation," Levanna added, reaching for the glass of cucumber water.

When it reached her lips, Lyla finally replied. "Some of us must court as normal. We weren't just handed a prince on a silver platter." Levanna paused before gulping down the water, watching the group of girls in silence. The friends shifted uncomfortably in their seats at Levanna's stare; it was unclear whether their discomfort was because of her future queenship or the kingdom's belief she was to become the most powerful Seer when she reached twenty-five. Regardless of the reason, Levanna relished the impact she had as she pushed back her chair. The sun streamed through the winding olive branches that formed a roof over the breakfast patio, warming the stones under her bare feet. She wrapped an arm around Lyla's shoulder, plucking a tart from her plate.

"You're welcome to him, if you wish," Levanna said. She shoved the tart in her mouth and disappeared through the glass doors, with the complaints of her sisters following behind. Still, the taste of lemon lingered as she ran her tongue over her teeth and shook back her hair, the white catching in the reflection of the windows overlooking the courtyard where her mother sat with her embroidery. *Shit.* Levanna stepped quickly behind a statue of the deity Dravos, the first Illusionist of Thassena, before her mother saw her. She was earlier in her routine that day. Levanna had thought she had another fifteen minutes before her mother would be down from her rooms. The main doors to the house clicked open, and her guards appeared right on time.

"Miss Zerpane, as expected, the man is already on his way to the library. Would—" Her guard, Radian, froze at Levanna's frantic hand gestures as she signalled him to stop.

"Levanna!" called her mother from the courtyard. She sighed, leaning her head back against the stone waves at the foot of the deity. She sent a single request to keep the conversation from delaying her day. If it had been a statue of Nerida, she might have prayed properly. She connected more spiritually with the celestial goddess, but her mother claimed Dravos had visited her once on the day of her supposed wedding and she had worshipped the deities most religiously ever since. Levanna glared at the guard, who mouthed an apology, before she plastered a smile onto her face, sidestepped the statue, and entered the courtyard through the glass doors.

"Mother!" she said cheerily. "You are up earlier than usual; did you not sleep well?" The scent of the capital's native clematis flowers rushed to meet the Seer as she stepped into the sun trap that was the courtyard. Her mother never allowed the gardeners to trim them, for she was adamant they should grow wherever the universe guided. As a result, all four walls were coated in pale pink and lilac flowers, climbing up the entire wall and out onto the roof, as if the courtyard was the very heart of the property that had belonged to her family for as long as anyone could recall. Her mother used to tell her that the first Zerpane lord married for duty but had been in love with a woman from Eresydon; he had the most powerful wielders of the second state plant the clematis plants as a shrine to her.

"Change." Her mother's sharp voice interrupted Levanna's thoughts about her future husband as she wondered if he would build a shrine for his true love when they married, for Levanna *certainly* did not love him.

"Whatever. Do you—"

"Change, Levanna. That is not an outfit befitting a future queen, nor is it respectable to have your back and shoulders bare in a place of learning."

"The scholars in the towers of Adricus certainly didn't mind my bare shoulders when I spent three months there last summer," Levanna replied.

"Those scholars see a woman once a month if they are lucky. I am not surprised they did not scold you for showing so much skin." Her mother did not look up from her embroidery. "I have picked a dress and hung it by your mirror. The servant girls are waiting to help you into it." Levanna groaned and turned on her heel. The fact that the gown required help meant she would not be comfortable today.

***

Levanna didn't think it was possible to sweat as much as she was right now, even as she used her power to draw the moisture from her skin. Luckily, the dress was a deep regal blue; otherwise, there would most definitely be a dark stain trickling down her lower back, beneath the ribbons that pulled the corset so tight she could barely breathe. At least her mother had granted a small reprieve, for it did not conceal her entire back. The fabric stopped halfway up her spine, her loose hair covering the remainder of her skin. She wished she had requested it be pulled into an updo. While the fabric was not as thick as the materials found in Eresydon and Asynthos, it was still thicker than the usual gauze-like material she favoured; it stuck to her arms and was secured by the loops on the triangle-pointed sleeves hooked over her middle fingers. With her skirts so much fuller than usual, she was having to hold the fabric up to keep from tripping over her sandals.

The Zerpane family home was in the centre of the city, as were most of the prestigious families in Thassena, who lived as close to the palace as possible. It meant the walk from Levanna's home to the library was a mere thirty minutes—a quick trip with her guards that attracted little attention due to the busy throngs of market browsers. But, add in a gown definitely fit for a queen, and a pace far slower than normal, and Levanna was drawing more eyes than she wished as they reach the city square. The gates to the palace stood opposite her on the other side of the square, with the library located on her left and the church to her right.

"If she ever makes me wear something like this thing again, remind me to go by horseback and take the back streets," Levanna murmured to her guards. They chuckled; she had a carefree relationship with her protectors, one that naturally arose after years of travelling together. Gathering her skirts again, she climbed the stone steps to the library. She outstretched her hand to lean against Radian's bicep before unbuckling her sandals. She sighed in relief at the cool, shaded stone beneath her feet and resumed her climb to the third floor, where she had been yesterday. Radian raised an eyebrow at the sandals in her hand.

"What! She said I couldn't show too much skin; nobody can see my bare feet under all this fabric."

"At least put the sandals in your satchel, otherwise the librarian will most definitely send word to your mother," Radian said, straightening to open the door to the third-floor archives. Levanna did as he suggested and dropped them into the front pocket of the leather satchel before flashing the librarian a sickly-sweet smile. Staring over her glasses, the old woman pointed her quill at a table where a stack of three books waited. Levanna ran to the table, much to the librarian's dismay, and picked up the folded parchment atop it.

There. I'm finished with them now.

-Kai

Kai. An unusually informal name for a man with credentials from Q'Ohar. Levanna did not dwell on it and collapsed into a chair before pulling the first book: *River Drakes: A Compendium of Ancient Breeds*. Reading, studying, learning —it was Levanna's sanctuary. The ability to lose herself in words, whether stories or factual, was something she could do every day. Reading and researching were the only things she could do to move closer to her vision. The mosaic light slowly travelled around the room as the day went on. At some point, Radian placed a piece of focaccia and a bag of olives from the market on the table, which she ate one-handed while flicking through the pages with the other. She jotted down notes from nearly every page, intrigued. Her initial three books had become a much larger stack. Her reading prompted questions, leading her to hunt for answers in other pages.

"Was it any help?" Levanna jumped at the voice so close to her ear. Her guards had not moved from their spot by the door, but she noticed their hands tighten on the pommel of their swords. She glanced up at the gentle voice to find Kai smiling down at her. He moved around the table before taking the opposite seat, resting his arms atop the stacks. He glanced at all the books. "Were the three I provided not enough?" he asked, resting his chin on the turquoise sleeves of his shirt. Levanna cocked her head.

"Are you bored with red?" she asked, turning her quill back to her notes.

"Would you have preferred me to remain in red?"

"It matters not what my preferences are."

"Oh, but it does. I should very much like the approval of Thassena's future queen." Levanna clenched her quill, and the wood snapped. "A difficult subject then," he mused. Levanna looked back up at him and glared at the playful smile on his face.

"If you knew who I was, then it would have been polite to give the future queen the books she required yesterday rather than making her wait." Levanna's returning smile was tight. "What interest does a man from Q'Ohar have in river drakes, anyway?"

"I was looking for information on the deity Anela," he said. That certainly piqued her interest. Leaning back in her chair, she toyed with the topaz on her finger.

"Why?" she asked. Kai leant back in his own chair, mirroring her movements.

"Why are you interested?" he asked. Levanna scoffed.

"This is pointless," she said, pulling her book back toward her.

"Because you are also looking for Anela? Is that not what the vision usually tells the oldest daughter of Zerpane?" he asked. Levanna narrowed her eyes.

"How do you know so much?"

"I'm a scholar. It is my job to know things," he said, leaning over the stack of books and plucking the one from her hands. "But I don't think either of us will find what we are looking for here." Normally, Levanna would not let a man dictate her conversation or actions, but she felt compelled to hear him out. "You need to find Anela. I simply want to know about her power and what was passed down through her lineages."

"Why?" Levanna asked again. A muscle in his jaw ticked, a sign he wished to get through this conversation without revealing his motives. He sighed.

"It sounds childish," he said.

"Humour me."

Kai shifted in his seat, leaning forward again. A waft of smoke and citrus met her nose, and she wondered if he'd been at a gentleman's lounge the previous night. Smoking was not a habit she looked upon fondly.

"I had a dream," he began.

"Ahh. Is this all some journey of self-discovery for you? Do you wish to wander the waters of Thassena in search of a woman who may look into your future?" she goaded. Kai removed his glasses.

"If I simply wanted a woman I could see a future with, I would not have to look so hard," he said, his bronze eyes boring into hers. Levanna cleared her throat at the uncomfortable feeling his stare had planted in the pit of her stomach. "I had a very vivid dream, so vivid it felt more like a vision. I have researched the deities and lineages to see if anyone from another state has ever been gifted the powers of a different deity. Finding Anela, or anything extra about her before her disappearance, would help."

"What was the dream?" Levanna asked. Normally, she would have scoffed. It was unlikely anyone other than a child of Thassena or Eresydon could be gifted visions, and even in Eresydon they were usually fragmented in prophecies, a completely different power related to the first Wiccan. But Kai seemed educated and certain of himself, someone who would not place weight on what-ifs.

"I cannot remember it all, as is usual with dreams."

"There are rituals to help that," Levanna said, and Kai tilted his head.

"There are?"

"Ah, something he doesn't know." Levanna smirked. "They are sacred to the Seers of the church to help us enhance our visions with more clarity."

"Is this a ritual you could complete?" he asked. Levanna paused, pondering the advantages of completing such a task. She could potentially see his dream, but that would steer her from her tasks.

"I can get you into the royal libraries," he said abruptly, as if he knew what she was thinking. Levanna stood from her chair. Now she knew he was a liar. "You do not believe me," he said, mirroring her actions. Levanna leant forward across the table.

"I am to be a royal, and even I have not been granted access," Levanna whispered.

"I have the credentials," Kai uttered, patting his left breast pocket. Very few could gain such access, highest priests and priestesses of Ithyion, other rulers, or...

"You're the King of Q'Ohar's personal scholar," Levanna breathed. Kai tensed. "Why on earth would the king and queen of Thassena let you into the libraries on his behalf after what he did to my mother's—"

"He did nothing of the sort," Kai hissed, his demeanour changing. The aloof scholar's face transformed into one of a solider, a defender of the crown. Levanna made to pull back and leave, but he caught her wrist, his grip firm. "We both need access to the royal libraries for information on Anela. I can give you access. In return, you help me extract the details of my dream."

Levanna scoffed and tried to pull away, but he tugged her closer. She did not anticipate his strength and stumbled against the table, their foreheads colliding. Levanna knocked over an inkpot in her attempt to steady herself.

"Goddess help me," Levanna murmured, but before she could reach up to rub her forehead, a warm touch was already there. She blinked up through her lashes to find Kai's brow furrowed, his eyes concerned rather than hard. He gently rubbed her forehead with his thumb.

"If you wish to permanently keep that ring off your finger, you know a bargain with me is the best way forward." His voice was soft again, understanding. A scholar was dangerous, as Kai was proving. Knowledge was power, and he knew enough about her family's history and the expectations of her destiny on the state. He knew she would do nearly anything to see her vision completed, her deity found, and her marriage prevented.

"You grant me access to the royal libraries, and I will perform the rituals of the church in return," Levanna said, searching his eyes for deception. But he only nodded as his thumb moved from her forehead to gently brush her cheek. "I make the bargain."

A tingle started in her wrist, and she glanced down to find the mark of the Goddess Nerida, and a single golden thread wrapping around her arm, binding her to Kai.

A celestial tie.

Chapter Four

"Did you know nobody knows the true origins of a celestial tie?" Kai said as they slung their satchels over their shoulders and hurried down the steps of the library and out into the square.

"Did you know you're wrong?" Levanna retorted. She lifted her hair with both hands to find some reprieve from the warmth.

"Did you know that, in fact, I am not?"

"Did you know—"

"There are early accounts of celestial ties, but"—Kai held up a hand, as if he were giving a sermon. Levanna rolled her eyes at his confidence as they wove amongst the throngs of people, following the two guards who forged a diagonal path for them across the square toward the palace—"there is more than one account that has sound logic and evidence, suggesting that nobody knows the true origins and actually the celestial ties are a direct representation of the many threads of fate due to the many ways in which they appear."

"Did you know the 'threads of fate' is a ludicrous saying, used by those who can't accept what's happened to them?" Levanna countered, trying to secure her hair in some manner to keep it upright.

"Did you know that is an attempt at an appeal to ridicule?" Kai countered, beginning to rummage around in his satchel as the guards edged closer to the palace entrance. Levanna glanced between the soldiers on the palace steps to the small path on the left that would guide her to a hidden entrance.

"Did you know arguments and fallacies were the most boring subject my tutors ever covered?" Levanna sighed, giving up on her hair.

"Did you know..." Kai's mumbled words stopped her as he seized her wrist and spun her to face him. She looked up, his height blocking the sun. He held two quills between his teeth. Though she did not flinch as his fingers brushed her neck to gather her hair, her skin prickled. His hands stroked the nape of her neck before tugging her scalp and twisting her hair in spirals. He withdrew a quill and pierced it through her locks, where the nib of the silver tip gently scratched her scalp. He did the same with the second quill. "That you should really carry hair pins with you?" Levanna was too stunned to comprehend how casually he touched her before his fingers intertwined in hers. He dragged her through the crowds to catch up with the two guards waiting for them.

"That way." Levanna pointed over Kai's shoulder, and the guards followed her direction. Kai did not question why they wouldn't simply use his credentials to enter the main gates. The noise from the square faded the further they journeyed through the narrowing alley.

"Odd that there is no soldier to guard this passageway," Kai said. His hand remained in Levanna's as they walked single file, his shoulders brushing the stones on either side.

"They don't know it's here," Levanna said. "Stop here," she commanded the guards.

"And how do you?" he asked. Levanna released his hand, the cool of the shade replacing his warmth. Reaching up, she brushed aside a violet clematis plant, revealing a damp stone wall with a tiny hole; a trickle of water filtered out, coming from the pipe system in the palace.

"Before we do this, I have a question about celestial ties," Levanna said, facing him with her hands on her hips. Kai's lips quirked, his eyes dancing with amusement behind his glasses.

"Something you do not know?" he asked. She ignored the tease.

"Do you believe the tale that celestial ties stop two people from betraying their secrets?" she asked. Kai raised his eyebrows, surprised by the question.

"I have heard the tales of what happens if they do," Kai said, and Levanna could have sworn the brightness in his eyes clouded, even momentarily. Slowly, Levanna nodded.

"Death?" she asked. Kai nodded, his jaw tight.

"But I would not betray your trust, regardless."

"Because I am a future queen, who could have you killed *regardless*?" Levanna asked. Her soldiers straightened at the words, and Kai's smile returned.

"Because you have asked me not to. My word means a great deal," Kai said. The mark of Nerida on her wrist tingled. She believed him. Levanna turned back to face the wall, her palms outstretched.

"Did you know there has never been a royal with more than two god-gifted powers alongside an elemental power?" she asked.

"That we know of," he said, and she smiled at his conspiracies. Though she supposed he was right. With a slow flick of Levanna's fingers, the water trickling from above danced away from the wall in a pattern of droplets until Levanna squeezed her hands to form one large layer.

"My water wielding, a gift from Nerida, is nowhere near as strong as the royal families, given their strength is passed on to one another in death. But it's there."

"It is not unusual for one of the three races to also be a wielder. Some would argue it is common," he mused. Levanna smiled, and with a wave of her hand, the water shimmered, revealing a door.

"Would you say it is common to be a Seer, wielder, and an Illusionist?" Levanna asked, testing the silver doorknob. She had read the private journals passed down through the Sisters of Rosso on her travels, the purest group of Illusionists in Thassena. In those, she had read of the door that Queen Aleena, the third wife of King Arorn, had hidden under an illusion of water to sneak out and see her lover over four hundred years ago. When Levanna pulled the door, Kai reached over her to grab the top of the frame and hold it open. She turned around to tell the guards to wait and found herself practically enveloped by Kai's body. He leant down slightly, watching with intrigue.

"You aren't about to lure me in here with a song and send me to my demise, are you?" he asked, though the gentleness in his voice suggested anything but fear.

"Don't be absurd," Levanna said, walking into the dark entrance. She glanced back with a grin. "Sirens haven't been able to walk on land for centuries."

"Nor has there been a record of a royal with more than two powers, and yet here I stand, being lured into darkness by a future queen of three."

"You have nothing to fear, Kai. If I were to lure a man to his demise, it wouldn't be you." She scraped her hands along the damp tunnel walls to guide her.

"I don't know if I should feel jealous or not," he said. "You make demise sound sensual, not deadly." Levanna blushed in the darkness, ignoring the heat of his breath on her bare upper back as they walked. The makeshift updo still held strong. Levanna ignored the comment as she reached the end of the tunnel. Light bathed the space as the view into the grand palace entryway shimmered behind an illusion that had formed with the water spraying from the fountain feature built into the stone. A patrol of guards walked right past the shimmering water, and Levanna gasped as a broad forearm wrapped around her middle, drawing her back. For a moment, Kai remained perfectly still, his chest rising and falling behind her head as the patrol filed past. She gripped his muscled forearms, exposed by his rolled-up sleeves. Levanna had never been so close to a man before; she hadn't even shared a hug with her father before he died when she was ten.

"They can't see us," Levanna whispered. "The other side is illusioned too. Can you see the shimmer, the mark of the power?"

Kai's breath tickled her ear as he leant down. "Show me," he whispered, his lips ghosting her ear. With his right arm braced around her waist still, he rested his left gently on her hip. She could have sworn his hand trembled where he touched her. Levanna swallowed, her legs beginning to feel unstable as she pointed up at the corner of the tunnel exit.

"There," she said, her throat dry. "The top left. If you allow your eyes to lose focus, the shimmer remains clear.

"Ah, so I would have to remove my glasses," he chuckled, the sound reverberating against her back. "I don't like them anyway. I suppose I can go without to test random illusions in Thassena."

"I like them," Levanna said. She pursed her lips and moved out of his grip before he could latch on to what she said. "We should get going." She stepped toward the clear space, waving her hand to pause the flow of the fountain on the other side. They stepped through. "The royal archives of the library are to the right and down the—"

"Levanna?" a male voice called. This voice was not the soft, gentle tone of the man who whispered in her ear moments before. This voice carried authority and certainty. It was not a cruel voice by any means, but it lacked affection. "What are you doing here? I didn't think we were due another scheduled lunch for a month." Levanna placed a hand against the fountain in the wall, the illusion no longer visible. She refrained from looking around her in a panic. Kai was also not visible.

"Just stopping for a drink," Levanna said, feigning confidence as she cupped her hands under the waterspout and stared at the wall where the illusion hid. She wondered if Kai was still on the other side.

"In... the palace?" he asked. Levanna sipped, stalling, before she wiped her hands on her gown and plastered on a smile.

"Well, of course I have another reason to be here," Levanna laughed, as though it was obvious. The guards' armour clattered as they moved against the walls, taking up watch. Levanna glided as regally as possible down the marble floors and between the soldiers, like she was already walking down the aisle.

Prince Theon reached for her hand to place a delicate kiss on the back of her fingers beside her engagement ring.

"Well, I am more than happy to see my future wife. I was just surprised, that was all." Theon smiled, his hand lingering on hers before letting go. He clasped his hands behind his back. His navy attire matched her dress almost perfectly, except for the elaborate gold shoulder tassels that looped down to adorn his right breast, which were far more ornate. His blonde hair was slicked back, brightening the grey in his eyes. He was a handsome man. That was not Levanna's issue. And he was kind, from what she'd heard. He showed interest in her research and did not judge when she admitted she had no other interests, always asking about her travels during their lunches. The simple matter was this: she did not choose him, and he did not choose her.

"I have an appointment at the royal library archives." Levanna smiled politely.

"I'm surprised my father granted such a request." Theon frowned. "Though I do not take issue with you proceeding with your research." The latter statement was genuine.

"Perhaps my persistence finally wore him down."

"You would be one of the few to successfully do so," Theon remarked. A silence fell between them, neither prepared for an encounter nor a conversation. "I could accompany you to ensure you reach the library." Theon turned his body and extended his arm. How could she refuse a prince, her intended? She was forced to incline her head and hide her frustration as she glanced around the hall.

"Are you wearing quills in your hair?" he asked. Levanna fabricated an entertaining story to explain why as they strolled the hallways, trying to fill the awkward silences that fell between them. A waft of smoke and citrus caught her attention. Kai was here somewhere. Yet she had no idea where he was or how he'd got there. Not with the twenty guards accompanying Theon everywhere he went.

Eventually, the guards were forced to halt. Only two led them down the spiral staircase, single file, until they reached the entrance to the royal library archives. Kai's scent was stronger here. Lanterns lit the curved archway where an old man sat behind a stone plinth. In any other state, it would be odd to store so many old books and artifacts underground. But in Thassena, it was the safest place. With the single entrance, and the regular wielders drawing the moisture from the air, the stone catacomb-like rooms were as dry as the deserts in Q'Ohar.

"Miss Levanna Zerpane, I assume?" the man asked, peering over his glasses while dipping his quill in ink. "Your associate has already shown credentials. You are free to enter."

"Who is your asso—"

"Thank you so much for the company, Theon." Levanna cut him off, gently resting her arm on his bicep in a sign of affection. He glanced down at it, brow raised.

"Well, you're wel—"

"I'll see you next month for lunch." Levanna curtseyed and turned, praying he did not wish to prolong their awkward interaction any longer. The sound of shifting armour confirmed his departure, and so Levanna allowed her feet to guide her through the archives, following the scent of smoke.

Chapter Five

"Did you know there are a group of Shapeshifters in Eresydon who believe Anela permanently trapped the body of her love in the river drake on purpose?" Kai asked, turning the page of fading parchment. Levanna hummed.

"I did, because you've already read that book."

Kai sighed, leaning back in his chair. "I knew there was something familiar about the way it put Shapeshifters on a pedestal."

"Don't we all put our races on a pedestal?" Levanna asked, glancing up at him across the table. Teasing, she added, "Q'Ohar in particular."

"I can't help if we home the superior races." He smiled.

"Your races are only powerful because Keres stole from his siblings to create them. The Angels of Asynthos to create his Xyra, Shapeshifters of Eresydon to create Smokeshifters, water wielders from Thassena to learn the movement and control of liquids to create his Forgers, as if melted metal has *any* benefit compared to water," Levanna scoffed.

"Some would argue that is ingenuity," Kai said.

"And some would argue it was cruelty," Levanna countered. Kai pursed his lips and turned back to his book. In the last six months, Levanna had learnt which topics made him tense. The shortcomings of his state and their past approaches was one such topic. Though he never vocalised his agreement, he never expressed his disagreement either. On occasion, he had brought up the cruel history of the other states as a potential argument, and Levanna found she could not disagree. Cruelty and questionable motives or the need for power existed everywhere. In the last six months, she had also learnt that neither of the pair had much patience.

They had learnt plenty from their private collection of royal books and artifacts, like the locations of the river drake pods—and their eventual extermination—the many variations of the love story between Anela and the man trapped as a river drake. One claimed Anela went into hiding after he had an affair with a Siren and that she was the one that had him turned into a river drake; another said he was actually a Shapeshifter, and she died of a broken heart when he was captured by sailors who were never found. Levanna's particular favourite was that neither were missing nor trapped—they had simply tired of the world and found somewhere to hide, living out their days in one another's arms. Despite the variations of tales, none mentioned his name or history or gave any indication of his whereabouts. The greatest visions Anela had recorded, from the birth of the greatest kings and queens, to the wars they would incite, and the visions of war and darkness that Levanna had not yet seen recorded in history. But nothing indicated where Levanna should search for the river drake or Anela, but she knew, she *knew* she would find him, for that was what her vision showed.

Kai also had little luck. He discovered no family lines where Seers crossed with those in Q'Ohar, no instances of crossbred abilities between races, though Levanna did propose that was not something anyone would choose to advertise and was likely information locked away in the King's own study. Kai had put in a request at the royal libraries of Asynthos, Eresydon, Carvyre, and Xyliar—even extending his offer of travel and research to Levanna. She considered it. Eresydon and Carvyre had accepted, provided certain paperwork was met. Xyliar had not responded, which was hardly surprising. What was surprising was the decline from Asynthos, which only piqued Kai's interest. Perhaps they had something to hide.

"Are their ways to make a Seer's visions stronger?" Kai asked, running a finger down a new book.

"You mean other than the church rituals you have yet to ask for to finalise our bargain?"

"And shorten our time together? Once the bargain is fulfilled, I have no way of remaining in your company." He flashed a lopsided smile, and Levanna could not prevent the small smile that graced her own lips.

"We could try the ritual. If it pulls your dream into focus, it may also sharpen my visions too. I do not believe I have missed anything, but it might be worth a shot," Levanna proposed. Part of her regretted the suggestion, unsure what her days might look like after spending six months together.

"And then we would go our separate ways?" Kai asked tentatively. Levanna continued flicking through the book.

"I suppose your company is tolerable enough that even with a fulfilled bargain, I may appreciate your company during my research." Levanna shrugged.

"You'll come with me then, to Eresydon?" Kai asked, leaning forward across the table with a child-like smile.

"I will need my mother's approval first, and"—Levanna shifted uncomfortably—"approval from my betrothed."

"You need his permission to leave the state?"

"Well, I am to be queen. Safety is an issue, unfortunately," Levanna sighed. Kai nodded slowly, as though he sometimes forgot he was sitting opposite Thassena's future queen, with whom he jested and teased so casually. He closed his book and reached for his satchel.

"Do we need to be in a church for the ritual?" he asked. Levanna shook her head.

"No, though I am sure the priestesses would argue the connection to the deities and Nerida would be stronger if we were. But I imagine it will be most effective wherever you are most comfortable." Kai held out his hand to her, and she slipped her fingers into his as he helped her to rise.

"To my quarters we go.

***

Kai's quarters were as she expected for someone employed by the King of Q'Ohar, though the books and journals scattered across the many surfaces of the room told her Kai had little regard for the luxurious life bestowed upon him. His rooms formed an entire floor in a building attached to the Embassy of Q'Ohar for royal residences. All royal families had one in the capital of each state. It seemed the King of Q'Ohar wished for his most prized citizens visiting Thassena to feel somewhat at home. Handwoven colourful rugs covered the traditional stone floor and matching chiffon curtains hung from the ceiling above the low-framed bed covered in silk sheets. Gold-framed paintings filled the wall at one end of the room, beside the window overlooking the royal gardens and the magnificent lake that sparkled every second of every day. Levanna placed down the crate, leaving her guards down at the doors with Q'Ohar's soldiers.

"I don't believe I have ever seen any soldiers guarding this residence before," Levanna said, shifting the curtain aside to peer at the back entrance to the residence, where a row of ten men, with perfectly trimmed beards, stood in their traditional garnet uniforms, complete with gold-capped shoulders.

"They're usually only around when someone is in residence," Kai said, rummaging through a wardrobe by the bed.

"I can't remember the last time I saw a royal from Q'Ohar visit. I met the Queen of Carvyre, but—" Levanna's words halted as she turned from the window to find Kai shrugging off his shirt. He draped it over the back of his desk chair. The moment from six months ago materialised—in the illusioned palace tunnel. She had felt his muscular build from the feel of his hard chest against her back, but seeing his bare skin and muscles was different.

"Sorry, I didn't realise you were—"

"That shirt was a little damp from the temperature," Kai said, combing his hand through his hair and removing his glasses. He buttoned up a new loose linen shirt. "I apologise. I cannot offer you something to change into." His eyes roamed over her dress. Her mother was asleep when she left that morning, meaning she had snuck out in something more comfortable. Not wanting to offend the prince should she bump into him, she had been somewhat mindful of royal decorum. The lavender gown was a light chiffon, the thinnest material possible, meaning the billowing cuffed sleeves were not as suffocating, though the high neckline was. She untied the gold-threaded rope around her waist that cinched in the dress, allowing air to flow over her stomach more freely to cool her. Levanna reached for two quills on Kai's desk and twisted her hair up.

"Ah, my favourite hairstyle," he said.

"Get on the bed," Levanna said. Kai stilled, his eyes widening. His mouth parted.

"I-uh—"

"You need to be lying down," Levanna clarified, "for the ritual."

"Right, yes, for the ritual," Kai blundered. A blush crept across his cheeks as he lay upon the silks, while Levanna approached with her crate of belongings. She had stopped at the church on the way. The priestess was torn between being polite, seeing as Levanna was future queen, and being standoffish; they hated the pedestal on which she was placed as the firstborn daughter expected to find Anela. Nevertheless, they had handed over the requested items.

Levanna placed three stones along Kai's body, one at the hollow of his throat, one on his heart, and one on his sternum.

"Each stone is taken from sacred water across Thassena: one from Dravos's lake, which he illusioned into a mirror so anyone might glance at their future, one from the Sirens Sea, where the deity Lailor was born, and one from the rivers of Aloro, representing the many visions a Seer will have in a lifetime and how they all will eventually interconnect." Levanna removed a sculpture of carved hands, cupped to hold water, which she pulled from the air to fill. She dipped a thumb into the pool and traced the symbol of Nerida on Kai's forehead before setting the sculpture at his feet. "We recognise the goddess that gifted us life through the creation of the deities. We place the water in her hands at your feet to symbolise you may walk these lands only because of her."

"I am not a child of Thassena, so that's not technically true," Kai said, his eyes closed.

"Well, this is the only way I know how to do it," Levanna tutted. She retrieved two candles next, a pillar of black and a pillar of white, and set each on either side of her where she knelt beside the bed. Before she could reach for the match, Kai waved a finger and lit the candles.

"That's the first time I've seen you use your power," she said.

"Flames are dangerous around books," he said. "What do they represent?" Levanna straightened and hovered one palm over Kai's midriff and the other over his forehead.

"They represent Sitara and Sonos," she whispered, beginning her deep breathing exercises.

"Not many people still give thanks to them; neither have been seen or heard of since the Great War," he said, though it seemed intended as a question.

"It is not a usual part of the ritual, but it is illogical for them not to be. We thank the deities for our life; we thank Nerida for the life she gave them; it makes sense to recognise the first celestial beings who gave us her as well as the first powerless mortals to grace the states. Power flows through the royal lines in death, and so that power likely flows through the lineage of the gods, even if they were created in part by the essence of their being rather than conceived and birthed naturally."

"Based on that logic, should you not also recognise Order and Chaos?" Kai asked. Levanna opened an eye and found him watching her.

"I wouldn't know what to use to represent them. They are a direct parallel of Sonos and Sitara, so we must hope this is enough," Levanna said, closing her eyes again. "Ready?" she asked. Kai's pinkie grazed her arm as a silent yes.

Levanna reached within her as she breathed deeply, recognising where each of her powers resonated. The well of water in the pit of her stomach, the tingle of her illusions over her chest, and the heavy weight of her visions across her forehead. She balanced her focus between all three and then zeroed in on the feeling on her forehead, searching for the light in her mind she believed was the essence of her Seer's power. When she found it, she expelled it through her body to her palm on Kai's forehead until it kissed his mind. Normally, she would stay like this for a while, focusing her breathing while her power washed over him, then she would withdraw and ask if his vision appeared. But instead, a different power reached out to her palm, planting kisses on her skin. A second later, Levanna's eyes rolled back in her head as a vision appeared.

Levanna watched a young boy, five at most, bouncing flames along the floor beside his bed in the darkness until a faint glow highlighted a woman standing by the window. She walked barefoot along the rug. The moonlight from the window shone on her dark skin, the flames at her feet illuminating the sparkle of her midnight gown. The woman perched on the edge of the bed as the flames bounced back toward the boy, a protective glow in his palms. The light reflected across the crown of stars on her forehead.

"Hello child," said Sitara, the Goddess of Dusk.

Chapter Six

Kai's small and frail body trembled as he pulled the silk sheets closer to his chin with one hand and held his flickering flame in the other.

"Do not be afraid," Sitara said; the softness of her voice seemed genuine, as if she did not intend to inflict pain upon the young boy. Sitara offered her hand, where dark wisps of shadows twisted around her wrist toward Kai's hand. Kai pushed back further against the headboard. "Do not be afraid," Sitara said again. Her shadows, hesitant, intertwined with Kai's flame, a dance of light and dark igniting sparks from his flame to bounce through the air like a performance at the evening shows his father held in the palace.

"See, there is nothing about darkness to fear," Sitara said, smiling. "It exists everywhere: in the shadows through the day, in the comfort of night. It is one with the very threads of the universe. See how it blends so beautifully with your flame, like it trusts you."

Kai slowly nodded, mesmerised by the joining of their powers.

"Who are you?" Kai asked. "Father said I am to shout if there is ever anyone in my rooms."

"Your father sounds sensible, but I think you know in here"—Sitara tapped his chest—"that you can trust me." Kai's shoulders relaxed while watching his flame. Sitara waved her hand, and the shadows retreated, forming the shape of a tiny dragon fluttering through the room.

"A dragon," Kai whispered, his eyes wide with wonder. "Have you seen one in real life?"

Sitara nodded. "They never leave Xyliar anymore, but there was *a time, long before the Great War, when they roamed Ithyion with their riders," Sitara said, separating the dragon into two smaller versions and guiding them in circles around the flame still burning on his palm.*

"Can you make a pegasus?" Kai asked, his voice playful as he relaxed opposite the goddess. A moment later, the two dragons merged into a spiral of shadows that reformed as the winged horse.

"Do you think you would like the ability to control shadows?" Sitara asked.

"I already have two powers. It's not heard of to have three," Kai said, bouncing his flame from one hand to the other.

"But if you could, would you like it?" she asked. Kai was silent for a while, his head tilted in far more contemplation than expected of a ten-year-old.

"It moves like fire. I think I could use it, but father doesn't like the power of Xyliar; he says it's dangerous."

"All power is dangerous, depending on who wields it," Sitara said. "Would you be dangerous? If you had all the power you could imagine?"

"I don't like hurting people." Kai frowned, his small mind already equating power with negativity. Sitara placed a palm against his cheek.

"That makes you vulnerable, child, but it also makes you the perfect choice for me," she said. "I need you to do something for me—"

Levanna's head throbbed as beads of sweat trickled down her temples and the nape of her neck. Kai had been right. This wasn't a dream or vision—it was a memory. She felt the difference. Dreams had a shimmering quality, while visions were sharp at their centre but blurred at the outer edges. This played out crystal-clear, as if she were there. Levanna tried to focus on the source of her power, to push it back into his memory, but the pain was becoming unbearable. Just when she thought she would have to give up, an image flashed in her mind—a woman she had glimpsed only once. The oracle, moments before she gifted Levanna the vision to find

Anela.

Birds chirped in the distant trees on the opposite side of the river glistening under the sun. Levanna peered down to find herself ankle-deep; the water twisted around her as it flowed downstream. She knew what came next in this vision; she walked downstream until it formed a waterfall until eventually the estuary opened into the ocean. Down below, she would see the river drake. Levanna paused. She had travelled all Thassena searching for this river, where, based on its width, it should be on a map, the native birds, the connection to a waterfall, but she had not found it yet. She had not recalled this vision since she was thirteen, and something about it was clearer now, encouraging her to slow down and take it all in.

A haze still blurred the corners of her vision, forcing her to turn slowly in a circle to catch the focus of the entire landscape. Only trees filled her vision, followed by the river reaching toward hills, then open fields behind her before she spun to face the drop of the waterfall. Levanna peered over the edge, and although she knew she was in her mind, her heart still raced at the uneven pebbles underfoot and the sheer drop below into the crashing water. Shimmers of iridescent blue scales shifted through the white foam of the waterfall, and Levanna held her breath as the river drake sprang free of it, spanning its wings as he glided over the water's surface. The sun bounced off his magnificence. A warbled cry sounded from his jaw before he tucked his wings in tight and dived back under the water. Levanna stared at the spot as he disappeared, yet there was no ripple. Instead, a shimmer refracted off the water. An illusion. Was that why she had found no such place on a map or across Thassena? Because the location in her vision was an illusion cast long ago and she needed to first find its true location.

Levanna stared into the distance, searching for a marker she knew existed. She raised her hand above her head, shielding the sun until her eyes fell on a collection of stones outside a cave in the distance. Levanna stepped off the edge of the waterfall and fell into the water. When she emerged, she was no longer in the waters of the illusion, nor in the cave she had been intent on reaching. Instead, Levanna stood on a ship staring down at the very same river drake. This had not been in her vision when she was thirteen. Something was focusing on her powers.

"Levanna!" Kai's voice cut through her. He should not be able to enter her mind in return. The ritual was only intended to work one way. "Levanna!" he called again. She looked up from the river drake in the open ocean and the blinding sun.

"Are you okay?" Kai asked. He rubbed her damp back as she panted, leaning forward with her hands shaking on the bed. Slowly, Levanna nodded.

"My body never usually reacts like this," she said between forced breaths. A flare of light forced her to turn her head. The white candle she had placed for Sonos burned far brighter than a normal candle. With a wave, she pulled water toward it, where it sizzled and extinguished. Her muscles relaxed, and Kai handed her a glass of water. The bed creaked as he shifted to sit before her, planting his legs wide. He gently rubbed her shoulders where she remained kneeling.

"Breathe, take all the time you need," he said in his usual soft lilt. Levanna tried to sift through her visions and his memory, but it was becoming hazy. Pieces fell away until all she could see of Kai's memory was Sitara on the bed before him.

"It wasn't a vision," Levanna said, looking up at him. She paused, struck by the concern in his eyes as he watched her. "It was a memory. Your subconscious is trying to bring forth a childhood memory." She sipped her water and watched the usual furrow of his brow return.

"Why would the Goddess of Dusk come to me as a child?" he asked, though Levanna had no answer. "I don't want to put you through that again to see more of it." He moved his hand from her shoulder along her neck before he pulled the quills from her hair and twisted his fingers through her curls.

"Did you know it isn't up to you?" she asked, attempting to coax a smile from him. It didn't work.

"Something within me cannot bear it. Watching you struggle physically pains me, and there's something there, something urging me to protect you from harm," Kai said. His bronze eyes roamed hers while he twisted one of her curls around his finger before brushing it over her cheek. Levanna leant into his touch, glancing at the mark of Nerida on his wrist, symbolising their tie. "It is as if I am a ship lost at sea, and your pain only pulls me further from the shore." His words drew her eyes back to his. Kai leant forward, forcing Levanna's head up to look at him.

"Perhaps you simply need a compass," Levanna whispered, unsure of how to respond to such sincerity. The intensity of his stare pulled at her, forcing her to move closer, as if she, too, was stranded and his presence offered her salvation.

"Perhaps you are my compass, the only thing I need to navigate this life," Kai whispered, brushing her lip with his thumb. The warmth of his skin lit a flame within, one she was not ready to unleash. Clearing her throat, she pulled back, only a breath, but enough for Kai to understand. He withdrew his hand.

"Speaking of directions," she said, internally cringing at her attempt to diffuse whatever lingered in the air between them. "I know where we need to go. It will help with my vision, but it is a sacred place. Another ritual on those grounds may pull the rest of your memories forward." While Kai pulled back when she stood, his stare still followed her, watching intently.

"Wherever you go, I'll follow. Lead the way, my compass."

Chapter Seven

There was something about dawn that always enraptured Levanna. Though she enjoyed looking up at the beautiful stars, she wasn't a night owl. Nothing compared to how every dawn brought with it a completely different palette of sunrise, with the clouds, or lack of, weaving a new and enchanting pattern across the skies. Not many points existed in the capital to watch the sunrise. It was too crowded, the sky a mere backdrop rather than the focal point of the painting. But here, camping at the edge of the olive groves, dawn was about to create a masterpiece.

Levanna crossed her legs and planted her palms on her knees, breathing deeply and slowly, as she watched the sky shift colour and thought of the god who had started it all, of the candle that had burned so brightly only two weeks ago when they began their ride across Thassena. In this day and age, the original celestial gods were so rarely worshipped by the masses. Even their children, the celestial four, were dwindling in favour of the deities who had a stronger bond with their people. Sightings of Dravos roaming Thassena were not uncommon, though many said he appeared lonely with Anela missing and Lailor bound to the sea. It was why finding Anela was so important. Levanna wondered if the other deities from the other states were involved in the lives of their people. If Stroman roamed Asynthos in desperate search of new Stormbringers since their curse began, or if Carlisle, the deity of Shapeshifters, mourned those trapped in their bodies. If Levanna was not so preoccupied with finding Anela and breaking the curse on the Sirens of Thassena, she might have spent more time studying their lands and why they became cursed. Had they angered someone? Who was punishing them?

"Did you know I'm beginning to like mornings? My father would not believe someone could change that about me," Kai murmured as he emerged from his tent and sat down beside Levanna. He passed her a steaming mug. "With lemon, just as you like it." He smiled.

"What is it about the night that you prefer?" Levanna asked, blowing gently on the mug before having a sip. She smiled as the perfect amount of tart lemon washed over her tongue.

"Perhaps it is because of my powers. My flame shines brightest in the dark," he said.

"By that logic, I should worship the moon for its control over the ocean."

"Perhaps not everything requires logic," Kai said, turning his head to face her. The rising sun cast a glow over his brown skin and a glare over the edge of his glasses as he watched her.

"That's not very scholarly of you," Levanna jested, nudging his shoulder with her own. "Though I suppose you may be right. There is no logic to explain the connection of our paths." Levanna turned back to watch the sun; she was unaccustomed to sharing her feelings. Feelings seemed dangerous if she were to indeed marry Prince Theon. Rustling sounded from behind, signalling that her guards had dismantled their camp to begin the final stretch of their journey. It would take them most of the day on horseback, following the river past Dravos lake until they reached their destination—the edge of the Crimson mountains, the site of the first Illusionist's sacrifice, more commonly named for the way the sunrise occasionally cast a red glow against the rock, said to be a sign of prosperity for the coming week.

***

Power has always had a brutal past. Regardless of whether the Seers were perceived as the purest or most devout of the three races in Thassena, that devotion had cruel roots. When Nerida created her daughters and son—Anela, Lailor, and Dravos—they did not know of the powers bestowed upon them; neither did Nerida nor her siblings. Perhaps if they had, they never would have created the deities at all. Anela's discovery of her power was a tragic one. She had lived three hundred years with no awareness of it, other than aiding Nerida in nurturing the mortals Sonos and Sitara gifted them and wielding water almost as powerful as her goddess. She did nothing else. She devoted her time to helping others, those who struggled to find their place in the world, which was how she sometimes felt, while her sisters grew into their power.

Anela led a group on a six-month trek across Thassena, ending at the mountains, where they would climb and finish their trip at the peak. A journey of self-discovery. On the final night before the mountain climb, the group's camp was invaded by two men from a nearby village. They hadn't expected the women to fight back. In self-defence, Anela stabbed one of the men, spilling his blood across the circle of rocks the woman had used to sit and reflect. A moment later, she had her first vision, though to this day, nobody knows what it was. Anela never killed again. The blood on her hands was enough to keep her on her path of kindness. But upon the awakening of her powers, and the story of what she had done moments before, others sought the location of the stones, making sacrifices in her name to awaken their own powers. It was only when she went missing that the hundreds of women she helped formed the Pathos Priestesses, named after the word for palm in the old language, offering guiding hands to turn people from sacrifice to prayer.

Levanna stared down at the circle of rocks; though the bloodstains were long faded with the rain and sun, the trauma remained. It saturated the air, a sense of sorrow and foreboding. Hugging herself, Levanna waited for her guards to finish setting up camp.

"If you are too tired to attempt the ritual tonight, we can wait until morning," Kai said, approaching quietly from behind. "Perhaps proceeding at dawn will help to calm your mind." Levanna nodded slowly as he placed his hand on her arm; she leant into him, and the weight of the pain soaked into the land was heavy on her chest.

Levanna was quiet as she ate with her guards and Kai before excusing herself. Despite the astronomical change in times, she felt tainted by the actions of her ancestors. The stars watched, blinking silently in the night, as the clouds shifted so the moon became her observer. The walk to the nearest river was not far and gave Levanna time to ponder how this site connected to the illusion in her vision. Visions always presented themselves exactly as the future; so, at some point, Levanna would walk through a river and jump into the depths of a waterfall. But she was unclear how to locate the illusion of the river and waterfall, and what it hid away. She tilted her head to the moon behind, the mountains looming high. A vantage point. Perhaps the illusion of the river and waterfall was somewhere in the mountains.

The gentle ripple of water attempted to centre her as she approached the decline of the riverbank and the water brushing the pebbles. Still, she heard the laughter of the men and the glow of their campfire. She knew the broad figure standing at the edge was Radian, who watched the forest line on the other side of the river for danger while the bank provided her with privacy. The night breeze kissed her skin as she slid the robe from her body, leaving her in a thin white slip that floated up and around her knees as she waded into the slow-moving river.

Silently, Levanna counted to three and braced for the cold as she lowered below the surface. Five minutes of counting went by, and Levanna allowed herself to breathe in her connection to the water, her midnight blue eyes glowing under the moonlit river. The waters were quiet, with no fish in sight, no crustaceans shifting the pebbles where she knelt. Just peace. Silence. In the distance, something dark shifted before a light shimmer replaced it. Levanna squinted, wondering if that was the gateway to her vision, the illusion she had seen. Saying farewell to the calm, she rose from the riverbed and pushed back her wet hair, blinking back the water on her lashes.

"I was starting to question at what point I should be worried." Levanna smiled, having become used to the quiet way he approached her without her realising. He sat perched on the edge of the riverbank, watching her glow under the moonlight.

"You did not need to worry. I have stayed under for hours before," she said, squeezing the water from her white curls, which only glowed brighter under the moon.

"When it comes to you, I always worry."

"Why?" Levanna cocked her head and wrapped her arms around herself, her damp skin beginning to prickle at the cold.

"Because I fear, after the last six months, I cannot envisage life without you in it." Kai's bronze eyes glowed brightly as he directed his hand, and the temperature of the water rose to a comfortable heat.

"Kai," she whispered. "I cannot—"

"I know you are promised to another, Levanna," Kai said, rising from the riverbank in his loose linen shirt and trousers. He was not tentative in his steps toward her as he entered the river. "But we—or I, at least—cannot tiptoe around whatever is between us."

"It is the tie, that is all," Levanna said, suddenly conscious of her sheer dampened shift.

"Did you know I think you're lying to yourself?" Kai whispered, finally standing opposite her. Levanna did not look up. She knew if she met those eyes she would be forced to confront that he was indeed right. "But even if you are content with lying to yourself, I am not. I cannot lie about the fact you consume my every waking moment and bless my every dream. I cannot lie and deny that I was drawn to you from the moment you walked through that library, the fire in your temper toward me burning as brightly as my intrigue." Kai's hands were slow as he slid them up her arms, her skin tingling under his touch. Branches cracking in the treeline made her jump, made her aware of how out in the open they truly were, but Kai stopped her from turning to look. "I cannot lie and say I do not think of that moment in my rooms, when I so badly wanted to replace my thumb grazing your lips with my own." Levanna's breathing hitched as his hands slid along her neck to cradle the sides of her face, his thumbs dangerously close to her lips again. "I cannot lie, Levanna, because I think I am falling in—"

"Don't," Levanna cried, finally looking up into those bronze eyes. "Don't say it." Her eyes began to water. "Because if you say it, I will have to spend my entire marriage knowing I could have had you if I had not been born with the Zerpane name." A tear trailed down her cheek, caught by Kai's thumb as his brow furrowed. He leant down, his forehead touching hers. "Don't say it, because I know I can never truly have you." She slid her hands over then under his arms until they rested on his chest, where she felt the loud thumping of his heart, beating only for her.

"You have me, Levanna. I am yours whenever you ask, from now until your wedding, and every day after that. If you call, I will come." Levanna clenched her eyes shut as their foreheads rested against one another, the river lapping around their waists. This was what her destiny deprived her of, what her family name and her place in power kept from her. Whether or not she found Anela and her love, she would be expected to marry. Deep down, she knew it to be true. Even if she lifted the curse on Thassena, there was no chance the royal family would give up the chance to join the two oldest lineages in the state. Even if Levanna did everything expected of her, she would still lose the only thing, outside of her freedom, that she had ever wanted. Him.

So, with the moon as their only witness, Levanna said, "What if I asked for only tonight?"

Kai let out a ragged breath as she slid her hands up his chest and around the back of his neck. She had never done this before; she had never been kissed or even this close to a man. Nor had she ever felt like this. Kai lifted his head from where it rested on hers. Kai was just as soft, as gentle, as slow and considerate in this moment as he was in every other. He stroked her cheek and lowered his lips to hers. Levanna had read about fiery passion, about hunger and need, but this felt more than that. She felt the words he wished to say, those she had forbidden, as he kissed her. Levanna clutched his hair as he hunched over her, guiding her lips to part, as she tentatively kissed him back. Then she realised where the need came from, the desperation of passion as the sparks between their skin lit something within her.

"If you ask for only tonight," Kai said. His breathing was rushed as she brought his lips back down to hers, pushing their bodies closer. His hands roamed the sheer wet fabric of her slip, and Levanna gasped as his hands hooked under her thighs, lifting her above the water until she wrapped her legs around his waist. "Then I will savour it as though it is our last night together."

Chapter Eight

Kai's kiss was gentle on Levanna's shoulder before he walked around her and laid in the centre of the rock circle. A blush crept across her cheeks as she thought of where else his lips had been in the river the night prior. The evening had intended to help with her mental clarity before today's ritual, but instead, her mind was filled with images of him, the feel of him.

"We won't get anywhere today if you cannot focus," he said with a sigh of contentment. Placing his hands on his thighs, he closed his eyes under the rising sun. A rustle from the treeline behind the river drew her attention; it felt like she was being watched.

"Who said I wasn't focused?" Levanna asked, leaning over him to place the pebbles on his forehead, his heart, and his sternum.

"Call it a sixth sense," he murmured, and she caught him watching her lips. She called on the water to fill the cupped statue hands and repeated the motions of painting the symbol of Nerida on his forehead before placing the statue at his feet. Her hands paused as she held the black and white candle, staring at the representation of Sonos. She wondered if completing this ritual at dawn would increase her connection.

"I'm focused," she insisted as Kai lit the candles, and she searched for her power while keeping her palm hovering above his forehead. There was no slow build this time as power rushed up to meet her palm and colours filled her mind.

***

Levanna recognised the bright hallways as a booming voice followed Kai down them: "Do not fail me," they said. "I'm telling you. If the Sorcerers' records are right, that sword will change everything."

"I understand!" Kai bellowed, a tone Levanna had never heard from him. The other man continued talking, but his voice faded as Kai continued down bright orange-tiled hallways until crossing an archway that led onto a terrace filled with leafy plants.

"Is my father making demands again?" a delicate voice asked. Levanna recognised her immediately, the only royal of Q'Ohar she had met. Then she realised why she recognised the hallways. The memory was between Kai and Princess Kazeema of Q'Ohar in the palace of Sahrih. The rumour across the state was that the Queen of Q'Ohar had summoned a Sorcerer in Eresydon to curse the king so he might never bear a son, though nobody knew why, a tale that was proven by his lineage being only Princess Kazeema. After her birth, the queen moved to quarters in Tamzi and sent the king a new son from a different man every few years to taunt him. Levanna was certain the only reason he kept them in the palace was because, deep down, he could not bear to pass his crown to a woman.

The princess was perched on the edge of a fountain, placing petals in an intricate pattern. Her saree was the same blush shade as the petals, highlighting the beautiful glow of her brown skin and her long, braided black hair. The henna on her hands formed patterns Levanna could analyse for hours.

"When isn't he?" Kai sighed, sitting down beside her with his head in his hands. "He wants me to journey across the states. He mentioned something about—"

The memory shifted, forcing Levanna away from the significance of the sword to the King of Q'Ohar and why Kai had omitted it from his personal reasons relating to his dream of Sitara. The next memory was older; Kai was younger, perhaps sixteen, but his glasses were still unmistakable as he clenched his fists at a desk before a whip of fire came down inches in front of his fingertips.

"What did I tell you about flinching?" a voice asked, though Lev-

anna never saw his face. *"This is a lesson in control, in keeping your emotions in check so you may master your powers more effectively."*

"Yes, father." Kai sniffed, and Levanna was filled with rage at his father's mistreatment of him.

"Shift," the voice commanded. Tears filled Kai's eyes, and he bit his lip so hard blood welled. He clenched his fists tighter until a waft of smoke trickled from his hand, wrapping around his arms until his body became one with the clouds of smoke which flickered with sparks of burning ash. He spiralled into a plume until reappearing on the other side of the room. A single clap filled the room, which darkened into the nighttime scene she had already witnessed. Kai was a Smokeshifter. She recalled the hazy memory where, as a child, he had mentioned two powers, but Levanna had not been able to previously recall the details after her mental exhaustion. Before she could watch the scene play out, a blinding light filled her mind, and two women she had never seen before lay in a field of deep red flowers, their heads turned toward one another. Magnificent wings of grey and lavender splayed across the grass beneath them.

"Did you mean it? When you said you would never let me fall?" asked the woman with lilac wings. *"Because every day I think I fall further and further into the darkness of my mind."* The dark-haired woman turned onto her side to face the other, their wings cocooning them in their own private sanctuary.

"I meant it," she said.

The vision faded as quickly as it had materialised, placing Levanna back in Kai's memory with Sitara. She watched the scene unfold, waiting for the moment it cut off.

"That makes you vulnerable, child, but it also makes you the perfect choice for me," she said. *"I need you to do something for me. I need you to keep something safe for me."* Kai nodded, more eagerly this time, won over by Sitara's charm and games with her dark powers. She pulled out his right arm and turned his palm to face her; his left hand still lit the room with his flames.

"This will pinch a little," Sitara murmured, pulling a small onyx

dagger from thin air and tracing a delicate line down Kai's forearm. "Shhh," Sitara hummed as Kai began to cry out; he did not flinch. "You won't remember this until you're close to your counterpart," Sitara said. She pulled from above her heart, and a pulsing essence slithered free, a thin thread that glowed brighter than the flame in Kai's hand. "But when you do, you will be drawn to one another, and once you have merged your essences into one, it will be time for the next step." Sitara guided the glowing thread down to Kai's arm until it melted into his blood and the cut sealed closed. "But first, you will need to find Levanna Zerpane."

***

The sun beat down on Levanna as she gasped for air and opened her eyes. Her body trembled, but this time with betrayal and rage, not exhaustion. The pebbles laid out on Kai's body fell as he rushed to push himself up, but Levanna was faster, nimbler. She rushed backward, keeping a sacrificial rock between them as she called on the water from the river nearby and raised defensive whips before her.

"You lied to me." She intended it to come out as a rage-filled yell, but it was more of a hurt whisper. Her guards caught wind of the change in demeanour, and the four of them ran toward her, swords raised. Behind the river, a war cry sounded from the trees as ten men came careering toward them, uncaring about the water as they rushed forward, outnumbering Levanna's men. Her eyes widened in panic, but Kai did not flinch as they ran past him and toward her guards.

"You brought guards with you from the city? From Q'Ohar?" she yelled, lunging her water toward him. She missed by an inch. Still, he did not flinch.

"Levanna, please listen to me."

"Listen to you?" she yelled, launching her power at him again.

This time he was forced to counter the whip of water as it reached his shoulder, flames bursting free from his hands and wrapping around the whips. He tugged before his flame could sizzle out at the contact, and she stumbled, releasing the power to form a new weapon. Three spears of water hovered at her side. "What could you possibly have to say? You lied about why you were here!"

"I didn't lie!" he yelled back; flames licked at his palms. "I told you I was here to understand my dreams."

"You failed to mention the part that specifically involved hunting me down." Levanna sneered, propelling a spear of water toward him as her guards' swords battled in sync with their wielding of water. "Or that the king sent you on a mission to find some stupid sword." She threw the second spear, but it dissipated against the flame. Levanna circled the stones, with Kai mirroring her on the other side. While she was poised to attack, he was stiff, as though every part of this interaction pained him. Liar. Manipulator. It was all an act. "Was last night a lie as well?" Levanna asked, her voice cracking as she pulled all her power from the well of all three in her lineage and hurled it toward Kai, who looked like he was breaking. He was forced to retaliate, his power meeting her fury in a blinding flash of white light. Bracing her feet in the grass, Levanna struggled to stay upright as she forced her power forward. The glow where their powers met grew and grew until threads of white light, resembling the essence Sitara had pulled from herself, began crawling along their lines of power, reaching toward one another. Levanna did not trust it; she trusted nothing. He was a liar. She dodged to the side as she released her power, and when Kai stumbled, she struck again, forcing him back through the air until he collided with the side of the mountain face. The rock cracked and crumbled, revealing the entrance to a cave.

"Your Majesty!" a guard shouted. Levanna turned to find her guards panting on the floor with blades at their necks. A guard sprinted toward Kai.

"Your..." Levanna trailed off, recalling the memories in the palace of Kai with the princess, the only true-blooded heir of Q'Ohar; the others all gifted a place in the palace, sired by different men.

"Your Majesty," the guards said again, helping Kai to his feet as he clutched his chest.

"Kai," Levanna said with realisation. "Kaigon Elharar," she said, her blood beginning to boil. "You're the crown prince of Q'Ohar."

Chapter Nine

Emptiness overcame Levanna as a click sounded from behind. Silvery-white, metal cuffs encased her hands. She reached for her power yet felt nothing—no call to her water, no way of freeing herself or her guards cuffed at her side. Tungstyn metal. The guard tugged on her arm.

"Don't touch her," Kai said, his tone clipped. The guard released Levanna immediately, though it made no difference when she could not reach her power. "We need to talk," Kai said, rubbing his chest and looking at his feet.

"Did you know you're a coward?" Levanna spat. When Kai looked up at her, she tried to read the expression in his eyes and decipher his motives for lying. What else had she missed? He turned and walked into the cave. Beside her, a guard in his blood-red uniform with a gold sash extended his arm, indicating for her to follow the prince into the darkness. She scowled before obliging, glancing down at Kai's blood spilled on the sacrificial stones as she entered the mouth of the cave.

Levanna had only ever met the King of Q'Ohar twice. Once when he visited Thassena when they hosted the annual meeting of the rulers. The second, when her betrothal to Prince Theon was announced, forcing her to attend a tour of the states, wasting her precious time. On the latter occasion, she had met Princess Kazeema. More time together might have led to a friendship between the two, something Levanna could say about very few people in her short lifetime so far. As the only two of the same age, they had been forced to have tea together while Theon met with the princes of the state. Now, she knew that would have included Kai. It explained why he had avoided the prince in the palace. Did Theon know the crown prince of Q'Ohar was in Thassena? Somebody had to, despite his credentials claiming he was simply a scholar and not the first male heir to the Elharar throne.

Staring at Kai, his face cast in the cave's shadows, she wondered who his biological father was. His demeanour was soft and gentle, rather unlike the fiery nature of the princess or the unforgiving king, or so the tales said. Did he inherit that nature from his mother? Or his sire? Regardless of who birthed him, it seemed he had been raised in the king's image—his kindness a façade, his true nature ruthless. How else could he explain his lies to Levanna?

"Did you know—"

"Don't do that," Levanna said. Kai pursed his lips. "Do not act as though this is any other normal conversation between us, as if we are sitting opposite one another in a library instead of standing in a dark cave, you with a wound on your chest and me in cuffs." Levanna was breathless as she spoke, trying to shield her tears and pain with fury.

"I was going to tell you eventually," Kai said.

"When?" Levanna asked. "When I walked down the aisle to my future husband and saw you sitting with Q'Ohar's royal family? When you were introduced at my reception dinner as the crown prince?" Kai flinched, the usual furrow of his brow returning.

"Sitara told me I was to find you, so when my father simply sent me away to hunt for a sword, I used it as an excuse to start in Thassena." Kai leant back against the cave wall. "The dream only returned to me a year ago, so I knew who you were—a Seer betrothed to Prince Theon. I knew it would be easy to find you."

"You can't possibly believe that Sitara genuinely has some great need for us?" Levanna forced a laugh and shifted on her feet.

"The sword my father wanted me to look for was created for someone in Xyliar. Sitara created the first deity in Xyliar, Makaria. So, with the sword being linked to her lineage, and the memory returning of her telling me to find you, I thought the two were connected, and that perhaps we were destined for something."

"Destined?" Levanna sneered. "She put the essence of herself inside you as a child and told you to find me. That is not destiny, Kai; that is by design." She shook her head in disbelief. This man, this *prince*, was so disillusioned to think she would help him.

"You don't understand what it is like, Levanna. To grow up in a household with no proper family except for a sister, who is not entirely your sister by blood. To be viewed as a tool by a man forced to become your father and spend every day of your existence trying to find ways to be useful, so you might one day be granted freedom to…"

"To what?"

"To find a different path and navigate a new direction in life; to find and feel the love you were deprived of as a child." As Kai's voice picked up, Levanna saw flashes of the king who raised him. The king with his short temper and disdain for his adopted sons.

"And if you had been honest with me from the beginning, perhaps you might have had that," Levanna whispered. Kai strode forward, and his eyes pained when she flinched.

"I still value every second of our time together. I meant what I said last night. Ask me to take you with me to Q'Ohar, and I'll do it. Ask me to run away with you to the forests of Eresydon, and I will ready a ship. Ask me to stay hidden in the shadows of the city, only to be called upon when your husband has gone to sleep, and I will be there to worship you, if only for an hour. Just ask me," Kai said, reaching to cup her cheek.

"It's a good thing you savoured last night as if it was our last," Levanna whispered. Kai bit his lip and nodded slowly, his bronze eyes fixed on hers as he backed away.

"I cannot let you return to the capital," Kai said, locking his hands behind his head. He stared up at the dark roof of the cavern. Levanna's heart raced as she looked around the small dark space. "Tensions have been high between Thassena and Q'Ohar ever since your mother's betrothed was murdered. If the attack had not happened on Asynthos, then war may well have already started. They will see this as a hidden invasion, a search for a weapon to use against them and the other states."

"Kai..." Levanna began as he started pacing.

"Why can't you just believe what I am telling you, Levanna? I have no dark motive. I am simply doing as I was asked."

"And what if your father wants that weapon to wage war? Would you ask me to trust you then?" She tilted her head. Kai screwed up his face, resting his hands on the cave wall.

"It's one sword; he doesn't want it for war."

"But if he did? If it could do something more than act just as a sword?"

"We cannot deal in what-ifs, Levanna, not when I have already presented you with other options, ones where I abandon my duty for you. You cannot ask me to do the same in the name of your state when you will not allow me to in the name of you. You cannot pick and choose the ways I do or do not obey my duty to my father, to my state."

"So, your duty means more?"

"If I do not have you, Levanna, then my duty is all I have left." Kai's voice cracked. Levanna wanted to believe him and to say yes to all his alternatives, perhaps a scenario in which they simply ran away together.

"I have a duty too, to my deities, my goddess, my state, my marriage." Levanna raised her chin, and Kai slowly nodded.

"Then I cannot let you leave, not until I know what to do with you."

"What? Your logic makes no sense!" Levanna exclaimed as Kai walked back toward the cave entrance. Panic roared inside her as she tried to reach for a scrap of power to help her escape and return to the capital, to inform Prince Theon of Q'Ohar's hidden agendas and continue with her hunt to fulfil her vision. A wall of fire blazed up to her knees as she tried to follow Kai toward the sacrificial stones. Her guards all knelt, cuffed, with blades still to their necks. They looked her over, searching for injuries; disappointment marred their expressions for failing to keep her safe.

"Kai, you cannot just leave me here!" she yelled. "It may be a long walk, but I can find my way to the next village. I know these lands far better than you." Kai halted in the circle of stones and turned back to face her, his brow furrowed.

"I will take your guards to Q'Ohar, speak with my father, and return for you in two weeks." He tossed the bags from their tents, along with the extras she assumed had come with the guards from Q'Ohar, into the mouth of the cave. He wasn't listening to her.

"You can't just—"

"I can!" he yelled, and Levanna shut her mouth. "I can," he said, softer this time. "If I let you go right now, we risk a war between our states."

"I won't tell anyone!" Levanna tried to beg, tears streaming down her cheeks.

"I'll be back for you in two weeks," Kai said again. He tossed the keys to the cuffs through the flames and twisted his hands, his fingers bent at rigid angles. Levanna watched as she scrambled for the keys, confused when his eyes blazed with power. Slowly, silver liquid seeped from the sacrificial stones, from the edge of the mountains, from the earth itself, as Kai pulled on the earth's natural metal. Slowly, the drops and plumes merged into one until Kai raised a wall in front of the cave.

"Kai!" Levanna screamed. "Kai, please don't leave me here!" she lodged the key into the cuffs as the wall of molten metal solidified. It seemed Levanna was not the only one with more than two powers. Kai was not only a Smokeshifter with the gift of Keres' fire; he was a Forger.

Chapter Ten

Three months later

The glint of the green gems in the stone tunnels was a welcome and familiar sight. The Cave of Anela. She was near it; she could sense it. Three months, and perhaps Levanna would finally see the light of day again. The first two weeks inside the cave that had opened in the side of the Crimson mountains had been torture. Constantly counting, trying to guess the hours, how much time had passed. On the first night, while staring up at the dark cave ceiling, she spotted a small white glow. A sliver of the moon in the outside world. She used that to track the time spent there. When fourteen nights passed, she expected Kai's return. He did not. Another fourteen nights followed without a sign from him. It was then she realised he had told another lie. He had left her there to die.

But Levanna had a vision to fulfil, and that kept her going. The knowledge she must escape to bring about the future she saw with the river drake. She had rationed her food, but with her supply of dried meats and nuts dwindling to nothing, she knew she had to find a way out. Having exhausted so much energy during the first few days in the cave— discovering her power did nothing against the metal wall—she needed to conserve what strength remained. Fumbling around in the darkness had eventually led her to a narrow gap, barely wide enough for her to fit through sideways, but after a month of rations, it proved no problem as she forced herself through, dragging her bag behind her.

She counted as she went, estimating the time it took. After thirty minutes, the gap narrowed, but she smelt water. There had been enough moisture in the cave walls to draw from to drink, but there was more here. Finally, she called on her power again and propelled it toward the narrowed gap, trying to slowly carve at the rock face until it widened. If she were a royal with the power of countless ancestors, she might have managed it in the first cave opening, but her true strength was in her visions, which was of little help here. Her determination paid off as she slid further through the rock face, the gap widening enough for her to quit shuffling and stride forward with more ease. She had to have walked for days until the trickle of water reached her ears and the moisture on the walls heightened. Eventually, her swaying body conveyed her exhaustion; she had been walking for far too long.

But then, her feet were wet. Puddles. Her palms scraped the cave walls as she stumbled, eventually reaching a small stream hidden within the mountains. The water was refreshing as Levanna fell to her knees, scooping it between her hands and drinking in rushed sips. When movement in the water caught her eye, she knew she would survive. A diet of fish and water seemed plenty normal for a daughter of Thassena.

Levanna rested, regaining her strength before pressing onward, following the stream until it became a river, until cracks in the rock gave way to splinters of light. She swam each day, pausing to rest and sleep in hollowed-out shelves in the mountain walls. Then, one day, she found herself here, in the familiar glow of green. The Caves of Anela. She knew then months had passed. The Caves of Anela were to the east of Thassena; the sacrificial spot had been on the west. Levanna had weaved in and amongst the mountains for months, and now she tasted freedom.

"Now, this is unusual," an ethereal voice echoed down the tunnel. Levanna followed it, retracing her steps to the spot where, a decade earlier, she had stood. The place where the oracle gifted

Levanna with the vision she still, even now, desperately chased.

"Do you appear differently every time?" Levanna asked, her feet sinking into the sand. She watched the redheaded woman carefully.

"It would appear so, but I only get to plant my feet on the sands with each new first daughter of Zerpane, but never the same one twice," said the oracle.

"Perhaps the universe knows I am close to failing and has granted me a second chance to see more of my vision," Levanna said hopefully. The oracle smiled, though it was a pitiful one. "It would have been nice to have seen the part where I was betrayed and stuck within the mountains for months." A bitterness entered Levanna's voice, despite it not being the oracle's fault.

"But then you would not have experienced the greatest love of your life. You would have gone in hesitant, already knowing his true self." The oracle leant back against the rock pool.

"Thank you for confirming I'll never find love again," Levanna mumbled, and the oracle averted her eyes.

"I've never gifted more than one vision in here," she said.

Levanna shrugged. "There's a first time for everything."

"You're very nonchalant for someone meeting the oracle for the second time in a lifetime."

"I suppose my wonder at fate and its visions has made me weary, given how little I have uncovered in the last ten years. I am supposed to be the greatest Seer of my generation and yet, outside of my vision of the river drake, I have been gifted only one other."

"Do you mind me asking what it was?" asked the oracle. Levanna sighed and planted herself beside the woman.

"Two Angels who appeared to be in love," Levanna said almost wistfully. The oracle hummed.

"Interesting. No other vision?"

"Only memories belonging to another."

"Perhaps we should change that," the oracle said, standing. The shimmering white hem of her gown brushed the sand as she turned to face Levanna. She reached for her hands instead of her temples and closed her eyes. Levanna followed suit. *There was no flash of light, no hazy edges in her vision. So, she opened her eyes. But instead of gazing upon the red-headed oracle, she saw her pin-straight, black hair as she stood to watch a ten-year-old Levanna walk away. But as the oracle faded, another woman took her place, one Levanna had already seen in a memory.*

"Wait, child," Sitara called. Levanna had no memory of this, but her younger self turned. "I wish to give you another gift."

"You've changed your appearance again," Levanna commented, assuming the goddess to still be the oracle who had just gifted her the vision of the river drake.

"When you live as long as I do, appearances grow boring," Sitara said with a playful smile. Levanna approached her without fear. Sitara knelt until sand coated the darkness of her gown. She reached for Levanna's arm. "This will help you with your vision and who you need to find," she said. Levanna's eyes lit up, assuming she referenced Anela and the river drake, but the older Levanna watching knew she meant Kai. She anticipated what came next. But instead of tugging from her heart, Sitara pulled a glowing vial from thin air. "This is the essence of the only love I've ever known, and it will help us both find who we need," Sitara whispered before swiftly slicing Levanna's skin. She cried out and tried to run, but Sitara held her tightly until the golden essence merged under her skin and into her blood. When she let go, she faded, and a hazy look coated Levanna's childhood eyes, erasing the moment. As the young girl turned and ran from the tunnel, light faded into the cave.

Levanna took a large gulp of air as the oracle stepped back and rested her hands on Levanna's shoulders.

"Now that was no vision either," she murmured.

"Some Seer, I guess," Levanna breathed in again. "You see all. What do you see about the goddess' intentions?" Levanna tried to determine if it linked to her vision of the river drake or if she was simply caught up in some god's game.

"I cannot tell you what her intentions are. I only see the many threads of fate that could unfold, depending on the decisions made."

"Would any of them alter my vision?" Levanna asked. The same sadness from before overcame the oracle, and Levanna wondered just how many dark events she saw in the future.

"I can show you what might happen if you try to alter your vision," the oracle said, glancing nervously around as though someone might rescind her power for the offer. Levanna nodded.

"Show me." She lunged forward to grip the oracle's hands.

***

The moon was full in the sky, shining down on the grey stone rooftop. Snow fell lightly on Levanna's bare shoulders and did not melt instantly, instead painting her skin the same colour as the lace white gown she wore. Her hands were intertwined with Kai's. He contrasted her in a black tailored jacket and cloak. Before them, reading from an old book, was a tall man with angular features, light stubble, and dark hair. Levanna's eyes were drawn to the scars on his arms as she smiled, a ripple of applause beginning from the guests on the rooftop as Levanna and Kai kissed in front of the altar. Bands of gold glinted on their ring fingers. Shadows began to swirl around their feet, and Levanna's smile wavered before tendrils of white light tentatively twisted from beneath her gown and danced with the shadows. Slowly but surely, the light and dark merged until a faint orb floated between the married couple as their essences merged and the power crept back toward each of them along the threads. Kai pulled Levanna into an embrace, and her eye caught the man. Black began to bleed into the whites of his eyes.

***

The wind rushed past Levanna's face, threatening to tug her hair free from its quills as she gripped the scales of the dragon's back harder. It felt unnatural; she should not be so high above the oceans. Behind her, Kai's arm wrapped tighter around her middle, steadying Levanna in her seat. He planted a kiss on her shoulder, but it felt cold.

Roars sounded around them, and the dark cloud they were in blew away to reveal a sea of black. Not the ocean they had just flown over, but a herd of dragons, deformed winged creatures, and Xyliarian Fae with leathered wings, intent on the destination ahead. Levanna's eyes watered. She did not know what land they were approaching. Not because she had never been, she knew by the blue of the ocean and the pattern of the waves that they had crossed a part of Ouro Ocean. She did not know the land because it was entirely up in flames. Buildings, trees, bodies all burned as screams tore through the sky.

***

"Is that enough to keep you on your course?" the oracle asked. Levanna frowned as she steadied herself in the sand.

"If I try to change my vision and reunite with Kai, something causes a dark power to overcome us and Ithyion?" The oracle's face was sad, her smile sympathetic, as though Levanna had mistakenly interpreted parts of the paths.

"You know I cannot answer that. I have already revealed too much. You are never meant to see what *could* be, only what will be." The oracle backed away. Levanna recalled Sitara asking Kai if he would like to control the same power she possessed. Was that her plan? Gifting Kai with her power through the essence planted in him? Did that mean... Levanna peered down at her palms and recalled the light tendrils as she watched herself marry Kai. Everything needed a balance. Did Sonos' power run through her veins? A light that could balance Kai's? Or one that could be completely snuffed out, like those brief threads of fate had shown.

"Levanna?"

She froze. When she looked up from her palms, the oracle was gone, and the very man she wished never to see again stood in one of the carved archways. He seemed different. His colourful shirt was gone, replaced with a black velvet and cloak. His glasses were no longer on the bridge of his nose, and his eyes appeared more hollow.

"You left me," Levanna whispered. "You left me to die."

"I didn't mean to."

Chapter Eleven

Emotions thickened the air in the cave, rife with fury, confusion, and desperation. Levanna was conflicted by the need to run and embrace Kai. Despite all he had done, the strings of her heart tugged her to him.

"I went to the sacrificial stones, but you were not there."

"More than a few weeks late." Levanna crossed her arms, trying to protect her emotions and her heart from lunging out of her chest.

"I can explain," he said.

"I don't want your excuses; I want to leave," Levanna snapped, raising her chin. Slowly, Kai crossed the sands, and Levanna stopped herself from backing up as shadows seeped from his skin. "What did you do?" she whispered, watching the way the tendrils of darkness twisted toward her, stroking her skin, coaxing her to let him in, to forgive him. Levanna thought of the vision she'd been shown, the darkness that overwhelmed Ithyion, the destruction. Was that all him?

"I went to Q'Ohar to speak with my father. He said he would allow me to bring you back to the state and hide you in the palace." His shadows reached to stroke her cheek. They felt so much like his hand. She would not say yes to that plan. A prisoner in someone else's home did not differ from the prison of her marriage. "But first I was to travel to Eresydon. He heard that someone there could find the sword he wanted. It was there that my eyes were opened." Kai's bronze eyes were dull as they widened. There was something unfamiliar and hazy about them now.

"And what did you see?" Levanna asked, keeping him talking while she tried to determine a way out of the caves without him following.

"He promised me that, with my power, I would not need my father's permission to bring you to Q'Ohar, that the Prince of Thassena would rescind his marriage to you and my power would force people to give me whatever I wanted, including you."

"Who is he?" Levanna asked, allowing him to step closer until his real hands stroked her cheeks. She tried not to flinch at how unusually cold he was. Memories of them in the river came flooding back—his gentle but desperate touch, the sweetness of his words.

"All I have to do is bring you to him."

Levanna reared back, and the shadows fell away, retreating into Kai's skin. "I'm not going anywhere with you! Not to meet someone who has planted such ideas of power in your mind," she said, the fury returning to her voice. Kai's eyes hardened, his jaw clenching.

"He said you would respond like that, and that I should use other means to persuade you." Kai spun from her, his cloak blending with his shadows. "Perhaps you'll change your mind if the safety of your precious state is at risk."

"Kai, wait!" Levanna begged. Shadows shot out from Kai, spinning and consuming him until they dissipated and left nothing behind. That wasn't him. That wasn't her sweet, gentle scholar, or even her hardened prince, whose determination and harsh actions were fuelled by the need to bring them together while fulfilling his duty. Whoever he had met when leaving Thassena and journeying to Eresydon had tainted him and drawn the power from Sitara's essence out. If only Levanna knew of a way to unlock the light that should be within her; maybe then she could use it to erase his darkness. Something told her it was deep-rooted, for the man who had just stood before her was not opposed to committing deadly acts to achieve his ambitions.

Levanna took off at a run as a tug from deep within guided her to him. She ran for only minutes before she met blinding light. She winced, having not seen sunlight in months. Her lids blinked rapidly, and she looked down, shielding her head with her hands. Water pooled at her feet, running forward. A river. Birds chirped the same pattern she recalled from her vision, and when she looked up, she found trees to the right of the river, mountains behind, and open fields on her left. She had no time to look for the shimmer in the atmosphere, to determine exactly what the path ahead of her looked like. So, she ran. Levanna followed the steps in her vision and ran as fast as she could through the river toward the drop she knew waited at the end. Logic told her to stop, that she did not know what she was truly jumping off, but she was granted that vision for a reason. Wind whipping past her, she took a deep breath to ease her panic and hurtled over the waterfall. Time slowed as her vision was fulfilled, as her eyes caught sight of the iridescent scales in the water below and the shimmer of an illusion. As she fell through the sky, she waved her hand to clear the illusion, yet still, she fell. Water would meet her soon, but it was not a lake awaiting at the bottom of the waterfall, it was the edge of the ocean.

Levanna kept her eyes open as she braced for impact, already twisting her power amongst the waves to cradle her beneath them when she landed. Glowing purple irises faced her just as her vision as a child had shown. Its body was nearly the size of the dragon she had seen in the potential paths of her future, but its scales were smoother, shinier. The pale blue was iridescent, flashing with lilacs and various shades as it flapped its wings beneath the water. She had done it; she had found the first river drake, the trapped body of Anela's love, the creature who could guide her to the deity. But suddenly, that didn't seem as important—protecting her people did. She needed to prevent the visions of the alternate fates she'd witnessed. Her hand steadily brushed the snout of the river drake, which let out a warbled cry beneath the waves. She wished she understood its meaning. A shadow fell over them, and Levanna looked up to see a large battleship and the sigil of Thassena fluttering in the wind. The river drake nudged her arm. Levanna frowned. She should have him guide her to Anela. But in her vision, she had been atop a boat looking down at the creature, so she obeyed and kicked her feet until her head broke the surface. A rope ladder was immediately lowered, and she climbed as quickly as she could, with the backdrop of cannons blaring through the sky.

"Miss Zerpane?" a voice called. Levanna turned to find an older man with inked arms standing at the helm of the ship. The captain of the royal fleets. The boat shook as a cannonball collided with the side and wood splintered.

"What's happening?" she yelled, running toward the mast.

"Prince Theon has had us searching for you for months. We were heading back to dock when Q'Ohar ships appeared out of nowhere and set fire to ours," the commander yelled. Levanna began climbing, her hands wet and shaking as she scaled the mast for a better look. Flames overtook her vision; boats burned on the water as threads of darkness climbed across the waves toward them, pulling them slowly and painfully under. *Kai.*

He was too far gone. The flames and darkness reflecting off the ocean were a foreboding warning of the differing threads of possibilities, of what would surely occur if Kai had her, or if whoever he worked for got his hands on her. She couldn't let that happen. Levanna would not be used as a tool of destruction.

The cannonballs paused, and the oceans fell quiet as a single ship broke free from the Q'Ohar formation and powered toward the last ship standing in Thassena's fleet. Its sails were not the same deep red as the others; this one was black. But from her vantage point on the mast, Levanna could not tell if it was a different colour or if Kai's shadows enveloped it so tightly that it was a symbol he went to war for himself and another, not Q'Ohar. A roar sounded beneath the waves, and it was as though Levanna was connected to it and sensed what it wanted her to do. She agreed.

"Levanna!" the voice she knew all too well screamed from the other ship, prompting Levanna to tighten her grip around the rope. Hanging off the side of the mast, she summoned all the power within her. The turquoise waves were rough as the river drake thrashed, eager to be assigned a task.

"I know, sweet creature. All in good time," Levanna murmured, reaching for the rope. She pulled it taut around her wrist and tied an unbreakable knot, securing herself to the mast. A flash of fire blazed overhead, and the ship rocked when it hit the quarterdeck. Her white hair flew into her face, and she hurried to brush it aside, eager to keep sight of his ship and the waiting river drake below.

"It doesn't have to be like this, Levanna!" he shouted again. He was too far away to discern his expression, but she knew Kai well enough to know the urgency in his voice would be paired with a furrowed brow. Levanna scoffed. He had a funny way of proving his words as his soldiers flourished their hands, aiming fire at her ship. His chestnut brown hair, hair Levanna once loved combing her fingers through, blew in the wind.

"Yes, it does, Kai! You know damn well I'm not returning to the mainland with you. I won't let you do this; I won't let you start this war!" Levanna screamed back. This was all a game to him; he could easily make the leap between the boats or have his soldiers burn the ship into ashes. He was toying with her. Either that, or a part of him truly still loved her before his heart had blackened, corrupted by greed.

"And what does sacrificing yourself have to do with ending my attempts?" Kai shouted over the ship's edge. He crossed his arms, the deep red of his cloak billowing in the wind behind him. Levanna paused to look at him. She wished she could save him. She wanted to reveal everything she knew—everything they could have shared if he had never left Thassena.

"Goodbye, Kai," Levanna called. She did not look back at his ship to see if he heard. Instead, she stared down into the ocean, spotting the iridescent wings of the river drake spanning wide from its blue-scaled body. Levanna loosened the grip on the water and sent a silent command, twisting her power until the drake glanced up at her with purple irises and catapulted through the ship. As the deck splintered into pieces, taking Levanna with it, she could have sworn she heard the pain in Kai's voice as he screamed for her, like he was himself again.

ERESYDON

AGE OF DEVASTATION 3051AD - 3503AD
[PRESENT YEAR: 3492]

TARLEIGH
WAINSOR
FEDWIN
BORDAN
C
ANDOR
HYSTONE
FOREST
HYBROO
FORE
TO CARVYRE

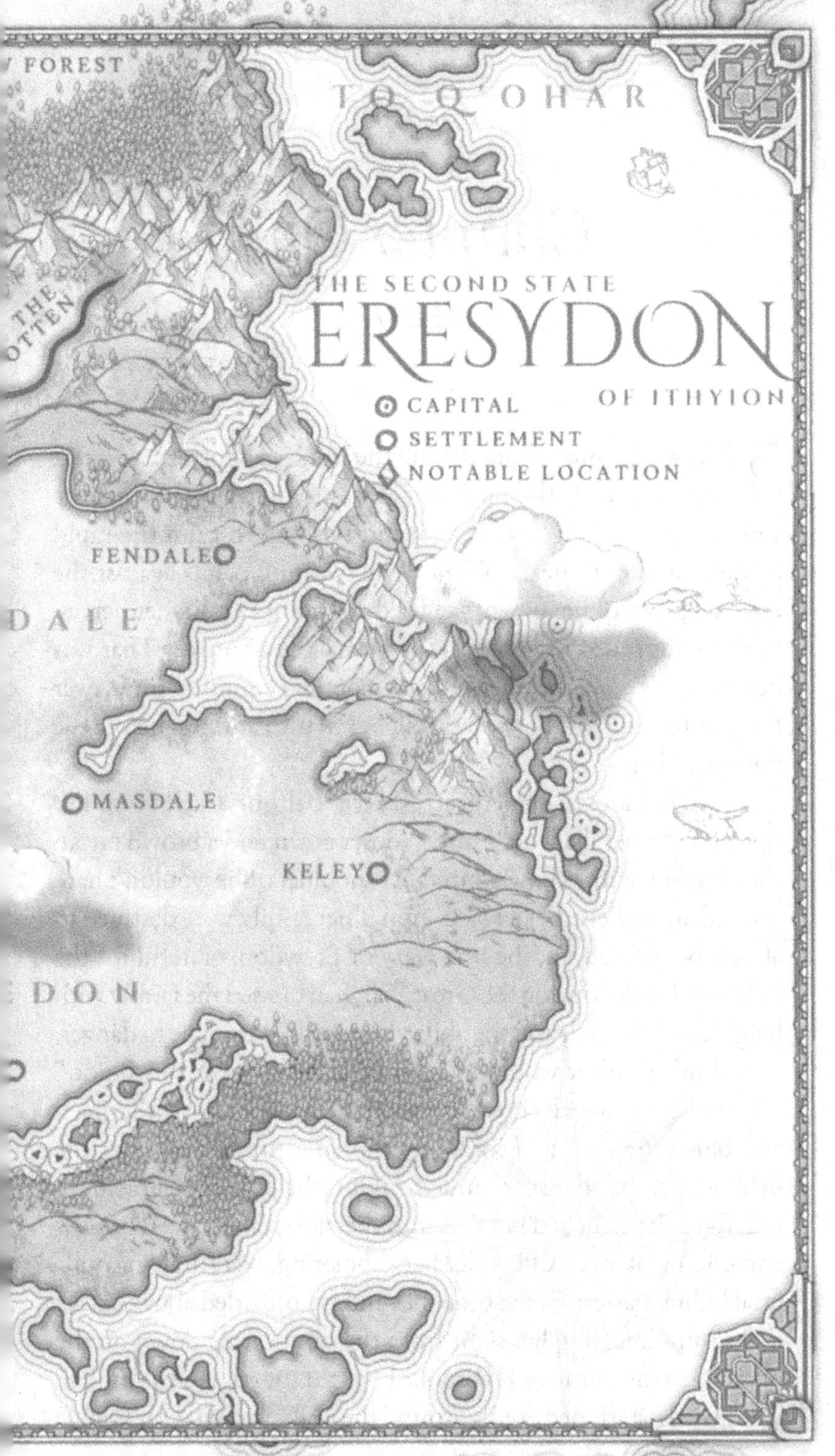

FOREST
TO Q OHAR
THE SECOND STATE
ERESYDON
OF ITHYION
CAPITAL
SETTLEMENT
NOTABLE LOCATION
FENDALE
DALE
MASDALE
KELEY
DON
TO Q OHAR

Chapter One

ALEYA

The string music from behind the stone wall formed a perfect melody with the birdsong above the treetops. While the sound was soothing and slow, it did nothing to calm the rapid beating of Aleya's heart. Wiping her sweating palms against the emerald green of her gown, she tried counting to calm her nerves. She was supposed to enter on the next piece of music. That was her mother's plan, the one she had recounted countless times over the past month. But her nerves told her to turn and run before the musicians began.

"Should I loosen the corset?" Havia Balfour asked from her right-hand side; she wore a much looser gown and a brown tartan shawl woven with yellow around her shoulders. She wouldn't have wanted anyone else by her side, even if her family were destined to always be so. Aelwen, the first deity of Eresydon, grateful for the Balfours' loyalty during the Great War, had blessed the family with heightened strength and the ability to detect a Mordane in danger.

"I don't think it would make much difference at this point," Aleya said with a shaky breath, smoothing her hands over the green and blue tartan of the Mordanes, chosen centuries ago after the fields and rivers that surrounded Andor, the capital of Eresydon. Barefoot, she clenched her toes into the moss, taking deep breaths and hoping nature would calm her. The strings were drawing out a final lulling pattern as the branches and ivy unfurled above. Aleya looked up, shielding her sight from the sun beating down on the opening in the centre of Hybrooke Forest at the edge of the capital. The guards, stationed evenly around the walls, turned with a single arm raised to warn anyone approaching that they were using their powers. Slowly, their arms lowered as the final branches and vines retracted from the top of the walls. The roof of greenery was now gone, leaving the guests to bathe in the sun while they waited. All eyes would be on her, Aleya Mordane, Princess of Eresydon and, after this, Queen.

"I can't do this," Aleya whispered.

"Ley..." Havia cautioned.

"The second I do this, Havia, my father relinquishes his crown to me. I cannot rule all these people. I cannot keep peace between three races on the brink of another war."

"You can do—"

"Sorry to interrupt," a male voice said from behind Aleya. She turned, her red waves falling over her shoulders. Lord Alastair of Tandale stood before her. "My son asked me to give you these before you entered," the man said. The sun brightened the grey streaks in his hair and stubble. Aleya looked down at his hands, holding a bouquet of red flowers secured with twine. Alastair said no more as she took them and headed back through the guest's entrance on the western wall.

"Your mother won't like that he's tried to change her perfect image of you." Havia said, placing Aleya's original lavender bouquet on the ground. "Maybe it's a sign you should run, a symbol of the infuriating life you will lead if he wishes to push her boundaries," Havia scoffed, but Aleya ignored her. She traced the delicate, velvet-like petals and smiled, recalling the memory.

***

Aleya's face was red from crying as she looked out of the balcony in her rooms at the Mordane residence in Thassena. She watched the ocean and pondered escaping, wondering what she might find. How sad that a sixteen-year-old wished to find a ship to sail away to a new life. One where no one expected her to rule an entire state with a man she was forced to be with. A knock sounded at the door, and she wiped the back of her sleeve against her eyes before the creak indicated the guards had let the person enter. Aleya stilled, staring at the ocean in the distance as footsteps approached from behind. She recognised them—how could she not, given the time she was forced to spend with him?

"Aleya," he whispered.

"I am tired, Evander," Aleya sighed, watching the sails of the boats billow in the breeze.

"I know neither of us has ever known anything else than the future we would have together. And I know the Queen of Thassena was trying to make it seem normal by telling you that the same is expected of their royal children, that one of their sons will always be promised to a firstborn daughter of the Zerpane Family. And I know all she did was remind you that it is a duty expected of you."

"If you could, I know you would run, but you won't, because as much as you hate duty, your need to please your father is far greater, regardless of the consequences of your own happiness. But..." Evander took a breath from his quick rambling, and, out of the corner of her eye, she watched him place a bouquet of red flowers on the balcony wall. "I also know that if we were not being forced into this and had met under normal circumstances, that maybe we would have fallen in love first. I know you like your tea with rose water and your bread with cherry jam because its tartness balances the flavours. I know you hate early mornings but love the calm of sunset. I know when you think nobody is watching, you like to weave delicate white flowers from the earth and around your ankles to distract yourself from your thoughts. I know you favour stories of adventure over those of romance, and if you were not a princess, you would be an artist." Aleya sniffed, trying to stop tears from falling at his words. "I know we do not love one another right now, and I know we may never, but I do know that regardless of the feelings between us, I will stand by

your side through it all, because my duty, Aleya, is to you and you alone." Evander gently squeezed her arm before leaving the room.

***

"I'm ready," Aleya said, placing her hands low in front of her, clinging to the bouquet of red flowers before nodding at Havia. The string music changed to a piece she recognised as the royal march. Guards pulled open the wooden doors. Butterflies fluttered across the open church, landing on the wooden pews and moss-coated floor, dancing atop the stone steps leading to the dais where Evander stood with his back to her. Aleya found her father's green eyes; he stood to the left with her mother and an empty seat to represent the sister she had lost in childbirth. To the right was Lord Alastair, who had resumed his position with his wife, along with Evander's two brothers. The church appeared just as divided. The left filled with Wiccan in clan tartans, the right in Sorcerers' silks and leathers. Wolves howled around the church. The Shapeshifters were here to bear witness as well, to the marriage intended to cement peace between them all.

Aleya calmed the tremble in her hands as she glided down the moss aisle, focusing on the sun brightening the blonde hair of the man she was to marry. As the music reached its quiet crescendo, Evander turned. Aleya could not deny that he was handsome. He wore a fitted leather vest over his green silk shirt with the mark of his family burned on his chest. The outfit accentuated his broadness, and the stone dais only heightened how easily he took up space in a room. His blonde hair hung just past his shoulders, with the top half braided in the traditional style of men across Eresydon, regardless of their race. His green eyes crinkled with a smile as she walked toward him. It all became far more real when Aleya's father approached, offering his hand to guide her up the five stone steps toward her future husband. When Evander reached for her hands, her father took his place in front of the glass wall that was the centre point of the church, looking out over the stream running through the forest and framing Evander and Aleya like a painting. Havia took Aleya's flowers, freeing the princess's left hand, so she could interlace it with Evander's. His hands were rough, evidence of his role training the soldiers in Eresydon's armies. But they were warm, a comfort.

"We are gathered here today to bless the marriage of Evander Heath, Son of Lord Alastair, Protector of the Sorcerers, and Aleya Mordane, Princess of Eresydon and Protector of the Wiccan. Can the families present the rings and the symbols of their home?" The king, her father, asked. Aleya's pulse quickened again as her mother approached with a velvet box and a long strip of fabric, the same tartan as the corset around Aleya's torso. The pair slid a simple metal ring onto one another's fingers, engraved with the sigil of Eresydon, before Evander released her left hand and turned her right until she clasped his, as though they were mere acquaintances shaking hands. Lord Alastair approached with a long strip of green silk, the exact same shade as the banners in their home. He placed the two strips of fabric over the pair's hands. She began to clench and unclench her left hand as small white flowers formed, winding under her dress and around her ankles. A soothing touch brushed her hand under the fabrics. Evander's thumb traced a small circle round and round, drawing her eyes to his.

I'm with you, he mouthed silently as their parents stepped back until only her father remained.

He wrapped the fabrics around their joined hands and recited, "When your union faces stormy weather that might threaten to uproot all you have created together, do you promise to brace through that storm, side by side?"

"I do," the pair said in unison, Evander's voice much stronger than her own as he continued tracing circles on her skin with a smile. A smile that was honest, perhaps loving, but above all, *trustworthy.*

"When sickness invades the mind or body of the other, do you promise to be a healer, comforter, and friend?"

"I do," Aleya said with Evander, her voice calmer as the strips of fabric shortened until her father tied the strands together. Binding her future to Evander's.

"Do you promise to love one another from this day until your dying breath?"

Aleya was not the only one to waver at that word. *Love.* But Evander squeezed her hand under the fabrics as a warmth spread through their palms.

"I do," they said together, and a thread of light seeped out from their palms and wound around their arms. Aleya's eyes widened as gasps and applause began in the church.

"Our god," the king paused, his jaw tense for a moment, "and deities have blessed this union." Aleya shifted at the mumbles in the room from the side of the Sorcerers. Their apprehension in acknowledging the deity was clear. "In these two individuals, they see the peaceful future they will bring to Eresydon and have blessed them with a celestial tie, a symbol of their great strength together."

Aleya swallowed. A celestial tie had not been granted at a wedding since the War of Hearts over a hundred years ago in 3350AD. Vaeda, the woman their first deity Aelwen blessed as a sister and gifted with immortality, claimed she could gift the Wiccan with new and strengthened powers. War had begun as the Wiccan were split between following Garridon and their deity Aelwen, and joining the cause of Vaeda. Aleya recalled her state visit to Asynthos, where they believed a celestial tie granted a shared destiny, or Thassena, where ties appeared within bargains, or Q'Ohar, where no one dared speak of them at all. So, was this celestial tie truly a blessing?

Chapter Two

ALEYA

Laughter filled the grand hall of the Andor Castle in Eresydon's capital. It was directly central within the state before the land was divided into three: Stendon for the Wiccan, Tandale for the Sorcerers, and Fedwin for the Shapeshifters. Eresydon was the only state of all six to divide its land by races. Aleya's father had always hated that and said they should be unified like the other states. Though that wasn't exactly true. Thassena's Sirens were banished to the oceans by the curse, the Stormbringers were so few and far between now they had secluded themselves in the Boznaya mountains—at least that was what the last report detailed. Asynthos was still cautious about who they allowed into their state after Xyliar's attacks from over a hundred years ago.

The Xyra of Q'Ohar were nearly a myth now, and nobody had stepped foot on Xyliar in centuries to know if the Staxion, Dragon-Bonded, or dark Fae continued to work in harmony. So, the only state that was truly unified was Carvyre. The divides within the states were becoming just as apparent for the entire kingdom. Thassena and Q'Ohar were still essentially at war after the then-prince Theon declared the crown prince an enemy of the state for the murder of his betrothed. Theon was on his deathbed now, with Kaigon taking his own life long before, and yet the King of Thassena had passed the hatred for Q'Ohar on to his own sons, ensuring a legacy of divide. Asynthos was secluded, Xyliar was practically non-existent, and Carvyre—well, Carvyre *thrived*, and everybody hated them for it.

The political discourse meant no other royals were present at

Aleya and Evander's wedding. There was no one else Aleya could turn to for advice, except her husband, who sat beside her now, drinking from a tankard. Her parents announced their retirement to their country estate, leaving Aleya alone to rule. Alone was an exaggeration, though. Her father would still attend monthly meetings along with the protectors of the Sorcerers and lords of the state. But one visit to discuss politics was not exactly a meeting Aleya looked forward to.

"What are you thinking about?" Evander asked; he leant away from his military friends to angle his body toward her, nudging her arm. She looked down at where the green of their garments touched and cringed when realising they would be in much closer company later that night.

"That if they were all drunk every hour of the day, we would never have to fear another civil war," Aleya murmured, reaching for her wineglass. She pursed her lips as she sipped. Far too sour. It seemed that being queen meant you drank wine at dinner tables, even if you were only eighteen and had never been fond of it.

"A sip of ale or wine does seem to erase much of history," he said. Aleya scoffed as she watched the men spilling drinks on the table and the women laughing until they were red in the face.

"More than a sip."

"You can learn a lot when people are intoxicated," Evander said, tipping forward so she could hear him over the noise. The silver of their diadems clinked briefly, Evander's completely rounded, Aleya's with a downward point on her forehead where an emerald was nestled.

"So, King Evander, what have you learnt from the drunken escapades of our guests?" Aleya asked, attempting to sip from the sour glass again. Evander waved down a servant and reached for two glasses on the tray. He took Aleya's glass from her hand, his fingers grazing hers for the first time since they'd been bound and blessed with a celestial tie. As he pulled his hand away, she stared at the mark of Garridon on the back of her hand, raised like a scar.

Glasses clinked as Evander raised her wine to eye level, pouring an array of different liquids into her glass.

"You wish for the Sorcerers to rule so badly that you would poison me on our wedding night?" she asked. Evander's hands stilled as he stirred the concoction.

"Is that what you think?" he asked. "That I am here to favour the Sorcerers and incite another war?" Aleya did not answer as he slid back her drink. "You know I do not practice, Aleya. I never have. It was the reason I was chosen instead of my brothers." Aleya blushed as he confronted her off-handed accusation and sipped from her glass again. It eased her mind that she would not be sharing a bed with a man who could cast a spell or curse upon her. Whilst she was meant to be neutral as queen to invite peace, her bias lay with the purity of healing and prophecies that their deity Aelwen blessed them with, alongside her elemental abilities from Garridon. Sweet flavours burst over her tongue, compelling her to sneak another sip. It was pleasant. She narrowed her eyes at him.

"What did you do to it?" she asked, peering at the remnants in the other glasses.

"Added sparkling elderflower and rose water." At Evander's shrug, she contained her small smile behind her glass and sat back in the throne-like wooden chair.

"So, King Evander, tell me what you have learnt from the drunken escapades of our guests," she prompted. Evander crossed his arms and rested back beside her, their arms touching briefly again. He pointed at a man and woman in the back corner.

"That is the head of the Brodie clan's son and the Lord of Fendale's daughter. Wiccan and Sorcerer." Aleya kept herself from interrupting; of course she knew who he was. The Brodie Clan was the first Wiccan clan descended from Aelwen, the first deity herself. They were the most powerful in Eresydon, outside of the Mordanes, who were more famed for their elemental strength. Their closest allies, though she supposed Evander's family were her closest allies now. "In public, they despise one another and accuse the other of concocting all sorts, but give them alcohol and a dark corner, and they appear as quite the opposite. Now, assuming their fathers will appear before you again within the year, arguing for more land from one another, you could instead enforce a marriage upon their children, granting them both lands and the rights to rename it under one governance."

"Enforcing the next generation to incite peace," Aleya murmured, glancing sideways at her husband. "What else?" This time, she took more than a sip of her wine.

"Lady Grey engages in conversation every now and again, but other than that, she simply patrols the hall, watching. If you ever need information, she is likely someone who would have it." Aleya watched the widow the children feared, simply because she screamed at them whenever they stole apples from the orchard that supplied most of the ale in Eresydon.

"Now," Evander said, moving his head closer to Aleya. The softer change in his tone forced her to finish her final gulp of wine and turn to look at him. He watched her intently. "The commander of the Sorcerer's army and his son have watched us with eagle eyes from the second we sat down. They have only had one drink and eaten a full meal." Aleya began to turn, but Evander brushed her red locks over her shoulder and ran his hand down her arm. She stilled, not used to so much physical affection. "Don't look yet. I'm going to make you another drink, and you can use that as an excuse to glance around the room and spot them. Then you're going to accept the drink and lean back, sitting comfortably as you have been."

Aleya smiled. "I'd love another drink." She did as he said and scanned the room. Nothing. The young couple from the corner had disappeared somewhere, and Lady Grey stood by the window next to where they had been, likely catching them sneaking off. Wolves patrolled the tables, representatives from the Shapeshifters still stuck in their animal forms. One growled at the table she had been looking for, and Commander Harris gave the large white wolf a disgusted look while his son watched Aleya and Evander. Her husband's hand brushed hers again, and she accepted the glass with a smile, leaning back in the chair. This time his hand remained on her left one, displayed on the table.

"They are watching to determine if we will be a successful partnership," Evander said. "Or if they could topple a throne or manipulate one of us into doing their bidding."

"I have heard of your valiant actions in battle, I would not be concerned about them trying to topple you," Aleya said.

"Those were simple uprisings in more rebellious Sorcerer settlements; it compares little to the overthrowing of a throne. We have to sell them on us," he said. Aleya sipped from her glass again and turned her hand where Evander's had been resting atop it until their fingers interlocked.

"Like this?" she asked, a blush creeping across her cheeks.

"Exactly like that," Evander whispered. "Look at me, my queen." Something about the words made her breath hitch, but Aleya turned as she was asked. "All we need to do is smile at one another while we have this conversation," he said, stroking a finger down her cheek. "You blush so beautifully," he said, his small smile genuine.

"What would they want to manipulate us into doing?" Aleya asked, angling her body into Evander's.

"Did you see the way Varna looked at him?"

"The white wolf?" she asked.

"The commander believes the Shapeshifter lands should be formally split between the Wiccan and the Sorcerers. He claims that because they can physically do nothing with it or govern in their animal forms, it would be better governed by the other two races." Evander's finger twisted around a curl, which he stared at with a smile.

"Which would then incite more dispute over who gets what portions of land," Aleya sighed. "I would never sign over Shapeshifter land. If the curse is lifted one day, they will be entitled to their home."

"I agree," Evander said. "Which is why we must appear as if we are not a couple that can be challenged, despite our age." Evander planted a kiss on her forehead before he mixed her another drink, squeezed her hand, and went to speak with her father, who awkwardly clapped Evander on the back and stood, clinking a fork against his wineglass. Silence fell upon the crowd as Evander returned to Aleya. He reached for her hand and encouraged her to stand.

"The king and queen will retire from the festivities for the night," the king said. Cheering sounded from the men through the room, a rhythmic banging of tankards on the table filling the hall. Aleya stiffened and gulped down her wine; her father mumbled something about well wishes and a happy marriage before Evander's hand guided her from the hall and up the grand staircases until they reached the eastern wing—*their* wing. Their room. Their bed.

It dawned on Aleya what was expected of her that night. Her mother had tried to talk to her about it, but she had changed the topic every time. Havia had attempted it, too, but she doubted her experiences with Athena were like those of a man.

"You're nervous," Evander said, tilting his head.

"I'm not," Aleya said, surveying the room lit by the glow of the grand fireplace at its centre. Evander looked down at her feet, and she followed his eyeline. Tiny white flowers twisted up and around her ankle. She blinked, and they rescinded into the floorboards. Evander approached slowly, reaching for her hands and clasping them between their chests.

"I respect you, Aleya." He kissed the top of her hand; there was no passion or expectation in the touch, only comfort. "I do not expect you to make love to a man you hold no feelings for, nor would I do the same simply because it is expected for us to have an heir." His touch was gentle as he removed her diadem and then his own, placing them on the chest at the end of the bed. He combed his fingers through her hair, and she shivered. "I thought you could pick out a book for me."

"A what?" Aleya asked, blinking rapidly as he released his hold on her and backed away.

"A book," he said with a childish grin. He unstrapped the leather from his shirt and tossed it over an armchair. He launched himself onto the bed, leaning on his side with his head propped on his hand.

"You want me to choose you a book?" she asked again, slowly. He pointed at the chest beside the one he had placed the diadems on, and she reached for the lid. The collection from her bedroom was in there.

"I know you love reading. I thought it could be a habit we did together. My mother told me the best advice she could give was to dedicate time to one another every day, even if it's only to talk in the evenings. But then I thought you and I have had no issues talking about politics and that of the state, so instead, I thought we could do something you might enjoy..." Evander trailed off as Aleya stared at him, clutching a book to her chest. "It's stupid. Of course, you may simply want to sleep, and in a bed of your own, particularly if you would prefer we not lean too much into the united front plan. I—"

"You wanted to read because I like to read?" she asked again, an unknown emotion spreading through her chest.

"Well... yes..." Evander said, watching her retrieve several books from the chest.

"Okay," she said, and Evander grinned.

"I desire a little romance in mine though," he said, and Aleya recalled he had always remembered she preferred adventures.

"What kind of romance?" she asked, rifling through the books.

"A slow one built on trust," he whispered. Aleya smiled to herself, yet her hair hid her expression as she pulled out the perfect book. There were no nerves as she lay down beside Evander. Together, they sat in silence, simply enjoying one another's company amongst the words they read.

Chapter Three

ALEYA

Within the last month, Aleya quickly learnt the parts of being queen she hated and those she tolerated. The monthly meeting, which she was attempting to stay awake in now, was on the list of things she hated. Weekly visits into the city to see the citizens were tolerable. She would probably enjoy it were it not for the incessant questions about when she and Evander would bless the kingdom with heirs.

Evander always knew what to say. "We're enjoying the bliss of marriage first" or "We want to ensure we are bringing a child into the world when there is peace and security across our lands." The peace and security line wasn't a complete lie, she realised, as Lord Alastair gave the accounts on the continued tensions between Thassena and Q'Ohar while the other states still failed to pick a side.

"We cannot pick a side when the battles have not ceased in the last ten years. At this rate, the negotiations will still be ongoing when I am in my forties," Aleya said. Her father frowned. It wasn't a particularly queenly thing to say, even if it was true. Prince Theon had declared war ninety-two years ago, and Prince Kaigon took his own life only fifteen years later. Yet the new King of Thassena and of Q'Ohar continued the strife that was fallout across all the states.

"What are the demands this time?" Evander asked from her side. A far more appropriate question.

"Q'Ohar is looking to exchange citizens."

"He wants people?" Aleya asked, leaning forward on her forearms to shift the discomfort from her throne. Her father's immediate frown made her straighten.

"He argues that low immigration across Ithyion to the third state has led to a gap in skill sets, which is slowing down their progression," her father said.

"They're already as far ahead in innovations as Thassena is, and possibly more so in other areas. Their coal mining transportation doesn't involve horses at all, given their ability to manipulate metal. They have created enough contraptions over the years and even replicated the pipework in Thassena before the state gifted us the plans. Even then, we had to go to Q'Ohar for an increased trade in metals to create it."

"The restrictions on water means they're struggling even more than usual to grow any crops," said Lord Alastair. "They are requesting citizens from Eresydon, who are happy to move to the north-western edge of Q'Ohar, and work to use their elemental power to nurture crop fields."

Aleya frowned. She sympathised with the citizens who faced the repercussions of their past rulers' actions.

"We would need to consider what they offer us in return. At the moment, I cannot think of how they would aid us, especially as we are focused on keeping our people happy," Evander said, his hand slowly intertwining with Aleya's as Commander Harris watched silently from the table.

"We are their neighbouring state, and we have remained impartial for far too long," the commander said. "If we don't intervene now, they will turn on us next."

Aleya sighed and flitted her eyes to the door as it creaked open. That was her cue to leave. "Update me this evening?" Aleya leant into Evander to whisper. He nodded and raised her hand to his lips. Her stomach fluttered as she smiled at him before leaving. Lately, his small displays of affection did that to her. She knew they were intended for the men at the table to enforce a perception of their partnership, but a small part of her hoped they were for her too.

Aleya smoothed down the thick fabric of her pale blue gown, a wedding gift from the Queen of Asynthos; it was their only contact from the second state in four weeks. Two heads peered around the corner of the door. One with braided blonde hair, the other with wispy chestnut curls.

"What took you so long?" Aleya hissed. "I was only meant to endure that for thirty minutes. It's been nearly two hours!" Aleya bowed her head to the guards at the door in thanks as the girls looped their arms in hers.

"There was an attack at the border between Tandale and Fedwin. The patrol wolves took a chunk out of two Sorcerers' arms," Athena said on her right, pushing her wispy curls from her face. Aleya groaned.

"That means Evander's father will ask for retaliation the second the meeting is interrupted and he is informed."

"In the wolves' defence, they were measuring a patch of land as though they intended on just moving right in." Havia shrugged. "I would have taken a chunk out of their arm, too."

"Anyway, Havia had to take the statements, which were, of course, dramatised, and I had to patch up their arms," Athena added, steering the women out toward the royal gardens instead of the apothecary tower.

"Are we not doing my daily check-up?" Aleya asked. The two women scoffed.

"We would know if you'd finally put that man out of his misery and slept with him, Aleya, so there's no need for us to keep pretending and check for a pregnancy." Athena stopped by a stone bench overlooking a large lake, with the surrounding willows blowing in the wind.

"Well, we should still keep up pretences."

"If anyone asks, we'll lie and say I'm waiting on a new delivery of herbs to check," Athena said.

"And he is not miserable," Aleya mumbled. "It's not like that between us." She cupped a rose on the bush to her left as Havia moved to sit beside Athena, looping their hands together.

"It may not be like that for you, but that man has been smitten with you since you were children," Havia said, brushing one of Athena's curls behind her ear. "He simply pretended he wasn't because he knew it was unreciprocated."

"That is a big assumption, Havia," Aleya said.

"It's not. The soldiers all talk about it in training."

"They shouldn't be gossiping about their king!" Aleya chastised.

"So you feel nothing for him? Even after the last month?" Athena asked.

"I—" Aleya trailed off. She thought of their evening routine together, where he would mix her a wine with sparkling elderflower and rosewater and stoke the fire until it was roaring and warmed the entire room. She would laugh every time he gasped at his book, and he would nudge her to feign offence. Eventually, she would end up leaning into his chest, her knees curled up and her book resting on her thighs. His arm would tuck around her to pull a blanket over her shoulders, but it would linger, keeping her warm while he held his book with the other hand. It felt... safe.

"She's blushing." Athena grinned.

"I am not!" Aleya slapped her leg.

But later that night, when Aleya's eyes were drooping, and Evander began to snore, she questioned whether the fluttering in her stomach and the warmth in her chest during their small moments together was more than comfort and stability.

***

A breeze skated over Aleya's skin; in her hazy sleep, she pulled the bedding higher over her shoulder and leant back until she met Evander's warmth. Still, she was cold. Her eyes blinked open slowly. A pale glow in the room indicated the fire still burned. So why was she so chilly? Aleya slowly pushed herself up, her red hair a tangled mess. She looked for the source of the breeze and froze.

Aleya slapped Evander's arm, who continued snoring. She slapped it again, her pulse quickening.

"He won't wake," called the voice of the woman on their balcony. "I have lulled his mind to stay asleep."

Aleya glanced toward the door, contemplating whether she could reach the guards on the other side before the woman did something. Was this the beginning of a war? Had she and Evander done a poor job of convincing the races they were the right rulers? Were the Wiccan or Sorcerers trying to take control?

"I'm not here to kill you, child," the voice floated through the air. "Come. Admire the stars with me."

Aleya reached for her robe on the floor by the bed and wrapped it around the thin green nightgown. She slid the letter opener on the desk up her sleeve as she padded across the moonlit floors.

"Who are you?" Aleya asked. Only the woman's silhouette was visible until they finally stepped out onto the balcony. A crown of stars glistened on her head, blinking just as those above them did. Her black gown hung off her loosely, as though she had not eaten or slept properly in months.

Sitara.

The ethereal voice ran through Aleya's mind, and she jumped back, clutching the balcony wall with a trembling hand. Should she bow? Curtsey?

"You do not need to do either," Sitara said with a soft smile, glancing back at Evander in bed. "You do not love him yet?" Aleya crossed her arms against the cold radiating off the goddess in waves.

"I do not know," Aleya said.

"Then you do not. Love is certain, Aleya. When you love someone, there is no doubt in your mind, just as there are no doubts in his." Aleya glanced back at Evander, his face gentle and stress-free as his chest slowly rose and fell. "There is also nothing I wouldn't do for love." Sitara tugged Aleya's hand forward when she wasn't watching. She gasped and tried to pull away, but Sitara's grip was far stronger. A blade appeared from thin air before Sitara sliced a line down Aleya's arm. She tried to scream, but Sitara's voice in her mind commanded her to stop. "I have tried this twice already, Aleya, so this time, we are attempting things differently." Aleya could only watch, her body frozen and unable to reach for the letter opener in her sleeve, as Sitara retrieved a glass vial from a blur of shadow, a golden thread sparkling within. "This time, I am going to walk you through it. I am going to tell you explicitly what you must do."

Aleya's eyes widened as the glowing thread wove its way under her skin before the wound healed over, leaving no speck of blood behind. Still unable to move, Aleya was forced to watch as Sitara approached Evander's side and did the same to him. A similar thread wormed its way into his body before she returned to Aleya. What had she done to them?

"You act as though you have a right to be offended that I, a goddess, the *first* goddess, cannot do with the people that all descend through my creations, as I please." Sitara tilted her head, watching Aleya regain her movements as she backed up against the balcony wall. "I have embedded your soul with the essence of my love, and your husband with my own essence." Turning, Sitara placed her hands on the balcony and looked up at the sky. "The awakening of the powers varies, and I am yet to understand what triggers it. I could wait months, years, decades. But I will wait as long as I need if it means getting him back."

"Getting who back?" Aleya asked, reaching for the letter opener in her sleeve.

"Do not insult me, Aleya. I will not be felled by a blunt knife," Sitara sighed. "Have you never wondered what prompted the curses that fell upon the states?"

Aleya frowned. "Nobody knows. There are theories it was the fallout of war between the gods and deities, but nobody knows who..." Aleya trailed off, beginning to wonder if the goddess standing opposite was the reason one race of her people could not shift back into their human form.

"The curses fell upon the land when Sonos was taken. It is the consequence of his absence. An imbalance plagues the world without him in his seat of power beside me." Aleya frowned. Who could possibly be strong enough to take a god? "I ask myself the same question. I know who did it, but the how remains a mystery," Sitara murmured. "But until he is recovered, the curses will remain. And you, Aleya, are my new key to finding him."

"Me?" Aleya exclaimed. "What could I possibly do?"

"You must merge your essence with Evander. Doing so will combine the power I have placed within you both. That power will act as a guiding light, a tug, a pull toward him. It essentially makes you both as powerful as our children."

"Then why can your actual children not find him?" Aleya asked, already resenting the expectation placed upon her.

"Because I birthed them. It weakened our essences within them, for they created their own. Whereas the power within you is now its purest form."

"How do we do that?" Aleya asked.

"I cannot give you all the answers, Aleya, otherwise fate may tug you on a different path," Sitara sighed. "But I will not take your memory of this." Sitara reached to stroke Aleya's cheek, her fingers cold as death. "You will find him for me before Valon finds either of you."

"Who is Val—"

Before Aleya could gather any more answers, Sitara crumbled away into a breeze of stardust and soared through the air.

Chapter Four

ALEYA

*T*wo Years Later

"You need to push harder, Aleya."

"You're doing so well, sweetheart."

"Not long now."

The voices in the room came and went as Aleya stared out at the balcony in her chambers. Sweat slicked her hair to her forehead, and Evander brushed it back for her, murmuring sweet words. She was too focused on the pain to decipher them. His hand gripped hers, the celestial tie still marking their skin. She screamed as she pushed again. Finally, a different scream merged with her own, high-pitched and squealing. Tears fell onto her cheeks, but they were not her own. She looked up at Evander, who cried as their first child entered the world.

"It's a boy, your Majesty," Athena said. Aleya watched her bundle the baby in a blanket and reach toward Evander. The king shook his head.

"Not until Ley is finished and okay," he said, returning his attention to his wife.

"I can't do it again," Aleya sobbed. "I can't."

"Shh," Evander hushed, stroking the hair back from her face once more. He shifted from his perch on the edge of the bed and gently propped her up higher. His free hand removed the unstructured pile of pillows beginning to kill her back. Instead, hard muscle replaced the soft support as Evander's knees came either side of her. He reached for her hands, clutching them. "You are the strongest woman I know. You can do this," he said. "You have done it once, and you will do it again. You can do anything, Ley," he whispered. Aleya rested her head back against his chest and pushed. Her vision became hazy with the exhaustion of being awake for twenty-six hours.

"I can't," she mumbled, her words muffled.

"I have the shoulders, Aleya. One more push for me!" Athena called from the end of the bed. Evander's grip on her hands tightened as she arched forward with another scream. The scream was not as powerful this time, and it trailed off with the echo of another infant's cry.

"Another boy. Two beautiful healthy boys." Athena smiled. Aleya saw the tears in her eyes, the happiness for her friend, not just her queen. But her face blurred, and darkness crept into the edges of her vision. She couldn't see the change in Athena's expression, but she heard her desperate yell for Havia, who stood outside the room. The door burst open, recognising the panic in her lover's voice.

"What's wrong?" Evander's voice was hazy as her grip on his hands weakened, her head heavy on her shoulders.

"She's losing too much blood," Athena's voice was quiet, as though Aleya was stuck inside a room, listening to everyone from behind a door. Aleya closed her eyes against the flurry of blurred movement. Strong hands shook her as she succumbed to the darkness. At just twenty years old, Aleya had never spared dying much thought. But this was what she imagined—a painless darkness that left you weightless. Her grandmother used to say people saw their entire lives flash before their eyes when they were about to die, replaying the happiest of moments. But Aleya didn't recognise the memories she was seeing in her mind as her body stilled.

Two Angels knelt in front of a bed, clutching daggers as their grey and lavender wings formed a cocoon around them. They were crying, but Aleya saw the love in their eyes. She'd heard stories of the next image, of Levanna Zerpane standing high on the mast of a ship. But the next part was not in the stories. There had been no mention of the dark shadows creeping across the ocean, drowning the ships in flames. Aleya did not recognise the white light before her either, or the man, with flowing white hair and a crown like the sun, offering his hand.

"Aleya, my child," the voice echoed, brushing against her skin like the first rays of a morning sunset. There were tales about what happened when someone died. They of course differed depending on the state you were in, but in Eresydon, it varied depending on the race you asked. The purity of her upbringing told her the Wiccan were the first new race on Eresydon, before the War of Hearts when Vaeda instigated the divide of the Wiccan, creating the Sorcerers with the apparent blessing of Garridon. It was the Wiccan tales of death she expected with their devout loyalty to the celestial god, Garridon. She expected to see two towering oak trees forming a gateway ahead. It was only right the God of Life would secure joy for his people in death. Aleya expected her ancestors to greet her, or anyone in Eresydon with unfinished business. She took comfort in that tale, that she could wait in peace, watching over her husband and the two children she had not had a chance to look at. Yet the man with a crown of sunlight stayed, with no towering oak trees in sight.

"Aleya, it is not your time," he said. In her mind, she floated on a cloud, her dress painted in the shades of sunrise, the loose fabric fluttering around her like butterflies. The light faded, just enough for her to make out the man standing opposite. His skin was pale, though not as pale as the white of his hair and the tendrils in his glowing eyes. The dark colour of his robes mirrored Sitara's dress and the stardust she had faded into.

"Sonos?" Aleya whispered. "I'm meant to look for you, but we could not figure out how."

"Who told you that?" he asked. His face remained neutral, as though chiselled from rock.

"Sitara," Aleya said. His eyebrows raised a fraction.

"She is looking for me?"

"She said there is nothing she would not do to find you. That you were her only and greatest love." The thought made Aleya think of Evander. The warmth in her chest and the fluttering in her stomach had slowly grown with each passing day of their marriage. He had been so patient when, finally, after a year, she admitted her feelings to herself and kissed him. Athena and Havia told her how perfect their first kiss had been, but she doubted anything compared to the kiss with Evander.

"Aleya!" a desperate scream met her ears, and the light of the man standing in her mind burst free, forcing her eyes open. The light wasn't only in her mind now, as a glow lit Evander's face as he hovered over her. His hands were on her chest, and a glow emanated from beneath them until threads of light twisted around his palm and along his arm until caressing his cheek. Aleya blinked as the thread retreated toward her chest, as if she controlled it.

"Please be okay."

"I'm okay."

The King and Queen's eyes widened at the sound of one another's voices echoing within their minds. Aleya opened her mouth to speak.

"Don't say anything. If we tell people, we will have to tell them about Sitara, about the essences within us." Evander's voice in her mind wrapped around her like a warm hug. He was right. Aleya had told only him of Sitara's visit and what she did. Unsurprisingly, he had trusted and believed her immediately. They had attempted everything since to merge their essences, their power. From battling one another to gently trying to summon one another's power. A part of her had wondered if their first kiss or the confession of their feelings, while tangled in bed sheets, would incite the merge. But they had told nobody else. They did not want to instil false hopes of finding Sonos and lifting the curse on the Shapeshifters.

"Do you think that's what that was?" Evander nodded in answer

to her question.

"It's not possible," Athena whispered from the end of the bed while Havia rocked two crying babies in her arms. "She should be dead; she should still be bleeding, but she is completely healed." Athena collapsed back on her stool, looking between Evander and Aleya. "What was that?"

The king and queen shared a look.

"There is plenty of time for questions," Havia said, moving toward the four-poster bed. "And answers," she said pointedly, looking at her queen. "But now, you must say hello to your sons."

Aleya's eyes prickled as Evander reached for one bundle of blankets and lowered the screaming baby to her chest. He propped himself up on the edge of the bed as Havia passed the second baby to him. Both stopped crying immediately.

"We'll leave you alone," Havia said. Athena stumbled as her lover guided her to the door, her eyes still wide and contemplative as to what had just transpired, and how Aleya had defied death. All Aleya could focus on was the beautiful green eyes peering up at her. Evander and Aleya were silent for a while, both cradling their newborn children. The Mordane royal family only ever gave birth to twins, a blessing for their unwavering devotion to the Wiccan and to Garridon, for being the family to stay loyal and pure where the Sorcerers had deviated. Her mother had been the first exception, the first of the Mordane line to lose a child in birth, the child who should have been Aleya's sister, who should have been queen.

"I will do anything to keep this state, this *kingdom*, safe for you two," Aleya whispered, delicately stroking her son's cheek.

"Your mother and I will reunite the skies to bring you both peace," Evander added.

"Where do we begin our search for Sonos?" Aleya asked. "Sitara said we would be guided to him, that our merged essence and soul would connect us to him."

"Perhaps we simply must wait and trust fate will guide us."

"Do you think any others have been able to speak in one another's mind?" Aleya asked.

"Presumably the Staxion in Xyliar. They can control minds, so it makes sense they can speak within them. Maybe the Hypherion of Carvyre, too, but only within dreams," Evander suggested.

"Maybe that is why we can, because the essence of Sitara and Sonos within us has merged. Their power created those lines. Perhaps we have been gifted with this ability to help keep us together in our search for Sonos." Aleya pondered.

"Whatever it means," Evander said aloud. "This is another way you're always with me." He leant forward, and she met his lips. The kiss was slow, savouring the fact they still had one another, and Aleya was still alive. "I am yours even when we are walking through the trees of death together."

Aleya was reminded of her mind before Evander and their merged essence brought her back, recalling Sonos, who said it was not yet her time. The air was suddenly heavy as she looked down at her sons. She knew then that this would not be the last time she was almost taken from her family.

Chapter Five

Nine days, twelve hours, and sixteen minutes, and Evander hated every second. Every breath he took that was not at his wife and children's side was an agony he did not realise was possible. Perhaps it was Aleya's brush with death only a month ago that made him more fearful of separation, or knowing he had two other lives to care for now, two lives that could be impacted by the success of his mission.

Tensions had escalated between the Shapeshifters and Sorcerers, which, in turn, only heightened tensions between the Wiccan and Sorcerers, the latter expecting a side to be chosen. Sorcerers initially measuring land and lingering long at the border with Fedwin evolved into building homes right on the path that marked the crossing. With the Shapeshifters unable to communicate, tensions only worsened as the Wiccan would need to negotiate on their behalf. It was the purpose of Evander's mission. He was journeying to the point on the northern border between the two regions. It also conveniently placed him at the edge of the Wynow forest before it slowly faded into the Q'Ohar's Razmah desert, allowing for a meeting with an envoy from the capital, Sahrih. Eresydon had agreed to send elemental wielders to the north of Q'Ohar, but only if any volunteered, which none had so far. Evander needed to communicate that.

Aleya? Evander tried calling out in his mind again with no success. It seemed their mental link could only withstand a certain distance. He had stopped hearing from her two days ago. Perhaps it was because he was so close to the next state rather than something else blocking their connection. There was so much unknown about the power and effects of gods and deities.

"Your Majesty, the camp has been set up for you and is ready for arrival," Commander Harris said. Evander nodded from atop his horse, turning from their brief break at the edge of the lake. The camp had been split directly along the border to allow for an easy meeting place in the centre, marking it as neutral ground. Green banners flew from poles with the Eresydon sigil clear to see: three trees and a soaring hawk. Today would be a meeting of those three—Wiccan, Sorcerer, Shapeshifter—while the Balfour family, the protectors, the hawks, remained in Andor, keeping watch over the Mordane Queen and heirs. Evander could kiss the deity Aelwen for blessing the first Balfour ancestor for their loyalty during the Great War. Knowing Aleya had Havia and her family beside her, with their heightened strength and sense of danger against the Mordanes, eased his worry even if it did not ease his heartache.

"Evander!" a booming voice called as he ducked into the large central tent of the camp.

"Father—"

"It's your Majesty," the commander cut in. Lord Alastair pursed his lips but bowed his head all the same to his son. Evander knew Commander Harris was correct to enforce such behaviours, and Evander should follow them too. But it was what made this meeting difficult, with his father acting as the representative for the Sorcerers, when much of what Evander had to say on behalf of himself and his queen favoured the Shapeshifters instead.

"Good to see you, Lord Alastair." Evander smiled, reaching to shake his father's hand. Low growls sounded from outside the tent as men hurled insults at one another. Evander sighed; it was not the welcome he had hoped his father's men would offer the ruling six. His father and his two advisors took their seats on the three carved wooden chairs at the east of the tent. Evander remained standing in front of his throne at the north. He tapped his hand against his thigh to calm his frustration at his father's lack of respect.

Men held the tent flaps open as a large white wolf prowled in, a low growl emerging from the back of its throat at the sight of Lord Alastair. With a turn of her head, she approached the king. Evander bowed his head in respect, and Varna, the leader of the ruling six, lowered her head and front legs in a bow. Four other wolves prowled behind, pausing to sit in a line along the western side of the tent. Two sable-coloured wolves, Baelyn and Tapesh, as well as two black wolves, Octavia and Serene. Evander waited, the tent flaps still open.

"We're missing—" A second later, a bundle of deep grey fur came careering into the tent, his paws too large for his body as he stumbled to a stop in front of Evander and licked his hand. The king smiled and stooped to stroke his head while one milky eye and one bright blue eye watched him. "It is good to see you too, Seiko," Evander said.

Varna huffed at the child's behaviour but did not scold him like she would the other wolves. She had a soft spot for him, which stemmed not from the alpha and youngest dynamic, but from the family lineage of the Shapeshifters that were documented. When the ruling six were in human form, they were the heads of the six settlements across Fedwin. Even in their permanently shifted forms, their statuses remained. Over four hundred years stuck in wolves' bodies froze their ages. They had lived far longer than they ever should have. But it meant Seiko was still stuck at the age of ten, an orphan whose parents died in the Great War before Varna took him in until he would come of age to rule.

"Shall we begin?" Evander asked.

***

"I think we should call it a day," Evander sighed, rubbing his forehead. Seiko whined in agreement from his position curled at Evander's feet. Varna sat rigid in the centre of the rest of the pack, staring at Lord Alastair, who still smirked. They had got nowhere. Still, his father persisted that land should be taken from Fedwin and gifted to the Sorcerers, given their population continued to grow while the Shapeshifters were still the same volume as they had been before the curse. The wolves growled every time the suggestion was made, and Evander was forced to summarise, yet again, why that was not fair. He offered plenty of alternatives, shifting farmland from Stendon to the Wiccan, who would allow the Sorcerers to build homes there instead. But that wouldn't do, for it would simply give the Wiccan more land even if being utilised by Sorcerers. Evander had tactfully attempted to expose the hypocrisy in that argument.

"A good suggestion, your Majesty," his father said, rising from his chair and holding his stomach. "I hear my camp has wolf for dinner." Baelyn and Tapesh lunged across the room, snapping their teeth. Evander did not flinch, but his father's eyes widened as he stumbled back a step. "There is someone I would like you to meet, *son.* May I send them in?"

Evander nodded and waited for his father to fetch whoever he assumed would try to sway his decision. He gave Varna an apologetic look and stroked Seiko's head as he rose and shook his fur.

"I'll find you later," Evander said. The wolves bowed their heads and exited.

"Your Majesty," a fragile voice said from the eastern entrance to the tent. "It is an honour to meet you." The man approached and, on trembling legs, tried to kneel.

"Please do not strain yourself on my account," Evander said, leaning forward with an outstretched hand to stop the elderly man from stooping lower.

"You are too generous, your Majesty." The old man clasped his hands, his beige robes falling over his wrinkled fingers. "I believe I may have found a way to help ease the tensions with Q'Ohar." Evander raised his eyebrows and leant forward in his throne.

"Please do tell," Evander said eagerly.

"There is a sword that was made between a King of Q'Ohar and the first Sorcerer of Eresydon following the War of Hearts," said the old man. Evander frowned. If Q'Ohar had been involved in weaponry during the disruption in Eresydon, it would make his next meetings difficult.

"I have never heard of such an artefact."

"You would not have, your Majesty. It is a closely guarded secret within the church of Fendale. Even your father does not know of it."

"Then how do you? Are you in the church?" Evander asked. The man shook his head.

"I am not, but I am a scholar for one of the priestesses, she is an orphan from Thassena who has converted to the church of the Sorcerers. Whilst she has no power, you can imagine, being from Thassena, that she wishes to see the tensions concluded. So she divulged the information to me."

"Why would this help end the tensions?" Evander asked.

"The king's family believe it is owed to them for it was their metals that created it, even if it was the first Sorcerer, Vaeda, who blessed it." Evander kept his face neutral, trying not to react. But the notion that it was blessed by a Sorcerer filled him with a sense of dread. Wiccan were blessed by Aelwen with the power of healing and prophecies. Vaeda claimed her gift had awakened to bless her followers with the power to enhance their words for more, to use curses and spells rather than simply imbuing objects. While it was his very ancestors that had received this blessing, Evander had never practised, nor had he truly ever sided with the Sorcerers, even if that much was kept to himself growing up. While he should not stereotype or make assumptions about their intentions, he did not have a good feeling about a sword that had been created following the very war that had divided the state. "If you could return that sword to Q'Ohar and offer it as a gift from all the states, it may prompt the King of Q'Ohar to push for peace."

"It would not placate Thassena though," Evander added.

"The first state simply wants it to end. The Zerpane family has not been blessed with a daughter since the death of Levanna Zerpane. They believe that the deity Anela refuses to be found in such tumultuous times and has stopped blessing the Zerpane family as a result. You can imagine the frustration this has caused the Sevia family, who have no women to wed their sons to, as the alternative they believe could break the curse." Evander scratched at the stubble on his chin.

"Do you believe they're exhausted enough that as long as this stopped the King of Q'Ohar they would not further disrupt the peace?" Evander asked. The old man nodded. "And where would I find this sword?"

"It is hidden within the Valley of the Fallen, the site of the Great War, and..."

"Where Vaeda blessed her followers and created the Sorcerers," Evander finished. Evander had heard horror stories of what happened to those who entered the hills since then. The land tainted by so much death. Some never emerged again; others came out with tales of dark creatures, their minds lost.

"I can introduce you to the priestess. She would be able to guide you." Evander was silent, thinking it over. If he was with a priestess of the church, he was breaking no laws in taking something from the Sorcerers' region. His head was aching with the exhaustion of the day. He rubbed his forehead at the dull throbbing.

"What is your name? I should like to relay the proposal to the queen first, and I may need to call on you to present it to her yourself," Evander said. He leant back in his chair, blinking as his vision blurred momentarily. He could have sworn the shadows moved.

"There is power in a name, your Majesty," the old man said with a smile. Evander chuckled.

"You work within the lands of the Sorcerers but abide by the old proverbs of the Wiccan." Evander smiled. "Am I to assume you do not lean in favour of either race, Sir?" The old man stepped closer, and Evander hissed, clutching his head at the pain as a voice sounded through his mind.

"*You may call me the Historian.*"

Chapter Six

EVANDER

A gap existed in Evander's memories. If he had not been staring at a letter from Aleya—dated four days ago—he would not have noticed. But he had no recollection of even writing to his wife in the first place, nor did he recall agreeing to journey to the church in Fendale to meet with a priestess. Evander frowned, reading the letter again.

My love,

The boys are well. They have settled into a better sleeping pattern thanks to Athena's scented herbs in their room. Havia provides reports daily on any rising tensions between the Shapeshifters and the Sorcerers, though it has remained quiet during your visit with your father and the ruling six.

The historian you speak of is not one I know, but I can certainly have the archives checked for the records of those in service to the churches across Eresydon to see if there is mention. What is his name?

I trust your intuition, and if your instinct suggests locating this sword could lessen the tensions across Ithyion, while we focus on the tensions within, then I am happy for you to journey there. Though it pains me to know our time apart will be lengthened. I have gathered quite a collection of new books for you in the last two weeks you have been away. Do you really think you could be gone for another month? I know the journey back to our home from Fendale will take at least ten days, but will you really require over two weeks with this priestess to find the sword? I do not doubt you; I only ask as I worry for the boys, who will not have seen their father in nearly six weeks.

Regardless of the pain it causes me for us to be separated, I trust whatever action you take. Please keep in touch.

Ley.

Who was the Historian? And why was Evander about to meet a priestess about a sword? A rising panic crawled up Evander's chest as he gazed upon the ivy-covered steps leading to the church. Had the hawk not arrived minutes ago, would he have remembered whatever was to happen next? Evander looked for his commander but found him absent; only six guards aided him now. He frowned. He would not have travelled alone with the protection of six men. Something was wrong. Was he sick? Had something ailed his mind? He'd heard stories of memories fading in old age, but he was only twenty-three.

"Ah, your Majesty," a voice called as the church doors opened. Evander frowned. Had he met this man before?

"Remember," a voice echoed through his mind, and a flurry of memories returned. Evander standing in front of the Historian before he entered his mind and forced his will, writing a letter to Aleya to explain the plan, discharging the commander back to the capital, telling his father to wait on the border with the Shapeshifters until further instruction, travelling to Fendale with only six guards, much to his father and commander's disagreement.

"I would like to introduce you to the Sister of Fendale." The old man did not tremble like Evander's memory conveyed as he extended his arm to the door. A petite woman walked delicately down the steps, with a gentle round face and blonde hair pulled back tight. Her robes were a soft blue, an unusual choice for a priestess of the churches in Eresydon.

"Tell her she looks beautiful."

"You look beautiful, Sister Fendale." Evander's eyes widened, shifting to the Historian.

"Reach out and kiss her hand." Evander's hand trembled as he

tried to resist the movement and winced as his lips met the back of the priestess's hand.

"It is an honour to meet you, your Majesty," she said with a smile, though her attention was directed at the Historian rather than him.

"I should like to cancel our plans and return to my wife. Please excuse my—"

"That won't be necessary, Evander," the Historian said, approaching. "You resisted far more easily than others have in the past. I did not expect you to recall your missing memories so quickly. My power is less focused as I am not quite used to this body yet." The Historian reached for Evander's temples. His guards did nothing, their expressions vacant, even as Evander's eyes rolled back into his head and threads of dark shadow consumed his mind, weaving amongst his memories of the past four days and their meeting, as if trying to rewrite the narrative.

"You have nothing to fear. Your wife knows of your journey to find the sword. You trust Sister Fendale, who will guide you on the journey to the Valley of the Forgotten to retrieve the weapon." Evander's mouth hung open slightly as shadows weaved the words into his head.

"It will be easier once you accept the power she planted in you," the Historian murmured, clutching Evander's head. "I cannot see if your essences have merged; something blocks me, but once we have the sword, I will take Aleya."

Aleya. Evander latched onto the name as the Historian released his grip. If he had kept his fingers ingrained in his mind for a moment longer, he would have seen the memory of Aleya glowing brightly, that light in the memory seeping into Evander's mind and dulling the shadows. The man had to hail from Xyliar; the shadows suggested as much, while his control confirmed he was a Staxion. Regardless, he was the first person Evander had met from the secretive state, and so he did not trust nor know his intentions. Evander kept his expression neutral, hiding the fact that the Historian's attempt had failed at the last moment. So, the King of Eresydon played along.

"Sister Fendale, I appreciate you passing along your knowledge of the sword. This will do wonders to heal the kingdom," Evander said. Sister Fendale smiled, but her eyes, again, were on the Historian.

"It is my duty to serve."

***

The Valley of the Forgotten was haunting. Created by the hills on either side, it was scattered with bones, some of which Evander was certain were human. The narrow stream running through it was far darker than any stream in Eresydon; he wondered just what polluted it. Evander had grown up in Masdar, much further south. But even as the son of the protector, he had never ventured here. It was like someone had planted stories over the years to keep people away. The perfect place to hide an old artefact. As he continued riding behind Sister Fendale on horseback, openings appeared in the sides of the hills. Small dirt holes that became cave-like as they neared the eastern edge of Eresydon. The opening became rubble and stone, forming carved entryways leading into darkness. His eyes pulled on the claw marks along the archway of one, just as a low rumble sounded within.

"What was—"

"We are here, your Majesty," Sister Fendale said, pulling her horse to a halt and sliding from its saddle. Evander followed suit. He had agreed to his soldiers staying at the church as the Historian had suggested, leaving Evander to keep up the façade and journey alone with the sister.

He stared at the large cave opening. Symbols were etched around the entrance, painted in what he believed to be blood. Sister Fendale reached for a flint in her pocket and scratched it against the stone until she could light the two lanterns hanging at the entryway. She handed one to the king and began walking. Evander accepted it with a false smile and followed. Behind him, he weaved his own power, a trail of vines with small red flowers, a path for him should anything happen.

"Do you know the great history of these caves?" Sister Fendale asked, her voice echoing off the stone as they walked deeper into the darkness.

"I grew up in Tandale—of course I do. While I do not practice like my brothers, I know my heritage. Vaeda was Aelwen, the first deity's closest friend. They called themselves sisters, and Aelwen gifted her with an expanded lifetime so that she would live as long as her. One night during summer harvest, Vaeda awoke with a prophecy. When she interpreted it, it foretold that she would become reborn as a true deity and bless those who followed her with the same essence that had created Aelwen and Carlisle, granting their words more power. Whilst the Wiccan have always been able to enhance their healing and the use of objects with incantations, they have never been able to use it without linking it to something else. Vaeda promised their power would be their words."

"I apologise, your Majesty. I did not mean to insult you. Even if you did marry a Wiccan." The latter part of her so-called apology was very much insulting. Many in Tandale disapproved of marriages between Wiccans and Sorcerers. Evander tensed but continued the tale.

"Slowly, people came to trust her word, following her to gather in this very valley. She entered the caves alone, and when she returned, she carried a glass jar, gifted by Garridon, with the very essence that had been used to create the other deities across Ithyion. She took a piece for herself and added the rest to water collected from this stream and bid her followers drink, blessing them with the abilities the Sorcerers possess today."

"Do you think it odd that nobody ever saw Garridon gift her this essence? That this woman suddenly received a prophecy so many centuries after her birth?" Sister Fendale asked, still slowly guiding them through the dark caves.

"There was no reason to distrust her; she proved her place as a deity when she gifted the power."

"The Wiccan distrusted her," Sister Fendale added. "So much so that they descended on the valley and the war began, calling what they had done unnatural." Evander did not respond, wondering if it was possible the deity Vaeda had known about the war she would incite, if that had been a part of the prophecy bestowed upon her. "Your account is correct from what has been revealed to the people of Eresydon. But you are missing a piece, a missing piece that was the reason she needed a following with strengthened power behind her," Sister Fendale said.

"This sword?" Evander asked, and Sister Fendale turned her head and smiled.

"The Valley of the Forgotten is a sacred piece of land. So much power seeps into its bones, residue that remains from the hundreds of wielders and races that fought alongside the gods and the deities. And then all those in Eresydon who fought in the War of Hearts. The rock within the hills and the caves radiate with lingering energy, the perfect place to create something just as powerful, especially with the words of so many Sorcerers."

"But why did this sword need to be made in the first place? What benefit would it have to someone in Eresydon? Why did the past King of Q'Ohar" Evander asked. He glanced behind him, ensuring his trailing vines still followed, signalling his path and location. Sister Fendale sighed.

"So small-minded, so gullible. The King of Q'Ohar was never involved, it was simply a means to engage in conversation with you. This stretches far beyond your state. This weapon speaks of a way to dominate all Ithyion if its wielder willed it." The Historian had said gifting this sword to Q'Ohar would ease tensions, a lie he had fallen for. "What if I told you the woman who had this prophecy wasn't Vaeda at all but had killed her and taken her place?" Evander processed the words, the sudden arrival of the prophecy only a hundred years ago. "The woman who took her identity descended from an Eresydon mother but her loyalties lay with her father and the strongest power crawling through her veins. She would do anything to help him get what he wanted. Together, they extracted the metals that still lingered with power in these caves and moulded it into a sword with a second material found on the isles between Xyliar and Carvyre, a precious onyx stone—the stone left behind when Tungstyn is mined."

"The metal that inhibits power?" Evander asked.

"Yes," Sister Fendale confirmed. "The royal families that guard and mine the material in their states never thought to experiment with the stone that remains, that it, too, could have enhanced properties. But my father is an innovator. Its responsibility was holding the metal. Imagine what else it could hold if imbued with the words and power of hundreds of Sorcerers?"

Evander hadn't realised how far they had walked into the caves until Sister Fendale came to a stop in a large cavern. Sunlight shone through the cracks in the roof, highlighting a broad black sword resting on a stone plinth. Evander glanced between the exit and the sword.

"What does it hold?" he asked. The woman ran her hand along the dark sword. Within, smoke swirled at her touch as if it was alive.

"Souls," she whispered, as though the word was precious. "Whilst the sword was forged from the metal from these caves, the woman and her closest followers stood in a circle with sacrificial blood on their hands as they chanted. Outside the caves, hundreds of Sorcerers lined the valley, all committed to the same spell, all binding a piece of their souls to this sword." Sister Fendale gripped the handle of the sword, and dark shadows drifted out from her fingers, wrapping around her body until her appearance changed. Her pale blonde hair blew out of its tight updo into deep chestnut waves. Her blue silk gown was replaced by one of deep black embroidered with amber swirls.

"Who are you?" Evander tremored. The woman laughed.

"I can give myself any face or appearance that is needed to obtain my father's goal: Sister Fendale, Vaeda, Viola by birth." The woman finally met his eye again, one deep black, and the other an Eresydon green. From her mother. Evander swallowed.

"What happens to the pieces of souls when the sword is used?" The woman, Viola, swung the sword.

"By offering a piece of their souls, all those Sorcerers bound themselves to it. When they died, their entire being was linked to this weapon. It also contains the souls of every person it killed in the battle between Xyliar and Asynthos. Those who have betrayed my father are trapped within too. It will continue collecting souls with every drop of blood it tastes so that when it is wielded, thousands of dark beings will emerge, all in allegiance to the wielder." Evander backed away at her words.

"Why has Garridon never intervened? Why would he allow this?" Evander asked, giving up his ruse that he was still under the Historian's mental persuasion. The Historian. He realised then that he had to be Viola's father, changing his appearance as she had done too. But who was he? Viola smirked.

"Who do you think tricked him into handing over the essence to me in the first place? You've experienced my father's control. He can easily fabricate memories and have anyone believe anything—even a *god*. Convincing him a third deity to balance the playing field in the next war was easy," Viola scoffed. "Poor Garridon, so desperate to be loved he would fall for such things."

"You want me to believe he could warp the mind of a god?" Evander asked.

"My father has far more power than anyone realises. I've been using the sword in the valley to test the control over the souls within: the deceased Sorcerers, the Angels from the last war, the deformed creatures he killed to bulk out the numbers. To ensure they are all ready for the day he takes all of Ithyion should he not get what he wants."

"And what does he want?" Evander asked. Viola clenched her hand, and darkness squeezed into his mind as shadowed creatures and figures crawled from the tunnels linked to the cavern. Her voice echoed in his head.

You and your wife.

Chapter Seven

ALEYA

*T*hree years later

"He's approaching the gates now, your Majesty," Havia whispered in Aleya's ear. She released a shaky breath and combed back Errard's hair with her hand before kissing Arden's forehead.

"Boys, go with Aunty Athena to your rooms please." Aleya rose from where she had been crouched by the rose bed, tending to the red flowers in bloom.

"Want to stay!" Errard began to cry. Aleya choked back her tears but knew it was for the best that they be as far from her study as possible when he arrived.

"Come on, boys. If you're good and there are no tears, Aunty Athena might have some sticky pastries for you!" Havia exclaimed with forced excitement, casting another worried look in Aleya's direction. Aleya nodded, though she was not certain who she was trying to reassure. Horses whinnied on the other side of the wall, signalling his approach along with the falling rain. Pulling her shawl over her hair, Aleya made a run for the doors into her study, held open by her guards. They too watched her with concern. She had chosen this room as her study for its proximity to the gardens, hoping it would ease her anxiety over the last three years. It hadn't. Though it had been an ideal place to run to when she felt like she was suffocating. A knock sounded at the mahogany door, and Aleya smoothed down her high-necked red gown, the one he had commented on last time, and clenched her hands together to keep them from shaking.

"Come in," she called, though her voice was far from confident or queenly. The room dropped in temperature, and she waited, trying to assess his mood and figure out which version of her husband she would receive today.

"Ley," he breathed. She bit her lip as her nose tingled and eyes watered. His eyes roamed over her dress, and he smiled, a real smile, the one she had fallen in love with. "Red like the flowers I gave you." He smiled and walked forward. For three years now, he'd only worn black Sorcerer's leathers, abandoning the tartan representing their family. His hands were cold as they reached for hers, pulling her closer. The leather was hard against her skin, and she was slow to wrap her arms around his waist. He smelt musty, like damp caves rather than warm pine trees. He smelt of distance and despair, like darkness and greed. He didn't smell like her husband. But he sounded like it. She wondered how long that would last this time.

"I trust you had a safe journey," Aleya murmured into his chest, trying to prolong the embrace, knowing she would struggle to keep the tears from falling once she looked at his face.

"I didn't cross through Fedwin. I wanted to avoid crossing paths with Shapeshifters," he sighed. Aleya frowned. Still, he was adamant they were a danger, despite Aleya meeting with the ruling six only a month ago. She wouldn't tell him that, though. The ruling six harboured no distrust of her.

"I'm glad you're safe," Aleya said. When he pulled away, she went rigid under his touch. He froze. He noticed.

"You do not like your husband's embrace?" he asked.

"Of course I do, my love," Aleya insisted, forcing herself to look at him and smile. His returning smile was lopsided, the left side of his face still pink from the four claw marks slashed across it. A Shapeshifter, he had said. Aleya knew no wolf with claws large enough to leave such a mark. "I just wish they were more frequent," she said. It was the wrong thing to say. Evander pushed past her and planted his hands on his waist, staring out over her gardens.

"Not this again, Aleya." His voice hardened, the voice she recognised but could no longer associate with her loving husband. "I told you; the work I am doing in the Valley will help ease the tensions. It will put us in a position of safety."

"But there are no tensions, Evander. Q'Ohar and Thassena signed a peace treaty. They have no quarrel. The Shapeshifters will have no reason to break the peace in Eresydon unless the Sorcerers—"

"Unless they what?" Evander snapped, whirling to face her. Aleya flinched.

"Unless your father makes good on his threats to take their land by force, which he has not followed through on since those threats began two years ago." She raised her chin, trying not to buckle in fear.

"I am the only one who stops that. He answers to me!" Evander shouted. His eyes darkened as decaying vines crept around his feet. Aleya grimaced. She did not know what had happened to him. All she knew was that when he went to the Valley of the Forgotten three years ago in search of a sword, he had not been the same since. He visited every other month, appearing sicker each time, his power dwindling as though dying with him.

"I know, Evander."

"Your king; I am your king!"

"You are my husband!" Aleya raised her voice, her eyes flashing, threatening to release her power to subdue him, something she had not yet had to do.

"If I am your husband, then you will listen to me," he sneered.

"You forget who is of royal blood, Evander. You are a king by marriage, not by birth."

"And by the time I am finished, I will be king of all." He slammed his hand down on her desk, and shadows rushed from his palm. She reared back as he approached, moving his hand from the desk to her throat and slamming her against the door. The soldiers in the gardens moved, and she waved a hand, stilling them. "I will be King of Eresydon; I will be King of Q'Ohar; I will take anything and everything I want, and then he will reward me." Aleya stilled, trying not to strain her breathing as she scanned Evander's eyes.

"Who?" Aleya asked, resting a palm on his chest. Evander's grip loosened on her neck as his eyes bored into hers. Something flickered within them as her palm warmed. A light emanated from beneath it, lighting the shadows under his eyes, which glanced at his hand around her throat and widened. He dropped her and stumbled back, breaking the connection with the power Aleya knew was what small remnants of Sonos' essence still remained in her soul. Residue of the power remained on Evander's black leathers, fading with every second.

"Aleya, gods. Aleya, I—" The realisation burned in his eyes, as if he had not meant to lay a hand on her, or yell and say those things.

"Evander, talk to me. Tell me what is going on," she begged, stepping closer.

"No!" he exclaimed. "I don't—I don't want to hurt you." His voice cracked as the pale light on his chest continued to fade. He tapped the side of his head. "He is in here; I cannot get him out; I cannot stop—"

"*Who*, Evander? Is someone making you do something? Is someone threatening you? Blackmailing you?" she implored. He circled around the desk, keeping his distance.

"I can't remember; I can't! I don't know what—"

"Shhh, it is okay, my love," Aleya murmured. A tear fell down his cheek as the light on his chest faded. She felt him disappear. Whatever sliver of him that had tried to break free was snuffed out as his eyes hardened again.

"It is not okay!" Evander yelled, reaching for the vase of red flowers on the desk and hurling it in her direction. An arrow shot through the glass panes of the doors, striking the vase mid-air before it hit the queen. Aleya shielded her arms over herself as broken glass and pottery exploded through the room. She turned her head to see Havia standing in the gardens. A second bow notched, aimed at the king's head. Evander stormed around the desk; crumbling vines crawled out along the lawn, shadows drifting off his back. Aleya lunged for his wrist, gripping it tight.

"No!" she exclaimed. The same white light emanated from her palm, latching onto Evander's skin just as he turned on her, his other hand raised, careering toward her face. Aleya stumbled, her head hitting the desk as she fell, clutching at the pain festering in her cheek. Light residue remained on Evander's wrist this time as he looked between his hand and his cowering wife on the ground. The tears in his eyes returned.

"Ley—"

"Go," she whispered.

"Ley, please."

"She said go, your Majesty," Havia commanded, her bow still aimed at his head from where she stood in the open doorway to the gardens. When Evander stepped toward Aleya, Havia released the string. An arrow shot through the study, scraping the back of Evander's braids and pinning a clump of hair to the door. The light on his wrist still glowed softly as it trickled down onto the back of his palm, where his celestial tie still scarred his skin. *Some blessing*, Aleya thought, cradling her cheek. Evander mouthed *I'm sorry*, as he forced himself out of the study, trembling.

Havia and Aleya were silent. Still, the queen remained on the floor with her hand to her cheek, her protector standing with her bow ready. They both listened for the sound of horses vacating the courtyard, a sound they wouldn't hear again for at least another month. When the clatter of hooves on gravel began, Havia dropped the bow and fell to her knees before Aleya. At the same moment, one guard at the door left to fetch Athena, and the other pulled a cloth from his breast-pocket, passing it to the queen. A repeat of the same routine as last time. Aleya dabbed at her eyes before Havia took the cloth and gently stroked her cheek. There was no blood on it this time when she pulled away.

"It is not him, Havia. I swear it is not him," Aleya sobbed. Havia gave her the same pitiful look she usually did, the face of a friend who believed her queen could not see the abuse for what it was. But Aleya knew it was not him. "He returned this time, and when the remnants of Sonos's essence touched him, it brought him back to me. If I could just spend more time—"

"Aleya, you know I cannot allow that. My very being won't allow it. My body was physically struggling not to be in the same room as you the second I knew he had crossed the threshold."

"But—"

"If you say something has happened to him, I believe you. Even if we cannot make sense of what, I know that man loved you with all his heart."

"*Loves*," Aleya corrected. "He still loves me; I know it."

"I could send more spies to follow him, but the last did not return from the Valley, and I do not know how many more families I can visit to declare their loved ones missing." Havia's voice was strained, the impact of the last three years weighing on her too.

"Perhaps we wait and see how he is next month and set a plan in place to restrain him. If we must lock him up until we can fix him, then that is what it will take."

"I cannot risk you being in a room with him again Aleya. I worry even when I am on a different side of the castle." Havia hesitated before pulling something from her pocket and placing it in Aleya's hand. A golden brooch of a hawk with an emerald eye. "I had the Brodie clan imbue this for you. While the powers Aelwen gifted my family with allows me to sense when you are in danger, it does nothing to help if I am ever separated from you. As long as you wear this, you need only think of me, and it shall transport me to your location." Havia cupped Aleya's cheek. The queen was not surprised they had managed such a feat; as the first formed clan, they had the most power aside from the Mordanes. The queen opened her mouth to thank her, but two small heads poked round the corner of the door with syrup around their lips.

"Papa gone?" Errard asked.

"Yes, sweetheart, but Mumma is right here." Aleya reached for her boys and pulled them into an embrace, trying to stop her lips from wobbling.

"My sister is in the city with her youngest whilst her husband and eldest train. Why don't I have someone collect them and bring them here? It will provide the boys with company whilst you rest," Havia said. Aleya nodded, and Havia reached for Errard, tickling him to make him laugh. "Shall we see if Wren wants to come and play?" she asked. The boys clapped their hands together, and Aleya bit her lip to stop from crying. Each visit from Evander was becoming more unpredictable, and she could not risk putting her sons in the firing line.

Chapter Eight

EVANDER

Darkness filled the Valley of the Forgotten in blurs. The creatures prowled, hungry. As usual, Evander couldn't make out their faces, only blurs of shadows moving like wolves in the night, except three times greater. The only time he'd seen it clearly was when he'd been marked, when the creatures and Viola made it clear who was in charge. He was a loyal servant. He would do as she asked. He would do as the Historian asked. The shadows creeping through his mind whispered their praises. His black boots crunched against bones before squelching in a fresh puddle of blood outside the cave opening. A part of him wondered what innocent soul had wandered too close, or had it been another spy from the capital?

The image of a beautiful woman in a blood-red gown appeared in his mind, the dress darker than the golden red of her hair pinned back by delicate clips and pearls. Something about her stood out amongst the shadows and the Historian's plans, ones he gave before Garridon discovered him on his lands and banished him. It was six months ago. Viola had him out in the valley attempting to control the sword of souls when he lost influence over them; thousands swarmed out at once. He had just been doing as he was told; it was not his fault hundreds of shadows had drawn the eye of a god. Evander wondered if Garridon still watched him now in disappointment as he continued following the assignments of the man he'd banished. Why had he not intervened?

Viola had commanded Evander to retreat into the cave, but he had waited in the shadows, watching the heated exchange between

Garridon and the Historian before Garridon whispered something in the old man's ear which changed his appearance. The brown robes disintegrated into one as dark as the shadows around the pair; his hair darkened; his skin became taut and pale and scars littered his arms. Evander did not recognise him in this form either, though his pointed ears confirmed he was indeed a dark Fae of Xyliar; it was clear he was Viola's father too.

The argument was not what Evander expected. There were no displays of power or even hand to hand combat, and he wondered if they had seen one another since the man tricked Garridon into handing the essence over to Viola and creating the Sorcerers. Eventually, Garridon punched the man's chest, where a glow emanated; he screamed and screamed, his shadows wrapping around him until he faded into nothing. Evander only knew he was not dead because Viola did not cry.

"You are back sooner than I expected," Viola murmured, sipping from a glass of wine at the desk she had procured. Their cave had become more like a home in the last three years, with furniture taken from surrounding settlements or gifted by his father. Lord Alastair never questioned his son, not when he promised to work on a way for the Sorcerers to claim Eresydon with him as their king. Evander frowned.

You are my husband. The voice of the beautiful woman sounded in his mind. He knew her. But as he stared at the surrounding darkness, he could not recall how. Only that he was to keep her on side until the time came.

"Your wife, how was she?" Viola asked, rising from the stool. Her robe slipped down her shoulder, revealing her pale skin. She only wore the face of Sister Fendale when they exited the cave. In the darkness, her chestnut hair fell in loose strands, and her face was flushed as she trailed a finger over his chest.

"My wife?" he asked, and she chuckled.

"His power is still rooted deep if you struggle to recall her from the moment you leave," she murmured, reaching up on her tiptoes and licking a trail along the column of his throat. Evander shuddered. *Wrong.* "Your love must not be that strong if she cannot break through his darkness," Viola whispered, pushing her body against his until he fell back onto the bed. She crawled over his body, but he lay still. Something shouted in his mind, stopping him. But he couldn't discern the words or the source. "I can make you want this, but it would be so much fun for you to embrace it first," she groaned, grinding against his leathers. She pulled on his braids, forcing his head back to nip along the column of his neck before taking another sip of wine. "Tell me you want me, *king.*" She reached for his hand, roughly shoving it against her breast, which had fallen out of her robe.

"I want to—" Evander's voice choked in his throat as he stared at his hand, at the scar on the back of it. He frowned. Someone else had that scar. Shadows crept through his mind, different from the Historian's—thinner and more delicate. Hers.

"Good king, say it," she cried, pushing herself harder against him as she squeezed his hand, still holding the glass of wine in her other. She tilted the glass, letting the red stain her chest and robe, marking it as red as the gown worn by the beautiful woman in his subconscious. *His wife.*

"No, I—" Dark shadows reached from the corners of the cave, climbing toward his shoulders and holding him down as Viola continued crying out. "No, I have a—" Evander tried to speak, desperate to reach the part of him who saw his queen: a memory of her on a bed, light emanating from her chest. Evander struggled against the shadows trying to hold him captive, but it further excited Viola as she unlaced his leathers and climbed on top of him. His cries and protests melted into hers of pleasure. Light tried to weave through his mind as Evander clenched his eyes shut and thought of her.

"My wife," he said as Viola collapsed onto his chest. The image of their wedding day appeared in his mind. "My..." A single tear trailed down the side of his face, and Viola screamed in frustration.

Evander opened his eyes as she pushed herself off him, just in time to see the wine glass careering toward his face. Pain splintered his skin.

"Clearly, you are still fighting," she hissed. Then everything went black.

***

Shadows twisted and crawled around the four-poster bed as Evander reached for one of the books piled on top of the wooden chest. He flicked through the pages before looking at what else the shadows tried to hide. A green robe was discarded on the floor next to the bed's right-hand side. A rattle rested on the bedside table beside a glass of wine. He picked it up and sniffed it. Sparkling elderflower and rose water. Bile rose in his throat as he recalled the last glass of wine he had seen. The red trickling down her chest as she... Evander gagged, his fists collapsing onto the bed as he tried to erase the memory from his mind, the guilt threatening to destroy him. Though it had not been his choice. Tears filled his eyes again. His wife. He wanted his wife. He didn't want this.

"It would appear that whatever happened on your last visit to the capital weakened my hold somewhat," a silken voice said. Evander wiped the back of his mouth and turned his head. The Historian stood in front of the ashen fireplace, though he appeared much younger, donning his dark clothes. His eyes roamed Evander's body. "The only thing that can truly break my control is the power of the light Fae, that was gifted to them by Sonos." He narrowed his eyes. "Have you been able to hide a memory from me? One that confirms she has accessed the power of her essence? Have your souls merged already?" He met Evander in two strides. "But how could that memory stay hidden from me," he murmured. "Does your merging make you stronger?"

"How should I know?" Shadows whipped out from the bed and

along Evander's back, forcing the king to cry out and collapse to his knees.

"Regardless, it would seem the power is not enough to free you completely. Perhaps the further you stay away from her, the easier it will be to keep you under control." The Historian turned to look out of the balcony doors, peering at the dark night beyond. "You will make one final visit, the one I have been waiting for," he said. Though Evander struggled, he pushed himself up from the bed and braced the bedframe for support.

"I won't do anything else."

"You will, Evander. It is only in this prison of your mind that you retain some of yourself, your will to fight back for your love," the Historian tutted. "You should understand, for I am doing all of this for love." He sauntered back to Evander, gripped the sides of his head, and forced all his power into him. Evander roared as shadows invaded his throat, ears, neck, consuming every part of him as the Historian whispered into his soul.

"You will declare the Sword of Souls, a sacred hidden artefact of the Sorcerers', has been stolen. You will claim the Queen of Eresydon stole it to use it against the Shapeshifters, forcing them to your side. You will declare yourself King of Eresydon and the Wiccan an enemy of the state for supporting their queen."

"No I—" Evander's words were mumbled as he choked on darkness, as the threads searched through his mind and sliced at every image of his wife. Her tentative smile when their hands interlaced on their wedding day. Her drunken blush as they crawled into bed together that first night and read. The way her pulse quickened every time he kissed her hand. Her anxious trembling as she told him she loved him and boldly kissed him for the first time. The smell of cherry blossom blooming in spring outside their windows the first night she allowed him to truly make her his own. Her grin as he returned home from a visit to the shifters, and she ran, launching herself at him and whispering that she was pregnant into his ear. The heartbreak as he watched her bleed out on their bed. His relief as their *essences merged, and she came back to him, vowing never to leave. The first laughs of his sons, before the darkness truly took over, before his visits became less frequent. The shadows sliced at everything as the Historian solidified his plan.*

"Once you have detained the queen, you will call for Viola. She will contact me and make the arrangements to have you and the queen transported to Xyliar, where we can begin our next steps." Evander clung to an image in his mind. Sat on the edge of their bed with Errard in his arms, leaning down to kiss Aleya as she cradled Arden.

"I am yours, even when we are walking through the trees of death together."

"Do you understand, Evander?" The Historian asked. The memory faded, the light of his life going with it, as he nodded slowly. "What are you to do?" he asked. The shadows slowly retreated from Evander's body, returning to the Historian. Wisps remained on Evander as he clenched his hand, his own darkness emerging.

"Capture the queen."

Chapter Nine

ALEYA

Aleya gathered her sons from their beds, who muffled their cries against her chest; the sounds were almost completely drowned out by the yelling outside the castle. The door slammed open, and Aleya was quick to pull vines through the cracks in the windows and floorboards, ready to protect the heirs to the Eresydon throne.

"It's just me," Havia said, panting as she ran into the room and lifted Errard from Aleya's grip, stroking his head as he cried into her shoulder. Athena appeared a moment later with a large brown sack on her back filled with as many things as she could carry from the apothecary tower. Under her other arm was a metal breastplate and attachments. She dropped the bag and forced Aleya's arms up as she lifted the breastplate over her head.

"Could you gather anything from the soldiers?" Aleya asked as Athena tugged the buckles on either side of her body tight, securing the protective breastplate to the queen before clipping a similar metal to her forearms. Aleya reached out to brush the tears from Arden's eyes.

"They're saying you stole a sword, one you wish to use to assert power over the Shapeshifters," Havia said, her frown mirroring the queen's.

"Why would I have a sw—" Aleya stopped, her voice trailing off. A sword. The very reason her husband had left three years ago and seldom returned. A sword that would apparently ease the tensions in Q'Ohar, tensions that no longer existed, but were instead the cause of a mob outside the castle. Dread ran through her body as she strode to the window in the tower and peered down below. Her heart stilled—or broke completely, she wasn't sure. Riding through the throngs of Sorcerers in brown leathers and silks, with raised and burning torches, was the man she loved. Evander rode through the crowd on a night black horse; the black of his cloak melted into his stallion's coat as darkness shifted around him.

"It's Evander," Aleya breathed.

"I knew he was going to push further after his last visit," Havia cursed. "Before he slapped you, Aleya, he stated very clearly what he wanted. To be king of it *all*. Regardless of whatever triggered it, he is corrupted with greed and the need for power."

"But it's not him. It's not—" Aleya spun as Havia gripped her shoulders, forcing the queen to look her protector in the eye.

"Aleya, I know you love him. He is your husband, king, the father of your children." Behind her, the boys sniffled in their nightclothes. "But if I do not get you out of this castle, he will mean nothing to you, for you will be dead." Havia's expression was stony as she stared at her queen, who was pained by the slap of such harsh words. Clattering sounded up the stairs, but Havia didn't move. She sensed no danger; it was the soldiers she had summoned. Their marching stopped outside the door, waiting for their queen and their next orders. The castle shook.

Havia and Aleya looked out the window. A large tree, carved into a battering ram, was being deployed against the castle's main doors. Bodies patrolled the walls of the castle, looking for other entry points. "We do not have time to wait, your Majesty." The use of a title from Havia prompted Aleya to think rationally. A reminder that *she* was the queen; if she wished to see peace in her state again, she had to survive this. Aleya's eyes scanned the crowd, hoping for one last look at her husband. When his eyes found her, a tingling spread through the back of her palm and her chest, the location of their celestial tie and then where their essences had once merged.

Aleya counted, waiting for something in his eyes to shift, anything to tell her he was still the man she fell in love with.

One.

Evander's expressionless face changed until a smirk formed on his lips.

Two.

His leather-gloved hands dropped the reins of his horse.

Three.

He reached into a bag on his horse to retrieve a glint of metal.

Four.

He lowered the newly made diadem onto his forehead, with an inverted black stone at its centre.

Five.

His eyes found hers again.

Six.

His smirk faltered.

Seven.

Aleya's pulse quickened with hope.

Eight.

Evander reached up as brown, decaying vines rose around him.

Nine.

The vines shot toward the window of the tower.

Ten.

The glass shattered, and darkness wove into the room.

"Move, move, move!" Havia shouted over the ringing in Aleya's ears from where she lay on the wooden floor. Gloved hands reached for her forearms as soldiers lifted her off the floor. Tension stopped them as they pulled. Aleya turned to find that the rotting vines, which should be easy to snap, were reinforced by wisps of shadows now climbing her legs. A moment later, Havia brought a sword down on them, snapping them off, but the shadows around her legs remained. She would have to worry about that later.

Aleya's eyes scanned the room in panic until she found her sons, each in the arms of a soldier. They guided them out of the tower and down the staircase. Pain seared in Aleya's ankles, and when she looked down, the shadows were twisting tighter.

There was no time to stop.

Shattering filled her ears as the crowd smashed windows on the floors below. Glancing over the banister on the third floor, a row of guards still protected the doors, ready to fight the second the Sorcerers broke through. Aleya stumbled; the guards on either side of her pulled her upright, the pain moving to her calves. The door down below splintered, and yells filled the castle entryway. Athena's eyes widened ahead of Aleya; they were running out of time. Decaying vines crawled up the banisters, searching for her. The entourage took a sharp turn toward a large tapestry depicting the Great War. The soldiers moved to either end, lifting it up and away from the wall to reveal a hidden door. But the tapestry fell in sync with the soldiers who were tossed to the floor by shadows. Chanting filled the castle. Aleya paused, looking at Athena, waiting for her to translate. Her lips moved slowly, and she closed her eyes, trying to decipher the words in the old language as the remaining soldiers swung at the vines still reaching for them.

"How does he know this is where you are? The soldiers below are still holding them back on the first floor?" Havia asked, rushing to her side and putting an arm around her waist to free the two soldiers. She winced in pain. Her leg.

"The shadows," Aleya said, looking down at where they twisted and climbed her skin. Havia knelt in front of her and reached to pull them off her. She cried out at the blackened blisters forming on her palms. Aleya's chest and hand tingled again. He was near. Or was the universe reminding her of Sitara's gift, of Sonos' light that only ever emerged when she was in Evander's presence? A balance to the darkness, the counterpart to Sitara's power.

Aleya balanced herself against the banister and stooped to her ankles, wrapping her fingers around the shadows. They burned for a second before their grip loosened, trying to kiss and climb her hand. What was she supposed to do? She had done nothing specific when she had left a mark of light on Evander; it had just happened.

"My boys."

Aleya froze, as did the air and time around her. She blew red locks of hair out of her vision, searching for the voice which belonged to the man who had not properly seen his sons in three years, except for the first time he had hit her. Never again after that. Aleya's head turned to the side as the soldiers backed away from the top of the stairs, still clutching her children. Vines moved along the floor, reaching for their ankles.

"The spell is to keep you from leaving the castle!" Athena yelled from in front of the tapestry. Aleya shot her own vines out toward her friends, trying to ward off the darkness attempting to entrap them. Her soldiers fell, her boys spilling from their arms. "They only need five more repetitions, Aleya, and it's over!"

The queen looked around her, and then everything slowed. Her soldiers on the floor, their powers useless against the shadow-coated vines. Athena, going blue in the face, as the vines moved to her neck. Havia, on her left, stabbing at them with her dagger, trying to reach her queen. The sea of bodies in Sorcerers' leathers ascending the staircase, their mouths moving in sync as they repeated the spell. Evander watching her. The hunger in his eyes, the desire to stride across the many bodies to take her. There was no love there. The man who once pledged his devotion to her, and her alone, was no longer. The velvet red flowers and the laughter they shared while turning pages in their books were a distant memory. There was only darkness and greed. He didn't want her. He wanted her crown.

Aleya forced herself to stand and reach for a discarded sword. The shadows around her leg slowly twisted around her torso now, as if looking for something in her armour. Summoning her power, she prepared to bring the trees outside the castle down upon the Sorcerers. A rush of wind brushed through Aleya's hair, and she gasped as her power shifted through her. Her eyes glazed over as a prophecy was gifted to her.

When there is dark, there is light,
When there is loss, there is fight,
There is balance in all,
A cost to one's fall.
When darkness consumes, know there is a price,
When all is lost, love is the greatest sacrifice.

Aleya gasped as her focus returned, just in time to watch Evander's cruel smile as he turned his eyes from her and slowly knelt on the ground. The shadows around her torso climbed up to her chest, as if burrowing for something, hunting for something it needed. Its counterpart. Aleya glanced down and touched the shadows' resting place, where they searched for Sonos's essence. She clenched her fist over the shadows and looked up. Evander spread his arms wide as his sons walked around the bodies on the floor toward him.

"No!" Aleya screamed. *Where there is dark, there is light.* Aleya ripped her hand from her chest. Slowly, a glow formed in her hand, pulsing brighter as Evander's eyes briefly flickered to hers. *Where there is loss, there is fight.* Aleya cast her hand outward, and white light burst through the room, toppling Evander and the Sorcerers down the stairs. The golden light hovered just long enough for the vines to recede, and for Havia and Athena to grab the princes and duck under the tapestry. Aleya glanced back for a second, searching for the bright green eyes she had once loved, but there was only a fading light and shadowed vines as Aleya turned and ran from her home and her husband.

Chapter Ten

ALEYA

Five Years later

The scent of blood filled Aleya's nose. Not the sharp metal tang of human blood, though that was still present, mixed amongst the grass and the weapons swung by her soldiers. No, this was the dark, decaying smell of shadowed blood. The only name they could give it. The name for the black tar that spilled when a blade met the neck of the shadowed wolves they had battled on one too many occasions over the last five years, the times where her husband relentlessly tried to reach her. She did not know what he, or whomever he was loyal to, had done to create such beasts.

Aleya wiped her blade against her leg, the black tar now stained with red from the last Sorcerer she'd killed. She craved fresh air to mask the smells and took a deep breath. She withdrew her power, cutting off the tie to the vines scattered across the battlefield. Havia, supporting an injured soldier, clapped Aleya's back as she walked past.

They had won this round, their first battle in ten months. Time allowed the Sorcerers to infiltrate locations across Fedwin with blood-marked spells designed to weaken her soldiers. Athena had spotted the first one in the region's capital not long after it had been made, the blood still drying underneath a table in a soldier's home when she had checked on an old wound. Instead of removing the mark, making it clear to the Sorcerers they had foiled their plans, they went along with it. Aleya sent soldiers to check for new marks, carrying the herbs from Athena to counteract the spell, which they'd ground into a fine dust and dotted at the four compass points of the symbol. They pretended their people were falling sick and slowing in training. Aleya knew eyes watched the settlements. They had to do enough to convince them that they were weakened.

It worked. The creatures and Sorcerers that met them on the battlefield today had not been prepared for their steady volume and strength. They had lost in only four hours. Evander had not come. He never did. She had not seen him since she had run from her home with her children, her closest confidants, and the soldiers she could move unseen until a message could be spread for others to find her.

Soldiers bowed their heads as she found her footing through the fields and then over the winding roots of Hystone forest, the largest and closest coverage on shifters' land to Stendon's border, the Wiccan region Evander had now claimed for the Sorcerers. Aleya's soldiers could still enter; they had infiltrated and regained settlements occasionally over the years, providing updates to the Wiccan families who were adamant they would not leave their homes. But the majority, along with their queen, had fled to Fedwin.

The ruling six had been waiting for her. It took ten days for their small entourage to run through the Wiccan lands, warning families as they went, while the Sorcerers hunted them down. They had tried to force Aleya to cross over the border sooner, closer to the capital, but she refused to leave her people behind. When Aleya, exhausted, finally stumbled to the border holding her two boys, she froze at the sight that awaited. Six wolves sat watching her and the crowd she'd gathered. Soldiers, families, entire towns. All outrunning Evander. Aleya raised a hand, waiting for a sign, for permission to seek refuge. Gradually, all six wolves had lowered their heads in a bow, welcoming them into their homes.

Fedwin was a sensible location to run to. With shifters still stuck in their animal forms, many had abandoned their homes long ago, leaving plenty of towns and buildings for her people to inhabit. For the first year, Aleya had one of those homes. But she was done hiding after the Sorcerers had attempted to burn down a quarter of the Hystone Forest. Since then, she had lived in a camp as large as a small city in its centre, the most easily defendable location, and the best for spying on the border.

Over the last five years, Aleya had called for aid every week. She had received no reply, though there was no indication whether that was because the other states did not want to get involved, or if all her communication attempts had been intercepted. Aleya would not give up. Civil war had ravaged Eresydon more than once over its existence. She would not be the reason it fell to ruin. *When all is lost, love is the greatest sacrifice.* The words of the prophecy made her shiver again. She refused to think of the many people and things she loved, for she refused to sacrifice them. Prophecies had been few and far between since the beginning of this war. Many claimed Aelwen refused to grant them during a time of such turmoil. Others said it was her right to for they needed the help; the lack of them suggested the Sorcerers had done something to block their power. Aleya wasn't sure what she believed. All she knew was that she had received no other prophecy since that night. Nor had she been able to access Sonos's essence again.

"You look tired."

"Just what a woman wants to hear, father," Aleya said, accepting the tankard of water he offered. He looked equally as tired with his rolled-up sleeves covered in blood.

"How many?" Aleya asked.

"Not as many as last time."

"How many?" she asked again.

"Seventy-eight," her father sighed. Aleya gulped back the last of the water and slammed the tankard down.

"I'll start the visits to their families," Aleya said, rinsing her hands in the bowl of water outside her tent before beginning to undo the buckles on her breastplate. "I just need to change first." Her father reached for her arm.

"Aleya, you cannot visit seventy-eight families. You need to rest."

"I will rest when my soldiers are rightfully mourned for protecting me and our right to peace."

"It is their job, Ley."

"Don't call me that," Aleya winced, and her father's eyes softened. "Just because it is their job doesn't mean their death is expected and my sorrow assumed."

"I know, but—"

"Aerial cover!" Voices screamed as Aleya re-buckled her breastplate.

"Positions!" Havia yelled. She exited her tent, her shirt half-unbuttoned and her lips swollen as Athena appeared behind her, scraping back her hair. Aleya's eyes immediately turned to her sons' tent; she breathed a little easier when she spotted her father already reaching them, ushering them back inside. "Hold!" Havia screamed again as the sound of notching bows filled the forest. Aleya reached for her shield on her back and approached the archery station beside Havia. The queen scanned the trees, ensuring all the makeshift archery points at the top of the trunks were manned.

"What could possibly be attempting an aerial approach?" Aleya murmured to her protector.

"No clue," Havia replied. "But aren't you glad I took one look at those damned shadow beasts and said 'why wouldn't someone also attempt to make ones that fly?'" Aleya nodded, scanning the gaps in the foliage. A shadow drifted then, then another, and another. Three. The queen held her breath, waiting for them to near so she could assess the danger. Aleya's mouth dropped open.

"Are those—" Athena trailed off as three shapes hovered in the sky.

"Permission to enter?" a female voice shouted from the sky.

Havia looked at the queen and shook her head, indicating she detected no danger. So, Aleya nodded back.

"Granted!" Havia shouted back to the female. "Hold position," Havia commanded the archers. The three bodies glided in through the narrow gaps in the trees. The leaves rustled, and a breeze pushed the strands of hair framing Aleya's face as wings flapped in the air. "Lower," Havia commanded, but she did not tell her archers to disarm completely in case danger was imminent.

The ground shook as the three bodies collided with the soil. They knelt with a fist keeping each of them upright. Aleya knew she should school her expression, but she was amazed at the power and beauty of the three Angels as they stood. The Angel on the right had the largest wings, a shade of blue that would rival the oceans of Thassena. His skin was sun-kissed, and his eyes glowed the same hue as his wings as he slowly retracted them until he stood in a polished silver armour over pale blue padding. On the right, the Angel with wings the colour of flames and blood scanned the camp, assessing for any move against them. Aleya sensed the Angels would make it out of the camp just fine, even if the archers loosed their arrows. These were no ordinary Angels with wings as pure as snow, nor did any of them look old enough to wield lightning before Asynthos had been cursed to bear no more Stormbringers. These Angels were unique—special.

Neither of the men stepped forward to greet the Queen of Eresydon. While the males had retracted their wings, the female kept hers on display. Her wings were as beautiful as the foliage above, each feather resembling the way a leaf transitioned from green to burnt amber with the turn of the year. If her wings were not evidence enough, her red hair was braided until it fell to her waist. When she twisted her hands, red flowers bloomed along the forest floor. Nobody spoke as the queen watched the three Angels, making it clear she was deliberating on what to do, putting them on edge as the two male Angels shuffled on their feet with an exchanged glance. Aleya wondered if the female's display of power meant the other two men wielded fire and water. She had never heard of powers crossing over within races. Was this natural? Or forced? Aleya thought of the shadowed creatures; they must have been created somehow, having never existed on Eresydon in the past.

"You hail from Eresydon?" Aleya asked the female, who bowed her head.

"I was born in Andor before the Great War," she said. She knew Angels had far longer life spans than the races of Eresydon, only parallelling the Xyra of Q'Ohar, and the races of Caryvre and Xyliar. The average one-hundred-and-fifty lifespan now of Aleya and Athena seemed miniscule as they stared at this woman who appeared to be in her mid-thirties.

"Present your name and purpose," Aleya finally said, searching for any sign of a lie in the woman's expression. She raised her hand to her chest where the royal sigil of Asynthos was engraved. Three mountains under three stars.

"Alyssa Balfour. I bring word and support from the Queen of Asynthos."

Chapter Eleven

ALEYA

Laughter, a rarity these days, filled the dining tent as Elias, the blue-winged Angel, beat Jayesh, the fiery Angel, in yet another arm wrestle. Soldiers passed thynai coins from their wagers. Aleya bit into a frostberry pastry, one of the sweetest things she'd had in years. When Aleya agreed the three Angels could stay and meet with them, they had first requested to fly back to their encampment, where they had carried over supplies with a group of additional Angels. They were fast and returned in an hour with twenty others and chests of supplies. Foods, stalactite healing water, short daggers, and herbs. Aleya worried someone would see them, but the female Angel promised they had stayed above cloud coverage until they were close enough to drop through the foliage.

Aleya smiled, watching the red head smiling beside Havia. Two Balfour women, generations apart. It seemed Alyssa had only known the station of her family name later in life. A woman she called Jes, with a sad lilt in her voice, had approached her when she was a child and said entering the queen's employment would guarantee her family the money to survive. If only Alyssa had known her father, who she had never met, had been a Balfour. If she had known she was a Balfour, she could have asked for a lineage test and money to support her grandparents instead of accepting Jes's offer. Yet doing so would have deprived her of all the adventurous tales she had to fill the dinner table. Fate had guided her life in a different direction.

The woman caught Aleya watching her, and the atmosphere shifted. Alyssa set her drink down and angled her body back to face the queen, planting her forearms on the table.

"You need help," Alyssa said.

"We've needed help for five years," Aleya said, her tone shorter than she intended. Alyssa frowned. "Where was your queen's answer to our calls the first time I asked—or the fiftieth?"

"She has received no such communications."

"Then how did you know we need help?" Havia asked.

"We were on route to Xyliar a month ago, to see if there was any movement on them opening their borders. It's a boring trip, because it always provides the same answer. No movement. So, we detoured and found a valley filled with shadowed creatures."

"You've known for a month?" Aleya asked. Alyssa flinched.

"We had to convince the queen to help," she said.

"So you are *not* here on the order of the Queen?" Aleya asked.

"Elias is very convincing," Alyssa smiled, but it quickly faltered. "We have seen this power before, when Xyliar attacked Asynthos."

"The shadowed creatures?" Aleya asked, but Alyssa shook her head.

"The darkness."

Aleya and Havia shared a look, thinking of Evander.

"The King of Xyliar, Valon, arrived on our shores, with an army of copper soldiers on the ground, and winged beasts in the sky, some that transformed in and out of Fae form," Alyssa explained, and Aleya's eyes widened.

"Xyliar has a queen, not a king; at least they did." Havia frowned.

"A long story for another day," Alyssa sighed.

"What did he want?" asked Aleya. Alyssa's eyes drooped as she wrung her hands.

"Two Angels. Unique Angels."

"But he didn't get them?" Aleya asked.

"No." Alyssa shook her head. "He sent darkness to the palace, but before he could reach them, they took their own lives. And we"—Alyssa nodded to Elias and Jayesh—"were able to expel his power long enough for him to realise he had lost what he wanted and turn back to the fifth state."

"How did you expel the power?" Aleya asked, thinking of the way her light had briefly stopped him.

"We merged the essence of our power," Alyssa whispered. Aleya glanced at Havia, and the Angel frowned. "You're not shocked," Alyssa commented. Havia shook her head in a silent instruction for the queen to not divulge what had happened between her and Evander when she almost died in childbirth.

"We've heard stories," Aleya lied. "Myths."

"It was enough to form a protective barrier around the castle and push back the darkness, but—" Alyssa shifted, seemingly conscious of all the surrounding bodies. "Nobody else in the state has done it since. Only us three. We think it's something to do with the fact we hold unique power, being of two bloodlines."

Aleya nodded slowly, but that didn't explain why she and Evander had merged so easily, and why Sitara had been so confident they would be able to. They were the ruling king and queen, making them the most powerful in Eresydon. Could that be it? The strength of Aleya's ancestors' powers in her body?

"We can do it again for you here, but the queen needs something in return." Alyssa said. There was the catch. What would Aleya have to sign away to guarantee her state peace? She nodded, waiting. "She wants to arrange a secret meeting between all the rulers, except Xyliar, and meet on the Isle of Gods."

"Why the Isle of Gods?" Aleya asked, frowning. Alyssa looked her dead in the eye, as though needing to emphasise the point she was about to make, to ensure Aleya took her seriously.

"She wants to call upon Sonos and Sitara."

***

"I can't believe it worked," Havia said, slowly crossing the forest floor outside the castle of Andor. Alyssa had held true to her word and, in the space of three weeks, had eradicated the shadowed creatures prowling Eresydon. They had also captured and detained nearly three quarters of the Sorcerers for questioning before returning to Asynthos, all while Aleya's soldiers held the castle in the capital under siege. It felt wrong, how quickly they had managed it, as though they were being granted free access.

"I should hope it did, given what we must repay the Queen of Asynthos," Aleya muttered.

"It was the right idea to not tell her Sonos is missing," Havia said. "It secured the help we needed."

"It was deceptive," Aleya murmured, unable to escape the guilt that she would arrive on the Isle of Gods in three months' time, knowing they would fail in trying to call upon the first two celestial gods. She did not want to think about the wrath she may face if they succeeded in calling upon Sitara, only for her to find Aleya had failed in even trying to locate Sonos, while her husband had fallen into darkness and its greed.

The towering trees blocked the light where Aleya crouched behind the large rock. Pushing her red hair from her face, she glanced between the cracks, assessing if they had truly won the war. Bodies littered the castle steps and rubble crushed most of the fallen. Her eyes trailed the walls up into the treetops, where the moss-covered castle was hidden from view. Others could still be trapped in the upper levels.

"Are you calling it?" a voice whispered. She turned to meet Havia's eye.

"It seemed too easy," Aleya replied. "The castle has been under siege for three weeks, and then suddenly today the soldiers are more spread out, and the pathway to the castle is clearer." Aleya glanced through the crack again, assessing the bodies for movement. She flicked her finger forward, directing a vine to snake across the floor. She held her breath, watching and waiting to see if the sudden movement prompted any surviving soldiers to charge. Her vines reached the castle doors with ease and looped through the heavy handles. Aleya tugged.

"I want my home back as much as you do, but something feels off. I have not seen him, dead or alive."

"The man's a coward and probably fled," Havia scoffed. The image of his valiant actions in past battles came to Aleya's mind.

"He wasn't always," she murmured.

"I'll call it then. I want to get home to Athena." Havia's blood-smeared face cracked into a smile as she ran forward with her sword raised.

"Havia Balfour, get back here!" Aleya hissed.

"Are you commanding it? If that is a command then you are declaring yourself queen again, which means we have in fact WON!" Havia shouted the final word, and cheers echoed through the trees, where Aleya knew the rest of her soldiers lay in wait. Her vines sensed something by the door.

"Wait!" Aleya called. "Havia!" Aleya screamed as a darker vine, not belonging to her, whipped from the door and wrapped around Havia's neck, tugging her back into the arms of the man Aleya had searched for.

"Come out, Aleya." His voice was just as she remembered it, his accent rough and sending tingles up her spine. Rising from behind the rock, Aleya lifted her arms in the air as she dropped her sword.

"Let her go, Evander. We both know it's me you want."

"Of course it is. Why would I not want my wife?" Evander's voice held no hatred as he stepped from the darkened doorway into the streaming light through the treetops. Aleya's heart pounded as she looked upon him. His hair was the same golden blonde, the top half braided back to reveal hundreds of different shades. He had shaved off his beard, revealing a strong jaw beneath which made his lips more prominent. Still, a golden crown sat upon his head, complementing the glow of his green eyes.

"I haven't been your wife for six years," Aleya said, stepping carefully towards the entryway and over the bodies that had fought for her. She had lost enough soldiers to understand it was a part of life, a part of war; regardless, she sent a silent prayer for them.

"Just because you were not here does not mean you weren't my wife," Evander replied.

"I was not here because of the decisions you made for our lands," Aleya spat. He had the audacity to wince, to appear hurt. Growls sounded behind the trees and Aleya took pleasure in the way Evander's eyes widened. "They sided with your cause?"

"Of course they did," Aleya responded, whistling low to the wolves prowling the castle perimeter. Evander backed away as Aleya strolled up the stone steps towards him.

"Surrender, Evander. I will not make your life hard." Aleya's voice was soft, exactly how he liked it. Aleya locked eyes with Havia, whose hands clutched the vines around her throat. She flicked her gaze pointedly at Havia's waist, where a poisoned dagger was tucked into her belt. Havia's eyes widened as she mouthed 'are you sure?' Aleya gave the slightest nod before distracting Evander again. "You can keep rooms in the castle under heavy guard. I will allow you access to the twins, provided I am present." Evander's eyes softened at the mention of the twins. Aleya swallowed the lump in her throat at the lie as Havia pretended to struggle, loosening one hand from the vines to reach for the dagger's hilt.

"Do they miss me?" Evander asked, his voice cracking. Aleya swallowed, trying to keep her voice level as she spoke the truth, all the while knowing what was to come.

"Of course they miss you. You are their father. Boys need their father," Aleya whispered, just as Havia pulled the dagger free and stabbed Evander's thigh. Before he reacted, Havia spun, still trapped in vines; she launched the dagger into his chest, pushing him against the stone wall. The vines withdrew as the glow of his eyes faded. Havia embedded her dagger further into his chest before backing away, clearing the path for her queen.

Aleya's heart broke at the tears pooling in her husband's eyes and spilling over the wrinkles that had deepened since she last saw him.

Evander's lip quivered. She knelt before him and cupped his cheek. The wedding ring, still on her finger, glinted in the sun, the symbol on it matching the pin on her husband's jacket. Evander reached up to Aleya's red hair, his favourite feature, and smiled.

"I still love you," he whispered. Those were his last words before his eyes went vacant, and his head lulled back. Aleya pulled the dagger out, trembling against the pain radiating through her chest as she felt herself being torn in two. She placed her hand over his chest. A faint glow coated the celestial tie on the back of her hand before it faded away, leaving her skin unmarked and the feeling that had sat in her chest, uniting her with her husband and their souls, was gone. Aleya let tears fall down her cheeks as she turned her head up to the sun, realising the pain Sitara must feel at never being able to find her love, as Aleya permanently lost her own. Now, she had to confront that goddess and tell her she would still not see the other half of her soul.

Q'OHAR

THE RULE OF THE DEITIES 0D - PRESENT DAY
[PRESENT YEAR: 87]

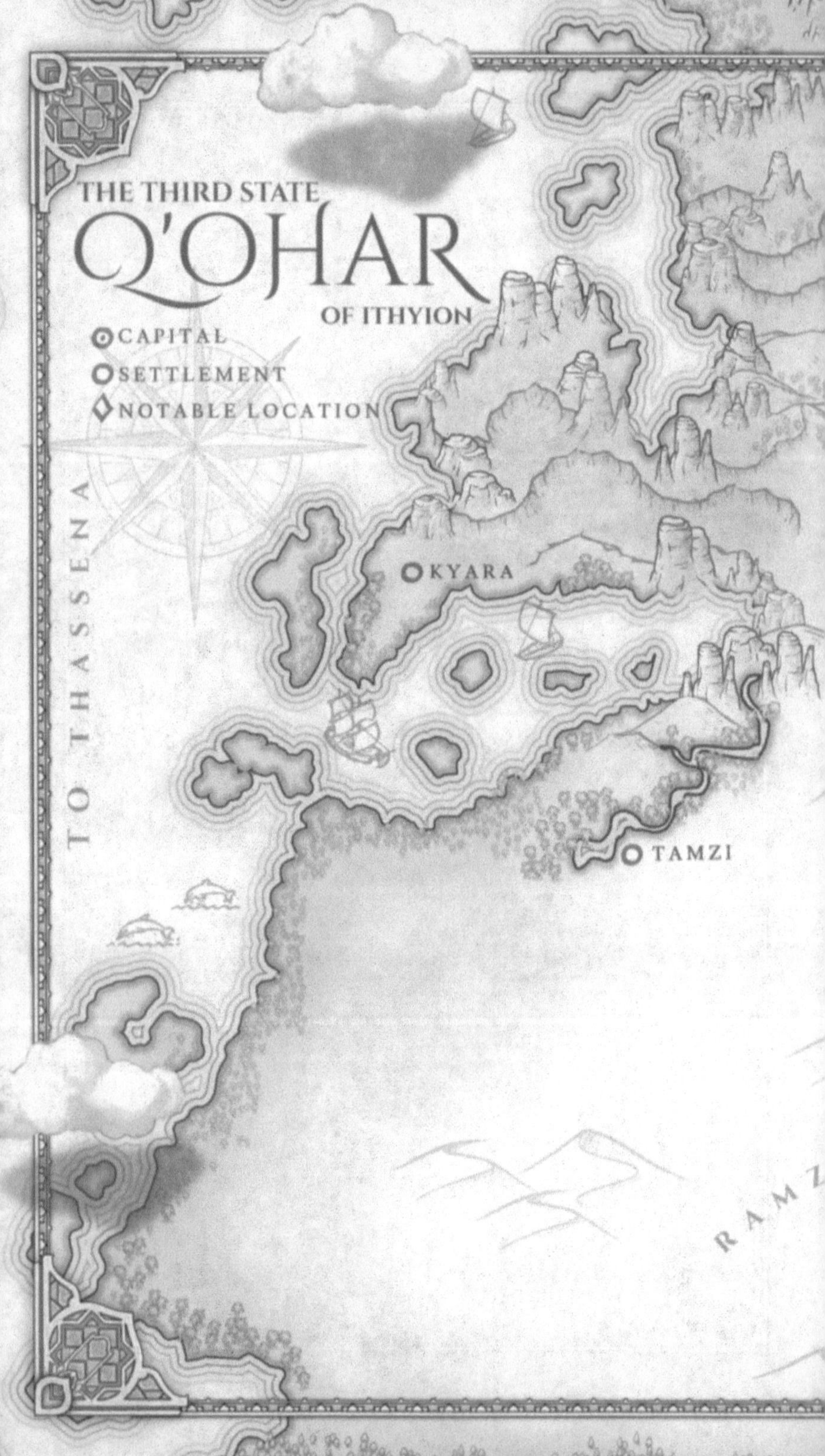

THE THIRD STATE
Q'OHAR
OF ITHYION
CAPITAL
SETTLEMENT
NOTABLE LOCATION
TO THASSENA
KYARA
TAMZI
RAMZ

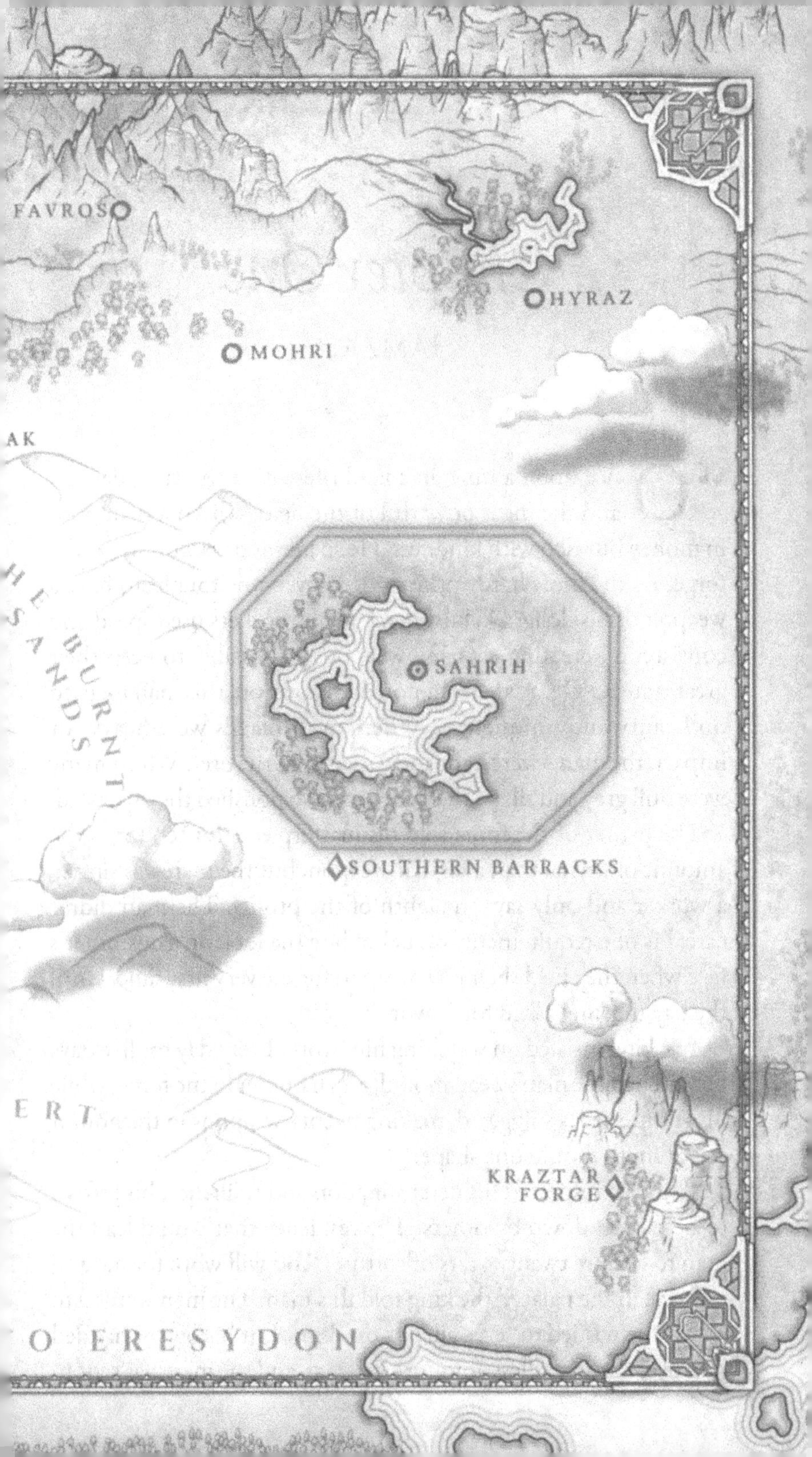

FAVROS
HYRAZ
MOHRI
THE BURNT SANDS
SAHRIH
SOUTHERN BARRACKS
KRAZTAR FORGE
ERESYDON

Chapter One

HAMZAH

"Once upon a time, in a land rife with adventure, danger, and the most powerful of the deities, lived a man poor in money but rich with kindness. He spent his days working at the forge. As the most hardworking there, everyone fought to have a weapon of his design. Whilst many metal workers used speed and consistency, creating as many weapons as possible to keep their great state, Q'Ohar safe from potential invasion, this man focused on beauty and uniqueness. Where most blades were heavy for impact, the man's were light and varied to fit the user. Whilst many were dull grey and silver, the man's were so polished they sparkled.

The owner of the forge sold his masterpieces for ten times the amount of thynai than a regular weapon, but the man was simply a worker and only saw an eighth of the profits. The man didn't care; his one requirement was beholding the look on a customer's face when they held their new weapon for the very first time. Until the day the king asked for a sword.

The king insisted on watching him work. Every day for five days he watched the man sweat, mould, and hammer in the forge, while his counterparts sniggered, making twenty weapons in the hour it took him to mould one shape.

The king respected his determination and resilience, his refusal to be beaten down by others. The resilience that would lead the man to endure twenty years of torture. 'You will work for me and only me in the palace,' the king told this man. The man wanted to say no; he wished to serve all, not one king, but his owner handed him over for an endless amount of thynai, and the man was sent to the palace.

But when he arrived, he was not sent to his workshop. Down and down the man walked, following the king and guards beneath the palace. The man stopped briefly, peering into a cell where white wings encased a body. A moment later, he was thrown into the cell opposite. The king turned to him, not a king at all, but a god in hiding, and said, 'You , Nefere, will be my greatest deity yet—'

"Hamzah!" a voice yelled up the stairs. "You better not be about to scare my poor children with that story!"

"But mumma!" Complaining, the children's shouts echoed through the room as they crowded around the bed. Hamzah closed the leather-bound book and straightened his uniform before rising from the chair.

"You heard your mother," Hamzah said, standing and checking the position of the sun outside. It was nearly time for his evening rotation. The children, three boys and three girls, scrambled from the bed, starting their routine of sitting on his feet and wrapping their scrawny legs around his ankles as he shuffled to the door. His sister always joked that their house would be even more chaotic one day when he had children. He had always rolled his eyes, but she swore the Seer she had paid in the market once prophesied he would one day have twins. Hamzah wasn't sure he would have time to meet someone to marry with how much he worked, let alone have children. His nieces and nephews were enough.

"But Uncle Hamzah!!" they complained, and he refrained from laughing as his sister emerged at the top of the stairs. Her dark hair was pulled back in a braid, and she wiped flour-covered palms on an apron that had far too many rips in it. Hamzah planned to gift her a new one for her birthday. He had walked past it on the culinary street in Sahrih countless times, enquiring on the price every time to ensure it had not gone up. Ten more thynai and it would be his.

"Uncle Hamzah needs to go to work, otherwise who else will protect the capital from darkness?" Inaya said, ushering her children off his leg and back into the two large beds the children shared. His employment was far from as noble as that, but the children saw his uniform and assumed he did something important.

Hamzah reached for the red sash and hung it over his left shoulder before tying his belt around his waist. Red for watchmen, orange for palace patrol, gold for royal guard. He wouldn't ever make it to orange. He didn't know the right people. But his role within the watchmen made him enough to feed his family, and the extra hours he always volunteered for allowed him to save occasionally for treats for his nieces, nephews and sister. They deserved something to keep them happy after his brother-in-law was killed by falling debris at the Kraztar forge three years ago. It was why the children liked the story of Nefere best—the story of a man who was kind and worked at the forge. That was all they were old enough to remember of their father.

"You need to adapt the second half of that story if they insist on you reading it to them," Inaya scolded, slapping him with a towel before wrapping two flatbreads in it for his break in six hours.

"You know I can't resist anything they ask of me." Hamzah smiled, packing the flatbreads into his satchel while his sister flattened a stray piece of his hair and patted his cheek.

"Don't overwork yourself. You still have three more night shifts before your next day off." Hamzah pulled her in a quick embrace. They never said goodbye without one. You never knew when someone wouldn't come home.

"I won't," Hamzah whispered. They both knew it was a lie. His twelve-hour shift would become sixteen so he could buy the children a pastry on his way home.

***

Many found the capital of Q'Ohar, Sahih, crowded and boring to look at compared to the other states. Hamzah wouldn't know if that was true. He hadn't ever travelled out of the city, let alone the state, but that's what he occasionally heard from those wealthy enough to explore the kingdom. Apparently, Asynthos was more magnificent and opulent, Eresydon was more calming and refreshing, Thassena was intricate and educational, Carvyre was bright and Historical, and Xyliar... well, nobody knew. Hamzah didn't trust the word of those who had journeyed to Q'Ohar from other states; he often heard them talk of his home being a dangerous place to visit, somewhere you could lose your belongings if you weren't careful, where they'd be traded in the forge if you failed to pay a fine or taken for experimentation like Nefere had endured long ago.

Hamzah quickly deduced, despite never having left Q'Ohar, that the other states had formed stereotypes of his home, of his people. It troubled him that nobody understood their reasonings for anything; belongings were only taken by children who could not feed themselves, for, out of all the states, Q'Ohar struggled the most with harvests. Being taken to the forge was a fair repercussion for a crime, and experimentation had not occurred in over a thousand years. Even so, the actions of one celestial god had tainted an entire nation. Nobody spoke of the beauty of the deserts on a windy day when the sand spiralled like sparkling gems, or the way the canyons near the coast mirrored the shades of sunset. Sahai to so many was simply towering walls and narrow streets; they didn't see the vibrant colours of the murals, or the fabrics creating roofed mazes in the outer parts of the city, or how the oasis in the centre was the most serene place to sit and listen to the birds, overlooking the domed palace with hundreds of thousands of tiny coloured tiles lining it like a mosaic. Over history, it seemed like people preferred their narrative to the reality that Q'Ohar was just like any of the other states, protective of its people and its land.

"Ten more minutes," his partner, Haroon, grunted beside him. They had both accepted additional hours. Haroon had a baby on the way and wanted to afford an inner-city physician for his wife.

Sweat dripped down Hamzah's back from the late morning heat. His normal hours would have had him finishing at sunrise, but he now wore an evening uniform under the blazing sun.

"It's your lucky day. You're relieved early," a deep voice said. Their general rounded the corner of the towering walls overlooking the Razmah Desert border with Eresydon. "At ease," he added, and Hamzah slumped his shoulders, turning to lean against the wall and face their general.

"Respectfully, Sir, I would rather—"

"You'll still be paid for the final ten minutes. There is a briefing down in the barracks. I'll keep watch until your cover arrives." Hamzah and Haroon gave a respectful nod and made their way down the stairs along the interior walls, which snaked until reaching the barracks below. It was still a good two hours from the edge of the first buildings in the capital, and three hours from his home on foot. Luckily, overtime usually guaranteed him free passage with the incoming traders who sped up their journey by bypassing the main checkpoints into the city at the north, east, and west entrances.

Laughter and loud conversation met Hamzah's ears as he pushed open the wooden door into the eating hall. Arched brickwork lined one wall, allowing the guards to overflow into the shaded, tiled outdoor area with potted, leafy plants and a fountain that regularly dried up. All the benches were filled, and other watchmen began to line the walls. Their watch post had not been expanded in the entire three years Hamzah had worked there. He wasn't as broad as others and slotted into a gap in the corner, the coolest spot against the stone.

"Attention!" The general of the southern barracks yelled, entering through the carved archway from his office. Silence fell over the men in the room, who all straightened beneath his watchful eye. He proceeded to inspect the men along the wall closest to his office before finally turning to relay the briefing. Usually they were updates on the other barracks, any issues they had come across for the southern watchmen to be aware of. He'd heard it all before, but the briefing gave him ten minutes inside and his full overtime pay.

"There is an opportunity for bonuses this month." Hamzah straightened immediately. The southern watchmen hadn't received bonuses throughout Hamzah's tenure. It was rumoured the last bonus involved fleeing Ithyion to search for a way to break the curses on the states. For Q'Ohar, the Xyra, the flaming winged race that had arisen from experimenting on one of Vala's Angels—renowned as once the greatest defence of the state—had been trapped somewhere within their mountain city Favros, unable to flee.

"The king—"

"That's what he thinks," someone muttered nearby. The general heard it, and one look had his men dragging the watchman from the room. Every state had a custodian, but in Q'Ohar, he insisted on calling himself a king. Hamzah was too young to know the details of Ithyion's move from royalty to custodians, but nobody spoke of why. Nowadays, many were confused when it was mentioned, as if they had no understanding of Ithyion's history. Rebels in the city who opposed the King had spread the narrative that the curses were worsening, that it was now coming for the memories of those on Ithyion. They called themselves Red... something. Hamzah couldn't recall.

"The king will journey to meet with the custodians of the other states. As usual, it is being hosted in Carvyre, which allows him the opportunity to return with his betrothed." Some of the men cheered while Hamzah cringed. The girl was twenty now and had been promised to the King of Q'Ohar since before she was born, an agreement that was made to guarantee Q'Ohar's continued supply of weapons, along with a battalion of Xyra one day when the curses were broken . Though Hamzah didn't think the Xyra would ever settle for being traded, particularly if they had no say in the matter. "As it is a long journey and Carvyre's curse makes some of its citizens unpredictable and volatile, the king would like to bring more than just his royal guard. Forty men will attend, ten from each barrack, to patrol the capital while the king is present, ensuring there are no attempts on his life or that of his betrothed's when they journey back." Nearly every man in the barracks raised his hand to offer, Hamzah included.

"It is three weeks at sea to reach the state, three weeks in the capital, and a further three returning home." At least three-quarters of the hands lowered. Too many had children of their own whom they could not spend so long away from. "Usual nine weeks' pay will be delivered to your family. Overtime at the rate of nine weeks will be delivered on return." Some hands raised again, calculating the worth versus the time away.

"Fire wielders only," the general added. Most hands dropped. Most fire wielders worked at the palace already, while the wall watchmen were mainly made up of those who possessed no power. Hamzah envied them sometimes. The divide between those who showcased Keres' power, and those who wished to avenge Nefere, had been heightened as of late. He had heard horror stories of fire wielders found with their skin flayed, all because they descended from the god they believed murdered their deity. Nobody knew that for certain. Nobody knew anything about what happened to stop the celestial gods from answering prayers, thus allowing the deities to become more present amongst the people. Scholars were even beginning to refer to the time prior to 3500AD as the 'Celestial Reign', erasing documentation of past eras and referring to 3500 onward as a fresh start—the Rule of the Deities. It should have been 3588AD, yet scholars wished for it to be known as the year 85RD. Hamzah kept his opinions about the over involvement the deities appeared to have, to himself.

Hamzah kept his hand raised along with nine others, earning glares from the other men. Hamzah would love a position at the palace, but while the pay was more, a chunk was spent on their living arrangements, for they were expected to stay there. Hamzah couldn't leave his sister alone permanently with the children, even if it meant more money. Nine weeks would be hard enough.

"Report to my office," the general commanded, and Hamzah fell into line with the other nine men. Finally, he would see how another state compared to his home.

Chapter Two

HAMZAH

The people Hamzah had overheard in Q'Ohar were right. Carvyre was bright and historical, but not with colours and vibrance—no, it was blinding in white marble. He did not know if the rest of the state was similar, but its capital, Lehorya, was indeed bright and magnificent. From the ship, it had appeared like a beacon. While most of the watchmen hung their heads overboard, not used to the ocean's sway, Hamzah stared, mesmerised, as they approached the docks, with the white of the city glaring brighter. He remained mesmerised, even after three days of patrolling the palace perimeters, regularly watching visitors toss a syiruna, the native currency, into the towering fountain of sparkling turquoise, the only colour in the city other than the lilac banners hanging in the streets and around the palace. The banners bore the sigil of Carvyre: three lavender stems, one for the light Fae, one for Hypherion, and one for the Pegasus-Bound. Their races were so different from Q'Ohar's. He would not have considered it a power to be bound to an animal, but it seemed there was great respect for those who were. He had yet to see a Fae showcase their power, though the men had been granted a tea to take in the evenings to prevent Hypherions from wandering through their dreams. It made him realise just how sheltered his life was. He wished he could bring his sister here, so his nieces and nephews could make a wish on the fountains.

"Change," the general of the north barracks commanded, the only general permitted to attend the mission. He was responsible for managing the rotation of the forty watchmen around the palace perimeters. His other responsibility seemed to involve taking his anger out on them, following his run-ins with the captain of the royal guard. Hamzah saluted as he marched past, following the other nine watchmen from the south barracks toward the quarters they had been assigned in the annex at the back of the palace. Despite it being merely guards' quarters, it was just as magnificent as the rest of the palace and city. Hamzah paused in the hallway, looking out through the marble columns onto the paved courtyard, where a bird sipped from the water of a fountain similar to the one outside the palace but smaller. The other watchmen were eager to switch; their next rotation allowed them to patrol the streets, seeing the stores and citizens. Hamzah was content with the peace inside the palace.

"Where the fuck is he?" a voice shouted down the hallway, followed by the sound of something slamming against a wall. Hamzah turned to see the cause of the commotion. A king's guard was held up against the wall by a whip of flame, brightening the gold of his sash across his red uniform.

"Brothel," choked the man. The captain released him, and he stumbled back in line beside the eight other royal guards.

"He was meant to be back ten minutes ago in time for rotation," one man said. The captain's face reddened. Hamzah would not have added that detail.

"He shouldn't have left the palace at all," the captain sneered. He turned on his feet and raked back his oiled hair. His eyes fell on Hamzah, who straightened, placing his hands behind his back. "You!" he snapped. Hamzah approached with quick strides. "Name and barracks."

"Hamzah Farseer, southern barracks."

"Gods," the captain sighed, rubbing his forehead. "You'll have to do. You're a fire wielder, yes?"

"Yes, sir," Hamzah replied, still staring straight ahead.

"Sir, the southern aren't used to any kind of danger—"

"You'll be relegated to the south if any of you speak again," the captain snapped. "At least he is fucking in the palace, which I can't say for your comrade. Give him your sash and fetch another for yourself from the quarters." He addressed no guard in particular. "You have five minutes to do it and find a new one for yourself before meeting us outside the council rooms." The man on the right rushed to pull his sash from his belt and hand it to Hamzah before taking off at a very brisk march. Hamzah looked down at the golden silk in his hand, his brow furrowing.

"March," the captain commanded the group. Turning on their heels, they began marching. "Hamzah Farseer, I'll alert your general that you're serving in the royal guard today." Hamzah hurried to keep up, attempting to multitask as he pulled his red sash free, folding the gold over his shoulder and under his belt.

"Sir, would you rather I detour and request one of the other royal guards on rotation inside the palace?"

"We don't have time. You're here. You'll do," the man snapped. He glanced sideways at Hamzah as he fell into line behind the others. "You'll be compensated with a day's royal guard wage." Hamzah said no more after that. The only giveaway he'd even heard the captain's words was the brief widening of his eyes. One day's wages as a royal guard was worth nearly as much as his overtime bonus for this mission.

The further into the centre of the palace they marched, the more colour, specifically lilac and gold, decorated the halls and rooms. Hamzah kept his eyes as focused as possible, trying not to allow himself to be distracted by the towering marble columns and arched entryways into rooms filled with even more luxurious items. Eventually, they stopped outside a wide set of gold doors. Two royal guards stood on either side of it, and a woman stood in the middle. Her hair was a blonde so pale it looked like faded gold, though it shone just as brightly. Her purple eyes glanced over the approaching guards and lingered on Hamzah, as though she knew he did not belong. She donned a deep purple gown that hugged her figure; a sparkling cape hung off her shoulders, and a gold sigil pin was on her collar. Her tanned hands moved to signal the opening of the doors, but they paused as marching echoed down the hallway on the left.

"Isoria, how lovely to see you again," the King of Q'Ohar's voice boomed. She was the Custodian of Carvyre, Hamzah realised. The royal guards all glanced at Hamzah, who looked away. As the king and the custodian spoke, he wondered if she took offence to the way he was the only person who insisted he was more than a custodian of the land and should be worshipped instead. Like a king. Hamzah's focus drifted to the piano music floating from the room to his left. He glanced out of the corner of his eye, just long enough to see a beautiful girl with glistening silver hair hurrying her fingers over the keys. The music started soft and gentle, but as she kept glancing up, her pace quickened until the piece became a rise of tension and battle. When a man approached, she slammed down her hands. The sound jarred through the hallway. Isoria and the king paused.

"Shall we?" said the Custodian of Carvyre, gesturing into the now open doors. Hamzah tore his eyes from the girl by the piano. The captain of the guard stepped aside to collect intel from the guards who had been at the king's side when he arrived. Hamzah followed the group, who now took over protecting the king. Every ten seconds, the line halted before moving forward. Eventually, Hamzah, at the back of the line, saw why. Still, Isoria stood before the door with a large gold-plated bowl in her arms, which shimmered with a swimming light.

"You're new," Isoria said. Hamzah nodded. Silent, respectful.

"The discussions in the council of custodians are sacred and secret. Nothing is to be shared outside of it. To guarantee the information's safety, a memory is given," Isoria said. She must have seen the way his brow twitched in confusion. "It is a memory of the ones you love the most, so if the information is betrayed, you know the repercussions."

"Reper—" Hamzah stopped at the raise of Isoria's eyebrow. He understood. Someone to kill if he spilt information. His fingers twitched, longing for something to distract from the anxiety spiking within him. Instead, he nodded. Isoria approached, balancing the bowl in one hand before resting a palm on his temple. Her hands were gentle and warm.

"The Hypherion of Carvyre are gifted with the ability to walk through dreams, but dreams are only plucked from a mosaic of our memories, meaning some of us can take pieces." Her voice lulled him into relaxing. "You will only feel a slight tingle." When she slowly withdrew her hand, a soft glow came with it, a string of white smoke-like material that she guided toward the bowl, merging it with the taken memories of the other guards. "A beautiful family." She smiled.

Hamzah swallowed. The kindness in her smile belonged to someone who could command an entire army to find and kill his family. She stepped aside, allowing Hamzah to enter and take up his position next to the row of guards lining the wall behind the king.

It appeared he was the last to arrive, with the long table already filled. On one side sat a woman with a white streak in her dark hair and a turquoise gown with Thassena's sigil pinned on her chest. On the woman's right was a man with red braids and a full but trimmed beard. Opposite them sat the King of Q'Ohar beside a woman with an open-backed dress, perfect for displaying wings. At the end, closest to the doors, was an empty chair for Xyliar. At the head of the table, in front of a painted mural portraying a map of Ithyion, Isoria pulled out a chair and sat. Hamzah's eye fluttered to the right, where a woman sat down on a smaller chair, scowling as she crossed her legs and arms. The woman who had been playing the piano. As though sensing someone watching her, her purple eyes found his. She tilted her head, as if intrigued by his appraisal. He immediately turned his head back to face the table and the king, the only person in the room wearing a crown.

"As the Custodian of Carvyre and the hosting representative, I call the eighty-eighth meeting of the council into session," Isoria said. "Before we begin, are there any motions that would like to be presented for discussion at the end of our meeting?"

"Eresydon would like to raise a motion to discuss the development of new tracks being made on the border with Q'Ohar to better facilitate continued trade," said the man with red braids. Isoria penned a note on the parchment with her long white quill.

"Thassena would like to raise a motion to discuss expanding the border of the Sirens Sea into the neutral waters to allow the growing population of Sirens to expand their homes," said the woman with the white streak in her hair. Isoria noted it while the King of Q'Ohar scoffed. The Custodian of Thassena clenched her jaw, tapping her fingers on the table.

"Asynthos has no motions," the Angel said. The King of Q'Ohar cleared his throat and stood. The other custodians glanced at one another, as did the guards of Thassena and Eresydon on the opposite side of the room. Hamzah quickly realised that the other states perhaps did not have a good opinion of the man who called himself a king.

"Q'Ohar would like to raise the motion of having my beautiful betrothed, Varlena, finally join me in Q'Ohar at the end of this visit." The custodians winced, and Isoria closed her eyes, seeming to prepare for something.

"Fuck, no!" The girl who sat before the map, with sparkling silver hair, exclaimed.

Chapter Three

VARLENA

Rage makes you ugly. That's what Varlena's mother used to say. Untamed rage was a weed left to grow and infest your mind. Perhaps if her mother had had more rage, she wouldn't be lying in the family crypt below the church on the other side of Lehorya. Rage might have made her defend herself when whoever snuck into her chambers killed her in her sleep. To Varlena, rage demanded attention; it placed her higher on a pedestal among the men in the military, the military she would abandon if she let the sorry excuse of a man standing proudly at the marble table get what he wanted.

"If you think I'm going to be paraded—"

"Varlena," scolded her aunt, Isoria, with her mother's familiar glare. *Rage makes you ugly.* Those words rattled in her head as she clenched her sharp nails into her palms.

"The negotiations were for when I turned twenty-five, when we confirmed I was not cursed." Varlena tried to approach it from a political standpoint—they must uphold the contract her mother put in place with the custodian, a title the arrogant man snubbed in favour for 'King of Q'Ohar.'

"Respectfully, princ—"

"Don't do that," Varlena snapped, pushing up from her chair. "Do not add a word you have no intention of using as a way to placate me like a child." From the looks on the other custodians' faces, she knew her eyes now glowed. A muted and feminine lilac that flashed a dangerous, blinding white, threatening to burn their very souls if she wished it. The *king*, she scoffed. Her future husband,

Malik, pursed his lips and pushed his chair out from the table. She scoffed at him. How dare he try to give himself a title above the others? If anyone was entitled to, it was her aunt, given she was of royal birth, a custodian until Varlena was old enough to take the throne or provide an heir from this pathetic excuse of a man. This man was simply the one selected to rule Q'Ohar when the true monarchs left in search of a way to break the curses on Ithyion, a fact that was seemingly fading from history and memories. Varlena expected the matter would be discussed in the meeting that day. Malik clasped his hands behind his golden sherwani and strolled toward her. To her left, his royal guards tensed, except for the new one, who watched her intently. Varlena's eyes remained on that guard when Malik did the stupidest thing he could. He reached to tuck a strand of silver hair behind her jewel-laden pointed ear.

"My dear," he began. He *touched* her. He fucking touched her. Varlena unclenched her hand and hooked her fingers, her power crawling to her skin. The guard's eyes flickered to her hand, and she plastered a sickly-sweet smile on her face as Malik took her hand again. A blinding whip of light should have erupted, coiling around his hand and wrapping it around his wrist. Instead, it hesitated as a wall of flames burst between the two, forcing Varlena to step back before her gown caught alight. Her forced smile became a sneer as she glared through the flames at the guard. The mesh of different coloured uniforms had all drawn their weapons at the display of power. The wall of flames faded as the king turned back to his chair, muttering something in the guard's ear before sitting. The guard reddened and faced ahead. Varlena wished she had been paying attention to catch what had been said.

"I apologise, he is new," the king said. When the guard's neck twitched, Varlena felt his stare. "But, as we know, Varlena, displays of power from *any* representative is prohibited."

"I'll do more than just—"

"Varlena!" Her aunt's voice was firmer this time, and she forced herself to lower in her chair, her teeth practically cracking under the pressure of how hard she forced her mouth shut. "She has a point, Malik," her aunt continued. "All Fae in Carvyre are to wait until twenty-five to marry or procreate to determine whether the curse has emerged in them." Her aunt made it sound like it was always present, as if there was some predisposition that forced it to awaken before twenty-five. Perhaps that was why her mother always told her rage was ugly, for fear such fury would nurture a dark curse lying dormant in her veins. But Varlena knew the logic was redundant. All the states were cursed in some way or another, and theirs had no predisposition. It was simple. Fate appeared to pick from random to see which resident of Carvyre would be corrupted by Xyliar's magic. Varlena had a theory that some Fae in Carvyre were cursed to awaken with the dark magic of Xyliar as a way for the universe to keep Sonos and Sitara's essence together. The reality was that it corrupted them. The power of Carvyre was the only one capable of battling and defeating that of Xyliar, so when it cursed a Fae, they were slowly driven crazy by the presence of darkness alongside their light. But it had only ever been present before someone turned twenty-five. The scholars spent years trying to draw a hypothesis as to what prompted a Fae to be cursed. What a waste of time.

"The terms, Isoria, state she will be married at twenty-five. It states nothing of where she resides until that date," Malik continued. Varlena bit her tongue, knowing the words of a contract were binding. This was a loophole.

"Why do you wish for her to arrive sooner?" Isoria asked.

"Relationships take... time," Malik said, glancing at the princess. "The more time we have prior to our wedding, the sooner we can conceive a child on our wedding night: the first-born child the terms state will then inherit the crown of Carvyre."

Varlena forced herself to look anywhere but at the king. The thought of that man atop her made her want to empty her breakfast onto his shoes. She scoffed. As if he wouldn't just take from her, regardless. They both knew a loving relationship would not exist between them. For him, he gained leverage and a connection to the Carvyre throne when their child reached twenty-five. For Carvyre, they gained a fleet of Xyra upon the curse breaking one day, not a fair deal in her opinion. For Varlena, she lost her army, any chance of taking back her throne once cleared of the curse, and the loss of happiness. Her eyes fell on the guard, who frowned. Why was he frowning?

"The terms are agreed. Varlena will return to Q'Ohar with you. I will continue as custodian until your first child reaches the age of twenty-five. At which point, they will return to Carvyre to rule," Isoria said.

Malik grinned, though the guard clenched his fist. Varlena screamed. At least she wished she did. Her aunt's magic coiled around her ankles under her gown in a silent warning of burning rope to keep her mouth shut; they would talk about it later. Instead, Varlena had to sit there in silence for the remaining five hours. She sat and listened to them speak of trade and borders, marriages and other arrangements, each topic more boring than the last. This was one part of being queen she would be grateful to skip, but that was the only part.

She resented her mother for signing the agreement, for signing her life away to Malik. Even to this day, it made little sense. Q'Ohar barely benefitted from it. It was as if someone had manipulated her mother into signing. Had she not signed her daughter's identity away, Varlena would have waited until twenty-five to see if the curse took root, and when it didn't, she would be crowned Queen of Carvyre, the only true ruler still in Ithyion. As much as Malik liked to call himself king, he was not. They were all placeholders until the true rulers would one day return with a way to break the curses. That was the plan, though it had been eight five years—and a full generation—since that plan was set in motion. That was what she could decipher, anyway. Nobody could speak of the deal Ithyion's rulers made with Sitara. Only the custodians knew of it because their relatives were the ones the rulers had passed protection of the states to before it was set into place. Varlena only knew because she was present in these meetings, and her mother had told her pieces here and there before she passed away. As a member of the remaining ruling family, it was Varlena's right to know.

Varlena wondered how different her life might be now if her mother had gone with the other rulers. But Xyliar was still impossible to get into, and as the only race able to battle them fairly, Carvyre's royal family remained the unintentional protectors of the entire kingdom.

"Any celestial updates?" Eresydon's custodian asked. Code for: has anyone heard fuck all about the rulers who upped and left eighty-eight years ago?

"The location hunt failed," Thassena's custodian responded. Their ships had failed to find the rulers'.

"It's time we moved on. They're gone," Malik complained.

"They were never meant to be easily found," Isoria added. "They're still somewhere." Outside, thunder rumbled, and the custodians shared a look.

"Perhaps the deities could help," began the Custodian of Asynthos. Lightning cracked outside the glass windows.

"The deities are part of the problem. Perhaps if they hadn't waged a war against their creators, we would have more help in breaking this goddamn—" The earth shook as rain hammered against the panes. When Varlena turned her head, she knew what she would see. Blood raining down over the marble city, staining it as a reminder. From what Varlena had deciphered over the years, everybody—and this time it *was* everybody—was cursed not to speak of where the rulers went or why. Not that it made a difference. The rulers had called on Sitara for aid against a darkness seeping across the kingdom. The next thing everyone knew, they had fled with what felt like a handful of citizens, given the grand size of the kingdom. The kingdom hoped they would return one day, breaking all curses across the lands. It sounded like a load of shit spun to gather hope from the people. Varlena was more inclined to live with the reality of a life they had now endured for centuries, and the centuries to come.

The falling blood eased, but the custodians took it as a sign to stay silent. It was always Malik who fucked it up, though that conversation was brief compared to the annual meetings she had sat in on over the last ten years. They all rose from their seats, vacating the room with their guards until only Malik, his royal guards, Isoria, and Varlena remained. Isoria approached her while the false king spoke with his guards.

"I know this is not what you want—"

"Then do not make me do it, Aunty," Varlena pleaded. Isoria placed her hands on her niece's shoulders. The affection felt cold.

"If I do not placate him, he will threaten trade halts again, just as his father did with Thassena. We cannot be divided when we are not intended for these seats."

"I should be in that seat, though," Varlena snapped.

"And you must accept your mother had a reason for not letting that be your fate," Isoria snapped back.

"Is she ready, Isoria?" Malik called. Varlena clenched her teeth again. Gods forbid he spoke directly to her.

"You are to pack your belongings. You leave in a week."

"But my battalion—"

"Will be granted a new commander, who you can debrief before you leave."

Varlena was losing the only thing that had sustained her after discovering she would lose all happiness at the age of twenty-five. She was losing her warriors, her friends. Her aunt tugged on her shoulder, forcing her to walk toward the false king. He no longer stood with ten guards. Only one. The one who dared to battle her power.

"Farseer will be your newly appointed royal guard now and when we return to Q'Ohar," Malik said. The guard's head snapped to the king, his mouth opening as if to reject the offer. Varlena watched him with intrigue. He didn't want to be her personal royal guard. Why? "He will accompany you to your rooms to pack. The king inclined his head and offered his arm to Isoria, no doubt wishing to scheme on some other matter. The guard faced her, his hands behind his back. He looked her up and down, but not in the way most men did. It was like he was assessing a threat, not a piece of meat to dine on. Varlena crossed her arms and raised her chin.

"Do you have an actual name, or am I to call you by your surname?"

"You do not have to address me at all, your Highness," he said. His voice was low and gravelly.

"Well, that would be rather boring. How will we argue whenever I try to evade your presence?" she asked with a sarcastic smile. His lip twitched, and he watched her silently for a moment. Varlena was not used to feeling uncomfortable under a man's gaze. Normally the rage overshadowed it.

"Hamzah, your Highness. My name is Hamzah."

Chapter Four

HAMZAH

Hamzah Farseer had observed countless things in the last six hours, but he had three main takeaways: Varlena Nylaria had a temper more burning than anybody he knew in Q'Ohar; she owned far too many dresses and not enough items of sentiment, and she knew perhaps thirty different curse words to describe her future husband. Silence had stretched between them on the walk from the council chambers to her own, each stealing looks at the other with neither acknowledging it. She had merely huffed when he provided his name and told him to keep up before turning for her rooms.

With each corridor, the palace became more beautiful; at least that was what he assumed, for his focus was mainly on the princess. The constant flip of her hair over one shoulder to the other in frustration, switching between tapping the sides of her curved thighs with her fingers and crossing her arms in a huff. He had never known someone so unable to keep still. He wondered if that was why she played piano—something to keep her busy and focused, a way to calm her mind.

Even in her rooms, Varlena was distracted. She had not commanded him where to stand, outside the door, or on the balcony, or by the windows. There were countless vantage points for ensuring nobody entered and harmed the princess, though he doubted she needed any protection. Hours on shift had taught him to focus on details to occupy himself, so he saw the moment her fingers curled like claws, ready to draw on her power. Hamzah hadn't been thinking of any rules or consequences when he blinked and set a wall of flame alight to protect the king. He had been thinking that his only job was to protect. *Never suggest I cannot protect myself again.* Those were the words the king had whispered in his ear when walking past. It couldn't have been more embarrassing than being cursed at by your future wife. And yet, Hamzah must have impressed him, for it was him, and not the other guards, who were asked, rather *told*, to become the princess's new personal guard. How he was going to explain it to his sister and the children, he did not know. Inaya wouldn't have his physical help around the house anymore, but the salary of a personal guard would change their lives. He could buy them a bigger home, one further into the city and closer to the palace, where he could still visit. Perhaps one of the narrower homes with multiple floors. His sister could have the top floor for privacy; below her, the girls; below them, the boys, and then a living area. He wondered if he could find one that had garden space and perhaps—

"Did you hear what I said?" The princess's voice snapped him back from his thoughts. Varlena stood in front of the open balcony doors, with ten open chests before her, overflowing with dresses. She held two up. "Which one is more appropriate?" Hamzah glanced between the two gowns. The left was a burnt orange, a gauzy fabric that left little to the imagination, and the right was a deep red; though the latter had more fabric, it *also* left little to the imagination.

"For?" he asked. Varlena hung her head back and sighed.

"My arrival in the city," she said. Hamzah's eyebrows rose as he glanced between them again.

"Neither," he said.

"That's not helpful."

"You asked for my opinion."

"I asked for your *choice*." Varlena narrowed her eyes, still holding the two dresses.

"You do not want to wear either, your Highness," he insisted.

"Why is that?"

"Because you will not be able to ride on horseback in either of those."

"I'll be in a carriage," she said.

"You won't. We didn't bring one," Hamzah replied. Varlena screamed through gritted teeth and flung the dresses down before storming out onto the balcony. As she tapped her fingers on the marble, Hamzah approached the chests, looking for one gown she had flung inside. He pulled it out and cleared his throat. Varlena turned, tilting her head as she eyed the gown.

"The wider skirts will allow you to ride either side saddle or regularly. While the people would appreciate you representing our state colours, warm colours wash you out, but this gold is a compromise that would please the people, while the deep cut to the waist, and the fact it is backless rather than modest, will make the statement you intend by embarrassing the king. Though it may also feed his ego a bit when he sees the men staring at you, so I'd consider if that's something you wish to inflate further or not." Hamzah waited, still holding the gown. Varlena stormed forward and snatched it from him, though she did not throw it. Instead, she hung it delicately over the dresser.

"I didn't ask to be analysed, Hamzah."

"No, you asked for my opinion on a gown, your Highness."

"Your *choice,*" she muttered, and his lip quirked. As much as she tried to hide it, hers tilted upwards too. Jewels came out of drawers next, and then glass bottles of fragrance, hair clips, and ribbons, slippers and riding boots. The princess had more possessions in just one chest than he'd owned his entire life.

A knock sounded at the door, and Hamzah was quick to open it. When he did, the man opposite surveyed him with the same calculated scrutiny. His hair was a pale blonde, not dissimilar from the Custodian of Carvyre. His eyes were a meek shade of purple in comparison to Varlena's. He stood half a chin taller than Hamzah, and by the way he puffed his chest in polished white gold armour adorned with engraved swirls on the shoulders, and straightened his back, he revelled in it. If Hazmah had met him in a tavern, he would have rolled his eyes, but here, he was professional. Hamzah waited for the man to finish his own inspection before introducing himself.

"Lowven Nylaria," he said, his voice dripping with expensive upbringing. Hamzah was most definitely stereotyping him. "Second-in-command to Princess and Commander Varlena of the first battalion fleet." Hamzah slowly stepped aside, sweeping his arm in welcome. The man raised an eyebrow as though sensing Hamzah's attitude.

"Hello cousin," Varlena sighed as she tossed another dress aside.

"That's my greeting?" he asked, collapsing on the edge of the bed and resting his chin in his hands.

"You know I am happy to see you, but I am rather distracted," she said, the attitude from her voice gone. Hamzah resumed his position by the door, watching the interaction. "You mean you are avoiding saying farewell," he whispered. Varlena glanced up at him from her spot on the chaise.

"No," she mumbled.

"You know the soldiers will be disappointed if you do not properly say goodbye."

"They are in good hands—*your* hands," Varlena said, suddenly very interested in how best to fold a gown Hamzah had watched her toss aside four times already.

"Varlena," Lowven insisted. The princess finally dropped the gown and looked pointedly at him. "You know I am only a mirror away—any mirror, or at least the portal mirror outside the city. I can be there in a heartbeat if you call," he said. The princess smiled gently and Hamzah did not have the heart to tell her that the king may have anticipated her desire to communicate with her family at home and would likely have a Sorcerer spell all the mirrors in the palace. It was a common form of communication in the fifth state, it seemed: using mirrors to bend light across space, allowing two people on either side to communicate. "Do you have time to meet the battalion before you leave? Even just for a final fly around the hills?" he asked. Varlena looked at Hazmah, who nodded. He had no idea if he had the authority to do so but supposed he would find a way.

Silence fell over the chambers as Lowven left. As Hamzah watched the princess, he could not tell if she was trying to stop herself from crying.

"Tell me about the palace. Do you think my chambers will be far enough away from his to sneak out if I please?" she mused, her voice an octave higher than before as she sniffed before sitting on a chest and buckling it shut.

"Respectfully, princess, I wouldn't voice your intent to escape to your personal guard," he said.

"See, when you say *respectfully,* I understand the tone. There is a layer of humour beneath it. When *he* says it, it is to try to remind me of my place as a future wife, as if I would not be a queen without this gods awful agreement." She blew a strand of hair from her face as the buckle on the chest finally snapped shut. "Which is why I want to know if my rooms are as far away from him as possible." Varlena waited, and Hamzah realised she still expected an answer.

"I do not know where your rooms will be in the palace, your Highness."

"Well, at least inform me of the options. The only part I have ever visited is the throne room." She crossed her legs on top of the chest and rested her palms on her knees, waiting.

"I—"

"Hamzah, you cannot be a very good personal guard if you cannot even describe the halls you walk," she said with a laugh. Hamzah glanced down at his feet, his embarrassment overshadowing how his skin prickled at her laugh. He cleared his throat and met her eyes again.

"I am not usually a royal guard, your Highness. I am a watchman at the southern barracks of the city walls." He waited for her face to change, for some kind of outrage at Malik entrusting him with her protection. She simply tilted her head.

"That is why you looked alarmed at the idea of being granted this position," she said.

"Who's analysing now?" Hamzah rubbed the back of his neck before stiffening.

"You do not wish to be my personal guard?" Varlena asked. It felt like a trap. She sprang to her feet and strode toward him. "Is there something about my personality you find off-putting?" She planted her hands on her hips and came far too close. He had to tilt his head to look down at her.

"You? Off-putting? Not at all," Hamzah said. While his tone was formal and polite, the quirk of her lips told him she had detected his sarcasm. Varlena batted her eyelashes, drawing his focus to her irises. Up close, they weren't just lilac. He distinguished flecks of white that brightened her eyes so much they twinkled like gems. Varlena's hand slid up his chest, and he cleared his throat. He didn't know if it was possible for his back to straighten any more, or for his muscles to tense further.

"Most men disapprove of my brashness because it mirrors their own; they resent my equal strength and sharper intellect." Varlena hummed while toying with the gold on his newly added sash. For somebody so strong, her touch was gentle. If he could not see her hand, he would not know it was there.

"Some men want an equal. Perhaps you will find that eventually in the king," Hamzah said, reminding her of her future husband.

"Am I making you uncomfortable, Hamzah? Is my personality and behaviour off-putting yet?" she asked. Hamzah's eyes narrowed, watching her relax as she leaned in. She was making him uncomfortable but only because he feared someone walking in, where he would surely lose his head despite not partaking in her game. He knew what she was doing—trying to get a reaction, trying to gauge what made him tick, discover his weaknesses.

"I do not believe any man would be uncomfortable with a beautiful princess hanging off him," he said.

"You think I'm beautiful?" Varlena asked, her voice quiet. Hamzah frowned, unable to read her expression. There was no mask of emotion anymore—no anger, no veiled sarcasm, no frown. Her face was soft, her eyes wide. Everyone, especially men, must have told her she was beautiful.

"You do not?" he asked genuinely. Varlena cleared her throat before sliding her hands off him and turning back to her chests, seemingly uncomfortable. She began picking up blouses and folding them methodically.

"My mother used to tell me my rage made me ugly," Varlena said, the teasing gone from her voice. Hamzah realised then: this was the first time he'd seen the princess without a veil. From only a day together, he had already deduced she could be stubborn, partly because she was likely spoilt as a child, but more so because she did not wish for her opinion to be overlooked. Her mind fluttered often, meaning conversation would never be dull. She could not keep still and he made a mental note to find distractions for her throughout her days. Her anger stemmed from a lack of control. Denied the right to speak against the agreement made for her life, being told to sit still and stay quiet, and leave anything she loved behind.

"I think," Hamzah began, pausing, contemplating if it was his place to engage in such conversations like this. "That rage is just one way passion manifests. Passion for what you believe in, what you think is right in any situation." Varlena paused in her folding and stared at the fabric. "I've never heard anyone say that passion is anything other than mesmerising." Varlena turned her head to look at him, tucking her hair behind her pointed ears. Her calm expression returned with a gentle smile.

"You think I'm mesmerising?" she asked. She was still. Her fingers didn't tap; she didn't reach for her hair. Patiently, she waited. Her silver hair glistened in the streaming sunlight, as though she herself was a star. Her pale skin possessed a light glow from the summer, directly contrasting her hair to brighten her appearance.

While the pale blue gown was beautiful, with the corset highlighting her hourglass figure, she would shine in nothing but a simple brown robe. He'd gone from watching the scorching Q'Ohar deserts in the blinding sun, to a woman with blinding beauty. His days would never be boring again.

"I think there is no word for what you are, your Highness," Hamzah said.

Chapter Five

VARLENA

Four weeks. Four weeks Varlena had been kept from her home. The first three were both tolerable and insufferable. Tolerable, because Malik had arranged for them to be on separate ships, and insufferable because, well... she was trapped on a ship.

At first, the sea air was refreshing; wind blew the salt from the waves with more ferocity than the gentle lapping of the ocean on Carvyre's shores. The men on the boat had been interesting to listen to at first, all guards or watchmen from Q'Ohar, except for the handful of crew members from Thassena to quicken the ship's pace. Leaning against the edge of the ship, she listened to them talk of their families, of escapades in the capital, of their hometowns across Q'Ohar. But then she noticed how they looked at Hamzah, and her fascination with their stories turned sour.

It was subtle to begin with—quick glances in his direction, where he stood three paces behind her. But then the glances turned to glares, murmurings, judgement, jealousy. From every snippet of conversation she overheard, though, Varlena deduced it was nothing to do with Hamzah or his personality. He could have been any random watchman plucked by fate and put in the king's path. They would have been jealous of whoever took the position. What fascinated Varlena more was Hamzah's indifference.

Had it been her, she would have made her rage known. The rage he'd said wasn't just beautiful or magnificent but *indescribable*. She bit her lip to keep from smiling at that moment in her chambers, the moment neither of them had spoken of since. She had been teasing him, testing his limits to see what she could get away with, but, from only one conversation, Varlena realised this was perhaps one man she did not have an immediate disdain for. She glanced at him on her left, atop his horse. Perhaps she might even have a friend, if she stayed sane and no curse tainted her.

"What are you smiling at?" Hamzah asked, handing her a skin of water.

"Nothing," Varlena said. Though she didn't hate him, he didn't need to know that.

"Probably thinking about stealing into the king's rooms tonight to wrap her mouth around—AH!" The guard in front began slapping at his arm to bat away the flames on his uniform.

"Okay." Varlena shrugged, glancing at Hamzah. "Now I'm smiling at that." Hamzah was not smiling, nor was his face filled with rage. Hamzah had a quiet anger about him, one that crept up on someone unawares, and only in the name of something honourable.

"You're to be their queen. They shouldn't speak about you like that," Hamzah said. Varlena laughed, and he finally looked at her—her lips, specifically. Her chuckle slowly faded at his stare.

"Hamzah, I am not embarrassed by the concept of having my mouth—"

"Do not finish that sentence," Hamzah said, clearing his throat.

"Does the idea of a woman doing such an act make you uncomfortable, Hamzah?" She smiled, the teasing lilt in her voice returning.

"Of course not."

"I'm sure you've enjoyed many women in your life—"

"Can we change the subject, your Highness?" Hamzah said. Varlena tamed her laugh; she had quickly learnt his use of her title was whenever he tried to be serious. So, she pulled her horse closer to his and leant over, gently grazing his knee with her hand before whispering in his ear.

"Don't worry," she said, her eyes fluttering to his. He stared at her hand's placement. "If my lips were around him, it would only be to lure him into a false sense of security before I bit it off and suffocated him with my power."

"That's treason, your Highness," Hamzah said. Varlena patted his knee and settled back in her seat.

"Aren't you loyal to me, Hamzah?"

"I am employed by the king."

"Hmm, that makes things complicated, doesn't it? Perhaps he will think you are my accomplice. Would you stand guard outside the room while I ripped his co—"

"*Varlena*," Hamzah hissed. Varlena snapped her mouth shut while Hamzah's hung open in shock. He spluttered an apology, but Varlena could only focus on how he said her name, the way his gravelled tone caressed the vowels. She planted her hand on his knee briefly again, halting his apologies.

"Rage looks rather beautiful on you, Hamzah."

***

Carvyre was seasonally warm all year round, but nothing prepared Varlena for Q'Ohar's afternoon sun. Ten hours of riding from the port settlement of Kyara and through the canyons had finally brought them into an oasis at the edge of the Burnt Sands, the desert positioned before the walls of the capital that the guards said were known to set stray travellers alight. Hamzah claimed the size of the oasis was nothing compared to the oasis within the city walls, with the palace at its centre. The horses were being watered, allowing Varlena a chance to change into her gown to enter the city. Malik hadn't addressed her once the entire journey, so she hoped her choice of outfit would at least elicit some reaction to fulfil her need to taunt him. The sun made changing into the outfit far more difficult than it should have.

Varlena grunted and stepped back into the shade of the tarpaulin the guards erected along the edge of the oasis, as Hamzah had instructed to allow her privacy to change. Hamzah had been correct in the dress choice. The glistening gold mirrored the desert sands, but the gauze that needed tying at the nape, securing her chest yet exposing her back, was constantly tangling with the sweaty underlayers of her hair. Why hadn't she tied it up? She screamed through her teeth.

"Do you need help, your Highness?" Hamzah asked from the other side of the tarpaulin.

"Seeing as this is your fucking fault in the first place, yes!" she exclaimed. As the tarpaulin rustled, Varlena twisted her hair up around her hand and held the two pieces of gauze behind her neck with the other. She must have looked a fool. Hamzah's darkened eyes told her she did not. He cleared his throat, the same way he always did when he felt awkward. She put him out of his misery. "I need you to tie these two pieces behind my neck, so I don't flash the entire city," Varlena huffed, turning to face the sands and exposing her back to him.

His fingers were rough as they brushed hers, reaching for the gauze tangled in her fingers. His tall body behind her cast a shadow over her skin. For a moment, her body longed to lean back, to see what it would be like to feel the muscle of his abdomen against her back.

"Is that tight enough?" Hamzah asked, his voice more strained than usual as his fingers scraped her nape one last time before drawing away.

"Double knot," she said quickly, waiting for his hands to brush her skin again. They were not gentle this time. His fingers went from the nape to her shoulders, one squeezing gently before the other trailed down her arm to her waist, pulling her back into him. She was right. His body was firm, but there was nothing daunting about his touch. She felt only warmth. Safety.

"What are you doing?" Varlena asked, her voice far weaker than she had ever heard it. Hamzah's shadow enveloped her as he bent closer, his grip on her waist firm. His neatly trimmed beard brushed her neck. She tilted her head instinctively.

"Making it look as though we are simply two people distracted by one another," Hamzah murmured. Her mind took a second to catch up with his words, too focused on the warmth of his breath against the shell of her ear, and his smell of honey and amber. *Look... look as though we are.* Her body went rigid. "Do not look, your Highness, but there are sand crawlers two dunes over in the northwest."

"What are sand crawlers?" she asked, her body still rigid as she reminded herself that the palm he splayed across her hip was a ruse.

"Smokeshifters who train themselves to hide amongst the sand, shifting with its movement and never hiding for noble reasons," Hamzah whispered.

"When they shift, do they still retain the embers of their smoke?" Varlena asked, her eyes flickering to the dunes before she reached for Hamzah's hand, interlacing their fingers. It was his turn to become rigid.

"Yes," he said, a quiet breath.

"Do you trust me?" Varlena asked.

"You are my future queen," he said. Varlena waited. "Yes."

Slowly, Varlena guided his hand up her stomach until their hands glided over her left breast. She tilted her head back as if she were moaning, her eyes finding Hamzah's. The bronze in them flared as he clenched his jaw.

"This is too much. I shouldn't be—"

"It's like you said," Varlena reassured him. "Make it look like we are simply two people distracted by one another." Varlena turned to face him, and Hamzah's hands slid to the bare skin of her back. "Just do whatever you would normally while I tell you the plan."

"What I would do normally?" Hamzah asked, his brow furrowed. Varlena glided her hands over his chest until they interlocked behind his neck, her fingers tickling the locks of his hair.

"With your wife, your lover, anyone," she murmured, pushing against his body on her tiptoes. Hamzah looked away, his hands beginning to stray from her back. Varlena moved again, gripping his jaw and turning it back to face her. *He's blushing; why is he—oh.* "You have no one?" she asked. Hamzah shook his head. "Have you ever..." His jaw clenched in confirmation.

"Move your hands back to my hips, the way you had them before," she guided. He did as she instructed. "Don't be afraid to be firm. Passionate, remember?" She smiled, but his face was still tinged red, and his eyes struggled to meet hers. "Now lean down into my neck, as though you are kissing it, so they cannot see your next move," she whispered. Hamzah hesitated before moving. He lifted his hand from her waist to brush the hair off her shoulder before leaning down. What she wasn't expecting was the way he kissed her skin, or how she would have to bite her lip to keep from making a sound far too inappropriate for a princess and her guard.

"Now, when I say so, you're going to glance at the dunes." His lips trailed further up her neck. Varlena swallowed, her breathing laboured. "And when you catch a shift of movement, you're going to set an ember alight." Hamzah nodded, his nose grazing her earlobe. Her knees wobbled. "The second you've done that, you're going to spin me around so I can see the light of the flame and refract it. Scattering the light will force them back into their physical forms."

"I understand," Hamzah breathed, tickling her ear. She clenched her fingers into the back of his neck, prompting him to tighten his grip on her hips. Varlena savoured it for a second longer, the touch of a man who was not trying to take.

"Now," she commanded. Hamzah latched onto the embers of the Smokeshifters with speed, for she instantly mourned his lips on her neck. He spun her so she faced the shifters. The flames fluttered through the sand. Splaying her palms outward, she focused on the light creating the flames and shattered it. The flames sprayed out like white shards until three men rolled along the dunes toward the water of the oasis behind the tarpaulin. The other guards shouted; their time was up. A tingling pain pierced below her ear, and she pulled back from Hamzah.

His eyes immediately widened.

"What did I do? Did I hurt you?" he asked, scanning her body. Varlena pulled her hair around her right shoulder, reaching up to rub the space below her left ear. "She is still changing!" Hamzah shouted, raising a wall of flame to his right, stopping the guards heading to the Smokeshifters from seeing them.

"No, don't be absurd. Can you check to see if something has bitten me?" she asked. The worry in Hamzah's eyes faded as he stepped closer, his hand hesitant as she turned her head, allowing him to investigate. He stilled. Not the still that came with restraining himself beneath her touch. He stilled in fear.

"No," he whispered. "No, no, no, no," he repeated, stepping back. He immediately brought his hand below his ear. "Check my skin," he said.

"Whatever for—"

"Varlena! Check my skin!" he hissed, glancing back at the tarpaulin as he hunched over so she could inspect his neck. Her fingers ran along his brown skin until pausing below his ear, where the mark of Keres was raised like a scar.

"A celestial tie," Varlena whispered, her hand moving back to her own neck, where she knew the same mark must be. Why did he look so panicked? In Carvyre's culture, celestial ties were granted as a mark of two souls mirroring one another. They were the foundation of some of the most powerful military partnerships in Carvyre's history, the foundation of beautiful composers, lovers, friends—a symbol fate wanted you to find one another. Hamzah gripped her hands.

"You cannot tell anyone, your Highness," he whispered. He was serious.

"Whatever do you—"

"Please, Varlena. You cannot—"

"Okay, I won't!" she exclaimed, yanking her hands away. Was the notion of sharing a tie with her really so sickening? "I'm sorry it is such a burden to you." She crossed her arms, and Hamzah's eyes widened.

"A burden?" he exclaimed. "A burden?" His voice rose, and he caught himself before anyone came to check on the pair. "Varlena, in Q'Ohar, anyone found with a celestial tie is sentenced to death."

Chapter Six

HAMZAH

The princess's welcome ball, with all the lights and music, was almost enough to distract Hamzah from the fact he had not spoken with her further about their celestial ties. After she agreed to say nothing, the king had stormed over with his own guards, commanding Hamzah to explain why he had not alerted the other guards to the potential threat of sand crawlers. While Varlena tried her best to minimise the argument by stating it was her idea, the king had insisted she ride beside him for the remainder of the journey into the capital, leaving Hamzah anxious and watching to see if the king's gaze ever fell upon her mark. Luckily for Hamzah, the king was too focused on watching the Smokeshifters burn alive, a consequence of looking upon his betrothed while she changed. For now, he was safe; her hair over her left shoulder hid it from view. He was lucky his hair was long enough to curl slightly behind his ear, covering his. It offered little reassurance; he was a dead man walking, and one who needed to speak with the princess as soon as possible.

Everyone in the ballroom gravitated toward her from the moment the king and the princess appeared at the top of the staircase. He presented her on his arm like a trophy. A trophy he had moulded to fit his ideal regal beauty. And she was just that, regal and beautiful, but she did not look like Varlena. The golden gown Hamzah had selected for her entry into the city had been replaced by a deep red lehenga, matching the shade of the king's sherwani. He was right; the colour washed her out, but she was still magnificent. Yet the cut of the cloth or the sparkle of the gems, as she twirled around the ballroom, did not make it so. Her smile did. The one he knew was not genuine but brightened her face as she danced with suitors presented by the king. But amongst all the smiles, the polite conversation, the incline of her head, the clench of her jaw when one of them said something that evidently made her want to release her rage, amongst it all, her eyes still glanced around the room as she spun, looking for him. Hamzah stood beside the smaller throne placed on a dais next to the king's, though neither had sat all evening. It gave him a clear view to assess the room for threats, though there were many avenues, all ones he was not confident defending against, given his incredibly brisk introduction to the palace. He was to meet with the rest of the princess's new royal guard in the morning for full briefing. His old general had warned him the other guards would likely be cold toward a new addition, particularly one that had been assigned to Varlena's side before any of them. It was nothing new to Hamzah, all the guards had been the same during the journey from Carvyre.

"Farseer," a voice commanded. Hamzah straightened and turned to greet his new captain of the royal guard, Nazim, the same man who had offered him the opportunity in Carvyre. He was more polished than his barrack general, his stomach rounder. "You're dismissed for the evening."

"Have I done something wrong, Sir?" Hamzah asked, glancing to check Varlena's position. Still, she danced in the centre of the tiled floor under the lanterns' glow.

"Not at all, but you'll need time to gather belongings and move them into the palace barracks." The captain clapped him on the back. "I'll take over for now. Pick up duty again in the morning after we meet with the rest of your group."

"Yes, Sir," Hamzah said, bowing his head before leaving the dais. His eyes scanned for Varlena's on the floor. She had finally escaped the Lord of Kyara's vice-like dance grip and stood with the two women who were her new ladies-in-waiting while she sipped, or rather glugged, a glass of wine. Their eyes met over the rim of the glass, and she set it down. Red stained her lips. Hamzah took a step toward her but stopped when the king approached her side, looping his arm in hers and steering her in the opposite direction. Hamzah didn't wait to see if she looked over her shoulder at him.

***

Laughter echoed through the house, but everywhere Hamzah turned, there was nobody there. No nieces and nephews running circles around him, no sister wrapping flatbreads or brushing her hands on her apron. The house was cold, empty, but there was a brightness to it that was unusual. His small home was on the outskirts of the city and packed between two other streets. It was usually dull, so the shine on the coloured rugs was odd.

"Is this your home?"

Hamzah spun round in the kitchen, his knee knocking on the table but feeling no pain. Varlena sat on a countertop in her red lehenga, one leg crossed over the other. Hamzah frowned, looking around himself.

"Where are we?" he asked. The brightness in the room radiated off her skin.

"You tell me, it's your dream," she said, tilting her head as though something confused her. "Someone else has been in your mind before, but they haven't left a trace I recognise. It cannot be someone from Carvyre." Hamzah didn't know whether to focus on the worrying idea someone else had been in his head without him knowing, or that she found it acceptable to be here without his permission.

"It's impolite to just waltz into someone's dream," Hamzah said, deflecting the question, suddenly embarrassed of his home, given the jewel-laden princess sat within its walls.

"The tea you had been drinking finally wore off." Varlena shrugged and jumped down from the countertop. Her feet stumbled, and she gripped the table's edge. Hamzah stepped forward to assist

her, but she held up her hand, her face holding no warmth. "You left," she said, licking her red-stained lips.

"The ball?" he asked. Varlena nodded. "I was told to come and collect my things and move them into the palace."

"You could have told me," she murmured, dragging a finger through the flour dusted on the table.

"You were with the king."

"Well, you still should have told me."

"How?"

"I don't know. You just should have," she snapped. Her eyes found his, and he tilted his head.

"What's really wrong?"

"Don't do that, Hamzah. Don't analyse me."

"Don't try to hide things, then." He shrugged.

"You're bolder in your dreams."

"Well, it is my head," Hamzah said, leaning back against the kitchen table as she walked around to face him. "Are dreams usually this empty when you enter them?"

"Usually, I stand at the periphery and watch, like it is a play. But sometimes I can clear the dream and speak with the sleeper."

"Like now?"

"Are you asleep in this house? Or in the palace?" she asked, shifting closer until her knees touched his.

"The palace."

"Come and find me," she said, moving forward until he was forced to widen his legs. She stepped between them. His grip on the edge of the table tightened as she reached out a hand and tucked a curl behind his ears, his usually slicked-back style messy from bathing before bed.

"I need to rest before I am with you all day tomorrow," he said, clenching his jaw as she trailed her finger down his neck. He suddenly realised he was shirtless.

"I could help you sleep better," she whispered, leaning in to plant a kiss on his shoulder.

"*Your Highness,*" *he said through gritted teeth.*

"*You sound so serious when you call me that,*" *she said again, planting another kiss before trailing them across his chest.*

"*It is your proper title, especially as I am your guard,*" *he emphasised.* "*The guard you have known for only a month.*" *It didn't stop her gentle touch as she lowered herself. His hands moved quickly, gripping her wrists and tugging her arms to her sides. It forced her to straighten and look him in the eye.* "*What is this really about?*" *He would not fall for whatever mask she was hiding behind tonight. Her eyes flickered.* "*Does that make you angry?*" *he asked, tilting his head.* "*Me taking back control of whatever game you are playing.*"

"*It is not a game,*" *she snapped. Streaks of white flashed in her purple irises. She tried to pull away, but he held her wrists firm, trapping her with his thighs.*

"*Tell me,*" *he said as she glanced away.* "*Tell me, Varlena,*" *he added, softer this time. Her hair fell down the sides of her face when she looked down. The mask slipped—the confident, flirtatious one fading to a gentler expression. Her eyes glistened.*

"*I just wanted someone else's touch,*" *she whispered.* "*Somebody I chose instead of—*"

"*Who touched you?*" *Hamzah asked, tensing. He had been off duty for one evening, and as a result, she'd been in danger.* "*Tell me, Varlena, and I'll—*"

"*You'll what?*" *Varlena asked, her head snapping up.* "*What will you do to the man who said he was owed a chance to test his goods before marrying me?*" *Her mouth snapped shut, as though she had not wanted to reveal how much this agreement tormented her. Hamzah breathed deeply through his nose. Nothing. He could do nothing against the king.*

"*Did he...*"

"*I didn't give him the chance to get very far,*" *she whispered, and Hamzah's grip on her wrists loosened to trace gentle circles on her skin.* "*I am to be locked in my chambers for a week as punishment.*"

"*As a punishment for refusing him?*" *Hamzah asked.*

"Welllll…" She tilted her head. "More of a punishment for how I refused him." She lifted one shoulder half-heartedly. Hamzah waited for her to elaborate. She loosened her hand from his grip, tucked her hair behind her ears, and rested them on his forearms.

"I suffocated him with my power until he passed out… in front of guards…shoving him and saying no wasn't working, so I figured I needed to be more forceful." Varlena stroked the thin hairs on his arms, and Hamzah shivered. "Is this what my life will be like now?" she asked, her voice sorrowful. "Trying to avoid my betrothed until we are married and I can no longer refuse him?"

A tear landed on his lap. Hamzah placed a finger under her chin, tilting it up so she would look at him.

"You always have the right to say no, Varlena," he said, brushing away the tear with his thumb.

"There is an agreement, Hamzah. I must give him and Carvyre an heir."

He frowned, infuriated. There was nothing he could do.

"Regardless, I will be by your side every step of the way. We will find a way to ease matters for you."

Varlena reached for his neck, brushing the new scar under his ear.

"Bound together for life," she murmured. "Why are celestial ties punishable by death?" she asked. "In Carvyre, it simply means you have found a mirror to your soul; in Eresydon, it is a blessing from a god; in Thassena, a symbol of a bargain, and in Asynthos, a shared destiny, a blessing. In Q'Ohar, I was told you simply do not believe in them." She shifted closer, turning her body to nestle her head into his shoulder. He hesitated before moving to wrap his arms around her. She wasn't the Princess of Carvyre or the future Queen of Q'Ohar in this moment. She was a young woman, frightened and alone, who had come to him for comfort and nobody else.

"That is what the people tell themselves. They believe if they give the ties no weight, they will not be marked. But in the past, it was believed a celestial tie bound two people with high levels of power, allowing them to draw on one another's strength. It makes them dangerous. A

threat."

"We are not of equal power, though, which proves the theory false."

"I do not think the king would see it that way, your Highness," Hamzah *whispered, breathing in the scent of wine on her breath. She squeezed his torso.*

"I will not let them kill you, Hamzah."

Chapter Seven

VARLENA

A year later.

It was growing. The dark vein that started on the left of her ribcage had expanded two inches. When Hamzah prodded it gently, the darkness under her skin squirmed. She flinched, and he looked up at her from his position on the floor at the edge of her bed. He squeezed her thigh in silent reassurance. But it didn't work. Perhaps her mother was right: rage made her ugly and was the perfect soil for the darkness to take root. Varlena Nylaria was twenty-one, four years away from marriage, an heir and providing her home with a replacement for Isoria one day, and she was cursed.

"From what I read in the academic journals your cousin Lowven sent me, it is still in the very early stages," Hamzah said, reaching for a tin of healing balm his sister had given him. He warmed it up between his fingers and gently stroked the veins along her ribs. Varlena relaxed at its instant soothing effects, dulling the throbbing sensation.

"How long until I go insane?" Varlena mumbled.

"We both know you're already insane," Hamzah replied, a playful smile on his face as he screwed the tin shut. Varlena reached out, brushing back his hair and then cupping his cheek.

"You would find me boring if I wasn't." He leant into her touch before clearing his throat and rising to stand. Varlena pulled her robe back around her. He never let it go any further than gentle touches and comforting embraces. No matter how clear it was that she wanted more.

"Your playful quips and arguments with the lords could never be boring, your Highness," Hamzah said, turning to open her chamber doors. Her two ladies-in-waiting already stood with a tray of tea and a fruit bowl.

"I will dress myself," Varlena said as one reached into her wardrobe. She hesitated and looked at the other lady.

"Your Highness—"

"You heard her," Hamzah said, still holding the door open.

"But the king commanded we—"

"And the princess has said otherwise," Hamzah insisted. Varlena smiled. Hamzah could not disagree with the king directly, but this was his small way of showing whose side he was truly on. Though how they were going to evade the king's next attempts at seducing her and finding the curse on her skin, she did not know.

"But—"

"Leave!" Varlena snapped, her power reaching out without her command. Strips of light shot from her skin, as the two ladies scrambled from the room. Hamzah slammed the door behind them and waited, watching her. He tapped his chest, and she mirrored his actions, delicately tapping on her collarbones to calm and shift the darkness within that was battling with her light to shift her emotions and control.

"I had one idea," Hamzah said. "It's absurd, but at this point, anything is worth trying."

"Hamzah, nobody has ever stopped the curse. I have four years, and then I'll be locked inside an institution." Her feet were cold as she padded toward the wardrobe, reaching in for a thin lavender silk to wrap around her body, one that brushed against the veins as little as possible. "At least I get out of marrying him. He won't want damaged goods," she muttered. She hadn't sensed Hamzah move and jumped when he slammed the wardrobe door shut.

"Don't say that. You are not someone who gives up," he said, raising his voice. Varlena's lip quirked as she tied the gown at her side.

"Rage still looks beautiful on you, Hamzah." She patted his cheek and moved to her vanity. The morning light streamed in from the arched glass doors, and light reflected off the mirror Hamzah had successfully replaced in his first month in the palace, ensuring it was not one spelled by a Sorcerer to counteract her power. She twisted her hand until she looked into the other mirror, the mirror placed in her cousin's study.

"Have you told her the plan yet?" Lowven asked, looking through the mirror at Hamzah instead of Varlena.

"Hello to you too," she said, beginning to braid her hair over her left side to hide her celestial tie. "Are you a part of whatever the absurd plan is?"

"It's not absurd," Lowven defended. "Just slim odds of success." Varlena sighed and clipped jewels into the crossovers of the braid.

"Tell me then."

"Tradition states the future queen of Q'Ohar is to take a pilgrimage of her choice before her wedding—some crap about purifying her mind and body for her husband. But nothing states when that pilgrimage can be taken."

"You want me to go on a pilgrimage. That's your plan? Heal the darkness from my body by doing some good deeds," Varlena scoffed. "You're right; that is absurd."

"Keep listening," Hamzah scolded, waiting for her to hold the necklace up, as she usually did, so he could fasten it around her neck.

"We can make it look like a pilgrimage, but really Hamzah will take you to Farvos to speak with the Xyra," Lowven said. Varlena clapped her hands together.

"Oh! My mistake, this is the absurd part! You want to seek the help of a race who are both cursed never to leave their home and also do not wish to since the murder of their deity."

"The Xyra have naturally heightened healing powers. It is not beyond the realm of possibilities that they have found ways to harness that and use it on others," Hamzah insisted.

"And how do you plan to face the fact they cannot leave Farvos?" Varlena asked, staring between Hamzah and Lowven in the mirror. The two men looked at one another before Hamzah spoke.

"Nobody said we couldn't enter."

***

Farvos reminded Varlena of Misorus in Carvyre, the birthplace of the pegasus, or the capital of Asynthos. All three locations towered upward. Asynthos up a mountain, Carvyre up a winding hill, and Farvos was built directly into the red canyon stone. Wisps of smoke and clouds shielded much of the mountainous city from view, obscuring the landing entrances that supposedly tunnelled inward until the city opened into a gaping expanse within. Not that there was anyone in Q'Ohar still alive to have visited before the curses t confirm that. At the base of the canyon rock, Varlena and Hamzah stood in front of towering, chiselled stone spikes.

"It's pretty evident they don't want anyone to enter," Varlena said, slowly unwrapping the woven fabric from around her hair and face. They had stopped at numerous settlements along their route in the last three months, keeping up the façade that Varlena was simply on her marital pilgrimage. They had to keep up pretences, given how difficult it had been to convince the king to agree to it. Luckily, Varlena and Hamzah had visited the church first; hearing how desperately Varlena wished to be blessed by the deities as early as possible swayed him. The priests had spent a month teaching her rituals and sermons and lore about the deities of Q'Ohar, as though she didn't already know them all as a princess of a royal family. Hamzah had been given strict lessons by his general on areas to avoid and places that were safe to stop and visit. After all, a woman on a marital pilgrimage could not be tainted by the minds of too many others and so was allowed only one guard. Her guard.

"What do you think happens if we just... walk through?" Hamzah asked, passing her a water skin. She gulped the cold water, freshly filled in Mohri, a settlement only a thirty-minute ride from Farvos through the dry forest. She wiped the back of her hand and stepped forward.

"Let's find out," she said, resting her hand on the carved stone spike as she crossed the very evident line carved into the ground. Smoke shifted above them; gentle clouds suddenly twisted into spiralled plumes that shot from the ground ahead. The stone shook with impact. Hamzah was next to her in a heartbeat, his arm outstretched as a trickle of flames at their feet formed a protective wall. The plumes of smoke and ash twisted tighter until three bodies formed. Two men stood further back while a surprisingly tall woman with gaunt features and black hair pulled taut stood at the centre; her hands were clasped, her eyes watchful. Smoke and ash flitted from her skin.

"Varlena Nylaria. We never have visitors, let alone a princess of Carvyre." The voice was hoarse, as though the Smokeshifter had spent far too long in her drifting form.

"We have come to—"

"I know what you have come for, Hazmah Farseer." The woman's eyes flickered to his. "It would seem your affection for your future queen has made you lax in spotting when the smoke of a tavern is actually the ash of a shifter hanging on your every word." Hamzah tensed at Varlena's side, and she knew he would be berating himself for the mistake.

"Can you blame him? He has only had the company of a princess for three months. My constant prattling has likely exhausted him. It's no wonder he did not see you or your acquaintances," Varlena said, stepping forward to defend him.

"You still call yourself a princess and not the future queen," noted the woman with a tilt of her head. "Perhaps you do not think you will live to see the day you are crowned."

Varlena held her head high. "Enough of the games. You said you already knew why we were here, so let's get on with it."

"We cannot give you what you seek."

"Cannot or will not?" Hamzah asked.

"I know what it is like to watch someone you love die. I would not force that on someone if I did not have to." The woman's eyes drooped for a moment. "It is true; the Xyra have found ways to harness their healing abilities to use on others."

"Then what is the problem?" Hamzah snapped. Varlena reached down to brush his hand, silently commanding him to calm, despite enjoying his rage.

"Whether it is the curse or something else, the power can only be used on people of Q'Ohar. It will not work on the princess."

"I want to hear it from one of their mouths," Hamzah said. Varlena squeezed his hand. She commended his attempts and determination to prevent the curse from spreading, but she was a lost cause, and the sooner he realised that, the sooner he could prepare for how different his life would look without her in it. She did not know if he would still be her guard when the insanity began, or if she would be shipped back to Carvyre immediately, leaving Hamzah as a guard for the king or perhaps relegated to palace patrol.

"What about the curse on them do you not understand?" the woman asked. "They cannot leave. Even if they wished to, they will not."

"Why?" Varlena asked, her curiosity piqued. They were cursed, but it would seem they were not fazed by it, not if they preferred life within their city walls.

"They have no heir, no leader, and no deity. They will never leave until the one who can complete the trials arrives."

"The trials?" Varlena asked. "The trials of Nefere?" She knew the Xyra's old ways from her childhood learnings. The trials determined who would become the leader of the Xyra, the highest-ranking official in their race. She had never heard of them waiting for someone to complete it.

"This isn't what we came here for, your Highness," Hamzah whispered.

"No, it is not," the woman said. "And we have already told you; we cannot help." The two men behind her began shifting back into smoke. "Unless you want to catch alight, I wouldn't cross the border." And with those final words, she drifted back into the sky, forming the protective smoke around the red stone mountain. Varlena pulled Hamzah back from the border and turned away. She couldn't look at the defeat on his face.

Chapter Eight

HAMZAH

Varlena's silence was never a good sign. It either meant she was scheming of ways to wind up a lord or the king, or over-thinking. Given Hamzah was the only one present as they climbed the stairs of the inn, he imagined it was the latter. She winced, her hand moving to the side of her blouse and drawing Hamzah's eyes away from the taunting sway of her hips. He reached out a hand to steady her on the final steps, but she shrugged him off.

"Number four," he called as she strode down the hallway, the wooden floorboards creaking under her riding boots. Her hair and side profile shone with moonlight as she opened the door ahead of him and hurried into their room for the night. Both were exhausted, their sweat-soaked skin caked in sand. The settlement they had stayed in the night before, Mohri, the closest to Farvos, had no remaining rooms. They were forced to travel further, to Razak. She radiated irritability as she pulled her blouse over her head and flung it on the bed. Hamzah closed the door behind him, dropping their bags on the floor and raising the light for the flame in the lanterns. The sound of her belt unbuckling prompted him to turn.

"I should—"

"Save it, Hamzah," she grunted. "I don't have the energy to hear your complaints of what is and isn't appropriate right now. Stare at my breasts, don't stare at my breasts, what does it matter?"

"I was going to say, I should run you a bath before you undress," he said, his lips pursed, though he made a point of only meeting her eye as she turned to him in nothing but undergarments. She kept one hand on her ribcage. He frowned. "Show me."

"It's fine," she muttered. "I'll run the bath myself." She slammed the door to the bathing chamber behind her, leaving Hamzah to rub his face until the grains of sand fell to the floor. A knock signalled the food had arrived, and he hastily opened and closed the door, balancing the tray of spiced stew and flatbreads in one hand and the jug of water in the other. The tray and jug clattered to the floor when Varlena cried out.

"Your Highness?" he called, darting to the door and shoving it open with his shoulder. Varlena was hunched over on the floor, one hand gripping the bathtub, the other on her ribcage. The water in the tub still sloshed from side to side, forming a puddle around her feet. She waved Hamzah away and sniffed. She wiped at her eyes before pulling herself up, angling her leg over the edge again. She winced, and the hand that had gripped her ribcage flew to the curl of the bathtub to steady herself.

"Varlena," Hamzah whispered. The darkness in the veins at her side twisted and moved, reaching further toward her hip than before. The surrounding skin was red and swollen.

"I'm fine, Hamzah," she murmured, gritting her teeth as she lowered into the tub. Her teeth chattered.

"This is why I offered to run the bath, you fool." He waved his hand, warming the water until it steamed at the right temperature, soothing the ache in her side. Her face finally relaxed as she lowered herself further in. He returned for the jug in the adjoining room and knelt in the puddle of bathwater at her side. Brushing her hair back from her face, he filled the jug and gently let the water flow over her scalp, and as it trickled down the sides of her cheeks, it mixed with her tears.

"Why didn't you say it was worse?" he whispered, reaching for a bowl of soap and gently massaging her scalp.

"The news at Farvos was already disappointing for you; I didn't want to make matters worse," she mumbled, holding out a hand for another bar of soap. Gently, she began rubbing her arms as

Hamzah rinsed the suds from her hair. Her tears stopped when he perched his arms on the edge of the tub to rest his chin.

"You could never disappoint me," he whispered. It gained him a small smile before she held the soap out to him.

"I can't bend far enough to reach my legs properly," she said. Hamzah held her stare for a second longer. He contemplated saying no, that it crossed the boundaries he'd been drawing in the sand between them for a year. But exhaustion weighed heavily in her eyes, dulling the once glistening purple. He nodded.

The smell of lavender filled the room as Varlena lifted one leg until her calf was out of the water. He glided the soap along her shin, and she rested her ankle in his hand. The water sloshed as she crossed her arms. He knew she had done it for him, so he could look up and not feel guilty seeing her chest through the water.

"For a man I have watched train in the ring, you have a very gentle touch," she said. "I won't break." He locked eyes with her as he finished washing the first leg and tried to lower it into the water. Varlena resisted.

"You are far from breakable, your Highness," he said. Still, she did not relent her leg.

"The rest of my leg still needs washing," she said, raising her chin. Hamzah quirked an eyebrow, running his tongue over his teeth with a sigh. Her eyebrows rose a fraction when he didn't say it was inappropriate but instead unbuttoned his shirt and rolled the sleeves to avoid soaking them. He gripped her calf harder, a silent protest to her request, but it only made her smile as he slid the soap below the surface and along the top of her thigh.

"I think you could break me," Varlena whispered.

"I would never hurt you, your Highness," he replied, shifting the soap to the outside of her thigh.

"It hurts me when you don't do as I ask sometimes," she said. The water moved against the bathtub as she uncrossed her arms.

"I always do as you ask," Hamzah said. In that moment, he was doing the opposite of everything he should be, simply because she had asked. He could not deny her when she was in pain. Varlena bit her lip, and she found his hand under the water, guiding him and the soap toward her inner thigh. She smiled at Hamzah's sharp intake of breath. His eyes never left hers as she sat forward, her face inches from his.

"Is that so?" she asked, her hand tucking a sand-coated curl behind his ear. "You're an obedient guard, aren't you?" she asked. "Why don't you prove it?" She released her hand from his, waiting to see if he accepted her challenge. He should pull back, tell her he would wait outside while she finished bathing. But he relented at the playfulness returning to her eyes. Just once, he told himself. Hamzah swallowed and began moving the soap in slow circles, washing the exhaustion of the day from her inner thigh. Her hand moved to hold the back of his neck, pulling him closer.

"Higher," she whispered. He did as she asked, continuing his slow circular patterns with the soap until the back of his hand met her other thigh. A soft sigh escaped her lips, and she spread her legs wider.

"I—" Hamzah choked when she dug her nails into the back of his neck, resting her forehead against his. The steam clung to their faces.

"Higher, Hamzah," she whispered. How could he deny her when his name sounded like a prayer on her lips? When the steam in the room was interspersed with the smell of lavender, a scent that tortured him every time he pulled away from her, every time he wanted to give in to the pull between them. He gripped the soap harder as he moved the final inch she wanted. Varlena shivered and slid her arm further around his neck, clinging to him. Moving her other hand to his face, she pulled back, revealing the darkening of her eyes. He'd witnessed lust in others before. Walking down alleyways after shifts, stopping in taverns for breakfast, but seeing it in her eyes, for him, was entirely different. Her lips parted, soft and quick breaths escaping them, as he continued moving. Her hand shifted over his face until her thumb pulled back his lip. He jolted at the spark that rushed through him, losing grip of the soap until his hand collided with her instead. Varlena let out a soft moan and shifted against him, willing him to continue his movements.

"We shouldn't—" His words were cut off by another soft sound as his thumb slid over her, repeating the motion. "Varlena..." he groaned, frustrated with himself. He regretted letting things get this far, yet the things he was doing to her, the sounds she was making—he would commit it all to memory.

"Don't stop," she breathed. He did exactly as she asked. He kept up the same movements and pressure until she moved her hips against the friction. He needed to stop; it was wrong; she was to be married, and he was just her guard.

"Varlena—" A quiet cry drowned out his words. She stilled against him, loosening her grip on his shoulders. He slid his hand away from her, back along her leg until he lifted it from the water and gripped the edge of the bathtub. Only at that moment did he realise his breathing was just as heavy as hers.

"Kiss me," she whispered. Hamzah's breath caught as she pulled back to look at him properly.

"I—" he clenched his jaw. Varlena huffed.

"That's where you draw the line, Hamzah? You'll let me take pleasure from you, but you refuse anything that might benefit you?" Varlena's face twisted into a scowl as she forced herself up and out of the bathtub. Hamzah hung his head at the slam of the door behind them. That was exactly why he'd promised himself to never take it further. Quickly, he doused himself with cold water, scrubbing at his body with soap and a cloth while trying to erase her sounds from his mind. When he finally exited the bathing chamber, he found her standing in front of the window, tapping her fingers against her arm in a silk robe. She flicked her wet braid from side to side.

"You're angry," Hamzah muttered, tying the towel around his waist and digging around in his bag for clean trousers to sleep in.

"It's the way I've always been, isn't it? Perhaps the curse will only make it stronger." Hamzah continued rifling through his bag. "Rage makes you ugly, Varlena," she mocked in a voice he assumed was intended to be her mother's. "Perhaps that is why you want nothing more from me." Hamzah's hand froze in the bag, and he forced himself upright again.

"Is that what you think?" he demanded, his own anger rising. "That I think you are unattractive and filled with rage? Is that why you think I will not allow myself to go any further?" His voice was raised now as he stormed to her side of the room. Though her body was angled toward him, she looked out of the window, refusing to meet his eye.

"Well, isn't it?" she asked, still tapping her arm.

"I stop myself because I do not know if I can handle the heart-break of losing you one day. I do not allow myself to linger when we touch or lean too close that I might kiss you, because I know if I do, I will fall deeper and deeper into your soul. I cannot fall so inexplicably in love with you, Varlena, when I know I will either lose you to a king or to insanity. That is why I channel my frustra-tions at not being able to touch you into absurd plans for finding a cure for you, Varlena." She did not look at him, but her tapping had stopped. "*Iahabi*, look at me."

She did not.

"What does that mean?" she asked, fidgeting with her braid.

"It is the only word I can think of that captures what I feel for you. I've told you once before that your rage isn't ugly. It is burning passion; it is earth-shattering magnificence; it is strength that keeps my world turning. *Iahabi* is my love, my everything, the other half of my soul. You, Varlena, you are my *Iahabi*." Hamzah was panting from the rising emotions in his chest, and still, Varlena did not move. Arms crossed, she stared at the floor. "Look at me," Hamzah said. Still, she did not. She chose to hide the vulnerability he knew was in her eyes, the pain of understanding his reasons for keeping their distance.

He reached her in two strides. She gasped as he yanked her braid, forcing her to look at him. His voice softened. "I said, look at me, Iahabi." And Hamza moved his hands to cup her jaw as he crashed his lips against hers. Varlena did not hesitate. Her arms were quick to snake around his neck as he hunched over her. There was nothing soft or gentle about his touch. A year's worth of anticipation and desire collided as Varlena teased his mouth open with her tongue, and he followed. Her arms trembled, and he pulled away, guiding her toward the bed. He knelt between her legs, gripping her face again, already mourning the absence of her lips. He wanted all of Varlena, every inch; he wanted to hear her soft breaths and sharp cries. He wanted to do everything he could to take away her pain and worry. His hand moved between her legs, and she bit down on his lip as his fingers slid against her.

"You learn quickly," she murmured against his lips.

"I pay attention," he whispered, shifting his lips to her neck until he kissed the tie that bound them.

"Well done," she murmured, clawing her nails down his back as he nipped at her neck. "But it is my turn to learn what you like." Varlena crawled away from him, gesturing to the bed until he moved onto his back. His hands gripped her thighs as she straddled him, finding his lips again. "Did you mean it?" she asked, trailing her hands down his chest. "Everything you said?"

Hamzah moved to grip her hand and pulled back to see the light in her eyes.

"Every word," he murmured, stroking her lip with his thumb. "Iahabi," he said with a smile. Varlena shifted and shuddered a breath as she leant to kiss him.

"My Iahabi," she said.

Chapter Nine

HAMZAH

There were many beautiful women in Q'Ohar, and Hamzah had noticed plenty over his twenty-eight years of life. But he'd devoted his life to his family; he had no time to give to another. Fate changed that. If he hadn't been on shift the day of the briefing, would he be in this bed? If he hadn't paused to take in the courtyard at the Carvyre palace, would he be listening to the soft feminine breathing beside him? If he hadn't jumped to defend the king, would he be slowly stroking a princess's hair, wishing for a way to save her? So many things could have altered his path, but the piece of his soul that was tied to hers told him they would have always found each other.

Outside the inn, horses whinnied and shouts erupted as the town awoke. Sunrise had long since passed. They had two months left of Varlena's false pilgrimage, yet he was out of options for ways to cure her curse. He glanced down at her ribs, the sheets tangled over their waists and between their legs. The dark veins seemed quieter this time, but they were still there, angry and threatening to tear apart their happiness. At least they had two months together, two months before they'd have to keep up the pretence of her wellbeing when they returned to the capital.

"I had an odd dream," Varlena mumbled. Hamzah hummed, a silent question. "I was in Eresydon, and there was this blonde woman, and she was pulling a dagger out of a man's chest. She looked sad."

"I hope that is not a bad omen," Hamzah chuckled.

"What are you thinking about?" Varlena mumbled. Hamzah

looked down at her from where he sat propped on his elbow, stroking her hair.

"Where I should take you next," he said. Varlena gave him a sleepy smile and stretched her arms with the smallest wince on her face before opening her eyes fully to look at him.

"I don't think we should go anywhere today." Her smile was playful, and he stroked a thumb over her bottom lip.

"What would you suggest instead, Iahabi?" he murmured, mesmerised. She propped herself up on an elbow, mirroring him before leaning in for a kiss. She smiled against his lips.

"I think you should find us wine and food, and we should stay in this bed until the stars come out again. It grants you the entire day to plan where to take me next," she said, sliding her hand over his waist and below the sheets. Hamzah chuckled.

"Why do I get the impression you would be far too much of a distraction?" He gripped her jaw, deepening their kiss.

"I think you're the distract—" Wood splintered as the door shattered open. Hamzah lunged over Varlena, protecting her from flying wood as pieces lodged themselves into his bare back. Footsteps thudded across the wood, and Varlena's hands clenched. A blinding light filled the space, giving the pair enough time to rush to their feet. Hamzah shoved the sheets in the princess's direction, hiding the curse crawling its way along her ribs as he reached for his discarded trousers. His sword was on the opposite side of the room, but before he could run for it and set it ablaze into a torturous weapon, Varlena cried out, and the blinding light disappeared into nothing. His eyes sought her immediately, finding her in tungstyn cuffs, the only metal known to inhibit power. Two royal guards, the king's, stood on either side of her.

"Hamzah Farseer," Nazim, the captain of the royal guard, entered the room, followed by two others holding similar cuffs to the ones on Varlena's wrists. "By order of King Malik, you are hereby arrested for the crimes of adultery and, as a direct impact, treason against the crown of Q'Ohar."

"No!" Varlena cried. "He didn't do anything; it's not his fault!" She screamed, kicking at the guards who held her.

"Varlena, stop," he begged, knowing the movement would strain her ribs. The guards' grips were rough as they shoved him against the wall, pinning his hands out. As they cuffed him, the connection to his power immediately dampened, which meant the princess was helpless too. They couldn't let them see her curse or the tie; he needed to get her out.

"This is absurd!" Hamzah shouted, trying to capture their attention. "They're not married!" Nazim turned to him, his face stern. Hamzah knew he was making it worse for himself, but he needed to protect her.

"I suggest you keep your mouth shut, boy, or these guards' fists might slip, rendering you unconscious for the entire journey back to the palace."

"You'd make the princess sit next to an unconscious body for the entire journey?" he asked. *Fall for the bait; give me more information.*

"The princess will be in a separate carriage, which will remain locked the entire way. We can toss you over the back of a horse for all I care." Nazim spat at his feet.

"Was it you who locked her away when she refused to sleep with the king too? How noble of you." Hamzah spat right back, and the captain reddened.

"Take the princess to the carriage," he commanded. Hamzah's shoulders relaxed. The sooner she was in the carriage, the sooner she could better hide her curse.

"No! I won't leave you!" Varlena screamed. "You can't make me! Hamzah!" Her screams echoed as they dragged her through the inn. He was certain he still heard them when they locked her in the carriage too, and when a guard knocked him out cold.

***

Cold water shocked Hamzah awake; he spluttered, blinking. He tried to move as another wave of water hit his bare chest, but his wrists were bound above him, and if he leant too far on one side, his balance shifted off his tiptoes. His wrists burned, suggesting he had been dangling unconscious for quite some time. Brief memories returned of him waking at checkpoints through the desert before an injection knocked him out again. An image of Varlena's face pressed against the window of a carriage came to mind before his head fell back against a horse.

"Varlena," he muttered. It came out hoarse, his voice scratchy.

"You dare name her without a title." A voice sounded in the darkness from behind him. Hamzah tried to take in the space, but it was dark. In front of him was a brick wall, and high above the smallest iron grate, a trickle of daylight entered. "My spies were correct then. You were indeed sleeping with my property." Hamzah twisted around the rope until he faced the king, leaning against the iron bars of his prison cell. *Property.* What had he done? His actions would sentence Varlena to hell in her marriage.

"Only once," Hamzah choked. "Well, one night. I lost count of how many—" Hamzah grunted, losing his grip on his toes as the king punched him in the stomach. Hamzah's sputter soon turned into a pained laugh. "Is it because I am simply a guard? It must have hurt when she refused you, a *king*?" He wheezed when the second punch landed. If he taunted him enough, perhaps he would be the only victim of his anger. He couldn't hurt Varlena, not when she needed to protect her image.

"Was this some elaborate plan? Is that why you embarrassed me that day? So I might notice your bravery and assign you to the princess?" The king asked, pacing back toward the cell entrance. A guard passed him something wrapped in black fabric.

"I was content at the southern barracks. I had no reason to seek the princess," Hamzah said. As the king removed the black cloth, he revealed a shining silver handle with black leather strips. Hamzah tensed as the king set alternating strands alight with his power.

"Or perhaps this is a long-term plan of yours. Perhaps the Custodian of Carvyre sought you out years ago, planted you within to spy, enabling you to attend the visit. Perhaps your loyalty was always with Carvyre." The king approached him again, stroking the whip's leather. He raised a hand and motioned with a finger. Two guards entered, cutting the rope from the ceiling. They didn't bother to catch him. The sound of Hamzah's kneecaps cracking echoed through the cell, and Hamzah wondered how many other prisoners were listening. Rough hands dragged him to his feet and pulled his arms taut, fully displaying his chest to Malik.

Hamzah didn't have a second to brace himself as the leather lashed his flesh. He cried out. His knees buckled, but the guards kept him upright and turned him, offering his back to the king.

"Tell me the truth, Farseer," the king said. Hamzah grunted and bit down on his tongue as the leather came down on his back this time. His eyes rolled as stars crossed his vision.

"Yes, I slept with the future queen. What more do you want from me?" he snapped.

"I want to know the real reason behind it all. I want to know if it is her you work for or someone else." The king lowered the whip again, and Hamzah's skin split. Blood splattered on the floor at his feet before the flaming strands cauterised his skin

"Is it so hard to believe that there was nothing more to it?" Hamzah gasped. The whip struck again.

"Why would she risk it all for you? For a guard?" The king snapped. The guards turned Hamzah around, and the king's fist collided with his jaw.

"What was she risking?" Hamzah laughed. "The two of you would never be happy." It was the king's turn to laugh.

"And what?" He gripped Hamzah's jaw, forcing him to meet his eye. "You thought the two of you could be? What was going to happen when she got married? When, on our wedding night, it was my cock in her—" Hamzah flung his head forward, head-butting the king hard enough that he stumbled back and dropped the whip. Blood trickled down his chin as he brought his hand to his mouth, glancing at the blood. He stalked back toward Hamzah and smeared it across his face before seizing his jaw again.

"All you have done is handcuffed yourself to a lifetime of torture and her to a marriage locked away, where she will only be used for my pleasure and paraded when I deem it so." The king's fist collided with Hamzah's face, knocking his head to the side. He was too exhausted to insult the king further. "Hold his head," the king commanded; his tone changed, curiosity replacing his former rage. One guard gripped his head, turning it to the side. *No.* Hamzah tried to force it from his grip, but the king's hand was on his neck, tracing the scar below his ear.

"Perhaps seeing you die first would tame her," the king mused. He reached for a blade at his side and brought it to Hamzah's neck. He cried out as the steel bit into his flesh, the king trying his best to carve the celestial tie from his skin. Blood leaked down his chest. They both knew that a celestial tie could not be severed with a blade. It was taken only in death or by a god or deity. The king dropped the weapon and walked away.

"Prepare the princess."

Chapter Ten

VARLENA

If Varlena's mother thought her rage was ugly before, Varlena dreaded what she would think of her now. She threw a vase against the locked door of her chambers and screamed. It was a wonder she still had a voice left. All she did was scream. Screamed in the carriage for the entire two weeks' journey back to the palace, when she was thrown into her rooms, and now every day when they brought her a tray of food before locking her away again.

Solitude and rage were a volatile mix, especially with a curse designed to slowly seep her with darkness, one that would clash with her power and render her insane. She was waiting for the insanity part. Would she forget things? See things? Speak as though someone else inhabited her body? For now, all she felt was pain and anger, the only emotion that stopped her from thinking of Hamzah for too long before she cried. When the click of the lock sounded in the door, Varlena spun back from her bed. She usually only had one visit a day. Her two ladies-in-waiting walked in, followed by two guards. Over one's arm was a large fabric bag used to transport lehengas and sarees, while the other carried jewels on a pillow. Varlena looked at them warily as they placed the items by her vanity. The guards turned, watching the door.

"Why are you here?" Varlena asked, her voice harsh. The ladies-in-waiting reached for her hands and unlocked the tungstyn from her wrists. She felt her power slowly return, but with it having been dormant for so many weeks, she was no risk to those present. They guided her to the vanity, where Varlena stared at herself in the mirror. Her usually silver hair was dull and matted, her eyes rimmed with dark circles, and her lips dry and cracked.

"The king wishes for you to attend an engagement," one woman said, untangling Varlena's hair; the other untied the fabric bag, revealing another deep red lehenga. She was rather fed up with the colour. Varlena glanced between them both and the mirror, her fingers twitching, trying to sense how much of her power had returned. She needed to get a message to Carvyre. Varlena sat and bided her time as they polished her skin, styled her hair, and preened her within an inch of her life. She needed them to face away from the mirror before they clipped the cuffs back on.

"Can we continue on the terrace? I'm far too stifled in here," Varlena said. The two women glanced at the guards, who nodded and proceeded to check the balcony first before taking up a position at either end, waiting for the women to join them. Varlena made a point of moving slowly, appearing as though she was weak from exhaustion, but as she hunched over the vanity, she reached for her power and tugged at the light in the mirror, reaching for the person on the other side. She turned her back and hoped Lowven took the hint to stay silent and watch as she joined the ladies-in-waiting on the balcony. She made a point of rubbing her wrists as she sat.

"Where will the engagement be taking place?" Varlena asked as the woman began coiling her hair.

"In the courtyard gallows," one of them said. Varlena frowned. The only executions she had been forced to watch in Sahih were the executions of rebels who called themselves the Red Stones, intent on denouncing Malik and his claim as king.

"Will there be many people attending?"

"Oh yes, most of the city will want to see the show, which means many of the guards will be present to control the crowds." A show could be a good distraction for Lowven to get in with a small fleet of Pegasus-Bound, though the gallows was an odd location choice.

"What kind of show?" Varlena asked, searching for any more information that might help her cousin. She tugged at her power, sensing his presence in the mirror.

"They're executing a guard with a celestial tie."

***

Sweat dripped down Varlena's back and her palms as she clenched the skirts of her lehenga. Her seat, up high on the balcony, was perfectly shaded, and two serving girls waved large fans over her as she waited for the king. Citizens began pouring into the courtyard, packed so tightly she had no idea where Lowven would land if he figured out a plan. Carvyre had a portal mirror in every state, located just outside the capital boundaries, allowing for quicker access to meetings and occasions, but Varlena had no idea if the king would have thought to sever the connection with a fracture across the glass. Hamzah's survival depended on it still being intact. If it was, then Lowven could use his power to shift them through the glass and would have thirty minutes before alarms sounded, alerting the king of its use.

People down below were shoving one another, angling for the best view of the wood pyre built in the centre of the courtyard. Her fists clenched hard in the silvery white tungstyn handcuffs. There was no sign of Hamzah yet. She assumed it was also no coincidence that the king had also not arrived. As though summoned by her thought, a hand clamped down on her shoulder, and she flinched, glancing down at it. Blood marred his knuckles, and she knew, as the roar of the crowd sounded, if she could see him, there would be blood on Hamzah's face too.

"This is of your own doing," the king said, waving to the crowd before taking his place in his throne and possessively claiming her knee with his hand. Varlena didn't care. Her focus was only on searching for Hamzah being woven through the crowd toward the pyre. To the west, a huddle of guards pushed through. He had to be in there with them.

"What are you doing?" Varlena snapped as the king reached to brush her hair from her shoulder.

"Taking one glance at your tie before it disappears with his death," the king sneered, grabbing a chunk of her hair and pulling until she inclined her head toward him. He leant in, as if about to kiss her neck. "I hope he was worth it, because I'll spend every night of our marriage wiping the memory of him from your mind." He bit down hard on her skin, and she cried out. The servants would say nothing, and the crowd were too far below to hear or care.

"You'll never live up to him," Varlena spat. "I'll name our heir after him just to spite you, and Hamzah Farseer will rule over Carvyre, knowing all the stories his mother told him of the one and only love of her life." The king chuckled beside her as he released her hair and signalled to the guards below.

"What makes you think I'll let you live to see your child's first birthday? I'm moving the wedding earlier, we will be wed tomorrow in a small ceremony and as soon as you have given me an heir, I'll decide just what to do with you." The king rose from his throne and clapped his hands.

"You can't do that the agreement says I must be twenty five—" Trumpets sounded out across the courtyard, cutting Varlena off. All eyes turned to Malik. She refused to stand; let her lack of respect speak for her defiance.

"In Q'Ohar, scriptures tell of the great danger that arises when those with a celestial tie draw on one another's power," the king's voice boomed across the courtyard. "And while we have not yet found the other half to this man's tie, we can rest easy knowing it will be severed with his death." Members of the crowd cheered below, but it did not go unnoticed by Varlena or the king that many murmurings began among the people, who shifted on their feet as they looked between the king and the pyre. "Let the preparations begin!"

As he leant back in his chair, Varlena flung herself forward, gripping the edge of the balcony as six guards hauled Hamzah up onto the platform. His head lulled, and from this distance, she had no gauge as to whether he was even conscious. The guards were not gentle as they pressed his body against the stake rising from the centre of the pyre and tied the ropes around his middle until he hung there.

Varlena scanned the skies, hoping and praying for a flicker of wings, the sound of a battle cry, anything to signal that Lowven had made it through the mirror and was going to rescue Hamzah. But nothing came. So Varlena screamed.

"Hamzah!" she called once, long and loud. His head spun to the balcony just as the king pulled her back by her hair. She collided with the throne, pain soaring through her ribs and down the top of the thigh, where the curse had now reached.

"Iahabi!" he roared back, perhaps the last words he could manage. Varlena sobbed. Even in his death, he would not give up her identity to the crowd, only that he had someone he cared for, someone who did not want him dead. Shocked murmurs ran through the crowd; those already uncomfortable with the display appeared more distraught at the idea that this man had a love—an *everything*. The affectionate term was the king's final straw. He raised his hand and flames immediately ignited at the pyre's base. She should have known he would not make it a quick death. Instead, the flames were slow and taunting as they climbed their way up the pyre toward Hamzah's feet. He did not struggle, he did not scream; he simply kept his head turned toward the balcony, to her.

"I hope he screams," the king laughed. Varlena turned to glare at him, but a shadow distracted her, a shadow she would recognise anywhere: the two sweeping curves that became deadly, sharpened points, the narrow build that could dart between mountain rock. A moment later, a gust of wind blew at the pyre, taming the flames as wings boomed overhead and her call was answered. Malik had no chance of understanding what was happening as a pegasus soared into view from the east. She counted to prepare herself. One. Two. Three. Varlena thought of nothing but Hamzah as she hauled herself off the throne and catapulted over the side of the balcony, free falling through the air until she collided with feathers, and a comforting hand hauled her up onto the creature's back.

"I assume we want the guard too?" Lowven shouted over the sound of wings. Ten more pegasi fell through the clouds while arrows soared, colliding with a shower of bright light as they took down the guards stationed in the watchtowers.

"A good assumption," Varlena shouted back as Lowven guided his mount left.

"He better be worth nearly burning a wing for."

"He is!" Varlena grinned as Lowven brought the pegasus to a halt alongside the pyre, where it treaded the air like water. His sword made quick work of slicing the ropes binding Hamzah before another member from the battalion fleet came alongside him, reaching out to catch Hamzah as his bindings broke free. Using his Fae strength, he hauled Hamzah onto the back of the pegasus. Shouts echoed through the courtyard, along with the unmistakable sound of cheers as balls of flame soared toward them. Lowven waved his arm, creating an arc of shielded light until they broke free above the clouds.

Varlena committed the cheers to memory as she reached a hand through the air to Hamzah, who smiled and, for a moment, the darkness that was knocking at the cage within her, was silent.

Chapter Eleven

HAMZAH

Three years later

The rebellion against the King of Q'Ohar was rife. During the day, raids from soldiers decimated homes, while fires consumed different parts of the palace at night. Shouts for Hamzah and Varlena echoed through the nights, chants hailing the 'Celestial Custodians.' It had been Lowven's idea to plant the story of their love and celestial tie. The story was quickly ignited further by the group who called themselves the Red Stones. Having successfully kept themselves secret over the centuries, they deemed now the most vital time to act in saving their state from tyranny. It seemed the attempted murder of an innocent guard, who had pledged to protect the city, only added fuel to the fire. Couple that with the king's own personal vendetta for falling in love with his future wife, a woman that had publicly disrespected him, and the people had a couple they could believe in. A couple to restore the rightful custodianship of Q'Ohar until... until what? He could no longer recall why the custodians were in power. Perhaps the Red Stones were right in their rumours; the curses were worsening and slowly wiping the memories of those on Ithyion.

What the people did not know, though, and what only Hamzah and Varlena knew, was that one half of that couple was slipping further away with each passing day. Varlena was six months away from her twenty-fifth birthday, the age she was to be marked free of the curse and married off to the King of Q'Ohar. Instead, as that date crept closer, Varlena's anger merged with the darkness trying to suffocate her from within. It whispered to her that revenge was the only true course of action. She was losing grip on who mattered, with no regard for the collateral damage her actions might cause.

"It was a step too far, sire," Lowven said. Hamzah flinched at the formal title. It wasn't something he was used to. But after Varlena had declared him as her intended, and the people called for their placement as custodians, it had become natural for the people to refer to him with some formal title, as Varlena Nylaria's future husband. Though neither of them had discussed what that marriage would look like, or if it was even possible, as her mind slipped further into madness.

"I know, Lowven," Hamzah sighed, pouring a glass of wine for the man he now called a friend. The Carvyre army had taken the southern deserts of Q'Ohar. Eresydon offered no resistance as long as they avoided the forest border. The rebels within had taken ownership of the northwest and east entry points, meaning the capital had been laid to siege for three months now.

"Perhaps we need to consider a tungstyn ring—not cuffs—but just something to dampen her power when the curse prompts her to react rather than think."

"We would need to suggest it at the right time, otherwise it will have the opposite effect," Hamzah said, scratching his beard.

"I'll have one made," Lowven said. The opening of the tent rustled, and Varlena stepped in, coated in blood.

"Iahabi," she smiled. "Has Lowven told you the good news? We managed to take the lords' state homes on the western side of the city." She leant in to kiss his cheek, and it took everything in Hamzah not to flinch at the smell of blood on her skin.

"Did it really require eight streets' worth of collateral damage? Innocents?" Hamzah asked, sipping from his cup as he glanced at Lowven. Varlena unbuckled the sides of her armour and removed her jewel-encrusted crown, setting them both next to the makeshift washbasin to be cleaned.

"There is always collateral in war, my love, but the people know we fight for a better future under our rule. One day, when our heir rules Carvyre, they will have a wonderful relationship with us as Custodians of Q'Ohar. It is prosperous for all in the long run." She smiled and began unwrapping her hair from her braids.

"There was an orphanage, Iahabi," Hamza sighed. Varlena slammed her breastplate down, which Lowven took as his sign to leave.

"I do not wish to fight, Hamzah," she said. "We are almost there. The palace has depleted its stores. It is ready for the taking, and for us to take our place as custodians while my aunt remains in Carvyre's seat until we have a child." Slowly, she unbuttoned the blouse and dropped it to the floor, revealing nothing underneath except the web of dark veins that coated all her skin bar her neck and hands. "The king was right, you know," she said, reaching to lock her hands around Hamzah's neck, pressing her breasts against his chest.

"About?" he asked, trying to stay focused on the conversation as she kissed his neck.

"I think the celestial tie did strengthen our powers. My light burns so much brighter," she hummed, rubbing a hand against his crotch. She was wrong. It was not the tie strengthening her, it was the added darkness in her veins—old, dark power. While the dark and light battled in her mind, it manifested physically in an unending well of strength. Hamzah was beginning to wonder if she held too much power, especially when her mind and ability to make rational decisions were not always correct.

"I don't think it is your power that makes you shine bright," Hamzah murmured against her lips. He moved against her, keeping her at ease for the request he had to make.

"You're too kind," Varlena giggled against him as he lifted her legs, and she wrapped herself around him.

"It is simply the truth," he said, laying her down on the bed and crawling atop her. Gently, he caressed her cheek, staring down at the Fae princess he had fallen inexplicably in love with.

"But think of how much more we could take if we use our power even more, with the whole kingdom at our feet," she giggled, reaching up to capture his lips again. Hamzah matched her movements as she flipped him over, straddling him, but in his mind, those words repeated in his head over and over. She wanted more. She would take more. He was losing her completely.

***

"Things were so different the last time we were here," Varlena's voice echoed. Hamzah spun around as the blurred kitchen of his family home came into focus. She was sitting on the countertop, as she had been the first time she walked through his dreams. "Something is different," Varlena frowned, patting the countertop beside her. His body felt light as he jumped up beside her, wrapping an arm around her waist as she leant her head on his shoulder. Slowly, the dream state focused, and Varlena tensed. She gripped his hand to stop him from moving.

"Has this happened before?" he whispered, as if the version of himself he was watching enter the kitchen would hear him.

"No," she said. The couple watched. Hamzah recalled the day; it was the day his brother-in-law died. His eyes were red as he pulled out a chair from the table and collapsed into it, rubbing his eyes. He had just been putting his nieces and nephews to bed whilst his sister, Inaya, rested. But he did not remember what came next. Darkness slowly seeped into the room, and a woman in a gown just as dark stepped up behind him. She seemed to admire him for a moment, scanning her eyes over his back before stepping around.

"Hello, Hamzah," her voice echoed. Hamzah watched himself jump in the chair, rearing back and stumbling as he rose.

"How did you get in here?" He reached for a knife tucked into the

back of his waistband but paused when the woman took a seat.

"I think the more important question is why you have not found your counterpart yet?" She smiled.

"My what?"

"You have a great destiny, Hamzah Farseer, you will find the princess of Carvyre, the tie between the two of you will unleash the curse already in her veins, the merging of your essence will awaken that which I put in you both so long ago." The woman stepped forward and something in Hamzah's mind told him to stay still as she reached for his arm and stroked the skin above his wrist. Dark shadows squirmed under his skin, only for a second, and he pulled back. "Perhaps the essence of you both would be enough to save her or at least weaken her if the tie was broken," the woman murmured before fading away.

"Did it seem like she was holding back—" Hamzah began to speak as the odd dream or memory faded, but Varlena had already jumped from the counter and planted a kiss on his lips.

"Did you hear what she said?" Varlena grinned. "The merging of our essence! That could be enough to break the curse."

"Varlena..."

"I know how," she said quickly, placing her hand on his chest, her palm warming.

"Varlena wait, something was wrong. She was so quick, rushed, as if she simply needed to tell us things we wanted to hear—"

"And it is what I wanted to hear, Hamzah," Varlena's voice cracked. "When we are in your mind, I don't feel the darkness of the curse; this is what it should be like all the time—you and I, together without fear of what it will tell me to do." She struggled to string her words together as she began to cry.

"But she also said it would unleash what she had put in us. We need to know what that is, who that woman was, if there is further danger to—"

"Please, Hamzah," Varlena cried. "I will risk anything if it means I am with you," Varlena fell to her knees, and he slid down

the countertop to pull her into his chest.

"Okay," he murmured into her hair, "Okay," he repeated. He could not deny her, not when this Varlena was the real her, not the one happy to let people die for the sake of power she only wanted because of the darkness corrupting her mind. Hamzah leant his forehead against hers as she placed her palm back on his chest, and he mirrored her actions.

"Release your power," she whispered, and he did as he asked, watching his flames intertwine with her light until they merged into a bright orb before the darkness crept out from her. The shadows of the curse. But a moment later, shadows seeped from his skin too, and he wondered then just what the woman had put into his veins.

***

Hamzah Fasaar had lived a humble and quiet life as a simple foot guard along the city walls. That was until he met the Princess of Carvyre. Now, he stood atop that same towering five-hundred-foot wall dividing the city from the border and prepared to jump, to take his own life, and end this all. The echo of steel on steel clashed behind him in the city, where the war raged on. Yet his eyeline focused on the calmness of sand dunes and a burning sky. If he squinted, he could spot the green forests in the distance. Perhaps someone stood atop a tree in the same place miles away, watching this very wall. Hamzah took a deep breath in and rested his brown forearms atop the stone, turning over the engagement ring in his hand. Flames licked his hands as he considered melting it.

The wall had long been breached by the princess's army; no soldiers would patrol the wall now, which meant he could live his final moments in peace. Would he have done it all differently had he known the outcome would be war, loss, heartache? Perhaps he never should have volunteered to escort the new King of Q'Ohar to Carvyre. Had he not, he never would have met the princess, the king's newly betrothed. Hamzah would not have caught her eye and become her guard in the city or been the one to comfort her during moments of pain at the king's hand. If Hamzah had never joined that trip, he would not have fallen in love with a princess or been caught with her and thus started a war. The king would not have threatened to kill Hamzah, and the princess would not have retaliated by calling her army to aid the day before the wedding.

If Hamzah had stayed but a simple foot guard, he never would have helped the princess to awaken old power in her veins to win a war, the same power appearing to manifest within his own blood. Hamzah clenched his fists, sensing something recoil in his arm, yearning to be released—he did not know what. But Hamzah was no longer a simple foot guard. He had caused a war and was the reason his love had lost herself to power, intent on taking the entirety of Q'Ohar down with her. The solution? Severing the tie between them, weakening her in the process. Glancing down, he saw nothing but the distant speck of guards below. If the princess was powerless, she may still win Q'Ohar's capital, but she would not destroy the rest of its land. Though, even that might not be enough to save the people Hamzah loved in the city. There was only one other option, one he knew deep down would be the outcome.

A door from the turret stairs opened, and Hamzah knew it was her, forewarned by whatever tied them together.

"We are going to win, Hamzah," she said gleefully. Hamzah no longer recognised the woman before him. Whatever light had once existed in her soul had been snuffed out until she was a shell of her former self. Her once luminous silver hair was limp and dull. Darkness had overcome the glistening specks of white in her purple eyes, matching the shadows within his veins. With a trembling hand, she tucked a strand of her hair behind a pointed ear laden with jewels. Her body did that often—shaking without warning, as if something within her yearned to break free.

"You might, Varlena, but I will not be here to see it," Hamzah said, throwing the engagement ring in her direction. Her face faltered with a glimpse of sorrow, a glimpse of the true Varlena before fury won.

"You believe you can abandon a princess, soon to be the queen of not one but two great lands?" she sneered and strode towards him in black leathers, showing the speed and strength of her legs. The purple gauze over each shoulder fluttered with her steps, secured by a silver jewel-encrusted belt that matched the ones on her crown. Hamzah expected her every move as he climbed atop the wall, and Varlena followed. She would never let him leave.

"This was never the plan, Varlena," Hamzah murmured, reaching for her cheek. Her features softened.

"It was, Hamzah. It was never meant to be the king; it was always meant to be you." She placed a hand on his still beating heart as he leant forward to plant a kiss on her forehead. She thought she had won him over with such simple words when she flashed a winning smile, one that almost had him believe she was the same girl he had first met years ago. He had been counting on her unwavering belief in their love, and he had been right to, for Varlena did not expect the dagger Hamzah slid from his waistband to stab the love of his life in the abdomen.

Varlena gasped and tried to pull back, but Hamzah clutched the back of her neck, forcing himself to look at the light that would soon fade in her eyes before they fell from the wall together. Taking her down with him was the only way to truly save the state. Panic widened her glistening purple irises as she clutched the dagger, blood gushing from it.

"The baby," she murmured. A chill ran up Hamzah's spine. She was with child. His children were in her womb. In a flash decision, Hamzah altered the course of history. Rather than dragging them both to their deaths to guarantee the end of a great power, he shoved Varlena back towards the turret before flinging himself backward towards the sands below.

As Hamzah fell, Varlena's scream shattered the sky.

Chapter One

AGE OF DEVESTATION :3492AD

Failure, the weight that hangs in the back of one's mind even when they think they have moved past it. It becomes easier to move on when distracted by the mundane until something—or nothing—prompts your mind to remember your failures. The words someone said or the memory playing out. It matters little if you are powerless, Fae, a deity of the first celestial goddess, for failure is an inescapable feeling, which Sitara learnt as she screamed and struck her glass of wine from the stone table in the centre of the home she once shared with her soul's other half.

Over a hundred failures, if she counted the amount of times she had scoured every inch of Ithyion for Sonos, to find where Valon had taken him. Her second failure if counting only the plans that she had been certain would work. The wine in her glass spilt like the waters of Thassena, lapping against the maps splayed across the table. The waters that her most recent try at salvation, Levanna Zerpane, had drowned herself in. Levanna Zerpane had been a safe choice—a Seer the people of Thassena believed would have the power to find their lost deity, whose location Sitara had never known. A Seer she hoped would have a vision of finding Kaigon Elharar and witness the merging of their essences, foreseeing their journey to find Sonos. Sitara had not picked wrong; she would not allow it to be her fault. Valon had dug his claws in yet again, and this time, *literally*.

Witnessing the curses befalling Ithyion had prompted Sitara's plan. With the natural disasters that had occurred from Sonos's injury, she quickly deduced the curses to be a direct consequence of his abduction. They claimed their own balance by taking from the people the way Sonos had been taken from her. Thassena's Sirens lost their ability to walk; Asynthos lost any new Stormbringers; Eresydon's Shapeshifters lost their human forms; Q'Ohar lost the protection of their Xyra, and Carvyre lost their free will and sanity. Xyliar's curse was the only one that brought a cruel smile to her lips, a fitting punishment. They lost love itself and were cursed to kill the one they loved the most if their lips ever touched. Sitara cared little about the curses, the repercussions of the imbalance on the world. Nor did she care what controlled such consequences. She cared only about finding Sonos.

Imbalance. Taken. Missing. The other half of her was gone, yet she still sensed him. His essence. Their merging, their bond, was one way they would always return to each other. A piece of him was inside her, a piece she could borrow from. The notion of a celestial tie had become blurred over time, alongside her meddling children who bestowed it for absurd reasons. It had at least given her cover after she most recently planted the sign of Nerida on Levanna and Kai, disguising her involvement. Sonos and Sitara's was the only pure tie; she should have been able to find her love. Valon had dampened it somehow, but what if she passed it on to another? What if she created two halves of a compass from the essence of herself, and what remained of Sonos within her? Sitara recalled the moment Chaos had sacrificed his bodily form for her. Golden threads had wrapped around Chaos and Order before exploding out into the universe until the pair faded. A balance, Chaos and Order's absence allowed Sitara and Sonos to live. With Sonos gone, the universe craved equilibrium. They would be forced to find one another, the light and dark, and when they merged their powers as Sonos and Sitara had, they would become just as powerful. Powerful enough to search for him.

The first part had worked. Sitara placed her essence into a unique child with deep grey Angel wings. Sitara took it as a sign that she was the one to pick, wings that symbolised the power of Sitara, of darkness. Her essence seemed to have prevented the curse from taking root, allowing the Stormbringer to come into her power. It was no coincidence then when another was born the same year with lavender wings—a balance. She chose Olirah for Sonos's essence; the golden tips of her wings reminded Sitara of him. What she had not planned for was that the same power lying within them would also grant Olirah the abilities of her other children. An ability that triggered events like pushing Jessemiah and Olirah away from one another until fate dragged them back together. It might have worked if Olirah hadn't ended up in Xyliar, or if Valon hadn't found her and recognised her uniqueness, if he hadn't been searching for the same thing as Sitara. He needed Sonos and Sitara's essence, and for them to merge, though she had not quite worked out that part yet. So, Valon was all too happy to follow Olirah. The fools did not remember her visiting them, and chose to sacrifice themselves to stop Valon instead of merging their essence.

So, this time, Sitara made sure at least one of them remembered. She ensured Kaigon would regain his memory of meeting, of her essence being placed in his veins, and of her instruction to find Levanna. Valon was one step ahead of her, and his Staxion-born powers had infiltrated Kaigon's mind and slowly corrupted his path. At least Levanna stopped them. Though she had also stopped Sitara from seeing if either of them would have developed other powers too, like Olirah had, or from understanding the way her and Sonos's essence worked.

She needed to try something different this time; she needed to be clear and direct with her next choices by inexplicably relaying what she needed from them both. She needed two people who were already destined to be together. Her mind turned to the Mordanes of Eresydon, and their daughter Aleya, who had been betrothed to Evander of the Sorcerers since she was a child. They would already be together, and the ruling family wanted nothing more than to break the curse on the Shapeshifters and work toward peace in their state. The promise of restoring the world's balance if Sonos was found might motivate them to act and instigate a plan immediately. Yes, this one would work. If not, she would keep trying, using new bodies, new hypotheses, and new paths until it worked. She had other options. Her next plan was to place Sonos's essence in the body of someone already from Carvyre, someone who connected to Sonos. She did not dare risk placing her essence in someone within Xyliar.

Valon had nearly decimated his entire family as centuries of suppressed power burst forth. Makaria's other grandchildren were powerful too, far more so than the other Staxions and Fae of the state. Yet Valon's magic had built over time until it was volatile, unpredictable. There had to be something different about him though, something that gave him the edge to entrap and hide a god, to foresee and infiltrate each of her steps. Since losing Sonos, her own power had weakened, limiting her ability to see the many goings-on across the kingdom. Sitara had to be present in the state, unlike before where it was as easy as looking down upon a child, picking a person to focus on and watching their life play out before her eyes. It was why she knew nothing of the happenings in Xyliar.

When the shadows consumed Xyliar's throne room, Sitara had laughed at Valon's absurdity for thinking he could kill her. But when the darkness faded, and he was gone, her mind turned. The deities fled, adamant that this was yet another sign of the danger caused by the celestial gods, as if they had not just begged her for justice. Her children left too, as they often did, in search of their deities to continue with their peace talks. The only people left in the throne room were the dead body of Valon's wife, his daughter, her husband, and one brother, the one Sitara had liked little after what she had seen him do over the years. Every other family member was dead. Slaughtered. Two young boys crept into the throne room; Sitara had been about to approach when she felt the pain in her chest—Sonos's pain—she fled to find the Isle of Gods stained with darkness and Sonos gone. Xyliar had been impenetrable ever since. Valon had cut off communication with the other states and placed his daughter on the throne for the running of Xyliar but called himself the king behind closed doors. She knew something else had to be happening behind its borders; he had to be readying for war against her, for the day he finally obtained the merged essence of her and Sonos for whatever means. She would rather die first and allow the kingdom to fall to ruin.

Chapter Two

AGE OF DEVESTATION :3502AD

The call arrived loud and clear. The voices of five royal families called out under the moonlight as they knelt in a circle around the stone table in the temple at the centre of the Isle of the Gods. She was unsure whether she admired their knowledge about this being the strongest place to contact her or felt offended by their arrival on her land without invitation.

Sitara had been in Eresydon, mourning her most recent failure with Aleya and Evander when she sensed they were all together. The deities were meeting separately, which meant the rulers had done something to keep them at bay. They wished to speak with only her. They all knelt on the cold stone, the king and queen of every state—excluding Xyliar, of course and Aleya, who was alone. The Queen of Eresydon was the only one that knew the truth, and it seemed she had not informed the others.

Sitara wondered how long it had taken for them all to realise the darkness that reached Asynthos, Thassena, and Eresydon must stem from the same place. Nobody had believed Asynthos at the time and called the claims absurd. Valon twisted the memories of those who had witnessed the events in the oceans of Thassena, but in Eresydon he became messy. He tried to use Garridon, and it had failed, leading to his banishment from the state and away from the sword of souls he so desperately wanted for his army. It left nobody to stop the queen from calling for aid, and for someone to finally answer. Sitara sensed her the most; the essence of Sonos planted within her still lingered, weakened from the power Aleya had exerted when she fled her home. It was a piece Sitara would gladly retrieve and plant in one of her next options. She had prepared for that plan upon sensing the summons, and now, here she was. Intrigued.

In each couple, one wore the darkness of her night, and the other wore the gold of her love. She smiled at the sight of its brightness; she had not worn his colours since losing him, donning only the darkness of her shadows. As she approached them, the gown she wore now reflected the night sky, reflecting the depths of her mind without Sonos there to warm her. Two stabbed hearts sat bleeding on the stone table where they knelt. If only they knew their feats were useless; there was no need for balance in sacrifice when Sonos was gone.

"I do not believe I have ever been called upon by so many," Sitara called. Their heads all spun to watch her weave over the stone floor, the moonlight providing a spotlight. They all bowed their heads. Sitara's eyes lingered on Aleya's.

"Have you told them?" Sitara asked, testing to see how honest she would be. The other rulers frowned, looking at the Queen of Eresydon. She cleared her throat.

"I have not."

"Why?"

"Because they would not have believed me," the queen said. "No one would believe that the God of Dawn could be taken." Mutterings began around the circle as partners conferred together, stealing glances at Aleya, who knelt alone.

"I still cannot quite believe it myself," Sitara said.

"If the God of Dawn is gone, then nothing can help us," the Queen of Asynthos said. Sitara spun to face her.

"Should I be insulted? That you think the first celestial goddess is not enough for you?" she said. The weight of Sitara's stare forced the queen to bow her head.

"Light is known to counteract the darkness, which means we need Sonos's power to eradicate the darkness spreading across the kingdom, to eradicate Xyliar," said the King of Thassena.

"You do need Sonos," Sitara said.

"Then where is he?" asked the King Of Q'Ohar.

"If I knew that, he would be standing by my side," Sitara sneered. She had forgotten how tiresome it was to speak with anyone other than her own blood, even if they were the most powerful families after the deities themselves.

"But you know how to find him," Aleya said. Sitara turned to face her.

"And look how well that plan turned out," Sitara said. "Yet again, Valon infiltrated the mind of one I had chosen and corrupted him. Every time I think I am close to succeeding, in drawing together two beings who I have planted our celestial essence in, he finds a way to ruin it."

"So you need somewhere he does not know of?" asked Vitoria, the Queen of Carvyre. Sitara tilted her head. She had not considered that. "If you could plant the essence in two beings without him knowing, they could find Sonos?"

"In theory, yes," Sitara said, "Though even with the essence merged inside the Queen and King of Eresydon, I could not sense it to guide their next steps." Sitara tugged at her chest. She plucked a piece of her essence free and then pulled a vial containing Sonos', from her shadows. Power rippled outward around the circle, and Aleya gasped.

"The door to the soul bears all to hear
Multiple generations is the rule of the Seer.
With those of white and those of black
The spirit of the first makes their way back.
When the darkness returns, sacrifice is made
In the wake of disaster, the return of the blade.
When light meets dark in the rarest of times,
When all that is left is the last of the lines.
The power to awaken that of old lore,
Lies in the soul of those with all four.
From fire and ice, the King and Queen must hide

Secrets from the past, the heirs must find.
Only together can they defeat and restore,
Only together can they gain so much more.
The Gods may whisper and help them on
Only if all possess that from Ithyion.
Watch for the dark one that will bring suffering to all,
The rise of old power, the Kingdom will fall."

Before anyone could decipher the prophecy Aleya was gifted, the Queen of Thassena's head dropped, her eyes rolling.

"A vision and a prophecy," Sitara whispered. The universe had a plan. Threads were falling into place. "What did you see?" she asked the queen. While she was not of the Zerpane line, her age ensured accuracy. The queen gripped her husband's arm as she blinked, processing what she had seen.

"A kingdom, different from Ithyion. Smaller. Four banners of each elemental state. An explosion and a new generation, multiple generations from now." Sitara recalled the words from Aleya's prophecy. Multiple generations is the rule of the Seer. Patience. Sitara needed to wait. "A sword of dark shadows, a war, and a death that is not final. Two powerful beings..." The queen met Sitara's eye. "The two you need."

***

It was sunrise when the plans were finalised. The Queen of Thassena had taken time to fully explain her vision, matching pieces to the Queen of Eresydon's prophecy. Then, the rulers of Ithyion and the Goddess of Dusk set a plan in motion, one that would allow the essence of Sitara and her love to grow in hiding, in peace, in the future when Valon would least expect it. Together, they conceived Novisia. Sitara would need to speak with her children first, for she would require Garridon to create a land linked to the Isle of Gods, a land that, with the King of Thassena's help, could be illusioned.

And with the Queen of Eresydon's support, a Sorcerer could cast a spell on it to strengthen the illusion's hold, though it may be a tense request given the Wiccan had won the recent war. It was the only way to ensure nothing could be manipulated, the only way to protect the future generation from playing out their path of fate. One day, all would become clear.

"You will need to appoint custodians for your states," Sitara said. "Vitoria can help them maintain the lie." The vision showed only the elemental rulers in the new kingdom. The Queen of Carvyre had rightly suggested remaining in Ithyion to keep the Carvyre population intact to fight any darkness that might attack within Ithyion. There, they would perpetuate the lie that Ithyion's rulers sought to break the curses on their states and left in search of other lands and powers that might help. One year from now was the plan. Enough time to slowly funnel trusted citizens to the Isle of Gods until its mirrored land was created, slow and subtle, so Valon would detect nothing.

"You understand there is always a cost to things like this," Sitara said. "I cannot guarantee that a new land existing on a plain different to ours will hold the same level of power; you might never see your home again. It will be your future lineage that saves this kingdom," she said. While the rulers' faces were all stern, they understood what they were doing; they were creating a future for their people.

"We will document it all," the King of Thassena said, whilst rubbing his wife's back. "There is a great scholar working in the libraries of Lera. He calls himself the Historian. I will bring him with us to keep records to ensure we all remember what this is for." Sitara cared little for what they did and did not document; she had one goal and one goal only. To find Sonos.

"I will not sense when the two have merged their essence. We will have to trust their ability to decipher the prophecy, even the parts we do not completely understand. I can reach them, but I too will trust their fate to play out once the essence has been planted in the selected two."

"We will create fail-safes," Aleya said. "I can have a weapon imbued and disguised to ensure they link to Carvyre, so should it recognise either essence in danger, it will link them back to Ithyion," she said, a soft smile on her lips. "This will be the last time. You will see him again. We will break the curse." Sitara nodded slowly, the idea prompting her to think of the sword Valon had lost on Eresydon, the army it could provide the future saviours with. Could she find a way to plant a piece of the stone that created it within them, something to call them to it?

"Once you have been on this new land for several decades, I will plant the essence in two on Carvyre and Q'Ohar to lead Valon to believe nothing is amiss. It will, of course, fail," she said, looking at the Queen of Carvyre.

"Two sacrifices for the creation of he who, alongside her, will save us all," Vitoria said.

Chapter Three

The deities demanded answers. Sitara thought they had been careful over the last year. They had sent one trade shipment a week, always from one state and with a regular departing time to not invite outside suspicion. But still, the deities claimed the celestial gods had stolen their citizens and kidnapped their rulers. Little did they know it was voluntary, and they were about to ruin the entire plan. If they had arrived a month earlier, they would have found the rulers healthy and the Isle of Gods sufficiently populated. But they had arrived a week too late. Garridon had already created the new land, an exact mirror of the isle that existed directly beneath it, and flipped the Isle of Gods so it sat below the ocean surface. The only addition was a small wedge of land Queen Aleya had requested for the ruling six Shapeshifters, not trusting that the second state may fall into civil war again with her gone. The other rulers ended up using it as overflow when they realised they were struggling too much to decide which citizens they took with them to Novisia. So Doltas Island became its own additional land, one that, given the land was a mirror of the Isle of Gods, was positioned in the direction of Xyliar. Those on the rock-like island would be the first to see if ships approached from the sixth state.

The King of Thassena had already used his most trusted Illusionists to mask the Isle of Gods to make it appear as normal rather than submerged below the waters banished by Nerida. All was in place, yet the deities were too late to uncover it all.

Still, they demanded justice, and their justice came in the form of war. Sitara watched, hidden away so she could journey to Novisia if needed, if it all failed. They were prepared this time; her four children ensured they kept the deities as separated as possible, to stop them from merging their power and repeating the damage they had done to Sonos all those years ago. They should have seen it coming when the deities funnelled into the valley on the Isle of Gods, mirroring what the gods had done to them in Eresydon the last time. The fighting intensified. Their soldiers were forced into thinner lines as they were pushed against the banks of the river running through the valley.

"Put an end to it," Sitara called to Nerida. Her daughter heard her call and called upon the river, raising it into twisting ropes that expertly wove their way around the necks of every soldier. She pulled, and the ropes tightened. Alternating her movements, she drowned others from within.

"Enough!" a booming voice roared. Nefere stood at the end of the river, where it slowly narrowed, his flaming wings spanning wide for all to see. His reflection towered over the water as his eyes burned bright and blue flames flickered up his arms. Up above on the edge of the canyon rock, smoke shifted until Exandria, the first Smokeshifter, knelt. Sitara could discern her silent plea, begging him not to do it. But Nefere spared a final glance at his dying soldiers and plunged his arm through the water and into the ground below. It started slowly at first as blue flames danced across the water until a raging inferno crawled up his arm and consumed him. Nefere did not scream as he exerted all his power. As the blue flame faded away, so did every ounce of water leaving only a dry scorched land beneath as soldiers rose and sputtered. Exandria shifted in the smoke, now standing where the river and Nefere once were. All that was left in his wake was a black mark on the ground, one she knelt before, weeping.

"Love makes people foolish," Keres said.

Sitara appeared beside him and said, "Do not condemn them for the thing that drives our very actions."

"It is you who wants him back so desperately, mother," Keres said, turning his back on her to talk with Garridon.

"It brings me no joy to do this to them," Nerida sighed as the soldiers raised their weapons to where the gods stood. "They follow blindly, but I admire his sacrifice." Nerida raised her arms, drawing on the ocean surrounding the isle until towering walls of water loomed, preparing to come crashing down. Before she released them, she nodded to the scorched mark on the earth and allowed a pool of water to form, a single oasis, a nod to Nefere's sacrifice, however misguided it was. Nerida frowned, and the towering waves in the distance faltered.

"Exandria is gone," she said. Sitara frowned, looking at the pooling water and the absence of the Smokeshifter on her knees. She scanned the valley.

"They're all gone," she said. "The deities. Where are they?" Sitara demanded. Nerida released the waves, their path slower than intended as she spun, scanning the vicinity.

"It was a distraction," Nerida said, her eyes widening as she watched her brothers. Keres and Garridon knelt on the ground, their faces scrunched in a pain Sitara had only ever seen once—on Sonos.

"Do not harm them!" Sitara screamed, drawing on her shadows. The deities of Eresydon, Q'Ohar, and Carvyre stood around them, threads of their essence pulling from their chests and wrapping around the two gods like rope, searing their skin and holding them in place.

"It is for your own good, Sitara," a voice sounded from behind as the remaining deities encircled Sitara, Nerida, and Vala.

"Makaria," Sitara breathed. "Why?" She had always sided with the gods over the deities.

"It's time for a new age, the rule of the deities," Makaria said, whipping out shadows toward her creator. Sitara deflected it in a heartbeat, but it provided the delay for the remaining deities of Xyliar, Thassena, and Asynthos to encircle her daughters, bringing them to their knees as they had her sons.

"You cannot hurt me. You saw what happened when Sonos was injured, and you do not know that the same will not happen if you harm my children." Sitara pulled on every shadow on the isle, scraping it across the floor toward her until it seeped under the deities' feet. They winced. They could not withstand her for as long as they thought.

"It is for that reason we don't plan to hurt them," Makaria said. Sitara paused her shadows, trying to ascertain how best to take them down without them tugging too hard and taking her children with them.

"What is your grand plan then?" she sneered.

"We will bind you all here, so you can never leave the isle or ever interfere," Makaria said. Sitara faltered. If they bound the gods to the isle, what effect would it have on Novisia?

"You cannot possibly know how to do such a thing," she said.

"No," a voice leeched over her skin, and her back straightened, drawing her shadows toward her. "But I do," Valon said, emerging from his own shadows with a young woman beside him. She had similar features to his daughter, who sat on Xyliar's throne. He had a second daughter. Another person she could inflict pain on for what he had done. The woman's one green eye glowed whilst the dark eye deepened as her father's shadows cocooned them. Sitara's eyes darkened as she raised her shadows. Her children cried out as the deities tightened their grips. She could not harm him without endangering the only family she had left. Nor could she risk their deaths and the roles they needed to play in the prophecy. The future generation would need to call upon them one day. The woman chanted in the old language, power in the words. The woman who had helped her father trick Garridon into handing over the remaining essence and creating the Sorcerers.

The spell was clear. As long as the isle stood, the gods would be bound to it. Valon didn't know. He couldn't yet know of the link between the isle and Novisia, of the hidden land he stood on and all it would become. If he had, surely he would not have cast a spell on the isle, would not have risked its destruction in the name of their escape. As the woman's words trailed off, Valon's shadows seeped into the earth itself. Sitara looked between her children. If she left, she might never see them again, bound here forever. If she stayed, Sonos would never be found. As magic seeped into the ground, Sitara stole a final glance at her children before spinning away in a flurry of shadow. She felt someone's essence reach out to her, to try to tug her back down as the spell cemented, but she broke free. When her shadows faded, she was hovering above the ocean along the coast of the isle. She sensed the power seeping into it—Valon's, the deities, the gods—just by being bound; it all merged with the words of the Sorcerer. Sitara closed her eyes and shifted herself to the coast, waiting above the shore until the spell was complete, ensuring she was not bound to the land. When she felt the energy in the air slow, she shifted to Novisia.

The queen was admiring a bed of flowers while her sons chased butterflies.

"Aleya," Sitara said. The queen looked at her, and her eyes widened. She immediately bowed her head. Her hands trembled, seemingly frightened. Sitara frowned. While she was not friends with these people, she and Aleya had come to a place of mutual respect between one another. "We need to hurry the plan," Sitara said. The queen frowned, brushing the dirt from her hands on her green gown, scanning for her sons as though she was scared of what Sitara might do. "Aleya," Sitara said softly.

"What plan?" Aleya asked.

Every spell had a consequence; everything demanded a balance. So, as power seeped into the Isle of Gods, stripping her children of their free will, it also stripped the memories of those on Novisia.

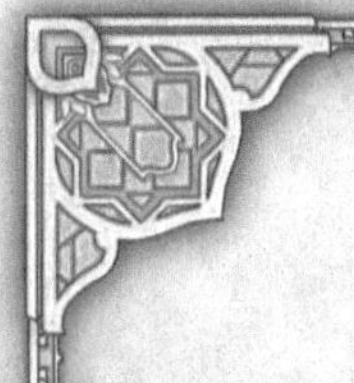
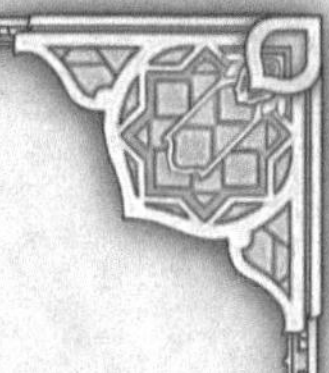

FATE

Epilogue

The threads of fate were crumbling.

What were once hundreds of thousands of sparkling threads in the darkness, falling into place from her fingertips to where they needed to be on Ithyion, were now dull string losing their spark. It had only been one at first, a long thread that stretched far into the future—centuries, in fact—before slowly trickling like dust, shortening and shortening until there was nothing attaching it to Fate's hands. She searched frantically for the ones she liked best, ensuring the threads that tied her to the Zerpane daughters still held strong. It did, and it was brighter than ever. The consequences of this one thread were far-reaching.

Each new day shortened a thread for someone else though, and each day shortened the time that ultimately remained for the existence of the kingdom down below. She could no longer keep track of the threads changing, shortening, or disappearing every hour. There was an imbalance in the world. It was not only the God of Dawn that had altered the scales of the universe, abducted to somewhere even she could not see; resolving that would rely on too many other threads falling into place first. Nor was it only the constant games Sitara played to try to control destinies that tipped the balance of the Kingdom.

No.

The imbalance on Ithyion was caused by a man who had wanted only to save others and those he loved.

The imbalance on Ithyion was caused by a man who sought out

someone he should not have.

The imbalance on Ithyion was caused by too much power.

Order and Chaos were bound to the land again, and Fate did not think even she could foresee the devastation that was to come.

CARVYRE
THE LOST KINGDOM SAGA CONTINUES IN
TRUTH OF THE LIGHT

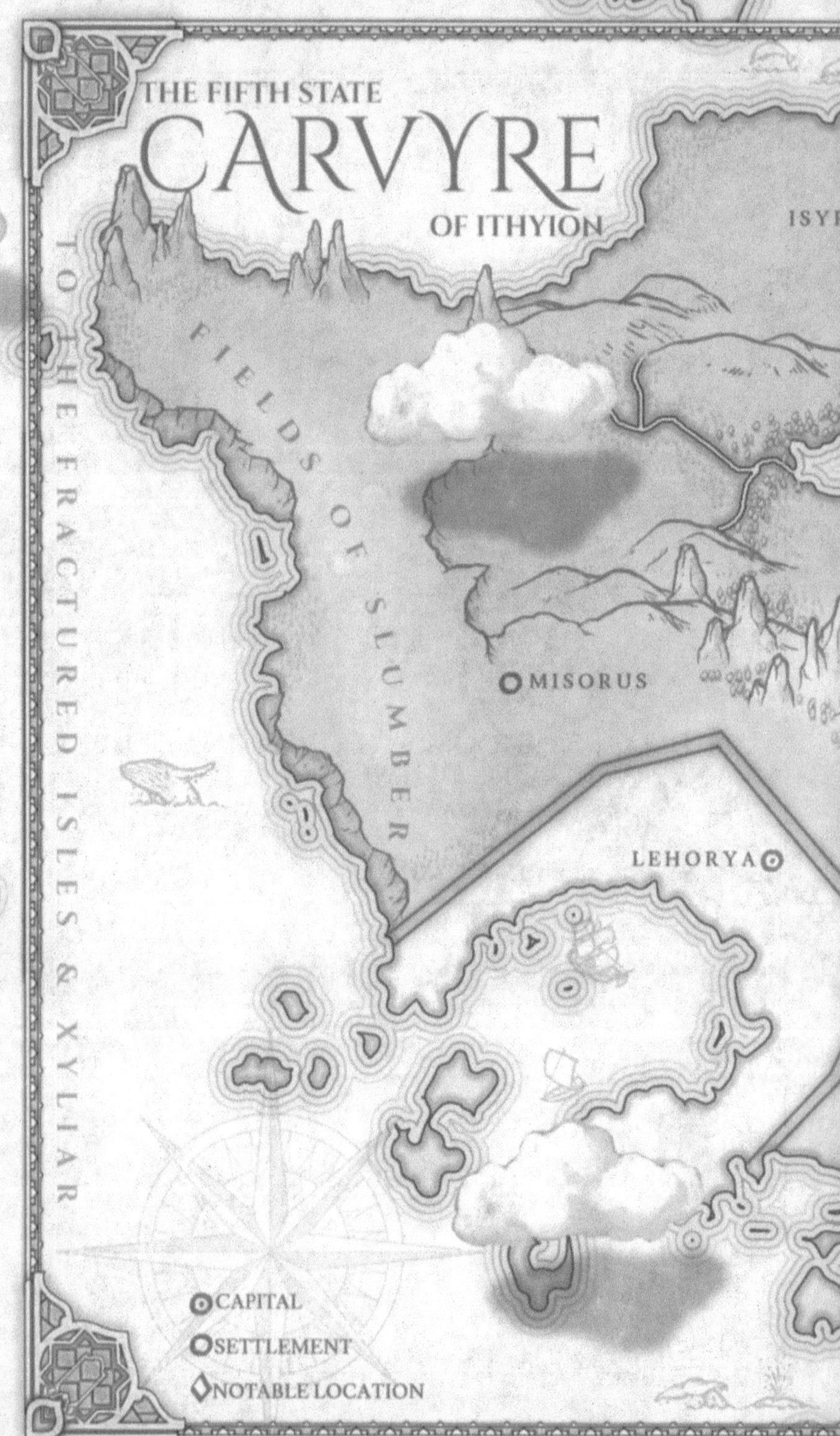

THE FIFTH STATE
CARVYRE
OF ITHYION
ISYR
FIELDS OF SLUMBER
MISORUS
LEHORYA
TO THE FRACTURED ISLES & XYLIAR
CAPITAL
SETTLEMENT
NOTABLE LOCATION

TO ERSYDON
NYLARIA NAVAL BASE
N'S STONES
MIRROR LAKE
BAY

Glossary and Pronunciation Guide

_A_

Abexu [Ah-bex-oo] – *Surname of the Xyliar royal family*

Adricus Marshes [Aye-dree-cuss Marshes] – *location in Thassena*

Aelwen [Ale-win] – *The first deity and Wiccan of Eresydon, created from the essence of Garridon combined with the stolen essence of Makaria and Oxyron*

Aleena [Ah-lean-ah] – *Queen of Thassena during the late 'Kingdom of Creation', married to King Arorn*

Alastair Heath [Al-as-stair He-th] – *Father of Evander, Protector of the Sorcerers*

Aleksandr [Alek-san-der] – *Head of Queen Avannah's royal guard*

Alyssa [Al-iss-ah] – *Angel with the earth abilities of the god Garridon, employed by and friends with Commander Jessemiah*

Aloro [Ah-lore-oh] – *Known for its many rivers, closest settlement to the Caves of Anela*

Andor [An-door] – *Capital of Eresydon, seat of the Mordane royal family*

Anela [Ah-neh-lah] – *The first deity and seer of Thassena, created from the essence of Nerida combined with the stolen essence of Makaria and Oxyron*

Angel – *Race in Asynthos with white feathered wings*

Arden Mordane [Are-den More-dane] – *Prince of Eresydon, son of Queen Aleya Mordone and King Evander Heath*

Araya [Ah-ray-ah] – *The third deity of Asynthos and the first*

Truthteller. Created from the essence of Vala combined with the stolen essence of Makaria and Oxyron

Arorn [Ah-raw-nh] – *King of Thassena during the late 'Kingdom of Creation', married to Queen Aleena*

Avannah Sturmov [Ah-van-ah Stir-mov] – *Queen of Asynthos during the early 'Era of Devastation'*

B

Balfour [B-al-four] – *Family name of those sworn to protect the Mordane family. Gifted with the power of additional strength and foresight when a Mordane is in danger, a power given by Aelwen as thanks for their loyalty*

Brodie Clan [Bro-dee Clan] – *The first Wiccan clan, close friends with the Mordane royal family.*

Boznaya Range [B -oz-nay-ah Range] – *Mountain range in Asynthos known for its mining of marble*

C

Calina [K-ah-lee-nah] – *The first Pegasus-Bound deity of Carvyre, created from the essence of Oxyron*

Carlisle [Car-l-isle] – *The second deity of Eresydon, the first Shapeshifter. Created from the essence of Garridon combined with the stolen essence of Makaria and Oxyron*

Caves of Anela [Caves of Ah-nell-ah] – *Location of Anela's birth and where young seers journey to meet the oracle*

Cecilia Abexu [S-eh-see-lee-ah Ah-bex-oo] – *Princess of Xyliar, daughter or Kylara Abexu, sister to Valon Abexu*

Crimson Mountains [Crim-son Mountains] – *Large mountain range running through Thassena. Eastern side is home to the sacrificial stones, the sight of Anela's first vision. Name for the colour when the sun hits the rock.*

Commander Harris [Commander Hah-riss] – *Sorcerer that serves as Commander of Eresydon*

_D_

Dalinea [Dah-lee-nah] – *The first deity and angel of Asynthos. Created from the essence of Vala combined with the stolen essence of Makaria and Oxyron*

Darius Sevia [Dah-ree-us See-vee-ah] – *Deceased Prince of Thassena during the 'Era of Devestation', was bethrothed to Sienna Zerpane*

Dragon-Bound – *A race of Xyliar Fae that have the power to mentally connect with a dragon that was born as a result of the splitting of the original land, Styros*

Dravos [Drah-voss] – *The second deity of Thassena and the first Illusionist. Created from the essence of Nerida combined with the stolen essence of Makaria and Oxyron*

_E_

Eamon District [Aye-man District] – *Poorest district of Vasturia, named after an orphan that rose to status of Lord*

Elharar [El-har-ah] – *Surname of the royal family of Q'Ohar*

Elias [El-lie-as] – *Angel with the water abilities of the goddess Nerida, employed by and friends with Commander Jessemiah*

Errard Mordane [Eh-r-are-d More-dane] – *Prince of Eresydon, son of Queen Aleya Mordane and King Evander Heath*

Evander Heath [Eh-van-der H-ee-th] – *Non practicing Sorcerer, King of Eresydon, married to Queen Aleya Mordane*

Exandria [Ex-and-ree-ah] – *The first deity and Smokeshifter of Q'Ohar, created from the essence of Keres combined with the stolen essence of Makaria and Oxyron*

Exoria [Ex-or-ee-ah] – *Capital of Xyliar*

_F_

Fae [F-aye] – *Name given to the race of pointed ear beings created by and descending from Makaria and Oxyron,*

Farvos [Fah-voss] – *Smoke shrouded mountain that hides the home of the Xyra, located in north Q'Ohar*

Fedwin [Fed-win] – *The Shapeshifter's region of Eresydon*

Fendale [Fen-dale] – *Settlement in Tandale, the Sorcerer's region of Eresydon*

Firella Abexu [F-eye-rell-ah Ah-bex-oo] – *Princess of Xyliar, daughter of Kylara Abexu and sister of Valon Abexu*

Forgers – *Race in Q'OHar with the ability to melt and wield metal*

F

Forever Fields – *Field on a mountain ledge rumoured to have grown from the blood of Angels and Vala's tears after Keres had stolen an ange from her*

H

Hallow Healers [Hal-low Healers] – *The most prestigious healers in Xyliar, located in Zandyn and known for their dismissal of pain relief in treatment*

Hamzah Farseer [Ham-zah Far-seer] – *Personal guard to Varlena Nylaria*

Hybrooke Forest [High-brook Forest] – *Small forest filled with streams located at the edge of Andor in Eresydon*

Hystone Forest [High-stone Forest] – *Largest forest in Fedwin, Eresydon*

Hypherion [High-fear-ee-on] – *Name of a race of fae in Carvyre with ability to walk through dreams*

I

Illusionists – *Race in Thassena that has the ability to use water to create illusions*

Isoria Nylaria [Is-or-ee-yah N-eye-l-argh-ee-ah] – *Custodian of Carvyre, sister to past Queen Vitoria, aunt to Varlena Nylaria*

Ithyion [Ih-thee-on] – *Kingdom*

Iahabi [Ee-hab-ee] – *Term of endearment in Q'Ohar*

Inaya [Ih-n-eye-yah] – Sister to Hamzah Farseer

J

Jayesh [Jay-eh-sh] – *Angel with the fire abilities of the god Keres, employed by and friends with Commander Jessemiah*

Jessemiah [Jess-eh-my-ah] – *Angel and Commander of Asynthos*

K

Kai [K-eye] – *Scholar from Q'ohar*

Kardyn [Car-din] – *Wealthy settlement in Xyliar known for its cliffs*

Kaven [Cave-en] – *Third deity of Q'Ohar and first Forger. Created from the essence of Keres combined with the stolen essence of Makaria and Oxyron*

Kazeema [Kaz-ee-mah]– *Princess of Q'Ohar suring the mid 'Era of Devestation'*

Kraztar Forge [Kraz-tar Forge] – *Largest weaponary forge in Q'Ohar*

Kyara [Key-are-ah] – *Port in Q'Ohar*

Kylara Abexu [K-eye-l-are-ah Ah-bex-oo] – *Queen of Xyliar, daughter of Makaria through natural birth, mother of Valon Abexu. Has changed her face many times over history, has also been known as Vyla Abexu in the past*

L

Lailor [Lay-ler] – *The third deity of Thassena and the first siren. Created from the essence of Nerida combined with the stolen essence of Makaria and Oxyron*

Lehorya [Leh-hor-ee-ah] – *Capital of Carvyre*

Lera [L-ear-ah] – *Capital of Thassena*

Levanna Zerpane [L-eh-van-ah Zur-pane] – *Daughter of Sienna Zerpane, bethrothed to Theon Sevia*

Lorenzo Zerpane [L-or-en-zoh Z-ur-pane] – *Cousin of Sienna Zerpane*

Lowven Nylaria [Low-when Nigh-l-are-ee-ah] – *Cousin and sec-*

ond in command to Varlena Nylaria

_M_
Makaria [Mak-are-ee-ah] – *The first deity of Xyliar. Created from the combined essence of Sonos and Sitara*
Marzoc [M-are-zov] – *Port in Asynthos*
Masdar [Mas-d-are] – *Southern settlement in Tandale, childhood home of King Evander Heath*
Misorus [M-is-or-us] – *Birthplace of the pegasus*
Mordane [More-dane] – *Surname of the Eresydon royal family*

_N_
Nazim [N-ah-zeem] – *Captain of King Malik of Q'Ohar's royal guard*
Nefere [N-eff-ear] – *The second deity of Q'Ohar and the first Xyra. Created from the essence of Keres combined with the stolen essence of Makaria and Oxyron*
Nylaria [N-eye-l-are-ee-ah] – *Surname of the Carvyre royal family*

_O_
Olirah [Oh-lie-rah] – *Angel that escaped Xyliar, gifted with the powers of all four elements*
Oxyron [Ox-eye-ron] – *The first deity of Carvyre, created from the combined essence of Sonos and Sitara*
Ouro Ocean [Or-og ocean] – *Name of the waters in the centre of Ithyion*

_P_
Pathos Priestesses [Path-os Priestesses] – *Religious group named after the word for palm in the old language, offering guiding hands to turn people from sacrifice to prayer in Thassena.*
Pegasus-Bound – *A race of Carvyre Fae that have the power to*

mentally connect with a pegasus that was born as a result of the splitting of the original land, Styros

Q

Q'Ohar [Ko-h-are] – *The third state of Ithyion*

R

Radian [Ray-dee-an] – *Levanna Zerpane's personal guard*
Razmah [Raz-mah] – *Desert in Q'Ohar that borders Eresydon*
Rosso [R-oh-so] – *Settlement in Thassena known for its coastlines and waterfalls*

S

Sahrih [S-ah-rhee] – *Capital of Q'Ohar*
Salvia Abexu [Sal-vee-ah Ah-bex-oo] – *Daughter of Valon and Luxiana*
Sascha [Sash-ah] – *Personal guard of Valon Abexu*
Seer [S-ear] – *Race in Thassena that are gifted visions of the future*
Sevia [See-vee-ah] – *Surname of the royal family in Thassena*
Shapeshifters – *Race in Eresydon with the ability to shift into an animal form*
Sienna Zerpane [See-en-ah Zer-pane] – *Mother of Levanna Zerpane. Previously bethrothed to Darius Sevia*
Siren [Sigh-ren] – *Race in Thassena that have the ability to hypnotise others*
Siren Seas – *Home of the Sirens since they were cursed to never step foot on land again*
Sisters of Rosso – *The most devout Illusionists in Thassena*
Smokeshifters – *Race in Q'OHar with the ability to shift into smoke and transport themselves elsewhere*
Staxion [Stax-ee-on] – *Name of a race of fae in Xyliar with ability to control minds*
Stendon [Sten-den] – *Wiccan region of land in Eresydon*
Stormbringers – *Race in Asynthos with the ability to wield light-*

ning

Stroman [St-row-man] – *The second deity of Asynthos and the first Stormbringer. Created from the essence of Vala combined with the stolen essence of Makaria and Oxyron*

Styros [S-tie-ross] – *Name of the fifth land in Ithyion before a war split it into two pieces, now known as Caryvre and Xyliar*

Sturmov [Stir-mov] – *Surname of the Asynthos royal family*

Syriuna [See-rr-h-nah] – *Currency in Carvyre*

T

Tandale [Tan-dale] – *Sorcerer region of Eresydon*

Tamzi [Tam-zee] – *Settlement in Q'Ohar*

The Burnt Sands – *Desert to the east of Sahrih in Q'Ohar*

The Crescent – *Ceremonial location in Vasturia, Asynthos*

The Valley of the Forgotten – *Location of the Great War and the War of Hearts in Eresydon*

Theon Sevia [Th-ee-on See-vee-ah] – *Prince of Thassena, bethrothed to Levanna Zerpane*

Thynai [Th-n-eye] – *Currency in the first four states of Ithyion*

Tirus [Tie-r-es] – *Sculptor, husband of Salvia, Lord of Kardyn*

Truthtellers – *Race in Asynthos with the ability to force someone to speak only in truths*

Tungstyn [Tongue-st-een] – *Silvery white metal, the only known material that can inhibit powers and abilities. Harvested from the exact, central point of a state/land*

U

V

Varlena Nylaria [V-are-lane-ah N-eye-l-are-ee-ah] – *Princess of Carvyre, bethrothed to Malik of Q'Ohar*

Vasturia [Vah-stir-ee-ah] – *Capital of Asynthos*

Vaeda [Vay-dah] – *Third deity of Eresydon and the first Sorcerer.*

Valon Abexu [Val-on Ah-bex-oo] – *Son of Kylara Abexu, Prince and then King of Xyliar*

Vanos [Van-oss] – *The first Hypherion deity. Create from the essence of Oxyron*

Viola Abexu [V-eye-oh-la Ah-bex-oo] – *Daughter of Valon and Luxiana*

Vitoria Nylaria [Vit-or-ee-ah N-eye-l-are-ee-ah] – Mother of Varlena, past Queen of Carvyre

Viserius Abexu [V-eye-sear-ee-us Ah-bex-oo] – *Son of Kylara Abexu, Prince of Xyliar, brother to Valon*

W

Wiccan [W-ih-can] – *Race in Eresydon that are gifted with prophecies and can imbue objects*

Wren Balfour [Ren B-al-four] – *Nephew of Havia Balfour, friend to the princes of Eresydon*

Wynow Forest [Win-oh Forest] – *Forest in Eresydon that borders Q'Ohar*

X

Xander [Zan-der] – *The first Dragon-Bound deity of Xyliar. Created from the essence of Makaria*

Xyliar [Z-eye-liar] – *The sixth state of Ithyion*

Xyra [Z-eye-rah] – *Race in Q'Ohar that have flaming wings*

Y

Yvenya [Y-ven-ya] – *The first Staxion deity. Created from the essence of Makaria*

Z

Zandyn [Zan-din] – *Most north-eastern settlement in Xyliar, home to the Hallow Healers*

Zonri [Zon-ree] – *Currency in Xyliar*

Playlist

Xyliar

- You're on Your Own Kid by Taylor Swift

- I can't carry this anymore by Anson Seabra

- Broken by Ansin Seabra

- Die Alone by FINNEAS

- All I Wanted by Paramore

- Villains aren't Born "They're made" (acoustic version) by PEGGY

Sonos

- My Moon by Jess Benko

- Starry Eyes by Cigarettes After Sex

- Here with Me by d4vd

Asynthos

- Invisible string by Taylor swift

- Gilded Lily by Cults

- I Can't Breathe by Bea Miller

- The Smallest Man Who Ever Lived - taylor swift

- Angels - The XX

- Russian Roulette - Nessa Barrett

Thassena

- I Wanna be Yours by Arctic Monkeys

- Deathbeds - Bring Me The Horizon

- A Soulmate Who Wasnt Meant to Be by Jess Benko

- Did you Ever Hurt for me? By Jess Benko

- Repeat Until Death by Novo Amor

- Indigo (feat Avery Anna) by Samb Barber

Eresydon

- Coney Island by Taylor Swift (feat the National)

- Would've Been You by sombr

- If This is Goodbye by Britton

- Mad World by Jasmine Thompson

- I Love You, I'm sorry by Gracie Abrams

- I Miss you, I'm sorry by Gracie Abrams

Q'Ohar

- Wicked Game by Chris Isaak

- Bad Decisions by Bad Omens

- Mad Woman by Taylor Swift

- Never Let Me Go by Florence and the Machine

- Two by Sleeping at Last

- Hell or Flying by Jeremy Zucker

Sitara

- Moondust - Stripped by Jaymes young

- Lost Without You by Freya Ridings

- Love of my Life by Harry Styles

Epilogue

- Fate - H.E.R

- The End of the World by Skeeter Davis

- Ominous (slowed and reverbed) by Insensible

Acknowledgements

Thanking myself first this time, because I don't know how my willpower and perseverance kept going with this one. Writing a whole other set of stories at the same time as drafting book four, Truth of the Light, was always going to be hard. But I may have underestimated just how hard. From drafting, editing, proof reading, making seven maps, making interior art, battling the nightmare that is Atticus formatting software. You made it over the line Laura and I hope you're celebrating with the girls with LOTS of Hugo Spritz' the weekend after release.

Thank you to my Mum who listened to one too many a breakdown every time something went wrong when trying to get this book over the line. My nan, grandad and dad for their continued love and support.

Thank you to Eden, my editor, for being just as insane as me when I said I was going to do this. For Aly who stayed up far too late into the night perfecting the cover for me, for Georgina who blew my mind with this hardcover art. It is a literal masterpiece.

Meg, Hannah and Kristin, whilst I gave you all your copies WAY too late for proof reads, I'll always be thankful for your belief in the series and how quickly you say yes to helping me in anyway possible.

Thank you ARC readers (albeit only a week before release) Looping you inot this surprise was my way of saying thank you for your long standing support.

Chlo and Mel, congrats on your fourth acknowledgement. I've not said anything nice yet, but are you already crying? Thank you for keeping me sane the entire way through this project, for being in on all the secrets of the Lost Kingdom Saga. Four books on and I still can't believe books and this series found me you both. I can't get too soppy otherwise you won't cry at the final two acknowledgments. Time for us to get a celestial tie tattoo xo

A Note from the Author

Reviews on Amazon, Good Reads, StoryGraph and other sites are one of the biggest ways to help indie authors. I would be eternally grateful if you could leave a review on your preferred platform as well asAmazon. Reviews have to exceed a set amount for Amazon to begin pushing indie books – so if you can, posting here will make a big difference.

I started this journey sharing this book through my socials, and I'm sure I've met many of you there. So, if you feel obliged, please share your thoughts and feelings around this book on your own socials so I can sit and cry tears of joy at this story reaching people.

Instagram:@author_lauracarter

Tik Tok:@authorlauracarter

Youtube: @authorlauracarter

So, you've finished Myths and Lies of Ithyion, and you're (hopefully) eager to get your hands on the next book in the Lost Kingdom Saga. Book four in the main series, Truth of the Light, is set for release in February 2026.

If you're a die hard fan of the Lost Kingdom Saga and want to show it off, you can find licensed merchandise for the series by the wonderful Chloe, at dumbblondeclub.co.uk

About the author

Laura grew up in rural Scotland before moving to London to study for her degree in English Literature, where she lived for ten years before moving to the countryside with her Romanian rescue dog, Rez. She grew up constantly immersed in different worlds through reading and always dreamed of becoming an author. When her love of fantasy and romance was re-ignited after three years of only ever critically analysing work, her dream of creating her own worlds returned. She now balances working full time for a cancer charity with writing her debut series, The Lost Kingdom Saga. She has a further thirteen plus books planned so you won't be getting rid of her any time soon.

9 781068 314476